PRAISE FOR *YOU CAN'T CATCH ME*

"Catherine McKenzie never disappoints, and this is her best book yet. Her writing is fluid and absorbing; the characters are fully realized; the plot twists and turns with expert precision; and underlying it all is a growing sense of dread that I couldn't shake until the book's terrific denouement. Highly recommended for fans of psychological suspense."

—Cristina Alger, *New York Times* bestselling author of *The Banker's Wife*

"Grabs you fast and simply won't let go. With breakneck pacing, a cast of compelling characters, and razor-sharp intelligence on every page, this puts all of McKenzie's skills on full display."

—Matthew Norman, author of *Last Couple Standing*

"Slick, smart, and ultimately heart-wrenching. McKenzie's at the absolute top of her game in this suspense that takes the cat-and-mouse genre to a whole new, mind-bending level."

—Emily Carpenter, bestselling author of *Every Single Secret*

"Catherine McKenzie is at the top of her game when a former cult member finds herself mixed up in a dangerous, high-stakes case of identity theft. Addictive and fast-paced, *You Can't Catch Me* proves that sometimes revenge is sweet. McKenzie's best book yet!"

—Mary Kubica, *New York Times* and *USA Today* bestselling author of *The Good Girl* and *Pretty Baby*

"Catherine McKenzie proves once again she is a master of the psychological sleight of hand. Reading *You Can't Catch Me* is like being blindfolded and spun around so many times that when you finally see straight, you can't tell who's good, who's bad, or who holds the cards. Unputdownable."

—Louisa Luna, author of the Alice Vega novels

"In *You Can't Catch Me*, Catherine McKenzie serves up a riveting tale of stolen money, stolen identities, and stolen childhoods. First a victim of a cult and now the victim of identity theft, Jessica undertakes a harrowing search for justice and healing. It's a breathtaking journey."

—Bryn Greenwood, *New York Times* bestselling author of *The Reckless Oath We Made* and *All the Ugly and Wonderful Things*

YOU CAN'T CATCH ME

Other Books by Catherine McKenzie

I'll Never Tell

The Good Liar

Fractured

The Murder Game (writing as Julie Apple)

Smoke

Hidden

Spun

Forgotten

Arranged

Spin

YOU CAN'T CATCH ME

Catherine McKenzie

LAKE UNION
PUBLISHING

Published by Lake Union Publishing, Seattle

www.apub.com

ISBN-13: 9781542019033 (hardcover)
ISBN-10: 1542019036 (hardcover)
ISBN-13: 9781542019019 (paperback)
ISBN-10: 154201901X (paperback)

Cover design by Rex Bonomelli

Printed in the United States of America

First edition

For Christie

PART ONE

Chapter 1

Airport Bars Are the Loneliest Bars

There's no real time of day in airports, only morning and drinking time.

I'm sitting in an airport bar. They're sad places, I've found, full of people who are waiting out flight delays or long layovers—whatever excuse they want to use to drink in the daytime.

The bar I'm sitting at looks like an Apple store, all white, glossy surfaces and molded plastic. You even have to order off an iPad, instead of from a person, though people still deliver the food. It's in Terminal One at Newark, one of those massive terminals where you can hit your daily step goal transferring from one gate to another. Across from me are a Lacoste store and a fancy candy shop, neither of which I can see any need for in an airport. I Forgot to Pack Any Underwear—now that would be a useful store.

My flight to Puerto Vallarta doesn't leave for three hours. I'm one of those people who arrives way too early for flights and stresses until they're through the security line. Laugh at me if you want; I've never missed a plane. I might also have nothing better to do these days than to day drink.

I stare at the iPad, trying to decide if I need a food cushion for the alcohol I'm definitely having. The menu is a weird collection of dishes. Imagining eating most of the choices makes me vaguely queasy (*airport sushi?*), but the charcuterie plate seems safe. Cured meat and pickled vegetables are items meant to withstand shoddy hygiene. I order it with the eight-ounce glass of wine, then swipe my credit card to pay. I scroll through my Twitter feed while I wait. My notifications have calmed down. There are only four or five hundred people @-ing me today and imagining the crimes they'd commit if they could get their hands on me. Charming assault and dismemberment scenario you've described, @TotalMan. Your mom would be so proud.

I should delete my account, but I take perverted pleasure in how mad I've made so many people. As if their lives are the ones that were turned upside down, not mine.

A woman sits down next to me and starts to tap on the iPad in front of her. I glance her way—she's thin, with thick black hair in a precision blunt cut that ends at her chin—and turn away. Women like this make me feel frumpier than I am. I'm wearing yoga pants and an oversize sweater, and my hair is in a messy top bun. I completed my "look" with a single coat of mascara. I like to travel comfortably, but still.

I turn back to my phone.

"Jessica?" the server asks.

"Yes?" my seatmate and I say together.

We turn to each other and laugh. This other Jessica has bright-red lips and small, even teeth.

The server's confused. She's twenty-one, if that, with a rash of acne on her chin. Her name tag says TAMMY. She looks down at the ticket in her hand.

"Jessica Williams?"

"Yes," we both say again, then turn and stare at one another.

"Oh, wow," the other Jessica says. I'm already thinking of her as Jessica Two.

"Does this order belong to one of you?" Tammy's holding my charcuterie plate in one palm and a large glass of white wine in the other.

"That's mine." I reach for the plate as she puts down the glass of wine.

"Definitely yours," Jessica Two says. "I don't do sulfites."

"Bring the other order as well," I say as Tammy turns to leave.

"Huh?"

"When you get the other ticket for Jessica Williams," Jessica Two says slowly, "do not throw it out."

Tammy backs away until she disappears through a swinging door.

"You think she'll figure it out?" I ask.

"I'm guessing no."

I swivel my stool. Jessica Two has tucked her sheet of hair behind her ear. A discreet diamond stud winks at me. "How did this happen?" I ask.

"Our parents weren't original in their name choices?"

"You have no idea."

I look at her more carefully. She's not my doppelgänger—more like the opposite of me. Light-blue eyes, where mine are hazel. That thick black hair compared to my finer light-brown strands that curl in the heat. Clear china-doll skin where I'm freckled and tan easily.

She's checking me out also, and grins as our eyes meet. "You're really Jessica Williams?"

"Yep," I say. "You?"

"Yep."

I reach for my wine. "Do you mind?"

"Please, go ahead."

I take a large sip. It's fruity and not what I was expecting, but how picky can I be? It's midday, and the airport feels desolate on this Sunday afternoon in early June. We're the only people at the bar.

"So," she says. "I have this thing I do whenever I meet another Jessica Williams."

I sit up straighter. "*Whenever?* This happens often?"

"Often enough."

"I've only ever known one."

"I travel a lot. Maybe that explains it."

"Could be. What is it?"

"I call it Jessica Williams Twenty Questions."

"That's not a thing."

"Sure it is."

I take another sip of wine, then pop a rolled-up piece of charcuterie into my mouth. Yum. Bring on the sulfites.

"What's the purpose of it?"

"It's a way of seeing how similar we are."

"You mean, besides the name?"

"Obviously."

I admit, I'm curious to see where this will go. "Okay, hit me."

She puts her phone on the counter between us, screen down. "Where were you born?"

"New York State. You?"

"Ohio. What street did you live on growing up?"

"Rural Route One."

"How original," she says.

"More so than you'd think. How about you?"

"Jefferson."

I take a large sip of wine. "Are there actually twenty of these questions?"

She raises a finger to her lips as the intercom blares with a flight announcement. Her nails are covered in bright-red lacquer. Another thing we don't have in common.

I drink again. I'm going to need another glass soon. "Go."

"What's your mother's maiden name?"

"Young."

"Gardner for me. High school?"

I shake my head. "I was homeschooled."

"Interesting!"

"Not really."

And "school" is a bit of an exaggeration. I was brought up in a cult, and reading, writing, and arithmetic weren't high on the list of Todd's priorities.

"Best friend growing up?" she asks.

"Sarah. You?"

"Molly."

"Did you go to college?"

"Columbia," I say. "J school."

She rests a finger under her chin. "Impressive."

"You?"

"A state school."

"In Ohio?"

She nods and looks away. "Where has that girl gotten to?"

"Her brain is probably short-circuiting from the coincidence."

"Probably. Anyway, what year were you born?"

"1990."

She gives a slow smile. "Ah. Same."

"That's weird."

"I thought it might be the case."

"Why?"

Tammy finally approaches with Jessica Two's drink, a scotch by the looks of it, poured over a large spherical ice cube. Even her drink makes me feel inferior.

"Jessica?" Tammy says.

I answer *yes* with Jessica Two out of habit. Or maybe it's spite. Tammy looks uneasy.

"Just leave the drink," I say.

She puts it down and backs away again.

"She's probably going to quit," Jessica Two says as she tries her drink.

"If she can't survive two Jessicas . . . ," I say.

"Born in 1990."

"Right? But how did you know?"

She shrugs. "I figured we were the same age. I'm good at guessing things like that. Also, Jessica was the most popular girl baby name that year. Well, many years, actually, but that year also."

"I didn't know that. When's your birthday?"

"July tenth."

A chill passes through me, even though it feels as if getting to this fact was the whole point of this conversation. "No. Fucking. Way."

She puts her glass down. I watch the gooseflesh rise on my arms.

"What is happening?" I ask.

"We're having a drink."

"Are you shitting me?"

"About my birthday? No." She takes another sip, then puts it down carefully. She takes out her wallet and flips her driver's license at me. There it is. My name and birthday on an Ohio license with Jessica Two's picture.

"What's your middle name?" I ask.

"Don't have one. You?"

"Anne."

She turns away from me so she's facing the bar. The television above it is playing CNN, which I've been avoiding for weeks. It's the media-critic show that runs on the weekends, and there's a panel on, discussing some tweet of the president's. But then the headline shifts—Plagiarism in Journalism—Fake News?—and my face flushes.

"I think we should stop here," I say.

"With the game?"

"I'm feeling . . . kind of seasick, to tell you the truth."

"Might be the sulfites."

"Probably not the sulfites."

She drums her nails on the counter. "Okay, it's strange."

"It's more than that. Have you ever done the math?"

"What's math got to do with it?"

I pick up my phone and do a quick Google search. "There were 4.16 million live births in America in 1990. If those are 50 percent girls, that makes 2.08 million girls born that year. Divide by 12 for the number of months, and that's 173,330 girls a month, assuming all months are equal."

"You did that in your head?"

"What?"

"That long division."

"Oh, yeah. It's this thing I can do."

Numbers and words; they've always been my forte despite my lack of formal education growing up. I should've applied my skills to learning how to count cards and made a killing in Vegas. Instead, my choices have led me here.

"Impressive," she says.

"Thanks. You said Jessica was the most popular girls' name?"

"That's right."

I do another search. "Williams is the third most popular last name. Five people in every thousand."

She takes a sip of her drink. "You see, there's probably thousands of us."

"With the exact same birthday? Maybe ten if you include Canada too. I'd have to look at the name distributions to be sure, and July might have more births than other months, but . . ."

"This is weird. Us meeting."

"I'll say."

She drains her glass. "You think our clueless waitress will serve us another?"

"One can hope."

Two drinks later, the world is tilting and they're calling my flight.

"I've gotta go," I say.

"Where you off to, anyway?" she asks. Her cheeks are pink. She's had three scotches, matching me in number. We've left the oddness of our name and birthday combo sit there between us, an unseen tie, an unspoken thread.

"Puerto Vallarta."

"Nice."

CNN is replaying the panel from earlier—the one discussing me. My faces flashes on the screen briefly, then disappears. Soon, I'll do the same.

"I'm going to confess something." I lean toward her. She smells like peat and grain alcohol. "I got fired last month."

"I'm sorry."

"No, I deserved it. But I got this trip out of it, so . . ." My petulant tweet announcing that *I'm going to Puerto Vallarta next Sunday, bitches* had been met with a particular amount of vitriol from the 4Chan crowd. I kind of enjoyed that one, I must say.

She glances at the screen. "Oh, you're *that* Jessica. I didn't connect it before."

I don't believe her, but this isn't the sort of conversation where you voice that kind of suspicion. "You've heard of me?"

"My Google Alert did."

"You have a Google Alert for your, I mean our, name?"

"You don't?"

"Well, of course, but . . ."

The corner of her mouth turns down. "But you're famous," she says. "I get it."

"I was never famous." I raise my hand and make the check symbol at our server.

"You've already paid."

"What? Oh, right."

I stand, wobble, regain my balance. The drinks were a bad idea.

"We should keep in touch," she says.

"Sure, give me your number." I reach for my phone on the bar, fingers at the ready.

"I have a simpler way." She angles her phone to me.

"What do we do?"

"Just tap it with yours."

"Like a toast?"

She nods.

"What do we toast to?"

"To the Jessicas?"

"Sounds about right."

Our phones touch.

"To the Jessicas!" we say together.

An alert flashes on my screen: *Jessica Williams has been added to your contacts.*

The speaker booms again. Ten minutes till the doors close.

"I've got to go," I say.

"So, go."

"Nice to meet you."

"Yes, it was nice, wasn't it?"

"Maybe we'll meet again someday?"

She smiles for an answer. I'm not sure why I'm lingering. I don't want to miss my flight; this trip was hard-won.

"You'd better run."

The way she emphasizes the word *run* snaps me out of my haze.

I turn without another word and start to jog toward my gate. I just make my flight, the gate agent *tsk*-ing me as I'm the last one to board.

I settle into my first-class seat and fall asleep promptly right after we take off, all thoughts of Jessica Two banished by alcohol and altitude.

But not for long.

Chapter 2

I Got Nothing

I promised myself to cut off all contact for the week I'm in Mexico, and it's a promise I keep. Holding to it isn't that hard. Most of my friendships were work related, emphasis on the *were*, and the others are not people I need to keep in touch with on a regular basis.

So I cut off all ties and I sit in the sun and read books on my Kindle and plan for what's to come. I eat my meals alone and drink alone and sleep alone. I run six miles on the beach every morning. The first day I puke at the end of it. The last day, I'm laughing even though my body aches all over. It's beautiful and restorative, a hiatus.

I take the shuttle to the airport.

I avoid the airport bar.

I keep my phone off even as I reenter civilization.

My resolve remains in place up to the moment I'm back in my closet-like room in my Greenwich Village apartment. I sit in the middle of my one luxury—a queen-size bed that touches the walls on either side—plug in my phone, and hold it in my hands like I'm praying.

"Here goes nothing," I say to precisely no one. The large canvas on the wall that's the only decoration in the room—a bold watercolor in sea hues that changes with the light—doesn't answer me. It never does.

I press the power button. My phone takes a moment to react, rebooting, installing some interminable software update.

The home screen loads.

For a blessed moment, my in-box remains empty, and no notifications appear. This feels impossible. At the very least, there should be hundreds of emails from J.Crew and for period-proof underwear. But there's nothing. I can't believe it. Keeping my phone was part of my deal when I left my job. Did they cut me off?

After a moment of panic, I realize what the problem is. I put my phone in airplane mode before I switched it off. I toggle the setting and shake my phone for good measure. Emails and texts start to flood in. I scan through them. They're mostly what I expected: 40 percent off clothing and threats to my life. But then the notifications from my bank start, one by one by one.

I've withdrawn money.

I've withdrawn money.

I've withdrawn all my money.

Your spending is much higher than typical.

That was five days ago.

After I calm down, I spend a bit of time poking around online trying to figure out what happened, and then I go to my bank. I wait in line for twenty minutes, only to be told by the teller that she can't help me with "my problem" and that I'll need to wait to speak to a manager. She can't tell me how long that's going to be, but if I'll wait over there, they'll call me when one's available. Would I like coffee or tea?

I sit in the waiting room, trying not to seethe at the casual way I'm being treated. Having your bank account drained isn't something most people would take in stride. It's even worse when the account in question contains your hard-won six-figure severance package.

Until about a month ago, I was the senior investigative reporter at FeedNews, the second-largest online news source with the number one spot in its sights. I got that position after my series on life inside a cult and the lawsuit that resulted after its leader died helped propel us to that status.

This past winter, I was assigned a piece on life as an intern in the state legislature. When I was doing the background research, I found this great first-person account someone had written years ago that no one had read (based on the number of likes and page views), and—there's no way to say this that makes me look like anything other than a horrible person—I lifted it and passed it off as my own. There's no defense to this. I had a lot on my mind at the time, and for good measure, or bad, I added in a few details about an up-and-coming congressman from a famous family that I knew were true but that I didn't have any double-sourced proof for. It got a lot of attention and, shortly thereafter, led to the end of that congressman's career.

Then, a couple of weeks later, I got caught. This guy, James, who used to work at FeedNews and who never liked me, published a take-down article exposing what I'd done.

The story about *my* story blew up.

I got pilloried. I got fired. But I also got a six-figure severance package because the head of the assignment desk is a piece of shit who'd been sending me lewd emails for years. I told his boss about it and blamed my moment of weakness on the stress that he'd caused me. I had #MeToo-type evidence to back it up, years of emails I'd kept in a folder called "asshole" in case I needed them. They "leaked" to the media, and that blew the story up even more. Interestingly, the calls for my death and dismemberment *increased* when that detail got out. Nothing makes an internet misogynist angrier than a woman making money off the misdeeds of another man.

Twitter was ablaze; the talking heads talked, talked, talked; and I stayed away from the pits of Reddit and 4Chan. In the end, I got them to throw in the vacation to Mexico because of the death threats. At that point, they would've bought me a Tesla to get the story to die down, but I don't have a parking space.

And now, I don't have the money either.

Somewhere, someone is laughing.

"How did this happen?" I ask the bank manager an hour later when I'm finally brought into her office. She has frizzy brown hair and is wearing glasses that are two sizes too big for her face. She introduces herself as Dolores.

"Most of the money has been removed from your account."

"I know that part." Someone had made two $1,000 withdrawals from ATMs, then wired $240,000 out of the account. I can't tell where to from my online statements. "What I want to know is how they did it."

Dolores taps at a keyboard that looks like it escaped the 1980s. "Your bank card and PIN were used at the ATMs."

"They must've had a cloned bank card ready to go and then figured out my PIN."

"They?"

"The person who stole my money."

She looks at me over the top of her glasses. Her eyes are watery and dark. "You know who stole your money?"

"I have my suspicions."

"Did you give that person your bank card and tell them your PIN?"

"Of course not. But it's not that hard to clone a card, from what I understand."

"Perhaps." She looks at her screen again, then back at me. "Your PIN could be stronger."

"Noted. What about the online transfer?"

"You must've shared your account numbers and passwords."

"Again, no."

"You seem upset, ma'am."

"Someone drained my bank account and you seem to be blaming me."

"We have to verify for fraud."

"So, verify," I say. "All of the money was withdrawn last week, right?"

"Yes."

"I was in Mexico then, which I can prove. Did the withdrawals originate at ATMs in Mexico?"

"No."

"So, it wasn't me. What about the online transfer? Where did that come from?"

She blinks, slowly.

"Perhaps the answers are in your computer," I prompt.

"Oh yes." Dolores pecks away again. "Ah."

"Yes?"

"You transferred the cash by wire to another account."

"Please stop saying that."

"What's that, ma'am?"

"That *I* transferred the money. I already told you I didn't."

"Well, all of your security questions were answered on the phone, ma'am."

"Show me."

She hesitates, then turns the screen my way. There they are: a long list of questions about my mother's maiden name and what street I lived on as a child, et cetera.

"What account was the money transferred to?"

"That's confidential."

"You're kidding me."

"I cannot disclose the banking information of another individual without a court order."

"How am I supposed to get that?"

"I assume the police could help you with that, ma'am."

"So, someone takes all my money, and the bank protects their privacy?"

"That's the law."

"Is there any other way you can help me?"

"Well, I think it's important to remind you to keep all of your passwords and account information in a safe place. Never disclose the answers to your security questions to anyone. A bank account is a responsibility—"

I raise my hand to stop her. "A simple *no* would've sufficed."

I leave the bank with my heart pumping. I stop at the ATM on the way out to get some cash. The thief left me with a few dollars. How nice of them.

I punch in my PIN, and the machine tells me I've made a mistake. I try again with the same result. What the—

Jesus. My PIN's been changed. Or the bank locked me out and Ma'am Dolores didn't tell me. Goddammit. I stare at my reflection in the glass screen, clenching my fist so I don't punch it. There's a pinhole camera above it, filming me trying not to lose my cool.

The camera! I should've thought of that before.

I go back into the bank, only this time, I bypass Dolores and go right to the top.

I'm not leaving here until I get what I need.

Chapter 3

Would You Like to File a Report?

It takes me an hour to convince the bank's branch manager to log into their central monitoring system and pull the ATM footage from the cash withdrawals. But eventually, after I threaten to write an exposé about his branch specifically, and he finds ample information on the internet to become convinced that I'm morally bankrupt enough to write the things I've threatened, he leaves his office and comes back half an hour later with two black-and-white photographs.

They're a bit blurry, but there's no denying that it's Jessica Two. In the first one, she's dressed the same way she was at the airport, only she's wearing a jaunty cap, almost a beret, that pushes her hair forward over her face and casts shadows where her eyes should be. I look at the time stamp: only an hour after my plane left. She wasted no time taking the first $1,000. She was at another ATM the next morning, on Greenwich and Eighth. She was wearing the same hat, but this time she had on a high-collared sweater. She wired away the rest of my money that afternoon.

I have so many questions. Like why did she risk going to the ATMs instead of simply wiring herself the money and disappearing? She must have needed the cash for some reason, because she was taking a risk even though I was out of the country and unlikely to be checking my account balance. Part of me feels like she did it because she wanted me to know that it was her, because she could've taken the cash from whatever account she transferred the money to. She didn't have to leave a trail and get caught on video.

She didn't have to come so close to my apartment.

I take out my phone and pull up Jessica Two's contact information, the one she passed on at the airport with what I assume was an infected tap. It's only her name and number, an area code I don't recognize. When I look it up, it says it's in California, but that doesn't mean anything. So long as you pay the bill, no one cares if you live where your cell was born. It's probably a fake number. I try it anyway, but no one picks up. I tap out a text.

Why did you do this?

I'm not expecting an answer, but it feels good to ask.

"You want to report a crime, ma'am?"

Tolanda Brown—the desk officer at the sixth precinct—is the second person to *ma'am* me today. I might not take that much time with my appearance, but I'm only a month shy of my thirtieth birthday, for fuck's sake. I'm wearing the pencil skirt and a dressy capped-sleeve shirt I usually reserve for interviews with important persons. I always thought this outfit made me look professional and approachable, not old.

"That's right."

"What type of crime?"

"A theft."

She hands me a form. "Fill in the details here and then take a seat over there." She points to a row of upholstered gray chairs against the wall. Her phone rings shrilly as she hands me a pen. I take a seat with my form. This room feels like where people go to die by waiting, but what choice do I have? In order to file a claim with the bank for the money Jessica Two stole, I need a police report. The bank manager had made it clear that because she had access to all my security passwords, the only money I was likely to get back was that taken from the ATMs. But I might as well make a claim anyway, he said, handing me the forms, because you never know.

I fill out the form.

Officer Richardson—property crimes—doesn't call me *ma'am* when we're introduced later that day, but he's not very reassuring either. In his midfifties, with a runner's build, he has a weariness about him that's discouraging.

He's got his suit jacket draped over the back of his chair. His dress shirt is yellowed, and his suit has the shiny look suits get when they've been dry-cleaned too many times. There are twenty other cubicles in the room, and it's loud in here, many people on the phone, being interviewed like myself. Despite the ambient noise, Officer Richardson talks low, almost mumbling, so I have to lean forward to hear him. It creates a sort of intimacy that I suspect is purposeful.

I give him the bare facts. I show him copies of my bank statements and the photographs from the ATM. He raises his eyebrows at the name thing, then chuckles to himself. These criminals and the things they get up to. I don't find it funny.

"Any chance I'll get my money back?"

He looks at me for a moment, sizing me up with large brown eyes that I suspect have seen twenty years of people asking him the same question as his hairline slowly receded. "You seem like a reasonable person. Are you a reasonable person?"

"I'd like to think so."

"Then the short answer is probably not."

"You should put that in the brochure."

"You asked."

"I did."

He meets my gaze. "I'm speaking of probabilities. I've seen a lot of things in my career, so you never know. For instance, way back when I was starting out, there was this gang that ended up doing a B&E on every house on the same block. That was in Brooklyn. Back before it was . . ."

"Brooklyn?"

"Right."

"Every house?"

"Pretty much."

"Was there something special about them?"

"Not really, other than the fact that they hit so many houses without getting caught."

"How is that possible?"

He raises a shoulder. "Low priority, lack of resources. It happened over several years, and most of what was taken was covered by insurance."

"Not like what happened to me, then."

"True," he says. "Anyhoo, about five years later, they caught the guys, and the funny thing was, they had this massive storage locker out in Jersey City. They hadn't gotten rid of most of the stuff they'd stolen."

"Why not?"

"They hadn't thought it through. They were good at casing places, getting in and out undetected. But they didn't have a way to offload what they stole. All the VCRs—this was in the early nineties—and family jewelry and such. I'll tell you one thing, though." He leans forward, mimicking me.

"What's that?"

"I was there when the folks whose stuff was stolen went to the warehouse to identify it."

"That must've been nice."

"It was a letdown, actually."

"How come?"

"The family heirlooms, people were happy to get those back. Their charm bracelets and such. Their memories. But the VCRs and other electronics that had been replaced with newer models by the insurance companies? You could see them, one by one, recognizing their things and turning the other way."

"Isn't that insurance fraud?"

"Probably. But who was going to do anything about it?"

"You?"

He straightens up. "Like I told you, personal-property crimes are a low priority. But I learned something that day. Even the most honest people, when it's their interest on the line, well, they're often willing to look the other way."

"Why are you telling me this?"

"Just making conversation."

"And what about my crime?"

"The other Jessica?"

"I call her Jessica Two."

He loosens his tie. "Probably not her real name, though. But you never know . . ."

"She showed me her ID."

"That's easy enough to fake."

"But she went through airport security . . ."

He nods. "There is that . . . though she could have used other ID to get through security."

"She had it planned out," I say.

"Clearly. How did she know you'd be at the airport, though?"

I explain to him about Twitter. Show him the tweet I'd sent. "She had at least a week to plan. And I was in the news a whole month before that."

He nods again. "Clever little scheme. You did make it simple for her, being so public and all."

"I guess I did."

"Your generation, living your life online. Makes it easy picking for the criminal class, I'll tell you that. Like that Kardashian woman with that robbery in Paris—"

I cut him off before he goes on another long tangent. "Could you get a warrant to get information on the account she transferred my money to?"

"I doubt it's still there. It's more likely that she transferred it right away to another account, and then another, et cetera. See those numbers there?" he says, pointing to my account statement. "That numbering means it was transferred to an offshore account. Untraceable."

So that's why she needed the ATM cash. If her money's offshore, it's probably not as easy as just going to an ATM and making a withdrawal to get access to it.

"It's worth trying, though, isn't it?" I ask with a note of hope in my voice.

He turns and taps on his keyboard. "There's nothing in the system under that name. If that *is* her real name, she doesn't have any priors."

"You have access to the DMV database, don't you? What about finding the other Jessicas born on my birthday? That's not a long list."

He looks at me over his shoulder. "Didn't you tell me her driver's license was from Ohio?"

"Yes, but—"

"We don't have jurisdiction there."

"How about the airport? Can you check if she used that name to go through security or buy a ticket?"

"That's the TSA's bailiwick."

"I thought that stuff was all connected now, because of 9/11?"

He gives me a look. "That's for stopping terrorists. Not catching grifters."

I slouch down. "So, you can't do anything."

"I didn't say that." He hits print, and his dot-matrix printer starts to buzz. He takes the paper off the printer and puts it at the bottom of a large stack. "I've put it in my to-do pile. That's the best I can do for you right now."

"Are you trying to make me mad?"

He swivels toward me slowly. "Course not, ma'am. I'm simply trying to give you a realistic expectation about what's going to happen here. I'm sorry it's not any different."

When the *ma'am*-ing starts, I know I'm done for. I stand to go.

He hands me his card. "If you learn anything else, you feel free to call me."

I take it and stow it in my pocket.

"You'll receive the police report by mail in four to six business days."

"Thanks."

"Good luck to you, Jessica."

I thank him again, though it's not luck I need now.

It's Liam.

Chapter 4

Enter Liam

Liam finds me sitting at the bar in Fiddlesticks, not my regular haunt, but a place I started going to a couple of months ago, right before everything started.

There's nothing special about this place. A shiny bar top, a mirror along the back wall with gold lettering that's half-covered by beer bottles and glasses hanging from a rack. Flags of the world paper the ceiling, each dipping slightly toward the floor in the middle. I like the fish tacos and the Coney Island IPA on draft. It's a neighborhood bar in a neighborhood in which I've been mostly anonymous. No one here knows my name.

It's five o'clock on a Monday in the second week of June. The city hasn't heated up yet to that suffering sauna it becomes in full summer. The bar's a quarter full, and even though it's a bit dark in here, I can feel the sunlight on my back through the stained-glass windows. I should be outside, soaking it in. Instead, I'm inside, planning, plotting, anxious.

"Job hunt?" Liam says, taking the stool next to me without asking, motioning to the notebook on the bar that I've been making notes in.

My heart hitches. I flip my notebook over. "Something like that."

"You drinking the IPA?"

"Yep."

"Any good?"

"It'll do."

He catches the bartender's eye, points to my glass, and puts up two fingers. The bartender nods and takes two glasses down.

"What's up, kid?" Liam asks.

"Shouldn't you stop calling me that by now?"

He gives me what I call his "charming" smile. Liam's six feet tall, and at forty-two, he still looks like he's in the merchant marines—his skin halfway between tanned and burned, with deep lines ingrained in his forehead. His dark-brown hair is peppered with gray, and his eyes are a hazel color that's the opposite of mine, closer to brown than green. "Does it bother you?"

"Sometimes. Plus, three people called me *ma'am* today, so I think I'm past the 'kid' stage."

He gives me a quick once-over. "It might've been the outfit."

"Shut it."

The bartender delivers our beers and Liam slips him a twenty. He's the king of overtipping, which gets him goodwill and access, both of which are useful in his profession.

"You rang?" Liam asks.

"What took you so long to get here?"

"I was on a case."

Liam works mostly as a private detective, with a side hustle as a fixer for certain prominent New York families and their lawyers. It's a lucrative business, though Liam doesn't care that much about money. He's the one who rescued me from the Land of Todd. And then he spent a year helping me reintegrate into society. One way or another, he's taught me most of the things I know.

"Something I can help with?" I ask him.

He laughs. "I've got it. Besides, you were never my best student."

"Can you blame me?"

He puts his hand over mine briefly. "You know I don't believe in blame."

A Liamism. There is no blame. Check, don't trust. You are your own choices. I had a notebook full of them, back when I used to write down everything he said like it was something to replace the Toddisms I'd been brought up on.

"I know."

"How was your trip?" Liam asks.

"Quiet."

"Good."

"Thanks for meeting me."

"No problem. What's up?"

"Can't I just be hankering for the pleasure of your company?"

He pulls a face as he lifts his beer to his mouth. "I haven't seen you in, what?"

"Six months." I knew to the day, but that might freak him out.

"Six months. That's too long."

"I've been . . . busy."

"So I read. How come you didn't answer my texts or meet me when I asked?"

That had been hard, ignoring Liam. I've been in love with him since I was eighteen, and I'm used to following his commands. "I needed to figure some stuff out on my own. Plus . . . well, I was ashamed, to be honest."

The bartender delivers the plate of fish tacos with a side of fries that I ordered right before Liam appeared. He reaches for one of the tacos. "Do you mind?"

"Everything I have is yours," I say.

Liam winces at the Toddism. "Okay, now I know something's wrong. Spill."

I grew up in the Land of Todd. That sounds so innocent, doesn't it? Like the Land of Nod, what Crate & Barrel used to call their kids' furniture line. And for my parents, it started that way. When they joined, it all seemed benign. I want to believe this, because thinking otherwise puts too much between my parents and me, and we've got enough baggage.

They were brought up in strict Mormon families and married young. They became members of the Land of Todd in their early twenties and were joined there soon after by my father's brother, Tom, and his wife, Tanya. My parents must've given the place glowing reviews for the fresh air and the clean life they were living. And Todd. I'm sure they sang Todd's praises as well. His energy. His purity.

His vision.

The Land of Todd—or the LOT, as we called it—rested on a large plot of land in the Adirondack Mountains. It was made up of small cabins that each family unit built for themselves, the communal dining hall called the Gathering Place, and Todd's house, a log cabin overlooking the lake. There wasn't any fencing when they joined. I've seen the photographs from the early days, and in every one of them everyone is *laughing*.

But they should've been paying more attention. Done some research. The Land of Nod is where God exiled Cain after he killed Abel. It's a place of wanderers, where some said even God himself could not see. Does that sound like the right idea to build a future on?

By the time the children came along—me; my cousin, Kiki; the others—things had started to shift. Todd didn't like the loss of attention, the loyalty to someone other than him, so he assigned two of the single women to be caregivers/guards and separated us from our parents. From the time I was five, I lived and worked at the Upper Camp, a part of the property that wasn't easily accessible and had none of the amenities (running water, electricity, plumbing) the houses I'd known till then did.

We were drilled in odd skills up there: how to dig a ditch, how to meditate for hours. We were being trained for something—we even had little outfits that I learned later were Girl and Boy Scout uniforms picked up on the cheap—but what? A new kind of society? A revolution? Todd was talking about that near the end of my time there, but it was incoherent. We'd be placed in strategic positions, and we'd know what to do *when the time came*. We'd *understand the signals*. It was all garbage, but we absorbed it silently, as we'd been taught.

Then, on a rare day when we'd been taken into town to get groceries at the farmers' market, Liam approached me while I was picking out tomatoes. "You don't know me," he said under his breath after telling me to look straight ahead and not react. "My name is Liam." But I knew exactly who he was. A few years before, an entire family had left in the middle of the night. After that, there was a name that was whispered late at night when our minders were asleep. *Liam*. Whenever someone left, it was because of him. Maybe that was true, or maybe they slipped away without help. It was hard to know what to believe.

But there was Liam in the flesh, looking like one of the heroes on the covers of the cheesy romance novels the girls hid in the walls and passed around like the contraband they were.

Telling me to keep looking ahead, to just listen. Offering a lifeline. A way out.

I took it.

When I'm done filling Liam in, I've eaten one of the fish tacos, and he's eaten two. The bar has filled up around us, and the music's been turned up a notch. Imagine Dragons is singing about being a believer. What do they know?

We've finished our beers and ordered another round. Not that it's a long story to tell, but Liam is big on getting all the details, especially about Jessica Two.

"She's done this before," I say.

"I was thinking the same," Liam says. He's got his own notebook out, the twin of mine. So many of my preferences are Liam based, I have trouble deciding if I do something because I like it or because he taught me to. "You thinking of trying to find her yourself?"

"That's why I called you. What do you think?"

"I think you should."

"You do?"

I was expecting a lecture. I'd broken one of his cardinal rules: never leave all your money in one place, especially not a place that's easily accessible through electronic means.

"Doesn't look like the police are going to do anything," he said.

"I got that impression. Where should we start?"

"I haven't agreed to help you yet."

"But you will, right?"

Liam holds his beer glass with his thumb and index finger and swings it back and forth. He loves giving silence for answers.

"I was thinking that if she's done it before, finding some of her other victims might help," I say.

"Other Jessica Williamses?"

"Yeah."

"You think she's used that name before? Why?"

"Makes sense, doesn't it? She has the ID; why not use it more than once if she can?"

"Or she might have a string of IDs," Liam says.

"She might. But you and I both know that a good ID is harder to get than most people think." After I'd left the LOT, I learned that my birth had never been registered. Todd didn't believe in the government, only Todd. It had taken six months, and a lot of help from Liam, to get the Social Security card in my wallet and the birth certificate in my safe-deposit box, which is also where I socked away my emergency fund, safe from Jessica Two.

"Plus," I add, "she said this thing about how she played this game 'every time she met another Jessica.'"

"That might be a clue. Or it might be a lie."

"Let's call it a hunch."

He finishes his beer. "You know what I think about hunches."

"Eliminate them. Don't believe. Check."

"That's right."

"So how do we check?"

Liam turns his stool around and rests his back against the bar. He looks out at the crowd of suited men and women. He's wearing dark jeans and a black shirt, a look he can easily turn into something resembling a suit with the addition of a blazer and a tie. *A look for all occasions,* he's called it.

I follow his gaze. There's a pretty early-twenty-something accepting a drink from an older guy at one of the tables near the door.

"She's fine," I say.

"Probably."

"You don't have to save everyone."

He looks at me. "If your 'hunch' is right, then there must be points of commonality."

"Besides our names?" I say cheekily.

"Don't be an ass."

"I feel like one."

"You got taken by a pro."

"You think?"

"Definitely. What she did took a lot of planning. She must've been tracking you for a while, waiting for an opportunity to connect with you and play that game. And the phone tap at the end, that's clever."

"That's how she got my banking info, right? Some kind of capture software."

"Yes, but that's pretty sophisticated. There's encryption in place that should've prevented her from getting anything other than your contact information."

The girl is shaking her head at something the older man's saying. But then she laughs, and the tension in my body eases. A downside of Liam: he makes you see bad everywhere you look. Which might be accurate most of the time, but it's a hard way to live.

"Don't say it, okay. I know I shouldn't have had my banking information in my phone, but I thought it was safer than e-banking over that shared Wi-Fi in my apartment. I know you always say—"

"Do everything in person—"

"Yes, but life's not built like that anymore."

"Expedience over security. It's always been our undoing."

A group of recently off-work friends stumble into the bar, laughing. The bartender ups the level on the sound system again and rings a bell: last call for happy hour. "Where the Streets Have No Name" starts playing. They could be describing the Land of Todd.

"I was easy prey," I say.

"What's done is done. What matters is what you do now."

"All right, enough with the sayings. Are you going to help me or what?"

I keep expecting him to offer, but instead he's made me ask again. Life is like that sometimes. Plans depend on other people.

"I'm at your service, *ma'am*," Liam says, then throws his head back and laughs.

Chapter 5

Card Tricks

Liam walks me back to my apartment, a few blocks away from the bar. Jose, the three-card monte man, is set up on the corner of Greenwich and Seventh, the way he often is. He's got a crowd of tourists around him, smiling and wasting their one-dollar bills like businessmen in a strip joint. Whatever floats your boat.

Liam watches Jose's hands, which I know from him is what you're supposed to do rather than watch the cards. Jose is very good, but if you look carefully enough, you can see what Liam pointed out to me years ago: he flashes the red queen, then palms it so it's one of the other cards that hits the table first. Thinking that you're following the card the dealer shows you is the mistake everyone makes, the reason the monte always wins unless you guess right through blind luck.

"You going to take him on?" I ask. Sometimes Liam likes to torture the three-card guys by beating them at their own game.

"Not tonight."

"Instead of saving all of us, you should've trained us up like Fagin in *Oliver Twist*."

"Find the lady," he says, tapping my sternum lightly. "Don't think I didn't consider it. With you and Daisy, we would've made a killing."

I watch his face. It's hard to know if he's joking sometimes, or what he's thinking in general. He was pretty clear, though, when I made a pass at him on the night of my college graduation a few months before I turned twenty-three. He removed my hand from his thigh gently and told me to get some sleep. I hid out from him for most of the year after that, but it was hard to stay away from Liam forever.

"What held you back?" I ask.

"Is that a serious question?"

I shrug.

"None of you deserved to be used anymore."

The crowd lets out a loud *Ahhh!* Jose just took a guy for fifty dollars.

"That guy's a plant," I say.

"Oh yeah?"

"Pretty sure."

Liam checks out the player. He's in his midthirties and wearing a Mariners cap and jeans ten years out of date. He bets another fifty dollars and wins this time. The crowd's bigger now, and pretty soon one of the local beat cops is going to break this up.

"You might be right," Liam says.

"I totally am."

"Why the confidence?"

"He was doing the same thing this morning."

Liam gives me one of his deep belly laughs. "That's my girl."

I wish.

It took me almost a year to call the number Liam slipped me among the produce. I should've left with him that day at the farmers' market like he asked, but I didn't want to leave my cousin, Kiki, behind. So instead, I'd taken his number and promised I'd find a way to use it when I was ready.

It took a lot of planning. We didn't have a phone in the Upper Camp, only a two-way radio for emergencies. The phone at the Gathering Place was closely guarded. Some said bugged by Todd. It was hard to know what was true at that point, which was one of the reasons it felt so dangerous to stay there. Then there was the way Todd kept looking at me. Kiki told me I was imagining it, but I saw how my mother looked the other way whenever he was near me.

Like a bargain had been struck and she had seller's remorse.

By that time, I barely thought of her as my mother. She'd birthed me, but then she'd let me be led away from her and into the woods, my hand clasping Kiki's like Hansel's gripped Gretel's. Even at five I knew she'd been given a choice, and I wasn't it.

I was seventeen when I met Liam, though it wasn't a birthday that was celebrated. When we turned eighteen, though, we got to come down the mountain and build our own house. Kiki and our friend Sarah were going to get to share a cabin, but not me.

Not me.

Two weeks before my eighteenth birthday, my aunt took me into town. My mother was supposed to do it—I heard her arguing with my father about it after the weekly assembly—but that was "too much to ask" apparently. Giving me up for whatever Todd had in mind could be borne, but buying what I now know, with the benefit of hindsight, was to be my "wedding dress" was a step too far.

I'll never truly understand my mother. But she did give me the gift of anger.

It has a way of focusing you that forgiveness can't.

Even though it's after seven, none of my roommates are home from work. The benefit of living with two investment bankers and a lawyer: I have this place to myself most of the time. My room is the "maid's room," that quaint term for a tiny room that probably never housed a maid, though one of my roommates—Josh, the annoying, know-it-all lawyer—says he looked up the census data from a hundred years ago and it lists "maid" as one of the occupants. He's always making shit like that up. Regardless, I'm most certainly not the maid of these slobs. They contribute to a weekly cleaning service, which was my one condition on moving in since we share a bathroom. They'd given each other a look that made me think I wasn't the first woman to ask and agreed. The room is small, but it's more personal space than I had in the Land of Todd. I'm debt-free, college all paid for, and had the comfort of knowing, until I crossed paths with Jessica Two, that if I were suddenly out of a job, I wouldn't be out on the street.

I've made the space my own. The queen-size bed that touches both walls is the most comfortable bed you'll ever sleep on. There's no window in here, just the painting Kiki gave me. Underneath it is a desk with a large monitor that doubles as my television. I installed a hanging bar near the ceiling that raises and lowers on a pulley system to hang my clothes on, and I built a set of drawers that fits under my bed.

I grab my laptop and return to the common area.

"You want a beer?" I ask Liam. He's standing in the middle of the living room, which is composed of two uncomfortable leather couches and a massive flat screen. Men and their priorities.

"Sure. Mind if I put the game on?"

"Go ahead."

Liam's a die-hard Mets fan and has season tickets at Citi Field that he inherited from his dad. Mostly, he gives them away or resells them, but he watches on TV when he can. He used to take me to games, telling me about this whole hot-dog-and-beer ritual he had with his dad and how they scored every game they attended together, keeping the results in a series of three-ring binders. It made me jealous of the normalcy of his upbringing, so I acted out by changing the score sheet when he wasn't looking. He stopped taking me after that.

Liam turns on the TV and finds the right channel while I go into the galley kitchen and fetch two beers from the fridge. Its contents are labeled like they were in my freshman dorm: the yogurt is mine; the fancy craft beer is Josh's. I take two of his beers, a tithe for the guacamole that was clearly labeled as mine that I caught him with a few weeks ago.

"I think we should start with Twitter," I say, handing him his beer and taking a seat next to him. I open the laptop and log on.

"What does that mean?" Liam asks, pointing to the number *293* over the little bell symbol next to *Notifications*.

"Have you never been on Twitter?"

He grimaces as he tugs on his beer. "What's it notifying you of?"

"All the people who've liked a tweet of mine or retweeted it or @-ed me."

"What's that mean?"

"Like direct tweeted at me. They sent a message to @reallyJessicaW specifically."

"That's your Twitter name?"

"Yep."

Liam pulls on his beer and barely avoids rolling his eyes at me. "Do you need to answer all of those tweet thingies?"

"Nope."

"Are you even going to check them?"

"It's not anything I need to see."

He reaches over and moves the mouse on the trackpad until the cursor's over the symbol, then clicks. My notifications are full of what I've come to expect—horrible misogyny and hate.

"What the hell is this?" Liam asks.

"This is what happens when you've been publicly shamed."

Liam's eyes scroll down the page. He stops when he gets to the first guy threatening to rape me.

"What the fuck, Jess. You need to call the police."

"It's just Twitter. They won't do anything. And they don't mean it. Not most of them, anyway."

Liam looks away and swallows half his beer rapidly. "What are we doing on here, then?"

"I wanted to see if I could find other women named Jessica Williams."

I execute a quick search in the people tab. The first result is the former *Daily Show* correspondent, but it goes on for pages and pages. "I'm not going to get anywhere here."

"Why does anyone use this?"

"It was kind of essential in my old job."

"And now?"

"A bad habit, I guess." I navigate away from it. "Anyway, it's not the right place for this kind of search. Maybe Facebook."

"Do you have Facebook?" Liam asks.

"Everyone over twenty-five has Facebook."

He frowns at my jab. Liam does not have Facebook. He turns his eyes to the TV screen. The Mets are up by two against the Phillies in the second inning. I'm sure it won't last.

I log into my Facebook account. I don't go on Facebook much these days, though I used to spend a lot of time on there. There's a survivors' group—Not in Todd Anymore—where some of us saved by Liam and others who left on their own started gathering seven years ago, after Todd died, but there's little activity there now.

"If I remember right," I say, "you can't search for age on here. Just names, and then you can see, sometimes, where they live and their age on their individual page if they want that information to be public."

"I thought Facebook was shit about privacy?"

"They know everything, but that doesn't mean it's easily accessible to ordinary users."

I type *Jessica Williams* into the search bar. A list of Jessicas appears, sorted by what algorithm, I don't know. One of the first on the list has a common friend, someone I used to work with, but when I check this

Jessica's page, she's ten years older than me. The next two both have their privacy settings on high, and no personal information but a photo.

I click on the expand tab—the list goes on and on and on.

"There has to be a better way," Liam says.

"You're the guy with the skills."

"You want me to call in a favor?"

"Would you?"

The distinctive sound of a well-hit ball draws Liam's eyes back to the TV screen. The Phillies have loaded the bases.

"Goddammit."

"Maybe you should switch to the Yankees?" I say. "I read this article recently about how they're New York's 'real' team now, based on fans."

"I'm going to pretend I didn't hear that."

"Liam Davis. Patron Saint of Lost Causes."

"And yet, you want my help."

"Yes, please."

He takes the laptop from me and concentrates on the screen. Liam's built up a web of contacts over the years that can help him locate people, some of which he's shared with me, and some of which he keeps to himself. I take a sip of my beer as I watch him.

Liam starts with a background-check website and enters some parameters. It chugs along and produces a report that says that there's no one with a criminal record in the state with my name and birthday.

"I thought we were looking for other victims?" I ask.

"It was worth trying before I called in the favor."

"Is it really that big?"

"They've been cracking down on leaks. Mario needs to be more cautious."

"But you'll ask?"

"I'll call him tomorrow."

I kiss him quickly on the cheek. "Thanks, Liam."

"Well, now . . ."

"Relax. I'm not going to jump you or anything."

I take the laptop away from him and sit on the opposite couch. It smells faintly of the cigars one of my roommates likes to smoke. He's trying out for Douchebag of the Year, an award he's going to win. Liam fiddles with his beer, looking uncomfortable, his concentration on the game now feigned.

"I have an idea," I say.

"What's that?"

I go back to Facebook and start a new post.

Is your name Jessica Williams? Were you born on July 10, 1990? Have you met another one just like you? Me too! DM me if you want to talk about it.

I make the post public, then pass the laptop to Liam.

"You think that's going to work?" He leans back into the couch with his beer cradled in his hands. Another crack of the bat and the Mets are now down by six.

"You'd be surprised what works on here."

"Please don't tell me."

"It's not like Twitter . . . well, mostly not."

"Didn't you meet that Pete guy on Facebook?"

It was Tinder, not Facebook, but that wouldn't make a difference to Liam. He'd taken an instant dislike to Pete when we met once for a drink last fall. It wasn't anything serious, and we broke up months ago. Was Liam . . . jealous? No. I put the thought out of my head.

"Pete wasn't so bad."

"He didn't steal all your money, if that's what you mean."

"Shut it."

"Seriously, Jess. You can do better."

"Maybe I like being alone."

"I doubt it." He takes another swig of his beer. "God, this is awful. And I'm about to turn off this game."

"That would be a first."

"Not these days."

My computer *pings*! Someone's tagged a Jessica Williams in the post. "We've got a hit."

"So fast?" Liam says.

"Technology. It's not all bad."

"I don't have anything against technology *per se* . . ."

"You sound like Todd."

Liam stands abruptly. "It's late, I should go."

"I'm sorry, okay? I shouldn't have said that." I stand up, knocking my beer over. "Shit."

I rush to the kitchen to get a rag. There's beer dripping down one of the leather couches, the only thing my roommates care anything about.

"Josh is going to kill me," I say, but Liam's already out the door.

Chapter 6

Connections

When I check the Facebook post the next morning after the guys have left for work in their noisy way, the post has gone semiviral, and thirty-five women named Jessica Williams have been tagged in the comments. A quick scan shows me that half the people who've commented on the message are the same trolls who were plaguing me before I left for Mexico, because anything I post online will forever be another opportunity to tell me I'm a piece of shit.

This much I know already.

Despite all the reactions, and the Jessicas, I have no direct messages. Added to that: Liam hasn't returned the two texts I sent before I crawled into the cocoon of my bed and willed the day to disappear.

I resign myself to the silence and settle in on the couch. I go through the tagged Jessicas one by one. None of them were born on the same day as I was as far as I can tell, and there's a string of conversations on the thread like Dude, what made you think that I was born on July 10? Or I'm not that old, bee-atch. So helpful.

It's a weird exercise. These other Jessicas are like a series of doors I never walked through. If I hadn't been born in the Land of Todd, or I'd never left, what might my life be like?

After an hour, I get sick of looking at all the Jessicas and waiting for a DM to appear or Liam to get back to me. It feels like I'm in a holding pattern, circling the city, waiting for the weather to clear.

To pass the time, I decide to reach out to The Twists, a group of misfits and weirdos Liam helped save from various cults over the years. We gave ourselves this title, mostly to piss Liam off, because it was part of our new freedom to poke fun at our savior.

I open the group-text thread we started years ago:

Anyone up for some trouble?

Covington replies first, as he always does. Next up is Daisy, then Miller. Everyone else begs off because of work, promising they might catch up with us later, though we know from previous experience that they won't.

The only one who doesn't reply is Liam.

But the word *Read* is right there under his name.

I smile to myself, knowing I can still get under his skin.

Feel free to join us, Liam! I write, then wait.

Have fun, he texts, but just to me, and I know that's the last I'll hear from him for a while.

We decide to meet at High Dive in Brooklyn. Miller and Daisy share an apartment nearby, so we go there often enough. With everything, it's been a few months since I've seen them.

I take the B train from West 4th, and as we lurch along, I read through the comments that continue to appear on my Facebook post like popping kernels, only now, two people have tagged a Jessica who lives upstate, and she's one of the Jessicas who turned up early in my name search yesterday. She's got her privacy settings on high, nothing showing in her feed except a picture with her face half in shadow. She has mousy brown hair and pale skin that probably burns on impact with sunlight. She looks tiny, almost elfin, but pictures can be deceiving.

I take a screenshot of her profile and plunk it into a text to Liam as we pull into the station.

Can you ask your guy to investigate her?

It only takes a moment before the word *Read* appears below my text.

I smile. As well as Liam knows me, I know him. He can't ignore a text or a challenge.

Then, feeling too much like an ex-girlfriend who's stalking a man who doesn't want to be with her anymore, I slip my phone into my pocket and vow to ignore it for a while.

Covington's already in High Dive when I walk through the bright-red door, reading something on his phone. He came from the Land of Todd, too, only he's five years younger than I am and—as the son of Todd's most trusted associate, and, if the rumor mill was right, maybe an actual son of Todd—got to skip the Upper Camp while I was there. As a result, he and I barely knew one another until he left the LOT; he was simply another face in the weekly gathering, one of the fervent ones I used to look at with disdain. He's the last person Liam saved, a year before Todd died.

Covington is sitting with his chair turned around, his gangly limbs spilling out in all directions. He always does this. Todd made us sit up straight with our feet on the floor and our arms by our sides. The way Covington sits is his way of saying "Fuck you, Todd" every single day. We all have our own ways of doing that.

"Where are Miller and Daisy?" I ask as I sit next to him at the table he's commandeered in the corner. Some of us came to Liam with disastrous names like Stardust and Riverstone. Another Liamism: it's never too late to pick the name that suits you. Hence, Daisy, Miller, and Covington.

"Miller's late as per usual. Daisy's in the bathroom."

"Ah."

"No, not like that. She's been . . . Man, Jess."

"Sorry, sorry."

"I put on an automator for this, but if you're going to be like that . . ."

Covington's a day trader, and he's always using words I don't know the meaning of or whether they even exist at all.

"Please stay," I say.

"You'll leave it?"

"Of course."

The waitress comes over and does a double take when she sees me.

"Oh, wait, you're that girl!"

Covington starts to laugh. "You're famous!"

"For all the wrong reasons."

The waitress shakes her head. "No way, man. You're, like, my hero. The way you took that asshole down." She holds up her hand for a high five. I meet it. "Solidarity, sister."

"Thanks."

"Now, what can I get you to drink?"

We give her our orders and then Daisy joins us. She survived David Koresh and Mount Carmel when she was a baby, but only barely, so her cocaine habit shouldn't be that much of a surprise. Only she looks like a librarian, glasses and argyle sweater and all, so it does tend to throw you for a loop.

She leans down to hug me. She smells like toothpaste and the cheap soap from the bathroom, but no other chemicals.

"I've missed you!" she says.

"Me too."

She sits next to Cov. "So, what's up?"

"Let's wait for Miller."

"Did someone say Miller Time?" Miller's voice booms behind me. He's short and slight, the product of his hippie, WASP mother who went to India and fell in love with his Hindu father at the Rajneesh's original ashram. His parents wore orange and then maroon and were at that crazy compound in Oregon. He was born after it all fell apart, but his parents hadn't quite worked the cult out of them. When Miller was six, his parents joined some splinter group no one's ever heard of, but which was just as weird. Maybe worse.

"You don't actually drink that shit, do you?" Cov asks.

"It's a perfectly respectable beer."

The waitress brings our drinks, and we spend a few minutes catching up, the small talk of old compadres, banded together like a group that's gone through war.

"What's up?" Daisy asks. "Why the SOS?"

"I needed to see some friendly faces."

"Is it that stuff with your job? I know you didn't do it."

"That's sweet, D. But I did."

Miller flips his bottle cap up in the air and catches it. "Wow, big confession."

"Shut up, Miller," Cov says.

"It's okay. It's true, I did it."

"Why?" Daisy asks. Despite her predilection for chemicals, she's the rule follower of the group. She won't even jaywalk. She allows herself to break the rules she needs to survive, but needs the regular conventions of society to bind her in. So, cocaine and hash—her medicines—are permitted. Letting your parking meter expire is not. I'm guessing plagiarism falls into the latter category.

"Did you read the piece?" I ask.

"I thought it was great."

"Yeah, well, that's because I found someone else's article that was great, but unread."

"You made out okay, though, from what I've seen," Cov says. "Thanks for trying to take on some of the trolls."

"I like arguing with those guys."

"You would."

Covington smiles. "Anyway, now you're on easy street."

"Well, that's where it gets interesting."

I tell them about Jessica Two. The airport, the drinks, the ATM, the wire transfer.

"Fuuuccck," Miller says when I've finished.

"Yep."

"That's kind of genius, though," Covington says.

"Genius?" Daisy says.

"Yeah, like, figuring out that you have a common name and that this could help you con people . . . It means you have all the ID you need, right? Like at banks and stuff."

"Assuming it's her name," Miller says.

"You don't think so?"

"It would be a big risk."

"Right," Daisy says. "Can't they go interview all the Jessica Williamses and figure out who did it?"

"They say no," I say.

"But she wouldn't have known that beforehand," Miller says.

Covington leans forward. "I bet she did. I bet she started off small, years ago. She has ID for this common name. Maybe it's hers, maybe it isn't. But she tries something, a small scam. Nothing happens. She gets away with it. She looks for other Jessicas. She researches them, finds one worth bilking. She pulls it off, gets away with it again. The police don't come knocking. She bides her time. She waits until the right moment. Then, boom. You're in the news. You're vulnerable. An easy mark."

"Thanks ever so," I say. But Covington's right. "It doesn't matter if it's her real name or not. Either way, she's gotten away with it so far."

"So far?" Miller asks.

"Maybe she messed with the wrong Jessica."

Covington raises his bottle and clinks it to mine. "You bet she did."

Many drinks later, the room's a bit blurry. I've been outside with Covington smoking cigarettes off and on all afternoon. My mouth feels dirty, and it's that moment in the evening when I regret drinking at all. I'm drunk, too drunk to sober up quickly, and I don't like being out of control. The music is thumping, and Covington signs that it's time for another smoke, and I follow him. We're all ingrained followers, us Toddians. You can take the girl out of the cult . . .

"Do you ever wonder who did it?" Covington asks when we're outside, a flame near his face. He has a scar along the edge of his chin that reaches down to his throat—he hit the razor wire on the perimeter fence when he left and almost bled out before making it to Liam's car.

"Did what?"

"Killed Todd."

"He had a heart attack."

"You believe that story?"

I take the lighter from him, light the cigarette he offers me, and inhale deeply. I never smoke, usually, but tonight—today, whatever—feels like a day to indulge in bad habits.

"What do you think happened?" I ask.

"Someone gave him a drug that caused the heart attack."

"How?"

"Those IVs he was always taking, his vitamin concoctions, or whatever. It would be easy to swap out a bag."

I concentrate on the cigarette. "You seem to have given this a lot of thought."

"I used to fantasize about it during meetings. Whether it would act quickly. Whether he'd be in pain. Whether he'd know it was me."

"Maybe you did it, then?"

"Nah, I was already free, remember?"

"So why do you think someone did?"

"That guy was obsessed with his heart health. His whole diet was designed to make sure he lived as long as possible. He checked his blood pressure every day. He ran six miles every morning up a fucking hill. It doesn't make sense."

I drop my cigarette and crush it. I feel nothing about what Covington's saying. The good thing about this many drinks is I've reached that point. Painless. Blameless.

"I think it's safe to say that there's lots of us who wanted him dead, who thought about it, even. Then it happened. That was a good thing, wasn't it? Who cares if it makes sense?"

"Not so good for everyone . . . what about Kiki?"

I wince, the shot of adrenaline my body releases acting like Narcan, jump-starting my heart. "What the hell, Covington? Are you trying to make me upset?"

He raises his hand in surrender. "Sorry." He tosses his cigarette into the street. "I suck, okay? We all suck."

"So says Todd."

"And Todd is all."

I shake my head at the call and response we said by rote a thousand times. "If he was murdered, he deserved it."

"He did." He pulls me into a hug. Touching most people still feels weird to me, all these years later. Physical contact wasn't allowed in the Upper Camp. Who knows what the kids might get up to if they could embrace?

"You okay?" Cov asks.

"I'm fine."

"I'm going to head back in."

"I'm going to stay out here for a bit."

He lets me go and enters the bar. I'm going to leave in a minute, but for now I linger. I watch the group through the window like they're on a sitcom, talking with big gestures, laughing, free. The leftovers, the side effects, the only family I have left.

My mind wanders. I check my phone, scrolling through my texts. Jessica Two's seen my message. So, her phone is working, real. And she has her read receipts on, so she wants me to know she's read it. A point of connection that I can use. But what words will unlock a reaction? A daily text? Hourly?

I poke at my phone and tap out: I'm coming to get you, get you, get you.

"No more drinking," I say out loud.

"I tell myself that every day," the homeless man I didn't even notice says. He's sitting on the ground against the side of the building, his possessions jumbled into a shopping cart.

"We should take each other's advice."

"Easier said and all that."

He raises a can in my direction. I toast him with air.

My phone vibrates. It's a text from Liam.

I found her.

Chapter 7

Road Trip

"Let's just go," I say, and for once Liam agrees with me. So here we are, in the middle of a Wednesday, driving out of the city.

It's a bright, sunny day, and we're on I-95, heading north. To Wilmington, New York, to be more precise, about five hours away. That's where this Jessica Williams lives, on a small dirt road outside of town.

While the world was still tilting in Brooklyn, I sent her a Facebook friend request. She didn't answer it. Then I realized I could send her a direct message even if we weren't friends, and so I wrote to her, setting out the basic details of what had happened and asking if the same thing had been done to her.

She didn't write back, but the message might have ended up in her spam folder. You'd have to be a monster not to respond to a cry for help from someone with the same name as you who'd been defrauded because of it, right?

In the sober morning, I took another tack and sent friend requests to the two women who'd tagged her in my original Facebook post. They were more open to communicating with a stranger and accepted my requests quickly. Then they both started messaging with me. One was named Miranda, and she worked at a high school where Jessie—that's what Miranda called her—worked a while back in a suburb of Chicago.

She couldn't tell me much about her other than where she lived now, and that Jessie had come into some money, she thought, but she didn't know the details. Jessie was kind of a private person, you know? She wouldn't like me telling you these things.

The other woman was named Leanne, and she lived in Wilmington, half a mile from Jessie. She didn't know Jessie too well, only that she was new in town these last two years, and kept to herself, and why did I want to know, anyway? What did my post on Facebook mean? Was there some kind of Jessica convention going on down there in New York City?

I laughed at that one. I had to get in a room with Jessie. Maybe face-to-face, she'd talk to me. A drunken Facebook DM is easy to cast aside. I'm much harder to ignore in person.

Even Liam knows this. That's how we ended up in this car, snarled in traffic.

"So," I say, digging into the food hamper at my feet when we've left the city behind, "I've got portable cheese and near-cheese products. Also, many kinds of chocolate. You like chocolate, right?"

Liam looks over at me. He's wearing a black T-shirt, aviator sunglasses that reflect me back at myself, and the Mets hat I gave him for his birthday a few years back. "What's gotten into you?"

I bounce in my seat. "I'm both nervous and excited. I'm nercited."

"That's not a thing."

"It could be a thing."

"This is a crazy idea."

"Who you calling crazy, sitting next to me, driving me there?"

Liam smiles what I like to think is his happy smile, and I feel like mission accomplished already. I can't think of the last time we were alone like this, spending the day driving somewhere. It's a beautiful day out, crisp and fresh, the sun high in the sky. You forget, living in the city, what the air can smell like, how clean it can be. How green the trees are when they're not covered in a film of dust and grime.

I watch Liam drive, his hands sure on the wheel, the route memorized. No GPS or Google Maps for him.

He glances at me, catching me looking. "What makes you think she's crossed paths with the other Jessica?"

"I have a feeling."

"That's it?"

"She's only lived in Wilmington for two years, and you said she works at the elementary school as a librarian. But that woman in Chicago said that she'd come into some money, and that's why she quit her teaching job there and moved away. I googled her and found a story in the local paper about her, you know, one of those 'Let's meet our new neighbor' sort of things, saying that she'd won the lottery. So, if she has money, why's she working in an elementary school library?"

"Maybe she likes kids. Or was bored."

"Or maybe Jessica Two stole all her money, so that's why she has to work."

"That's a stretch."

"Don't be so negative."

I fiddle with the radio until I find a good station. Tom Petty and the Heartbreakers twenty-four seven. Liam nods in approval.

"What's your plan?" he asks. "For when we get there?"

"Ring her doorbell until she lets me in?"

"And then?"

"Get her to tell me if she's met Jessica Two?"

"And if she has?"

"We'll put our heads together and pool what we know, so we can track her down."

"How, though?"

"I haven't worked everything out yet."

He stares at the road, saying nothing. We pass a sign for the Catskills, and I wonder if Liam notices, but he doesn't say anything.

"You don't think this is going to work?" I ask.

"Truth be told, I doubt anything's going to come of it."

"Why agree to come along, then?"

"I thought it would distract you, give you something else to focus on besides all that job stuff."

I'm touched, truly, but it's best not to let him see that.

"Wait, wait, wait. Hold up. Is Liam Davis confessing to deceiving me?"

"I wouldn't call it a full-scale deception."

"Semantics."

"Sorry."

"It's fine. It's what I was going to do anyway. But thank you."

"For what?"

"For coming along."

"You don't care that I think there's no point to this?"

"Nope. I'm still nercited."

Two hours later, I'm less nercited and more plain nervous, anxiety about what's coming up soon on the road pushing past the adrenaline. The sugar high has worn off, and we're in a zone on the highway past Albany where there's intermittent cell reception. Even the radio went fuzzy and then silent.

"Do you have a girlfriend?" I ask Liam.

"Where did that come from?"

"Just making conversation."

"Uh-huh."

"Well, do you?"

"Not at the moment, no."

"But you have, right?"

"What are you asking me, Jessica?"

I bite the corner of my thumb where it meets the nail. "I was just sifting through stuff in my mind, and it occurred to me that I've never met one of your girlfriends. Why is that?"

"I like to keep my personal life and my professional life separate."

"Ouch."

His hands squeeze the wheel. "I didn't mean it like . . . I'm sure you've had plenty of boyfriends that you haven't introduced to me."

"No one special."

"So, Pete was special?"

"I didn't say that."

Liam shakes his head. "You know I care about you. About all of you."

"I know. Forget I brought it up, okay?"

We're silent for a few minutes. Then, it happens: we pass the first exit for Schroon, a place I know too well and never intended to come back to. I can feel myself shrinking, folding into myself, as a deeper kind of silence descends in the car, one created by the memories that are rushing past like the pine trees. Without a word, or even a sound, Liam reaches over and takes my hand. I clutch it, weaving my fingers through his, letting the warmth sink in. I look away from the road and hold my breath until that exit and the next are in the rearview.

Eventually, I let go. I lower the window and fold my arms on the sill. I feel the wind in my hair and breathe in that smell of loamy earth. The smell of home. The only home I knew.

"What was the reason," I say to Liam, "that you spoke to me that day at the market?"

"What's that?"

"September 15, 2007, at 11:28 a.m. The Schroon Lake Farmers' Market. You came up to me. Not Kiki or Sarah or Hughie. Me. Why?"

I'm not making up the time. I remember everything about that day. The late-summer sun on my neck. The scratchy fabric of the dress I was wearing, what we called a "civilian dress," one of the few I had for when we left the compound because a group of teenagers in Scout uniforms and Park Ranger outfits would've set off alarm bells even in that sleepy town. There was a battery-powered clock on the wall behind the cashier. I was holding a ripe tomato and trying to resist the temptation to eat it right there like an apple.

Then I heard his voice.

"You were alone," Liam says now in the car.

"Well, that's crushing."

"I didn't mean it like that."

We pass a field of cows. The smell of their manure tickles my nose. "What, then?"

"I went to that farmers' market every weekend that summer, waiting for a chance to speak to you. But you were never alone."

"Travel in twos," I say in a monotone. "It keeps away the blues."

"That's the worst Toddism ever."

"Right? Anyway, I was alone this time?"

"You were. I watched you get out of the van, and you made a beeline for the tomato stand. So, I took a chance, and it worked out."

"Why me, though? Why not the others?"

"You were someone I could save."

He's holding something back, I know, but I decide to let it lie.

"You were brave," he says. "You are still."

"I hope so."

Now we're going through one of those granite canyons they carved out when they built the highway. Water runs down the rocks, and it smells like the beginning of time.

"I never asked you—why were you so hell-bent on saving people from the LOT in the first place? I mean, saving people is kind of your thing, but there are so many choices."

"You remember my cousin, Aaron?"

I sit back in my seat. "Not that well, to be honest. They kept the boys and the girls pretty separate, even in the Upper Camp. And his parents were very close to Todd, like Covington's parents. He didn't have to spend much time up there with us."

In truth, many of us kind of hated Aaron, or the idea of him at least. He'd seemed too pious, so devoted to the cause. There was speculation that Todd was grooming him to be his second in command and eventual successor, though the idea of the Land of Todd after Todd wasn't ever something that was discussed. Because Todd was going to live forever.

So said Todd.

"He was never the same after I helped get him and his parents out of there."

"What happened between them and Todd, anyway? They were so tight with him."

Liam grips the wheel harder, like he's trying to strangle it. "Todd . . . wasn't right."

"We all knew that."

"I mean, he wasn't right with Aaron."

Despite everything I went through, this shocks me. "I didn't know."

"I've never told anyone. Todd destroyed that kid." His voice is tight and filled with emotion, like mine gets when I'm on the verge of tears. I've never seen Liam even come close to crying, though. My hatred of Todd deepens, and I'm so glad he's dead, it feels wrong.

He clears his throat. "Anyway, when my aunt and uncle found out, they knew they had to get Aaron away from there. So, they found a way to contact me and I came to get them. Afterward, I worked with Aaron, trying to help him get back on his feet. He had this . . . not quite a list, but other kids that he'd talk about. Kids he thought Todd liked too much. I couldn't let anyone else go through that."

"Was I on the list?" I ask.

"Yes."

The cheese crackers I ate earlier rise like bile in my throat. Even though I knew about Todd's plans for me, there's something worse about knowing that others could see it too. That I didn't only imagine that my parents had turned the other way. That everyone in the LOT had.

"So, you *were* looking for me."

"Yes, but Aaron's descriptions weren't much to go on. Pretty girl with light-brown hair—that applied to more than one of you."

It was true that there was a bland sameness to many of us, especially those of us who were related. By the end, more than half of us were tied by blood in some way or another. Aaron was different, though. He looked like the movie-star version of Liam, and those good looks were part of the reason we hated him.

"How come Aaron has never hung out with the rest of us survivors?"

"He didn't make it."

My own selfishness sickens me. How did I not know this? How could I never have asked before? I turn back to the open window. If I breathe deeply enough and concentrate on a single point, I may not puke.

"I'm sorry, Liam. And I feel like a complete shit for never asking you about it until now."

"It's okay."

"No, it's not."

I reach out and place my hand over his on the gearshift. I squeeze it hard, then release.

"He couldn't take it out here in the real world, but you did. Cov, Miller, and Daisy did. The others."

"You saved a lot of us."

"Not enough."

That's how I feel also, but I don't blame Liam for that. I search for the words to comfort him, to change the mood back to what it was a couple of hours ago when we first left the confines of New York and all there was in front of us was possibilities. But before I can put the words together, my phone buzzes.

I take it out of my bag. Jessie's written me back on Facebook. I open the message.

I heard you were asking about me. What's this about?

My fingers tingle in excitement as I tap out a reply. Did you get my DM? Can I come see you?

I got it. What for?

I want to talk about what happened to me. Did it happen to you too?

There's a pause. She's writing something, then stops. Writing again.

It won't do any good.

Can we discuss it in person and then we'll see?

Another long pause.

Fine.

I smile as I close my phone. "We have contact."

Chapter 8

The Third Jessica

"Contact?" Liam asks as he pushes his aviators onto his head, his eyes squinting against the sun.

"With Jessica Three. She's agreed to meet me."

"Jessica Three?"

"You know, the one in Wilmington who we're driving to see? I find it's easier to refer to us like that."

"I thought you said her name was Jessie."

"Yeah, so?"

"I would've thought that you, of all people, wouldn't be so cavalier with people's names."

"A name is a name is a name."

Another Toddism has Liam shaking his head. "Okay, I deserved that. But that's your one free pass for the day."

"We'll see."

The last time I was in Wilmington, it was a run-down town with a Santa's Workshop near Whiteface Mountain. My parents took me there once before Todd moved the kids up the hill. It still fits that description. Many of the houses are falling apart, with rusted-out trucks littering the lawn, and the motel we pass where Liam mentions that he's reserved a room has definitely seen better days. But there's a fancy chocolate shop now, and cute decorated roadside stands where you can buy firewood. When we turn down the dirt road Jessie lives on, I catch a glimpse of several large houses with high peaked roofs and walls of windows facing the ski hill.

We pass a short woman with brown hair tucked into a baseball cap who's running on the road. Liam slows down to give her a wide berth. A minute later, we arrive at our destination.

Jessie's house is surprisingly large and imposing, a timber-frame with gray cladding and the requisite tall windows facing the hill. There's a perennial garden in the front yard full of daffodils and tulips that dance in the pleasant breeze. The lawn is freshly cut, and the box hedge along one side of the house is neatly manicured. Despite this, the house has a deserted air, even though there's a car, a dark-blue hybrid, in the driveway.

We get out of the car. Crickets grind in the air, and somewhere in the thick wood behind the house, a woodpecker taps at a tree.

I ring the front doorbell, but no one answers. There's no shifting presence inside. Even though Jessie is expecting us, I didn't give her a precise ETA.

"We should've called ahead," Liam says.

"Ha, ha. I did, dummy." I wave my phone at him.

"Maybe she changed her mind."

"Yeah, maybe."

"Looking for me?" a woman's voice says behind us. It's the jogger we passed a few moments ago.

I feel that prick of excitement again. "Jessie?"

"Jessica?"

"Yes."

"And this is?"

"Oh, Liam. He's with me."

She looks at him nervously.

"Don't worry," I say. "He's harmless."

"What do you want?"

"I'd like to know what happened to you."

Jessie approaches us cautiously, her eyes shifting from me to Liam and back again. There's a sheen of sweat on her forehead. "Why should I trust you?"

"She took your money, didn't she?" I say. "Jessica Williams?"

Jessie closes her eyes for a moment, perhaps wishing us away.

"Yes," she says finally, then opens her eyes. "You'd better come in."

Inside, Jessie offers us water and asks for ten minutes to clean herself up. She takes eight and returns in a loose pair of boyfriend jeans and a screen-printed T-shirt with the New York skyline on it. Her hair is scraped back, revealing a high forehead and watery blue eyes. Like me, she's not wearing any makeup. About five feet tall in her bare feet, she looks to be about my age, which, of course, she is.

She pours herself a glass of water from the tap and sits down across from us, tucking her legs under herself in a lotus-like position. She holds her glass of water as if she might lose her grip on it.

"How did you find me?"

I decide to leave Liam and his background favors out of it. "I put up this post on Facebook, and two of your friends tagged you in it. When I reached out to them after you didn't answer my message, they told me where you lived."

"Friends! Sure."

We wait for her to say more. It's a technique Liam taught me years ago—wait for someone to fill the silence when you want to get information out of them. Sometimes the questions in their minds are larger than the ones you might ask.

"It was Leanne, wasn't it? That's who you talked to?"

"That's right."

She makes a small noise of disgust. "The town gossip."

"All small towns have them."

"Yeah, that's true. But she . . . likes to stir up trouble."

"Oh?"

She looks out the window. Some of the trees have grown up and obscured the view of the hill. "I don't know why I'm telling you this, but . . . a couple of years back, when I moved here, she had me over to some Welcome Neighbor thing. I guess it's a big deal when a new person moves to Wilmington. Anyway, most of the town turned up, but it wasn't welcoming at all. It was like . . . You know those super friendly people who are kind of rotten underneath?"

"Sure," I say. "I've met people like that."

More techniques from Liam. Agree with whatever someone says when you're interrogating them because it creates intimacy.

"They're horrible," I add. "Leanne was like that?"

"Yeah. She didn't want to get to know me, not *me* me—none of them did. They wanted to know *about* me, to inspect me. And when I didn't want to share, well, she turned kind of nasty."

"What'd she do?" Liam asks in a gentle tone.

"This rumor started . . . God, it sounds so weird to even say it out loud, but it was this stupid thing about how I was a witch, or a Wiccan, running some secret coven up here. I found out about it at the library where I work. The kids would whisper when they saw me, and some of the younger ones even started crying during this reading exercise." She shrugs. "I was reading Dr. Seuss."

"You don't look like a witch," I say, smiling, trying to defuse the tension. She looks more like a bird. Thin, small, and jittery, as if she might take flight at any moment.

"Why do you think she did it?" Liam asks. He's leaning forward, reducing the space between them. Another way to create intimacy.

"Who knows. To run me out of town, I guess, once she knew I wasn't going to fund the new covered bridge over the river."

"I feel like I'm missing a few pieces," Liam says.

She blinks slowly. "Because I wouldn't use the money to do it . . ."

"The money?"

"That I won. In the lottery." She looks back and forth between our puzzled faces. "She didn't tell you?"

I answer her, feigning ignorance. "She just said that you lived here and were a bit . . . private."

"Oh. I assumed she'd told you the whole story. Her side of it, anyway."

She looks into her water glass, clearly regretting her confidences. She puts it down.

"No, she didn't say anything," I say. "But don't worry. You can trust us."

"That's what *she* said."

She looks up. Her eyes are brimming with tears.

Liam leaves the couch and sits on the coffee table in front of her. He reaches out and takes her hands in his. She startles but doesn't pull back.

"Are you talking about Jessica?" he asks.

"Yes."

"I call her Jessica Two," I say, feeling a stab of jealousy.

She breaks Liam's gaze to look at me. "Which would make me?"

"Jessica Three. Sorry, I know it's probably annoying."

She nods almost imperceptibly.

"Will you tell us how it happened?" Liam asks, bringing her focus back to him.

"Okay."

Jessie tells us her story with Liam's gentle prompting.

She was born in rural Illinois, but she was working as a teacher in a suburb outside Chicago when she won a million dollars in the state lottery. It was the one silly thing she did every week, she said, playing the lottery.

"It's hopeful," Liam says. "That's why people play."

"Is it?"

"It's about fantasy. Dreaming. What could be if only money wasn't a factor."

"Yes, I suppose that's right. Anyway, then I won."

"That's amazing," I say.

"It wasn't like I won the Powerball or anything, and with the taxes . . . But it meant that if I was careful, I could leave teaching, which I hated, and take a bit of time to figure out what I wanted to do next. I started looking for a place to buy up here because I'd visited the area once as a child, and it's so close to the mountains. I always wanted to live in the mountains."

"It's beautiful," I say, though I hate the Adirondacks.

"Yeah. And I got this house for almost nothing."

"This house?" I say, looking around. The beam work alone must've cost a small fortune.

She follows my eyes around the room. The number *2008* is carved into a large beam above the exit to the patio, the year it was built, presumably. "I got it in a divorce. They had to get rid of it quickly. I was in the right place at the right time with a cash offer."

"So, you moved here?"

"Yes, two years ago."

"What happened then?" Liam asks.

"Besides being labeled a witch?"

Liam smiles and nods. She has trouble taking her eyes off him. I know what that feels like. "Besides that."

"There was some press when I won. Local teacher wins the lottery, that sort of stuff. Then the letters started."

"Letters?" I ask.

"Begging letters. All lottery winners get them, I've heard. *Can you please donate to this charity? I'm down on my luck. I'm your long-lost cousin.* That sort of thing. Mostly, I ignored them."

"I'd do the same."

"I did make a contribution to the American Cancer Society."

I nod. "They do good work."

She looks away. "Then, after I moved here, I got a different kind of letter. It was from this . . . I guess you'd call it a support group?"

"For lottery winners?"

"Yeah. I know it sounds sort of hokey, but I was feeling pretty isolated."

"What did the letter say?"

"It was an invitation to a conference in Denver. I'd never been there."

"Was there a conference?" Liam asks.

"No, it was all a lie. I only found that out after."

Jessie's flexing her fingers back and forth, as if she has arthritis. Her nails are short and chipped.

"What happened, Jessie?"

"I had a connecting flight in Minneapolis. While I was waiting, someone called for Jessica Williams to come to the service desk. When I went up there, she was there."

"Jessica Two?" I say.

"Yeah."

"What did she look like?" Liam asks.

"I mostly remember her red hair."

"Anything else? Height, weight?"

"She was taller than me. Wearing a fancy black business suit and these super high heels."

"Confident? Pretty?"

"Yeah."

"And she made the coincidence seem cool, right?" I say. "Like you were part of some club?"

"That's exactly what she did."

"How long did you talk to her for?"

"She offered to buy me a drink because 'How often do two Jessica Williamses meet?'"

"Too often," I say.

"Seems like."

"So, you went."

"I don't usually drink, but I did that day."

The woodpecker knocks loudly against a tree. Jessie turns to look out the window to the deck, maybe seeking him out.

"Was she drinking scotch?" I ask.

"What? Oh yes. She was."

"And you?"

She turns back to me. "She ordered me something called a French seventy-five. Because I had to try it, apparently."

My brain tosses up the recipe from when I worked as a bartender for a catering company when I was in school. Sparkling wine, gin, lemon syrup. A deceptively strong drink. Especially for someone who isn't used to drinking. The drinking is part of her MO, clearly, and for good reason. People open up more when they drink and are less likely to remember the fine details.

"Then what?"

"We talked a bit, about this and that. And we played that game, of course. How she got my information."

"Jessica Williams Twenty Questions?"

She shakes her head. "I can't believe I fell for that."

"You weren't the only one."

"Then I went to get on my plane, and I only realized once I was on it that I'd left my phone behind."

"She took it?"

"I think so."

"How did she unlock it?"

"My password was lazy."

"Your birthday?"

"Yes."

"What happened when you got to Denver?" Liam asks.

She lets out a long, slow breath. "There was supposed to be someone to pick me up. Someone from the conference. But there was no one there. I didn't have my phone, so I couldn't call anyone. I found one of those airport computers, but then I realized I couldn't pay for it because my wallet was missing, too, with all my money and ID and bank cards. Eventually, someone was nice enough to pay for me to have a few minutes on the internet, and I looked the conference up and I couldn't find anything other than the website I'd looked at before. It didn't exist."

"She sent you the letter and made a fake website," I say.

"I think so."

"How did you get home?" Liam asks.

"I called my old boss from Chicago, and she faxed airport security the information from my personnel file. You can't imagine how hard it was to get them to believe me when I didn't have any ID."

"You couldn't ask your family for help?" Liam asks.

"My parents are dead, and I don't have any siblings."

It's a terrible story, but believable, given what I know. I try to imagine how I might react in the same situation. Anger, fear, loneliness. Mostly anger, I'm guessing. But I'd also know that Liam would come to my rescue. There's security in that, which I take for granted.

"And then what happened?" Liam asks.

"I confirmed what I already knew. She'd gone to the bank and taken out all my money."

"Because she had your wallet."

"Yeah, and her driver's license, which she showed me, which said we had the same name and birthday. My account information, my passwords, they were all in my phone."

Liam speaks with a bit more urgency. "She went into the bank?"

"I wasn't signed up for internet banking. I don't like doing much online."

"There must've been security footage, then."

"There was. The bank pulled it and gave it to the cops. They didn't care. One of them even said it could've been me, dressed up, taking my own money."

"Why would you do that?" Liam asks.

"That's what I said. And you know what the cop said? He said, there's all kinds of criminals in the world. Smart, dumb, and somewhere in between. Apparently, people do this sort of thing to try to get the insurance money. You know, how the bank has coverage on your accounts for fraud?"

"My cop said something similar," I say. "Plus, I got told I was a low priority."

"They said that too."

"She took everything?" Liam asks, keeping us on track.

"Pretty much. I filed for the insurance, but I was denied. I have the house. And I was lucky enough to get a job at the local school, not teaching, but at least it puts food on the table."

"It's not what you fantasized about," I say.

"Not by a long shot."

"And that gossip, Leanne—she knew about this?"

"Her husband is one of the policemen in town. I guess he told her, because she started saying things about how I could apply for"—she raises a hand and half covers her mouth—"*food stamps*. I thought what I told the police would be kept confidential."

"It should have been," Liam says.

"Thank you for telling us all this," I say.

"Is it going to help?"

"Maybe. We know something more now, anyway."

"What do you know?"

Liam summarizes. "That she's done this more than once. That she targets Jessica Williamses for some reason. That she's organized, smart, skilled with people. That her ID is good enough to fool a bank. She's very good at disguises and also a risk taker, confident she won't get caught. If you still have the pictures of her, then we can add it to the ones we have and see what other points of commonality we can find."

"What are you going to do with all that information?"

"We have enough to go back to the cops," Liam says.

Jessie shakes her head vigorously. "No, it's not going to make a difference with them. This happening to more than one person? It sounds even crazier than my original story. They'll end up telling Leanne and all them about it, and then there'll be more stuff in the papers about me. More reasons to treat me like an outcast. I don't want that. I just want to be anonymous."

"Don't you want your money back?" I ask.

"You think I'm going to get my money back if she goes to jail?"

"Depends on how good she is at hiding it."

"She's a professional. Isn't that what you said?"

Jessie's up and pacing now; I can almost hear her heart beating from here as I watch a pulse throb in her neck.

"Please don't take this to the police," she says. "Please."

"Hey," Liam says in a soothing voice. "Don't worry. We won't do anything you don't want."

Jessie looks at me for confirmation.

"We won't. Besides, I have a different idea, personally."

"What's that?"

"Catch her."

Chapter 9

In the Land of Todd

"This whole menu is screwed up," I say to Liam an hour later. We're ensconced in the A&W in town, sitting on the back porch under an awning that blocks out the suddenly hot sun. He ordered the Papa burger. I rebelled and ordered the Teen. "Why does the Grandpa burger have three patties? And the Mama burger doesn't have lettuce or tomato? Or bacon? I bet a lot of mothers like bacon."

"Just order what you want."

"I did. But this menu is pure patriarchy. What if you're not a mama or a papa? This is a good way to make people feel bad about themselves."

"I think we're going to feel bad enough about ourselves if we eat everything we ordered."

I pat him on the hand. "Poor Papa."

"Ha. That would be something."

"You'd make a great dad. I mean, you basically are a dad already."

"To a bunch of grown-up children?"

"That's right. You adopted all of us."

"I'm not your father."

Something in his tone reminds me that I don't want him to be. I change topics. "So, what did you think of her? Jessica Three. You certainly were friendly. I think she's half in love with you already."

"Don't be ridiculous."

"Is it so ridiculous?"

"As you very well know, I was being friendly to get her to open up. And it worked."

"You were holding her hands."

"I was calming her down."

I look away. Two large motorcycles roar into the parking lot. Their drivers are all in black leather and have matching long beards.

"She's a bit strange, though," Liam says. "And scared of the cops, for some reason."

"Maybe she doesn't want to be treated like a hysterical woman again. It wasn't that fun when it happened to me."

"I think it's something else. You check her story out?"

"Like I said in the car, I googled her when you sent me the info. She definitely worked at an elementary school in Chicago; I found an article about the school play that she was mentioned in. And then the article in the local paper about her when she moved to the area."

"Wonder what it is, then?"

The server brings our burgers, and for a few minutes we eat silently, filling up on empty calories. I try to remember how old I was when I came here with my parents. Five? Four? Not long before we were frog-marched up the hill. That's why they brought me, I think. A last treat.

"Maybe she has something in her past," I say. "There's lots of people who aren't comfortable around the police. It doesn't matter to me. She met Jessica Two; that's what's important. Especially if she can find those photographs."

"We should go to the cops."

I sit back and look at him. He's got some ketchup in the corner of his mouth. I have a sudden urge to reach across and wipe it away, which I quash.

"Since when has that been your modus operandi," I say instead, "Mr. kidnapper extraordinaire?"

He wipes his mouth with a napkin. "I never kidnapped anyone."

"Todd would've begged to differ."

"I rescued you."

"I know you did. I'm just saying, coloring inside the lines isn't usually your thing. Or going to the authorities."

He raises his drink to his lips, taking a long slug of his root beer through his straw. Mine's so sweet it's making my teeth hurt.

"You're right," he says. "But this feels different."

"The only thing that's different is that this is my operation, not yours."

"I'll accept that."

"You will?"

"You're an adult. You can make your own decisions."

"Or mistakes."

"That too."

I take a large bite of my burger. It might be a sexist establishment, but its product is delicious.

"This burger is pretty amazing."

Liam smiles at me. "You got some . . ." He motions to his face. I reach for a napkin and try to clean myself off.

"Here," Liam says, taking it from me. He reaches across the picnic table and wipes gently at my chin. I can feel myself blushing and look down at the table to avoid eye contact.

"That's better."

"Thank you."

I pick up some fries and resolve to eat them more daintily.

"I'll tell you one thing, though," Liam says. "This Jessica Two, or whoever she is, is pretty lucky. You having money, this one too . . . you worked out the odds on that?"

"She's pretty patient, right? Two years between jobs. And maybe she has a string of aliases that she uses in the same way, waiting for the perfect moment. Until she gets a Google Alert telling her that someone she can approach is flush. And from what we know, she's done well, but it's not like she's hit some massive jackpot."

"How much did she get from you?"

I finished off my burger. Equal parts beef and salt, and probably lots of sulfites. I banish the thought.

"Enough. And don't give me a lecture. The money was in that account because I was going to invest it like a real grown-up person who doesn't keep their money in cash and hide it in their mattress."

"Did I say anything?"

"You didn't have to. You think Jessie will come through with the photos?"

Liam stands, lifting his tray to take it to the trash. "I don't think she's going to do anything."

"Let's give her some time to think about it. At least until tomorrow."

"All right. That gives us the afternoon, anyway."

"To do what?"

"You'll see."

Something about the look in his eyes makes my blood run cold. "It's not what I think it is, is it?"

He says nothing, so now I know for certain.

We're going back to Schroon.

Schroon is the town I escaped from. Where my aunt, whose birth name was Caroline, but who went by Tanya then, because all adult Toddians were expected to adopt a *T* name, had taken me to buy a "pretty dress," she said. "Something that will look nice in a photograph."

There were so many confusing things about that sentence. Girls in the Land of Todd didn't wear dresses, only uniforms—Girl Scouts when younger, and secondhand Park Service outfits when older. I didn't even know if anyone had ever taken my photograph; Todd was against cameras because they were a way to spy on you and created "evidence" that could be misconstrued. The one exception was the Wall of Honor—a line of photographs of Todd with his "special recruits" on their eighteenth birthdays that hung on the wall in the Gathering Place. That wall fascinated us when we were small and was a place to be avoided when we were older.

The photographs were mostly of Todd with girls, but sometimes boys, often with a cake with many candles. I never thought much about them when I was younger. They were weird, for sure, but everything in the LOT was weird. We knew this even though most of us had never known anything different. But, odd as those photographs were, they never had anything to do with me because if I thought about it at all, I guess I always assumed that I'd never end up there. That if it was a place of honor, it belonged to Kiki.

Kiki—named after how she pronounced her middle name when she was two—was the golden child. Long, perfectly spun sunshiny hair. Clear blue eyes and excellent posture. We were as close as sisters, and yet we wouldn't be allowed to share a house when we turned eighteen. She was sharing with Sarah, the other girl our age. I'd be the odd woman out, even though we'd asked to be housed together. But it wasn't to be. Instead, I was the one whose mother wouldn't look her in the eye when she talked up the virtues of living alone "most of the time." Shivers.

Even before Todd took an interest in me, I'd thought about escaping from the LOT off and on for years. I'd listened to those rumors about "Liam," the ghost who came to rescue you if you wished it hard enough. A specter who appeared when you needed him most. If you turned around three times at midnight and clicked your heels together under a new moon, he might come and get you. Sarah knew for sure that this was how Aaron had escaped, only he'd screwed up the spell and his parents had disappeared too.

I didn't believe in spells, but after that day at the farmers' market, I knew Liam was real. I told Kiki about him at the first opportunity, but she refused to leave with me. So I was on my own. I spent that winter working out the details of my plan over and over, waiting for an opportunity. When Tanya told me she was taking me to town, I was happy despite the underlying unease related to the reason for the visit. Sitting next to her in the van, I tried to memorize the turns as if I'd be driving them. Right, right, left, then a long stretch . . .

The store she took me to was out of date and out of the way. There was one older woman at the cash register and dust flashing in the sunbeam that cut through the front windows. I took the white dresses Tanya handed me and willed her with a look not to follow me into the dressing room. I hung the dresses on the hook, then slipped out the emergency exit before I had time to talk myself out of it. I rushed down the street to the coffee shop Liam had told me about, one who'd know what to do if a scared girl came in unexpectedly asking to use the phone. I dialed Liam's number, and he thankfully picked up immediately. We made a quick plan for a week ahead, the day I'd be moving down the mountain. Then I ran back to the store, grabbed the dresses from the changing room, and told my aunt that either of them was fine, she could choose.

I'd been away for five minutes.

What did she make of the beads of sweat on my brow? She was too guilty to notice, I thought. Or she'd mastered the art of looking away, because that was how you survived in the LOT.

Looking right at things was discouraged.

The LOT has shrunk in the intervening years. As we walk around the dilapidated compound, I'm shocked at how quickly we canvass what once seemed vast: the Gathering Place, Todd's house, my parents' cottage, where I was supposed to live. There's still half a dock on the small lake we used to jump into on winter mornings to cleanse ourselves of our desires. "When you plunge into the cool," Todd used to say, wrapped in a fur coat that looked like it belonged to a Muscovite, "you have no choice but to forget everything else. There's nothing but yourself and your survival. Hold on to that feeling and you'll be invincible."

I move instinctually, Liam following me, letting me set the pace. I've been back here since I ran away, but I had things on my mind other than a trip down memory lane. Like Todd said, I'd been dipped into the cool, and I was trying to hold on to the feeling.

The hike up to the Upper Camp is steep—I remember that right. I'm out of breath when we get to the small collection of cabins I spent my childhood in. The "school," where we learned our odd lessons and ate our meals. The washstand, where we brushed our teeth outside in all weathers. The girls' bunks and the boys' bunks.

The guardhouse.

I open the door to the girls' bunks. The roof is half–caved in.

"Careful," Liam says.

"It'll be all right."

I walk into the dark wooden structure. It smells of rot and decay. A mouse scurries across the floor. I suppress a yelp.

My bunk was at the back, above Kiki's. My initials are carved into the beam, but Kiki was too afraid to do that. She didn't want to get in trouble. I didn't either, but I didn't think I would. That was how we were different. She let fear in, anticipated it, even. I tried to keep it at bay by ignoring the obvious realities.

I look down at her bunk. I don't have to close my eyes to remember her lying there in a rough muslin nightgown like something Laura Ingalls Wilder might have worn. Her hair was always pleated into a tight braid that looked as if it hurt her head, but she took it out for sleeping. She'd make me brush it a hundred times, though I never understood why. It was perfect whether she did anything to it or not.

I told her I was leaving that last night I spent here, my bags all packed with my meager belongings to move down the hill. She was moving down also, but not moving on. I'd asked her again and again to come with me, but she'd always refused, her fear holding her in place.

"What will you do?" she asked. "Where will you go?"

"Anything and anywhere. It has to be better than here."

"They won't accept you."

"So Todd says."

Kiki sucked in her breath. Questioning Todd was an offense that brought on the highest punishment—banishment to the Back Forest. Kiki was terrified of the place even before we were forced to spend a week there for punishment. It was claustrophobic and terrible, and the thought of being there for any length of time was more than enough to keep her in line.

"Jess!"

I slipped down off my bunk and broke another rule. I climbed into Kiki's bunk and hugged her close. "I'm not going to tell you anything else because I don't want you to get into trouble, but if you want to leave, anytime, find a way to call this number." I whispered it into her ear and then traced it on her palm over and over again until she nodded that she had it memorized. "It's for Liam. He can save you."

Kiki pushed me away and turned onto her side. I didn't take it personally. She was afraid for me and for herself. Despite the nightgown, she wasn't a pioneer. She wanted stability, rules, predictability. But those things were already slipping away. Todd wasn't Todd anymore. Maybe he'd never been, and our parents had simply participated in some mass hallucination about sunshine and rainbows and good pot. When the smoke cleared, all that was left were weird rules and unhappy children and adults who looked like they wanted to talk in whispers while checking over their shoulders that they weren't being spied on, but somehow never did.

Right before it started to get light outside, I dressed in a pair of Park Ranger pants and a heavy flannel shirt I'd lifted from the boys' laundry and tucked my hair into a baseball cap. Then I scurried down the hill with my duffel bag on my back, on past the small sleeping houses, out to the road where Liam was waiting.

"Why did you bring me here?" I ask Liam when I step out of the cabin into the half light of the woods.

"Unfinished business."

"We all have that."

"Some more than most. I could sense it when we drove past here earlier . . ."

"I had a moment. That's all."

"Are you sure? Because it's perfectly normal to have feelings about being raised in a place like this, and we've never talked about everything that happened after Todd died."

I slap on a smile. Everything that happened after Todd died isn't something I want to talk about with anyone, even Liam.

"I'm not . . . I'm not holding on to anything here, if that's what you're thinking."

Liam's face is in shadow, but I know how he looks. "And yet, you stole that article."

"I did."

"That's all you have to say?"

I can't look Liam in the eye. "If I explained it, would it make a difference?"

"It might."

"I doubt it," I say.

Liam watches me for a moment. "Was that guy harassing you?"

"Of course he was. You think I faked the emails?"

"You never said."

"I don't tell you everything."

"We're supposed to share the big stuff."

I feel a prick of anger. "I made a mistake, Liam. People make mistakes. And yeah, I was losing my job, and I was going to be left with nothing, so I played a card I'd been holding. And if it was wrong, I'm being punished for that, aren't I? The money's gone. That should make you happy."

"It doesn't."

"So why are you accusing me of . . . what? Being like Todd? Taking my moral cues from a sociopath?"

"I never said—"

"You definitely implied."

Liam runs his hands through his hair and looks away. It's always so complicated between us. He's too many things to me. Brother, mentor, father, savior, and not the thing I want most.

"I want you to be well," he says.

"I'm working on it."

I stand next to him and we turn to face the downslope of the hill. Schroon Lake glints at our feet.

"You don't have to worry about me so much," I say. "I'm doing okay."

"If you say so."

"I do."

"Can I give you one piece of advice?" Liam asks.

"Sure."

"Whatever you're holding on to, and I know it's something even if I don't know what it is, let it go."

I look out over the view. I remember too many things, but mostly I remember what I can't forget.

"I will," I say, the lie slipping easily through my teeth. "Thus endeth the lesson."

Chapter 10

One More for Good Measure

When we get back to the motel, there's a surprise waiting for us.

We'd stopped at the store to get food we could eat in the room for dinner, and then the liquor store because all I wanted for dinner was whiskey. I felt dirty after visiting the Land of Todd. Twenty minutes under a hot spray and then three fingers of Canadian Club sounded like a perfect evening.

These plans get put aside when I open the door to our room and find an envelope from Jessie.

"What's that?" Liam asks as I pick up the manila envelope from the floor.

The words I FOUND THEM are written across the front. We'd told her where we were staying in case she located the pictures from the bank. She'd given me a funny look when I'd said the words *our motel room*. I'd quickly explained that Liam was cheap, and that since we'd known each other so long we were more like brother and sister. Liam had frowned at that, which, frankly, gave me a bit of hope.

I open the envelope and shake out a set of three photographs that are similar to the ones I got from the bank, only these are in color.

"Pictures of Jessica Two," I say.

"Ah."

"You want to take a look?"

"Sure."

"Drink?"

"That too."

I put the bags on the shelf holding the TV and pull out the Canadian Club. There are two glasses in the bathroom that seem clean, but . . . "No ice," I say to Liam.

He's sitting on the edge of one of the beds. It's covered in a multicolored comforter that's seen better days. The rug on the floor is another multicolored pattern, picked, I'm sure, for its capacity to hide stains. The furniture, such as it is, is laminated pine and probably was made before I was born.

"I think I saw a machine next to reception," I say to Liam.

"Maybe later."

I screw the cap off and pour us each a drink. I hand Liam his, and down half of mine. It stings in the way I was hoping the shower would.

"That's the ticket."

Liam gives me a look, but I wave it away with the envelope. We move to the small round table in the corner. It has a lamp suspended over it that provides some faded light. The large window that looks out over the parking lot is covered in a slatted blind that Liam rolls up. It's close to sunset, and the sky is pink and purple over the pine forest across the road.

I place the photographs on the table one by one, then take out my own set from my bag.

"This doesn't even look like the same person," I say.

My Jessica Two has black hair that falls in a straight line to her chin. Her face looks narrow, her nose straight. She's all angles. I remember thinking she was taller than I am, but we never stood next to one another. She wore heels and slim, fitted black pants. Her red lips and nails were the only other things that stood out.

In contrast, Jessie's photographs show a redheaded woman with long, wavy hair and a rounded face. Her clothes are loose, giving the impression of a plumper body underneath.

"She's good, I'll give her that," Liam says.

"What am I missing?" I finish my drink. I'd love nothing more than to pour myself another one of equal strength, but I sense judgment from Liam, so I hold back.

Liam points to how the woman in Jessie's photographs and then mine is wearing her hair. "See here, you can't see her ears in either photograph. Or her forehead."

"Why's that important?"

"It's hard to change the shape of an ear, or where a natural hairline is."

"She was wearing earrings. Diamond studs, I think."

"That's smart. It gives you something to focus on rather than their shape or other things like freckles or moles."

"What about the nose? Isn't that hard to change?"

Both of these women have straight noses, but one looks narrower than the other, and longer.

"That's easy to shade with makeup."

"How would she know how to do that?"

"There's lots of good tutorials on changing your face contours on YouTube."

"YouTube? You watch YouTube?"

He gives me an exasperated look. "Everyone watches YouTube."

"Sure. YouTube, but not Facebook. Got it. And makeup tutorials, apparently. You were saying?"

"I watch them for professional reasons. Anyway, if you take a look, you'll get an idea of what you can do. Someone with skill can completely change their appearance."

"But what about things like height and weight?"

"That can be adjusted with shoes, clothing, padding."

"Do you see any similarities?"

He holds up the best picture of Jessica Two from my series and one from Jessie's. "It's a woman."

"Yeah, thanks, I could figure that out for myself."

"Don't be so sure. She could've been a man."

I sit back in my chair. This has never occurred to me.

"But you said she's not."

"I don't think so. The features are too fine. And see here?" He points to where Jessica Two is reaching toward the keypad in the ATM. "Her wrist is delicate. That's another thing that's hard to fake."

"So, a woman. Anything else?"

"She probably is about your age, late twenties to early thirties. It's hard to add more than four to six inches with shoes, so she's between five feet and, say, five six. She's white. She has light eyes since you said she did, and the redhead does, and colored contacts can only do so much. Given her wrists, she's on the thin side, but I couldn't say much more than that. I don't think she has dark hair naturally—her brows aren't dark enough. So, she likely has lighter hair, blonde or light brown."

"Not red?"

"Strawberry blonde is possible, but she doesn't seem to have any freckling on her arms or chest, which is definitely harder to cover up than most things, so probably not red hair."

"Not all redheads have freckles."

"I'm working on averages here."

A pickup truck rolls into the parking lot. There's a pack of kids riding illegally on the flatbed, like a scene from *The Outsiders*. They jump out and pull out a cooler.

"Tailgate party?" I say.

"What?"

"Check it out."

Liam looks out the window and winces.

"Great location you picked here," I say.

"It'll be fine."

"If you say so. Anyway, not much to go on. A light-haired and light-eyed girl around my age and my height and weight, give or take ten pounds. This could be me."

Liam's eyes rest on mine. "Is it?"

"What? No."

He laughs. "Gotcha."

"Not funny. But how did you know it wasn't?"

"Because of this," he says, taking hold of my wrist and turning it over, then pushing up the long sleeves I almost always wear. I've got a bad scar on my wrist—a burn that travels across my tendons and is visibly raised from my skin. He traces it gently, then drops my arm quickly. I shift my arm up reflexively, holding it against my body.

"You can see the underside of her wrist clearly in one of the photos," he says. "It would be hard to cover up your scar with makeup."

It *is* hard to cover up. I gave up trying long ago.

"So, Todd saved me from your suspicions. Thanks, Todd."

He turns away, and I know I've done it again.

"I didn't mean . . ."

"It's fine."

I reach out and touch his arm. "Hey, Liam. Thanks for today. All of it. I appreciate it."

"Even Schroon?"

"Even Schroon."

He looks skeptical as he pats my hand, then stands. "We should eat, then get some sleep. Long drive tomorrow."

I agree because I've done enough damage.

But I'm not going back tomorrow. I'm going forward.

Hours later I'm lying in my bed, trying to ignore the full fucking party that's going on in the parking lot. The level in the bottle of Canadian Club is lower, but if I drink any more I'm going to regret it in the morning. Liam went to sleep an hour ago after the baseball game finished (another loss), but I can't help but ask.

"You awake?"

"Mmm."

"Sorry."

"It's fine. I'm sleeping."

I stare at the ceiling, listening to his breathing. The scar on my wrist feels like it's throbbing, but it's not because it hurts. It's because I want to get up and slip into the bed two feet away and throw caution to the wind. Peel my T-shirt over my head and let it drop to the floor. Rest my lips against his neck and throw my leg over his hip and . . . I'm starting to sweat. I have no idea how Liam would react to any of that, and my best guess is rejection, so I try to distract myself from the vivid fantasy in my brain by logging on to Facebook on my phone to see if there are any updates on my post.

There's nothing, but there *is* a message from someone named JJ.

I saw your message. What do you want?

I click through to her page. Her privacy settings are at the max, so all that's there is a picture of her in a chef's hat and her location: Philadelphia. I google: *Philly, chef, JJ*. A bunch of links come up, including several to YouTube videos.

"Hey, Liam," I say very quietly as I slip on my headphones and plug them into my phone. "I'm watching YouTube."

He doesn't react. He probably can't hear me over the thumping Ariana Grande.

JJ's a chef with a YouTube channel that has over a million followers. I watch one of her videos. She's an army vet, and lost part of her left arm in combat, but she doesn't let that stop her. She's relentlessly positive and clearly loves what she's doing. Eighteen months ago, there was a large profile on her in the *Philadelphia Inquirer*. All about how she'd become a successful YouTube star, with an annual revenue of over a million dollars.

Uh-oh.

I head back to Facebook and type: Is your name Jessica Williams?

She reads and answers it quickly.

Yes.

Have you met someone else with the same name?

Yes.

Were you born on July 10, 1990?

Again, yes. That's what your message said.
Why else would I write you?

Just confirming.

Well, it's confirmed.

Did this other JW steal your money?

There's a pause, then: Yes. You?

Yes.

When? she writes.

Recently, I write. A couple of weeks ago. You?

18 months, four days.

Did you go to the police?

Of course. They were useless.

Same.

I'm not going to them again, she writes.

Me either.

So why are you writing me, then?

I have a plan.

Oh?

Yeah, but it's . . . can we come see you?

What do you mean, "we"?

I found another Jessica.

A long pause this time. Then: Okay. But please don't tell anyone you're coming.

Why?

She hasn't been in touch with you?

I think of the texts I sent to Jessica Two. She hasn't responded yet. And maybe she won't. I check my text threads to be sure. No answer. I text her again. I'm going to find you. I blame the Canadian Club.

No, I write to JJ. She hasn't been in touch.

She will be.

What did she do to you?

It doesn't matter. Just promise me you'll be careful.

I promise.

We make a tentative plan to connect in Philly in a couple of days. Will I be able to convince Jessie to come with me? If I were her, I wouldn't be able to pass up the chance, based on curiosity alone, and I'm counting on that to overcome her natural hesitancy.

"Jess, what the hell are you doing over there?"

I lay my phone down flat on my chest and pull my headphones off. "Sorry, did I wake you?"

He sits up and turns his back to me, putting his feet on the floor. He stands and walks to the bathroom, closing the door firmly behind him.

I put my phone on the bedside table and snuggle down into the covers. Liam comes out of the bathroom smelling like the cheap soap I used earlier. His bed creaks as he climbs back in.

"You got a pen pal or something?" he asks.

"I'll tell you about it in the morning. Go back to sleep."

"You sure?"

"Yes."

I roll over onto my side for good measure. I'm finally feeling sleepy, and if I tell Liam about JJ now, it'll be at least an hour of questions.

"Night," I say.

"Sleep well, Jess."

I listen to the thump of the music, and this time it starts to lull me away. I'm almost gone when my phone flashes on the nightstand, the light like a beam in my eye.

I pick it up.

Jessica Two has texted me back.

You can't catch me, her text says.

There's no more sleep after that.

Chapter 11

Don't Go Chasing Waterfalls

Liam drives me to the High Falls Gorge after breakfast the next morning, where Jessie suggested we meet after I reached out to her. It's a part of the Ausable River that's been a pay-to-see attraction since the 1800s. Jessie didn't say why she wants to meet here. There are only a couple of cars in the parking lot, and an old-timey buggy guarded by a placid-looking horse. One of the cars is Jessie's Prius. I can see her sitting in the front seat, looking at her phone. There's a chill this morning, and it was one of those winters followed by a cold spring, so there's still snow on the ground deep in the woods where the sunlight doesn't reach. I wouldn't wait outside either.

"You sure about this?" Liam asks.

"I'm sure."

He looks a bit tired. I'm tired, too, but I tried to hide that from him as I told him about the messages from JJ that I received last night. I didn't tell him about the text I sent or received from Jessica Two, or tell him about JJ's fears, but Liam's uneasy anyway. He's got a job lined up with a longtime client that he can't skip and thinks I should postpone doing anything further until he can come with me. But I've reminded him that I'm nearly thirty years old and that it's time for me to fix my own problems, and he's reluctantly agreed so long as I promise to let him know the moment it gets dangerous.

"Why do you want Jessie to go with you?" he asks.

"I don't think she's told us everything she knows yet. Plus, there's safety in numbers, right? That should make you feel better."

He ignores my jab. "You think she's holding back?"

"Not deliberately, but maybe something JJ tells us will jog her memory."

"What if she doesn't want to go?"

"Then I'll ask her to drive me to Plattsburgh. Or I'll take an Uber. We talked about this. It'll be fine."

"This doesn't seem like a great place for Uber service."

"I've figured out worse situations."

"I know you have."

I tap him on the nose. "It's like you said yesterday. I'm all grown up now. You can let this little bird out of the nest."

Liam crooks his index finger under my chin, making sure I'm looking him squarely in the eye. "You keep making jokes. But this, what you're planning, it's dangerous. Maybe she's only a con artist, someone who's never had to do anything violent. But that doesn't mean she won't if she's pushed. The smart thing to do is to take what you know and go to the police."

"They won't do anything."

"Perhaps not, but what are *you* going to do if you find her?"

"Get my money back."

"And if she refuses?"

"Then I'll turn her in."

"So simple, huh?"

"That's right. Keep it simple. You taught me that. And I know how to protect myself. How to fight." That was part of Todd's lessons too. Hand-to-hand combat. Liam added in the self-defense portion; he believed in walking away from the fight in an honorable way, but I knew how to do both.

He lets me go and turns away. "I tried to teach you a lot of things. Maybe I was wrong to get involved in the first place."

My stomach drops. The last thing I want to do is make Liam question his role in my life. "Why do you think that?"

"A lot of you are struggling. Think of Daisy. Look at where you are right now. Aaron. Maybe you would've been better off if I left well enough alone."

I've never seen him like this, full of doubts. "Hey." I reach out and repeat his move, my finger under his chin so he's looking me right in the eye. "Of course you shouldn't have done that. Think of what would have happened to me if I'd stayed where I was."

His eyes shift away. "Yeah, maybe."

"Definitely. Plus, why are you so worried? You don't even think I'm going to find her."

"You probably will."

"Thanks for the vote of confidence. Come on, what's up?"

He raises his hands to grip the steering wheel. His fingers are strong, capable. "I've got a bad feeling, that's all."

"You don't believe in bad feelings. You believe in checking. That's what I'm doing."

"You're right."

Jessie opens her car door and steps out. She's wearing a purple Patagonia puffy jacket and dark jeans. She looks tiny and vulnerable.

I lean in and kiss Liam on his cheek. His stubble is rough against my lips, but he smells warm and clean and inviting.

I pull myself away. "I've got to go. Drive safe. And thank you."

"You're welcome. Stay in touch."

"I will. I promise."

And maybe this time I'm telling the truth.

Jessie and I pay separately for our tickets and listen to a short lecture about how part of the trail is closed for repairs and to follow the signs. We go through the doors and walk over a small bridge that crosses the Ausable River. The water is rushing by fast and loud, dark and cold.

"Why did you want to meet here?" I ask Jessie as we turn right down the path once we've crossed the bridge.

"You want to take the easy path or the regular one?"

"What's the difference?"

"One brings you to the falls, and there's stairs and these glass-bottomed landings, which are kind of terrifying. The other is just a path in the woods."

"The terrifying path, for sure."

She laughs gently. "I get the sense that you're a bit reckless."

"Sometimes. Liam thinks so."

She glances at me, then shifts away. "Is he your boyfriend?"

I shove my hands into the pockets of my fleece. It's even colder in the woods, without the sun. The air smells like the river and melting snow and that undercurrent of granite I smelled in the car yesterday. New York is a state made of gravestones.

"No."

"But you want him to be?"

"I . . ."

"It's complicated?"

"Definitely."

"He likes you," she says.

"We've known each other a long time, but it's never been like that between us."

She looks skeptical. "You don't have to tell me."

"No, it's fine. Liam works as a private investigator, and he rescued me from a bad family situation when I was eighteen and helped me set up my new life."

"That's cool."

I laugh. "Yeah, Liam is pretty cool."

There's a rustling up ahead. An Amish family emerges on the path—father, mother, and a passel of children. The buggy in the parking lot suddenly makes sense.

We pass them and nod politely. It's difficult not to stare even though I've been on the receiving end of that kind of attention. Once they're out of earshot, I ask Jessie, "Is that usual?"

"First time for me, though I've heard there's some in the area. I'll never understand it."

"What's that?"

"How someone could belong to a cult like that."

"They're not a cult. They're a sect."

"Po-tay-to, po-tah-to."

"No, I—" I cut myself off. I don't tell people about the Land of Todd. It tends to elicit odd reactions. "I'm a journalist and I wrote a long piece about cults. There are important distinctions."

I'd investigated several small cults, but it was the segment on the LOT that went viral. "Williams has a way of climbing inside the mind of a charismatic leader and exposing them for what they are—sociopathic, narcissistic, opportunistic." That was in the *New York Times* after my article got turned into a six-episode podcast that I narrated. I never told anyone, not even my editor, how I got that insight, and The Twists and Liam kept my secret.

"If you say so," Jessie says.

We reach the first set of stairs. They're steep, metal, and look like they've been here longer than I've been alive. The roar of the falls is deafening.

"You up to this?" she asks, pointing down.

"Sure."

I take a first tentative step. I'm not usually afraid of heights, but this is not the sort of height you normally encounter. My heart speeds up and my palms feel slick against the cool railing. When we get to the bottom, we stand on the glass-bottomed platform and watch the water rush over the side of the cliff. I feel dizzy and disoriented. Jessie stands next to me.

"That's amazing," I say.

"I couldn't believe it the first time I came in here."

"You'd never know it was here from the road."

"I thought that too."

She walks closer to the railing overlooking the water. I take a step closer, pressing my body up against the railing. I feel shaky, and there are unstable thoughts in my mind. "Let's go back up."

I turn and start up the stairs in front of her. Two steps in, she stumbles into me, almost knocking me off my feet. I reach out and grab the stairs, the sharp metal cutting at my fingers. She puts a firm hand on my back as a family appears at the top of the stairs.

"You okay?" the mother asks. She's blonde and tall, her husband wearing a dark scowl behind her.

I push myself up. "I'm fine," I say, holding up my hands, which are stinging but not cut. I turn to check on Jessie. She loops her arm around me quickly, the other holding on to the railing tightly.

"Everything's okay!" she calls up to the family, looking worried, then turns to me. "You all right?"

"Yes."

I turn and we climb the stairs and past the family waiting for us at the top.

"Be careful down there," I say, eyeing her rambunctious children. She nods, and Jessie and I walk away from the roar of the falls.

"That wasn't fun," I say.

Jessie looks down at her feet. They're in white tennis shoes, tied up neatly. "I'm not sure what happened."

"I felt dizzy down there."

"I guess that's it." She sits on a bench under a tree and wraps her arms around herself. "I'm sorry."

"You didn't do it on purpose."

She bites her lip. "Were those pictures helpful?"

"The ones you left at the motel? Yes, a bit, but not as much as we would've liked."

"Sorry."

"It's fine. That's not why I wanted to meet you. Another Jessica reached out."

"What?"

"Jessica Four. She goes by JJ."

"Who is she?"

"She asked me not to say."

"So why are you telling me, then?"

"Because she's agreed to meet me, and I'd like you to come."

I sit down next to her. The bench is cold, under a canopy of trees and next to the side of a hill. There's a small patch of snow up the side of it, and I can still hear the rush of the river.

"Where?"

"Philly."

"Is that where it happened?"

"Not sure. She didn't say where Jessica Two caught up to her." I stand up and stamp my feet on the ground to warm them up. I'm getting colder by the minute. "Will you do it?"

"What's the point?"

"I think we're getting close."

"What could possibly give you that idea?"

I pause. I'm not sure what the right move is here. "She texted me yesterday. Jessica Two."

"What?"

Jessie stands quickly and starts to march down the path away from me. I rush after her.

"Wait up."

We arrive at another bridge. We cross it and stop in the middle. It feels like we're only a few feet above the river. I take out my phone and take a picture. I'll send it to Liam later. He likes nature.

"What did the text say?" Jessie asks loudly over the roar.

"I'd texted her a couple times, stupid stuff about how I was going to find her, and she told me I couldn't catch her."

"She's probably right."

"Don't you see? If she texted me back, then it means something I'm doing is getting to her. Maybe she saw my message on Facebook and all the people who were tagged there."

"Saw me, you mean?"

"Well, yes."

Jessie lets out a long, slow breath. "I don't like this."

"I get it, I do. But JJ, she also told me to be careful. It seemed like she was worried about Jessica Two, and doesn't that make you mad?"

"Why would that make me mad?"

"Because she's getting away with it. She took our money, and she's going to do it again, and she's done it to others, and then she has the gall to make us scared about it as well. I don't want to live my life like that, do you?"

"Doesn't feel like I have much choice."

"But you do. You *do*. We do. If we work together, go talk to JJ and find out what she knows, I think we're going to be able to figure out how to solve this thing. Maybe get our money back, and get her out of our lives once and for all."

"She's not in my life."

"Isn't she, though? You're stuck in this town that you hate living in because you can't leave. You're too scared to tell that bully, Leanne, to cut it out. She did that to you."

"Don't lecture me."

"Okay, you're right, I'm sorry. I just . . . I'm worried about what she might do next if we don't stop her."

"What do you mean?"

"Look, I'll be okay no matter what happens. And you'll be okay too. I don't know about JJ, but maybe she will as well. But what if her next victim is someone vulnerable? Someone who can't take being duped?

I've seen what can happen to someone when they're betrayed. It's not something everyone can stand."

I look away so Jessie won't see my tears, but I can't hide my shaking hands.

"Are you talking about someone in your family?" Jessie asks.

"My best friend."

"I'm sorry."

"It's okay." I wipe my eyes quickly and turn back to her. "But if there was something I could've done to stop that from happening, I would have, you know?"

"It's not our job to save her victims."

"Our job? No. But our responsibility? I kind of think it is."

A couple and their dog appear on the path. The dog is small and energetic, bounding happily on its leash.

I look at Jessie. She's watching the dog, a bit fearful.

"I'm going to do this with or without you," I say. "And I'm not going to stop until I find her, I can promise you that. But I'd rather have your help."

"Why?"

"Because we're in this together. You, me, the Jessica in Philly. We're connected."

"You sound like Shakespeare. The Saint Crispin's Day speech. You know it?"

"*We few, we happy few, we band of brothers . . .*"

"*For he today that sheds his blood with me . . .*"

"*Shall be my brother*," we say together. "*Be he ne'er so vile.*"

The couple passes us, giving us a look like you might expect if you came upon two women randomly reciting Shakespeare in the woods.

I hold out my hand. "We in this together?"

She still looks unsure, but she reaches out her hand just the same.

Chapter 12

Waiting Room

Jessie agrees to drive us to Philly in her car, though I offer to rent a vehicle. Taking her car is better on the cash flow. Like a good Liam disciple, I have some money stashed away for emergencies that wasn't in the account Jessica Two got to, but it's not going to last forever.

I have a few minutes to look around Jessie's place while she packs. There isn't much personal about it. No family photographs. No photographs at all. The cupboards contain only the essentials, not even a complete set of plates. I have this feeling that if I look in her closet, I'd find three or four outfits and that would be it. As if she were living her life ready to pack up at any moment, nothing she'd regret to leave behind.

But have I been living my life any differently? Would someone who went through my room think I was there for the long haul? A whole benefit of living with jerky Josh and his former frat buddies is that it's temporary and doesn't require any investment or ties. I could pack up in an hour and owe them nothing.

"You checking up on me?" Jessie asks, startling me as I close the kitchen-cupboard door.

I glance over my shoulder, keeping my voice calm. "What? Oh no, I was looking for a glass for some water."

"One cupboard over."

"Thanks." I go through the motions of getting a glass out, filling it from the tap, and drinking it down. I can sense Jessie's eyes on me as I do so. I turn around. She hasn't moved. There's a small bag at her feet, and she's scraped her hair back into a ponytail, revealing a distinctive widow's peak.

"Should we bring some snacks?" I ask, trying to breach the tension.

She takes a beat. "Snacks?"

"You know, for the drive. It's a long one. And I left my snack bag in Liam's car, unfortunately."

"About five hours and forty-nine minutes, according to Google, if we observe speed limits and take the toll roads," she says, frowning as she speaks. I can tell that she's questioning the choice she made at the gorge. I shouldn't have let my curiosity loose. Whatever trust I'd built up on our walk has been drained away, like the water I just chugged down.

"I didn't mean anything by it," I say.

"What's that?"

"Looking around a bit. My curiosity got the better of me. When you work with Liam for too long, it kind of becomes part of your DNA."

"Suspicion?"

"More like the need for information. Get all the information."

"Huh?"

"It's a Liamism. That's what The Twists call these sayings he has."

"That a musical group?"

"What? Oh, ha. No. There's . . ." I should shut up. How can I explain us? "I mentioned before that Liam saved me from a bad situation? Well, I'm not the only one. There's about a half dozen of us, and that's what we call ourselves, after *Oliver Twist*. But he's not like that Fagin guy. It's an ironic name. Liam's scrupulously honest."

"That right?"

"Trust me."

"Hmm."

I put the glass down on the counter. "Hey, I know we just met, and you have no reason to believe anything I'm saying, but I'm trying to do something good here, I promise."

"Don't do that," she says.

"What?"

"Forget it. Are we going or what?"

"You still want to?"

"I never wanted to, but I said I would, so let's go and get this over with."

We don't get snacks. And we don't talk much in the car either. Jessie hands me a map and tells me to navigate because she doesn't believe in GPS, so I spend my time figuring out the map and give her updates now and then on our progress.

Familiar names flash by on the road as we retrace the drive Liam and I did the day before all the way back to Albany. We stay on I-87 rather than switching to the 95, and then we're out of my known universe, driving by places I never paid any attention to on the map that was on the wall in the Gathering Place. My eyes used to be drawn to farther-away places—London, Paris, Budapest. I've never been to any of them. Instead, I ended up five hours away in New York. The trip I took to Mexico a few weeks ago was the first time I'd ever left the country, my newly minted passport still fresh, the pages stiff.

We stop for lunch at a diner near Newburgh, a town on the Hudson River. It has a lot of fried fish on the menu, but also sandwiches and pasta. There's a blue strip of neon running around a recess in the ceiling, which makes everything and everyone in the place look slightly alien.

"Fresh jumbo shrimp cocktail," I say to Jessie once we've had a few minutes to peruse the menu. "You think that's a good choice?"

She makes a face. "I'd stick to things that don't go bad so quickly, personally."

"You make a good point."

I order a corned beef sandwich and a Diet Coke. She orders the turkey on whole wheat and sticks to water.

"It's my one vice," I say, as she eyes my drink with a bit of distaste. "Well, maybe not my only one, but one a day can't hurt, can it?"

"Eat what you want," she says. "I don't care."

"Did she have any weird eating habits?"

"We didn't eat together."

"Just drank."

"That's right."

I take a sip of my Diet Coke. It's refreshing, especially after the long drive. "And you haven't flown since?"

"Nope."

"Did you ask the airport to check its records?"

"Where? In Minneapolis?"

"Yeah."

"I did. They said I was the only one with that name through the airport that day."

"So, she has other ID."

"I guess."

"That's good to know."

"Why?"

"The more we know, they closer we are to getting to her."

"If you say so."

She eats her sandwich delicately, taking small bites. I've already finished my sandwich and the large pickle it came with.

"I can drive, if you want," I say.

"What's that?"

"After lunch. To give you a break."

She smiles. "Thanks, I'd like that."

After lunch, I take the wheel and lead us onto the highway. The Prius handles well, and it's easy to get going over the speed limit. Too easy.

We pass a patrol car tucked into one of those turnarounds that are hard to see until it's too late. I glance down at the speedometer; we're going seventy-five.

"Shit," I say as the cop pulls out of his hiding place.

"What?"

The flash of lights answers for me.

"Dammit," Jessie says. "This was a mistake."

"It's just a ticket," I say as I slow down and start to pull off to the side of the road. "I'll pay it."

"No." She looks over at me in frustration. "You and me. You're going to have to show them my car registration and your license, so they'll know we're two Jessica Williamses traveling together. Police don't like coincidences. I should've thought of it before."

"I'm sure it will be fine. I mean, you don't have a criminal record or anything, do you?"

"No."

"Me neither. So, why would the cops care about us? If they do, we'll explain."

"I never switched my registration to New York."

"I don't think that's a huge deal."

"I hope you're right."

I stop the car and roll down my window as the cop approaches.

"How are you folks today?" he asks. He's about forty years old with close-cropped blond hair and a beefy neck.

"We're good," I say.

"Where you headed?"

"Philly."

"You in a hurry to get there?"

"No, I'm so sorry, Officer. It's my friend's car, and I'm not used to the gas pedal. I didn't realize how fast I was going."

"Uh-huh. What you going to Philly for?"

"A reunion," I say, smiling.

"Sounds fun," he says. "Please hand over your driver's license and registration."

"I need to go into the glove box," Jessie says.

"Go ahead."

She opens it and reaches in as I take out my wallet and give him my driver's license.

"You, too, little lady."

I can see Jessie grit her teeth as she takes out her wallet and hands him her driver's license with the registration. As she leans over me to do so, I can smell her sweat.

The police officer starts to enter the information into his computer, then stops. He puts the two licenses one on top of each other; then he frowns. He tips his head down into the car.

"You ladies have something to tell me?"

After he calls it in, the police officer tells us to follow him to the station.

"See," Jessie says. "I told you."

"It's not illegal to be driving with someone who has the same name as you."

"Tell that to Mr. *Little Lady*."

"He's a jerk," I say. "But if we tell the truth, it'll be okay."

"Which is?"

"The story I told you, why we're going to Philly."

"I don't know why we're going to Philly."

"Sure you do. We're going to meet another Jessica so we can compare notes."

"If I had her name and address, it might be more believable."

"You know her name. I don't have her address."

Jessie turns toward me. "What? How are we going to find her?"

"We arranged to meet at a Starbucks."

"That doesn't sound suspicious at all."

"She's cautious. I don't blame her."

Jessie gives me a withering look as the cop car pulls off the highway. The cop station doesn't take long to get to. It's a low, nondescript building with a wall of windows looking out over a parking lot. If I had to come to work here every day, I might kill myself.

We follow the officer into the building. He directs us to sit and wait.

"Together?" I ask.

"Is that a problem?"

"No, of course not."

There's a family of Middle Eastern origin sitting in the waiting area and four police officers standing behind a set of glass enclosures, raised up higher so they have a vantage point over us. They seem to be in the middle of a coffee break, clustered together and chatting.

Jessie sits in one of the chairs and I sit next to her.

"I guess we have some time," I say. "We could discuss our strategy for Philly."

She shakes her head. "Not here."

"Right, good idea."

"No, bad idea."

"That too."

Thirty minutes later, we're still sitting there, as is the family. No one has been called up to a window. Three more people have come in, including one guy who looks homeless and seems to be missing a shoe. I'm beginning to think that the waiting is a tactic.

Jessie seems better equipped than I am to deal with it. She takes a book out of her purse and opens it.

"Any good?"

"Yes."

"What's it about?"

"It's called *The Marriage Lie.* What do you think?"

"Would you like me to stop talking?"

The answer is clearly *yes*, but instead, Jessie closes the book with a sigh and folds it onto her lap.

"Wonder how long they'll keep us waiting," she says.

"Until we crack, obviously."

"We haven't done anything wrong."

"True. It's the name thing, right? Making sure we're both legit."

"I'm assuming so. Systems don't like coincidences."

"Why are you so worried?"

She flips her book over and then over again. "I haven't had the best luck with authority."

"You mean when you reported the theft?"

"That, and other things. My parents died when I was young, and I was put in the foster system. This one family I was with, their son . . . wasn't very nice."

"He was abusive?"

"Not like you're thinking, but he . . . did things. Disturbing things with the family cat and hiding my stuff, and I guess now you might call him a sociopath in the making. Then, he was just this bad seed. Anyway, I told on him to my social worker, and I got punished."

"How?"

"They pulled me out of the family, then put me in the orphanage for a while. I was hard to place after that."

"But you hadn't done anything wrong."

"That's my point. Just because you haven't done anything doesn't mean you get treated as if you're innocent. I would've thought you knew that."

I stare straight ahead. I do know that, but it's not something I like to talk about.

"You're right." I stare at the police officers behind the counter. They've gone back to their stations now, but that doesn't seem to have changed the pace of service. "I was raised with a bad guy too."

I rub at the spot on my wrist where my scar is. As usual, it's covered by a long-sleeve T-shirt. It's a stylized version of Todd's initials, Todd Blakemore. A *T* and a *B* woven together in an intricate pattern. Only, he never told us that's what it was. Until Liam told me, I thought it was a symbol of togetherness. It was on lots of things in the Land of Todd—our uniforms, over the entrance to the Gathering Place. I'd always been told it meant "us." What a joke.

"What did he do?"

"Lots of terrible stuff. He was definitely a sociopath."

I got the scar—the brand—when I was twelve. There was this ceremony Todd did for all the kids at that age, a kind of initiation because that was the age of reason, according to him. When you could choose to join the group formally. And we did. We all did, because what other choice did we have?

"I don't like to talk about it," I say.

"I get it."

"It's—"

"Jessica Williams!"

We look at one another. Here we go.

"Yes," we say together, and stand.

Chapter 13

Not a Lucky Number

In the end, the police let us go without anything more than a speeding ticket. Us being together caused a glitch in their system, the policeman behind the counter says, but our documents checked out, so we're free to go. Jessie should update her car registration; she has two weeks to do so. We thank him and leave.

By that time, though, it's starting to get dark out. Jessie suggests we stop at a roadside motel, get some dinner, and rest. I agree. We drive through a McDonald's, then find a place a few miles away, the twin of where Liam and I stayed in Wilmington. I offer to share a room to cut down on expenses, but Jessie says that she "values" her "privacy." So, I eat my burger alone, take a shower, change into my pajamas, and climb into bed. It's early, but I'm exhausted. I fall easily to sleep.

I wake up in a cold sweat with my arm throbbing.

I was having the dream. The Dream.

It's always the same.

Black-cloaked figures in the Gathering Place in the middle of the night. The other children all lined up in their uniforms. The lights down low. I'm wearing a white robe that's scratchy against my skin and smells like mold. My mother and father are standing on either side of me, holding an arm apiece. Todd appears, his skin burnished, his robe white as snow. He talks about the importance of family, the sins of the world, the reason we chose to leave it. Then he asks me if I'm joining the group willingly, which makes my twelve-year-old self want to laugh. *You're holding me down,* I want to shout. *Who would do this willingly?* But instead, I nod and say, "Yes, Todd." This is the only acceptable response.

Then that glowing light. The heat as it approaches my skin. The pain.

It stops as suddenly as it starts, though the echo is almost as bad. The burned-flesh smell makes me want to vomit, and then I'm in Todd's arms and he's telling me that I'm welcome, that I'm beautiful, that I'm amazing, and that together we will do fantastic things.

"You're through the worst of it," he says.

I wake up with the word *No* caught in my throat.

I lie on my back trying to slow my heart. Headlights arc into the room from the highway and light up the ceiling through the slatted blinds. It almost makes me miss the tailgate party from the night before, which leads to thoughts of Liam. I check the time. It's only eleven. Not that late. I send him a text.

Checking in.

He answers a few minutes later.

Where are you?

Some small town on the way to Philly.

Jessie agreed to go with you?

Yes.

Why are you stopped?

I got pulled over by the cops for speeding. Apparently, they care about the speed limit on this side of the Hudson.

You have a lead foot.

☺ Miller says that too.

?

You don't know who Miller is?

Ha, ha. I meant when.

I drove him to the Hamptons last summer. I think I scared him.

Ah. I did not know that.

We went to a party. No biggie.

Hmm.

Jessie's in another room, I write. She didn't want to share. Do you think that's weird?

No.

Not even a little?

No.

We shared a room.

That's different. And not the first time.

True. Liam didn't take me to New York right away after I leaped into his car and told him to "drive, drive, drive" me away from the LOT. Instead, we hid out in a hotel room in the Catskills for three days. It was in one of those resorts that was popular in the 1950s, like the one they go to in *The Marvelous Mrs. Maisel*, which Daisy and I watch together.

It was a hot July and the resort was full of rustic cabins with no air-conditioning. Mostly, I lay on the bed, watching the ceiling fan rotate while I tried to absorb the information Liam was feeding me. I'd been in a "cult," only that was a word I'd never heard. What did it mean? I wasn't "programmed"—that's what everyone in the outside world was, enslaved to the government. Todd was a bad person. That, I didn't have any trouble believing.

I'm not sure I ever thanked you properly for that, I write.

You thanked me plenty.

Well, thank you again.

You're welcome.

We are better off because of you.

Maybe.

You done saving people?

?

It's been a while, I meant. No new people.

Are The Twists feeling like they need new members?

I smile at the use of the name I know he hates. No, I write, I just realized that we haven't met anyone in a while.

There have been a few in the last couple years. They don't always want to meet the group.

Oh?

They've been through enough.

Okay, I get it.

It's late. You should get some rest.

Okay.

Sleep well.

You too, I write. Love you.

The words whoosh away, and I wish I could take them back. I've never written this to Liam before. Never said it. Does the fact that I didn't put "I" in front of it make it less of a confession? Is there a way I can diminish it further?

Oops, I write, but don't hit "Send." Liam's typing something. Or thinking about it.

Then: Same.

I put my phone down with a smile on my face, but before I can settle in, my phone flashes again, that distinctive light pattern getting my attention. Is Liam taking it back? I shouldn't reach for my phone, but I can't ignore it.

It's not a text from Liam.

It's from Jessica Two.

Stop it, it says. This is your last warning.

I hold on to the phone tightly. One of the things she doesn't know about me yet: I don't respond well to threats.

PART TWO

Chapter 14

The Back Forest

Two weeks after the branding, I was sitting in our weekly session with Todd when I spoke out.

Well, first I sat out.

I never understood what Todd's obsession with sitting was about. I only knew that ever since I could remember we were told to sit with our backs pressed against our chairs with our feet planted firmly on the ground. Our arms were to be by our sides, and there was to be no crossing of the ankles or, Todd forbid, legs crossed over one another. Even now, I find myself sitting like that when I'm not paying attention.

My arm was still smarting. That's why I think I did it, but it wasn't as if it was planned. I didn't know how to plan then, only react. My arm hurt. It was Todd's fault. I couldn't understand why that had to be. Why my parents hadn't stopped it, why no one had. I'd spent two weeks nursing it, climbing into Kiki's bed and resting my bandage against hers. Kiki tried to pretend that she understood why it had happened, but I knew she was only pretending to try to make me feel better because it seemed to affect me more than it did her.

"We need to be prepared, we need to be ready, we need to have everything set to go on a moment's notice," Todd was saying. He was wearing one of his uniforms—white pants and a top that looked like hospital surgeon scrubs, only it was pressed and starched, so it looked almost military-like. His skin was tanned to a perfect bronze, and his eyes stood out with a blue intensity. I used to try to count how often he blinked, certain it was less than other people.

"Why?" I asked, the word I'd thought over and over escaping my mouth before I could stop it.

"Who said that?" Todd asked, spinning on his heel and pointing at us. The twenty kids in the room were sitting four by five, in precise rows, with the smallest kids in the front, the oldest in the back. Kiki and I were in the middle.

The room was deadly silent. No one spoke out during Todd's lectures. Silence was even more important than sitting properly.

"Who. Said. That?" Todd asked again, his voice shaking. Todd wasn't used to being disobeyed, and he didn't react well when it happened.

"It was her," a quisling named Jaimie said, turning and pointing at me. The small children were always the worst. They didn't know, yet, that sucking up to Todd didn't insulate them from punishment.

Todd was next to me in an instant. His hand reached down and encircled my branded wrist. I cried out.

"You had a question?" he hissed.

"No, no."

I could feel Kiki shaking next to me.

"Yes, you did," he said. "Go on, ask it."

"I asked . . . why."

"Why what?"

"Why do we need to be prepared?" I asked, my voice hiccoughing and rushed. "Why do we need to fear everyone?"

His fingers tightened. He was so much stronger than I was. "Have you not been listening to a word I've said?"

"Yes, I have."

"Then you know why."

"But I—" Kiki stomped on my foot. I stifled the cry, but my knee jerked up in the air.

"But I what? How are you sitting? What is happening here?"

He jerked me up by my arm and dragged me to the front of the room. Kiki followed along as if she were tethered to me. Todd was so mad that he didn't even notice her at first; he just tossed me into his chair like a piece of garbage. We weren't ever allowed to sit in that chair. One of the grown-ups brought it up for his talks each week, then took it away again. Todd himself never sat in it for more than twenty seconds, the time it took him to wind himself up and begin pacing back and forth.

"How do we sit?" he said.

I held my arm, feeling frozen by pain.

"How do we *sit*?"

Todd was yelling so close to my ear that my eardrum started to rattle. I planted my feet on the ground, but I couldn't seem to let go of my arm.

Todd started to move me like clay, forcing my back against the chair, squaring my shoulders, then prying my hand off my arm.

"That hurts!"

Todd froze, and I froze right along with him. Then his hand reared back and cracked against my face.

"Stop it, Todd!" Kiki said, astonishing everyone since she'd never spoken out of turn her whole life.

And then we both got punished.

There wasn't a beating, but there was the Back Forest.

Kiki and I were banished there for a week. For willfulness, for troublemaking, for talking back to Todd. The list of our crimes was long, and we were lucky, my mother hissed at me, that she'd managed to intercede on our behalf and keep our banishment to a week.

"What were you thinking?" she asked us, over and over. "I just don't know what you were thinking."

"Oh, stop it, Therese," Tanya said. "Can't you see the girls are terrified as it is?"

My mother looked at me, then Kiki. We were sitting together on Kiki's bed, huddled together, too scared to cry. We'd never been to the Back Forest, but we'd heard enough horror stories about it. The bogeyman lived there. The devil. Children who were sent out there came back changed, or never came back at all. Who knew what was true?

We were about to find out.

"Get up," my mother said. She had a hardness about her that Tanya lacked. People were always saying how much we looked alike, as if reminding themselves that we were related. I never saw the sameness, only the differences. Her hair was thick and wavy, and her eyes were set closer together than mine. Her arms were strong and muscular from all the manual labor she did around the compound. I was thin and weak, and I missed my mother even though she was standing right in front of me.

"I said, get up."

"You sound like Todd."

My mother didn't know how to take this. Usually, that was a compliment, but she knew I didn't mean it that way.

"What has gotten into you?"

I didn't answer her. Instead, I showed her my arm. She pulled back.

"Come on, girls," Tanya said. "We'd better go and get this over with."

I wanted to bite back at the "We," but Kiki stopped me. She stood up and pulled me along with her.

She looked at me and I was amazed. She didn't look scared. She looked resolute.

"We'll be okay," she said. "It's only a week."

Chapter 15

Philadelphia Feeling

We're sitting in a Starbucks near the Delaware River Waterfront. This is where JJ said she'd meet us at two p.m. It's two forty-five. The Starbucks is full of the usual midafternoon crowd: people pretending to write the next great novel, students "studying" with their friends, stay-at-home moms wrangling their kids with promises of a cake pop so they can get their triple shot of whatever.

"She's not going to come," Jessie says after I look at my watch for the tenth time. She's had a cappuccino with two extra shots of espresso and is tapping her foot in time to the music that's playing on the stereo system—someone new I don't recognize. I ordered some calming tea, but it doesn't seem to be working.

"Let's give it ten more minutes."

"Don't you have her number?"

"No, only Facebook."

"That wasn't the best idea."

"I know, okay?"

She raises her hands in surrender and returns to reading her book. I take out my phone and check Facebook again. JJ's read my message asking if we're still meeting but hasn't responded. I hate this fucking feature. There's nothing worse than knowing for certain that someone's ignoring you.

I write her again. Still here. I'd appreciate it if you could let me know if you're going to show up.

I watch the little icon appear next to my message, letting me know that once again she's read it. But once again, she doesn't respond.

"Okay, you're right. I don't think she's coming," I say, putting my phone away.

Jessie puts her book down on the table. She's halfway through it already. "So, what now?"

"I have no idea."

We finish our drinks, then head outside and down to the waterfront. There's a tall-ships festival going on, and the air smells like the beach, that tang of ocean mixed in with decaying fish, though it's only a river.

The crowd is substantial. A nice Friday afternoon in June—everyone's playing hooky. There are vendors selling popcorn and cotton candy; it contributes to the carnival atmosphere, a feeling that's confirmed when I see a three-card monte man standing on a patch of grass next to the river. He's in his midtwenties and is wearing a Phillies cap backward. He has a fairly large crowd around him. We stop and watch for a minute. I quickly spot the guy who's in on the scam, a kid in his late teens who wins three quick hands in a row, giving confidence to those duffers watching that they, too, can make a quick buck.

"Want to see something?" I say to Jessie. "I can beat this game."

"Nah, it's a trick."

"I know."

She smiles. "How do you beat a trick?"

"Watch."

The guy who's been winning loses and hands back the money he'd just won. He walks away in mock dejection.

"Step right up! Step right up if you think you can find the lady and beat a master at his game!"

I walk to the portable card table he's working on and smile nervously at the guy. "How does this work?"

He shows me his teeth. One of his front teeth is turned half sideways, but his eyes twinkle and there's a certain charm about him.

"My name's Hal."

"Hi, Hal. I'm Jess."

"Well, Jess, you ever play before?"

I shake my head.

"It's two dollars a hand. You guess right where the queen is, I give you four dollars."

"And if I guess wrong?"

"I keep the money."

"Sounds simple enough."

He starts to shuffle his cards. "Sure it is. You got a good memory?"

"I like to think so."

"Quick on your feet?"

"Do I need to catch anything?"

He laughs. "No, I just meant you have a better chance if you can think fast."

"Oh, right. Sure. What do you think?" I say to Jessie.

"I say go for it."

"Okay, then."

I take two singles out of my wallet and put them down on the table. He goes through his routine, showing me the red queen, then dealing the three bent cards onto the table one by one. Then he moves them around as he patters about following the lady. First slowly, then more quickly. I watch his hands, and not the cards, and so I see him palm the queen while he shuffles the other two cards, then pull it out again as he moves in for the flop.

"Follow the card now, don't lose sight. Follow the card, or hope you guess right."

His hands stop moving.

"All set?" he asks. "You know where that pretty lady's at?"

I hesitate, acting uncertain, then point to the far right.

"You sure?" he asks, smirking.

I've picked the right card, but this is another tactic. If someone guesses right, then they try to undermine their confidence and convince them to switch their initial choice.

"Yes, I think so."

He turns it over. The red queen looks back at me, minx-like.

"We have a winner!"

A few people clap and press closer. Jessie bounces on her heels.

"Beginner's luck," I say.

I reach for the money.

"Again?" Hal says. "Double or nothing?"

I look at Jessie. She nods enthusiastically. I make a show of considering what I'm agreeing to.

"So, I bet four dollars and if I win, I get eight?"

"That's right."

"Oh, come on," one of the lookie-loos says. "It's only eight dollars."

"True! Okay, let's go."

We go through it all again; then I point to the card in the middle. He doesn't ask me if I'm sure this time. He frowns and flips over the queen.

"Oh! You won!" the woman standing behind me says.

"Go again," Jessie says.

"What do you think?" I ask Hal. "Eight dollars for a chance at sixteen?"

He considers. He isn't sure, yet, that I'm onto his game. And it's not as if my bet is big at this point. Besides, the people watching will think they can win now, and that will help him draw more people in. I can sense the crowd getting bigger behind me. I've become the assistant, good for business.

He calculates his odds and agrees. "All right."

He shuffles his cards. The longer I look at him, the older he seems. He's got deep lines in his forehead, and his skin is tinged in that way that happens to longtime smokers. He gives me a look as he exposes his queen, then shuffles the cards quickly. I take even longer to decide which card is right, and in the end, I pick the one in the middle. He's giving me a hard stare now. These guys like taking people. They do not like to be taken.

He turns the card over, the queen appears, and the crowd claps. He shuffles some bills together and hands them to me. He knows he's been beaten, but he's still in charge.

"Show's over," he says to me in a way so we understand each other. "Who's next?"

We spend the next couple of hours wandering around the waterfront. Jessie is strangely keyed up after my modest takedown of the three-card monte man.

"That was pretty great," she says. The sun is glinting off the water, and the crowd has multiplied as the day's gotten nicer.

"Thanks."

Jessie's gesturing with her hands as she talks. "No, I mean it. Beating someone at their own game like that . . ."

"He was onto me pretty quickly."

"But you didn't care about getting caught. I bet you could've had him going for much longer if you mixed up your winning and losing."

"Yeah, that's how it's done."

"How come you didn't do that?"

"I wanted to show you I could beat the guy. I didn't care about tricking him for real."

"How long do you think you could have kept him going, though?"

"Liam's taken some of them for a couple hundred. But he gives the money to homeless guys."

Her hands fall. "Oh, Liam."

"What's that supposed to mean?"

"I didn't ask about him; I asked about you. How much do you think *you* could make?"

"Maybe the same. Why do you want to know?"

Her eyes are bright and glistening. It's a look I've seen before, the glint of power when you realize you can get something over on someone.

"Just curious."

I think about that for a moment, and then I say, "We could do it."

"Do what?"

"Con someone."

"What? Why?"

"For the fun of it."

"Umm . . ."

I smile. "Oh, come on. You're telling me you've never thought about it?"

"You have?"

"Sure. I read up on them a while back, for an article I was writing. Confidence tricks."

"You did?"

"You think it's weird?"

Jessie gives me a look. "I'm not sure what I think, to be honest."

"Fair enough. But didn't what happened to us make you wonder? How easy it would be to get away with it?"

"Okay, maybe I have."

"Of course you have," I say. "We're different now. Different than all of them."

I motion to the crowd around us. So many families having a nice Friday together. I'd never had a day like this, full of candy and sunlight. I guess Jessie hadn't, either, based on what she'd said about her upbringing. The LOT was dark in general, and then there was the Back Forest, where the old-growth trees were so thick it felt like no light could get through.

"I guess you're right," Jessie says. "But what does that have to do with conning someone?"

"It's the challenge, I think. Seeing if you can get a stranger to trust you . . ."

I turn and look at the river. The water's dotted with sailboats, paddleboards, and kayaks. I wonder what it would be like to be on one of them. The wind in my hair, the rough chop beneath my feet, the horizon a destination.

I'm not entirely sure why I'm pushing this, but I don't seem to be able to help myself. It's an impulse that's gotten me into trouble before.

"What do you say?" I ask Jessie. "You want to do it?"

"I'd like to try," Jessie says in a small voice.

I smile. "Cool."

"Should we do three-card monte?"

"What about something a bit harder?"

"Such as?"

"It's funny," I say. "They all have these fancy names. Like the Widow or the Driver."

She looks at the boats. "I don't know those, but there is this one I read about once, I think it's called the Bar Bill Scam? It's this thing where you make nice with a guy and then pretend you can't pay at the end of the evening."

"That sounds like college. Or dating."

She smiles. "True."

"Are you serious?" I ask. "You want to do this?"

"Ah, hell, why not? It'll help defray our costs since this trip was a waste and all. And it might give us some insight into Jessica Two, right?"

"It could. So, we hit on a guy and get him to buy us dinner?"

"Basically."

I look down at what I'm wearing. Broken-in chinos and a stretched-out long-sleeve T-shirt I think I stole from Liam years ago. Jessie's a bit neater, in a pair of slacks and a short-sleeve shirt with flowers on it, but neither of us is dressed for fine dining. "I don't think we look the part, though that might be an advantage."

"How so?"

"I think you need to be unexpected. That way, they don't see you coming."

I look at Jessie. She's nodding in agreement. We probably shouldn't be doing this, but I have to admit I don't see the harm in it, so long as we pick someone who can afford to pay at the end of the evening. Is it really any different from the nice meals I've had on a guy I had no intention of sleeping with or ever seeing again?

Moral relativism. That's Liam's voice in my head. But for once, I want to banish it.

"Okay," Jessie says. "Let's do it."

Chapter 16

Bar Bill Scam

The Back Forest wasn't just a place; it was an idea. Sort of like the cave that Luke goes into on Dagobah in *The Empire Strikes Back*—somewhere where your worst fears could be realized. We were provided with a tent, a shovel, some matches, and a water jug. That was it. Any food we ate, anything else we needed, we were on our own. I remember how quiet it was in that thick wood. How Kiki tried to hide her tears from me. I remember notching a tree when I thought a day had passed and then giving up on the other days because night and day were barely distinguishable.

"Will they come for us?" Kiki asked me every "morning" as we rose from the beds we had fashioned out of leaves and dirt when our internal clocks woke us.

"They will," I assured her, though I barely believed it myself.

Solitary confinement, it was supposed to be. Only the forest was alive. We were cut off from the others, and in the end, even from ourselves. For Kiki, it was a descent into an even stricter obedience. She would barely blink without permission.

But for me, it was the solidification of an idea. I would find a way out. And when I did, no one would ever find me.

Here's how the Bar Bill Scam goes down.

We find a restaurant that has a happy hour from five to seven. It's a low-key place where a man might stop in for a drink before he heads home for the night. There's a large square bar in the middle of the room surrounded by high-top tables. English pub food, and a mix of regulars and one-timers with a sleepy-looking bartender wiping down the bar. Perfect.

We take up seats away from one another around the bar. Jessie pulls out her book; I look at my phone. We both order a glass of white wine. These are the signals that we want to be disturbed. Because nothing says *Talk to me* like "I'm busy reading," if you're a man on the make.

Sure enough, within five minutes, a man in a suit with his necktie loosened sidles up to Jessie. He's holding a full tumbler and strode past fifty a few years ago. I don't see a ring from where I'm sitting, but he looks married. Jessie puts down her book reluctantly and begins to make small talk. She gives him clipped answers to begin with, then opens up slowly until he makes her laugh. He signals for a waiter, and she orders a glass of champagne and asks to see the menu. The champagne is a test we devised in our hastily made plan. If he balks at the price, then we'll abandon and move on to another mark.

I get up to go to the bathroom. As I suspected, the man is wearing a wedding band, tight on his fat finger, which is what also makes it okay: he's a married jerk buying a woman an expensive drink in a bar, and the fact that he's married means there's no way he's going to complain to anyone when he gets taken.

I catch Jessie's eye as I pass them and give her a short nod. He's too engrossed in Jessie to notice me. I go into the bathroom and waste a few minutes washing my hands and drying them carefully. When I return, I stumble on the floor and grab on to Jessie for support.

"Oh, hey," I say as she straightens me up, "it's you."

"Wow," Jessie says. "Long time."

"Such a long time."

"So great to see you."

"You too. You look great. This girl," I say to the man, "is amazing."

"I was just thinking that myself," he says, smiling at Jessie indulgently.

"Oh!" Jessie says, turning and patting him on the arm. "Is it all right, Robert, if she joins us?"

He looks caught between wanting to please Jessie and being stuck with me. "Sure, of course. What were you drinking?"

"We're having champagne," Jessie says enthusiastically, draining the rest of her glass. "Is that okay, Robert? We can pay our own way."

"Absolutely not." He motions for the bartender, pointing to Jessie's glass and holding up two fingers in a move that reminds me of Liam. What would he think if he could see me right now?

"Thank you," I say, shoving that thought aside.

"Think nothing of it."

"Say, you look familiar," he says to me. "Do I know you from somewhere?"

"Don't think so."

"No, I'm good with faces. Give me a minute."

I turn away. We should abandon this mission pronto before he figures out that I'm *that* girl. I never thought I'd be recognized in Philly, especially now that all the press has died down.

Robert snaps his fingers. "Can't get it. You must look like someone."

"I have that kind of face."

I reach into my purse and pull out a pack of cards, putting it down on the bar. I put my hand back in, looking for something. "My stupid phone always gets lost in here."

"Oh," Jessie says, picking up the cards. "Can you still do it?"

"Do what?" Robert asks.

"She can do magic," Jessie enthuses.

"Magic?"

I aw-shucks kick at the floor. "Well, not magic exactly, but you know that card game? Three-card monte?"

"Of course."

Jessie jumps in. "She can beat the game, every time."

"Impressive," he says.

"Anyone can do it."

"You'd finally be willing to teach me?" Jessie says.

"Sure, why not."

I open the deck and find the three cards I need, then bend them in the middle, so they make a tent on the table. I show Robert the red queen. "This is the card you need to follow."

He nods. His face is puffy from too many stops at this bar on the way home, but he wasn't a bad-looking guy once, if you go for the prep-school type.

"Watch the queen."

I show it to him again, then start my shuffle. I flop the cards onto the table. The queen is in the middle, but if I've done it right, he should think it's on the left.

The bartender brings us our glasses of champagne. I take a sip. It's cheap and sweet. No chance that it's actually champagne, but grifters can't be choosers.

"Could I get an order of fish and chips?" I ask the bartender. He winks at me quickly. He's seen this scam before, some version of it. And what does he care? He knows this guy is good for the bill.

"Oh, that sounds good. Me too," Jessie says. "Do you want anything, Robert? I bet you like the ploughman's."

"I do, actually."

"I knew it." Jessie rubs her hand along his arm. "So, we'll have that too. Your drink okay?"

"I'll have another," Robert says, pointing to his glass.

The bartender turns to go, and Jessie picks up his glass and smells it. She wrinkles her nose. "Ugh, how do you drink this?"

"I'll teach you to appreciate it if you like."

Jessie smiles at him. "Maybe later. Let's let . . . Oh my God, I forgot your name."

She means me. She's slurring her words. She needs to slow down on the champagne.

"It's June."

"Right, of course, how silly of me. Robert, this is June."

We shake hands formally though we're already past that stage.

"June, finish the trick."

"So, Robert, which card do you choose?"

He looks down at the cards on the bar. "I was distracted."

"That's all right, I'll do it again."

I go through the routine. His eyes have been following the wrong card the whole time. He points to the card on the left.

"I just took your money." I flip over the card to show him his mistake.

"How did you do that?"

"It's simple."

I go through it again more slowly. Flash him the queen, then exaggerate the motion of switching it for another card.

"It's designed so that the player is following the wrong card," I say. "That's the trick."

"That's cheating."

"If you know what to look for, you can win."

He sips on his drink slowly. "Show me again."

Several hours later, after more card lessons, a full bottle of what they're passing off as champagne, and more food than I've eaten in a single meal in years, Jessie excuses herself to go to the restroom. Because it's part of our plan, I know that the bar's phone will ring in a moment, and so it does.

"Shanty's." The bartender's eyes flit to Robert. "Yes, ma'am, I'll tell him." He hangs up and walks over. "Time to settle up."

"What's that?" Robert's slurring his words, deep into his fourth glass.

"You need to pay your bill, sir, and get home. That was your wife on the phone."

"My . . ." He slips his ring-bearing hand into his pocket, then makes a big show of looking at his watch. "It's late. I should be getting along."

"One bill, sir?"

"What? Yes, of course."

Jessie returns from the bathroom as the bartender puts the bill on the bar in front of Robert.

"Is the party over?"

"I'm afraid so, my dear. I, uh, have an early meeting in the morning."

"That's too bad."

Robert takes his credit card out and passes it to the bartender without looking at the total. I can see it, though. Close to $500. This place certainly charges champagne prices.

"It can't be helped," Robert says. "But I'd love to see you again."

"Yes, of course."

Jessie takes a pen out of her purse and writes her "number" on a bar napkin. The bartender gives Robert a credit card slip to sign, which he does hastily, adding a crappy tip. He passes it back and takes Jessie's napkin, tucking it into his pocket.

"I'll be in touch."

"Do."

She presents her cheek to him and he kisses it. Then he gathers himself and walks unsteadily out the door.

I watch him leave, then take a twenty out of my wallet and put it on the bar.

"I noticed he left a bad tip," I say.

"Thanks," the bartender says. "Another drink?"

"I think we're done here."

He nods knowingly as Jessie and I stand to go. We walk to the entrance and wait a moment to make sure that Robert is truly gone. When we make eye contact, we burst out laughing.

"Should we go?" I ask when we've regained control of ourselves.

"Let's."

Outside, the air is cooler, and I wish I had a coat. But the alcohol and food are warm inside me as we lean against the building.

"We did it," Jessie says. "I can't believe it."

"We did. We really did."

"Are we terrible for doing that to someone, even though that guy was a jerk?"

"He was—"

"Pleased with yourselves?" a gruff voice says behind us, making me jump.

I turn around. It's a woman with close-cropped blonde hair wearing a military peacoat.

JJ.

Chapter 17

How Do You Say Goodbye?

Covington was the one who told me that Todd was dead. Another text in the middle of the night, a light flashing next to me on the nightstand. I'd forgotten to turn off my phone because it was the end of term and I'd just graduated from J school. I'd gone to a party with this guy, Max, a guy I'd never paid much attention to, but who was good enough for that night. One thing had led to another, and he was breathing heavily next to me in my bed. He wore round glasses and had earnest ambitions about becoming the next Walter Cronkite or Brian Williams or whatever. The sex had been disappointing, so instead of dozing off in a comfortable haze, I was lying awake regretting my choices.

When the text came in, I read it, then read it again. Covington had written: Yee-haw! Jester is dead! followed by a series of emojis that I think were meant to denote joy.

Are you watching Top Gun? Again?

No, dummy. Todd. Todd is DEAD.

What? Are you sure?

Yeah.

How?

My parents called.

Holy shit.

I KNOW.

When did this happen?

Couple days ago. Funeral is tomorrow.

You going?

Damn right. It's going to be lit.
You should come and dance on his grave with me.

Todd was dead. I didn't know what to feel. Happiness? Worry? Todd couldn't touch me anymore, or anyone else. How did I feel about that?

So, you coming, or what? Covington wrote.

I'll let you know in the morning. What time are you leaving?

He told me, and I set an alarm and settled under the covers. Todd was dead. Somehow, I never thought of that as a solution. The regrets that had been keeping me awake drained away. I turned on my side, my back to Max, and fell into a deep sleep.

In the morning, I shooed Max out, took a shower, and texted Covington that he should come pick me up. As the city, then the wilderness flashed by, I concentrated on one thing. Kiki.

After I'd left the LOT, I'd tried to find a way to keep in touch with her, to let her know that the offer of rescue was still good, but it was impossible to reach her. The first summer, I borrowed Liam's car and drove to the farmers' market. I had my hair up in a baseball cap and sunglasses on—I was scared of being seen, caught, kidnapped in reverse. I waited around all day, but no one from the LOT ever showed. Feeling desperate when the market started packing up, I asked a few of the merchants I recognized whether they'd seen anyone from the Land of Todd.

"You mean those cult people?" one girl about my age asked.

I nodded.

"They don't come here no more. Not since last summer."

Not since I'd flown the coop. They must have figured out how Liam had gotten to me and had cut off that avenue of escape. What was I going to do?

I could ask Liam, only I hadn't told Liam about Kiki. He knew I had family in the cult, that my parents were still there, but I hadn't gone into the details of anyone else who mattered to me. When I first left, I was in too much pain and guilt to talk about it. I'd left Kiki behind. Even then, I knew I shouldn't have done that. I should've forced her down the hill with me, even if it meant increasing the chance of discovery. She didn't know what she was doing when she said she wanted to stay. She was programmed, brainwashed. What would Liam think of me if he knew I'd abandoned her? I was ashamed, so eventually I tucked Kiki away. I tried not to think about her. She'd made her choice, and there was nothing I could do.

I played all the time that had gone by over in my head on the drive to the LOT with Covington. It had been five years since I'd escaped. Five years since I'd seen Kiki. Would we be strangers to one another? Could she forgive me? Or was she now as brainwashed as our parents?

We timed our arrival so that we wouldn't have to run the gauntlet of stares and questions our being there would raise. Todd hadn't left instructions, so they were burying him in the Back Forest, Covington's parents had told him. The main camp was abandoned and silent when we got there. Memories flooded back as we picked our way through the woods. Then we were there. A hundred people huddled silently around his grave. I picked out Kiki immediately, went to her side, and slipped my hand into hers. She squeezed it tight without looking at me, and my worry seeped away.

I looked around the circle defiantly, meeting the startled stares of the Toddians and avoiding those of my parents. What I wanted to do was make eye contact with Kiki. But when I finally did, I felt a chill run through me.

She didn't look much different; she *was* different. She used to be positive and innocent. She wasn't the most confident girl, but she was sure of her beliefs and her place in the world. She had confidence that Todd was right, that the path would be revealed, that everything had its purpose, including her. Her eyes told a different story now. She'd seen and experienced things she hadn't thought possible, and I was afraid to ask what they were.

I leaned my head against hers and whispered into her ear. "You don't need to be afraid anymore, Kiki."

I felt her go slack. "Oh, Jess. Of course I do."

JJ, Jessie, and I are sitting in the dark corner of another bar a few blocks away. JJ's sitting across from us and she's not smiling. She's been observing us since we got to Philly, and she's found us wanting.

"We were just having a bit of fun," I say.

JJ ordered an old-fashioned, but she's barely touched it, and the fizz from the champagne and grift has evaporated.

"I saw that."

"I'm sorry. That was unacceptable."

"It was."

"I could explain, but no excuses."

"I appreciate that," JJ says. "I don't like excuses."

"I get it."

She squints at me. Her face is permanently lined from the sun from when she served in Afghanistan. The false arm and hook she wears when cooking is absent; her green army-surplus jacket is tucked neatly over where her left arm should be. Her hair is that white, albino blonde you usually only see in children, her eyes a deep brown.

"You do?" she asks.

"You've seen enough bad in your life."

"I've certainly seen enough of you two."

"We deserve that. As I said, no excuses."

"Right."

She finally picks up her drink and swallows half the glass.

"I am curious, though," I say.

"What about?"

"Why didn't you walk away when you saw what we were doing? Why stay and watch? Why reveal yourself?"

JJ smiles slowly. Her teeth are straight and white, and the charisma I saw on YouTube finally shines through. "I've been asking myself those very questions."

"Any answers?"

"Curiosity."

"Killed the cat," Jessie blurts. I stomp on her foot, but not too hard because I'm pretty sure she's drunk. Whether it's on the champagne or the high of taking Robert for $455 including a shitty tip, I'm not sure.

"That it did." JJ finishes her drink and looks like she's thinking about another. "Okay, so yeah, I'm curious. But I shouldn't be. I should stay the fuck out of it."

"That's what I said," Jessie says.

"Then why didn't you?"

"Curiosity for sure. Plus, she's pretty persuasive, this one." Jessie points her thumb at me.

"Oh yeah?"

"I'm a librarian in Upstate New York."

"What's that got to do with it?"

She motions to herself. "Do I seem like the kind of person who'd willingly come all this way to try to talk someone into searching for the person who stole my money?"

"You do not."

"Exactly."

"So, what are you doing here?"

"She gave me this whole speech about how we were a band of brothers and we had to stop Jessica Two before someone lost more than just their money."

"Jessica Two?"

"It's what I call her," I say.

"I am so fucking confused right now." JJ leans back in the booth. She catches the eye of our waitress, and that silent signal for *more* passes between them.

"I'm Jessica One," I say. "To me, anyway. So, when I met the other Jessica, and she did that thing she does—you know, *Oh, we have the same name, how unusual*—I started thinking of her as Jessica Two. Jessie's Jessica Three. You're Four."

"Why do you get to be One?"

The waitress delivers JJ her drink. She holds the glass in her one hand, staring at the liquid in the murky light.

"This might be the stupidest fucking conversation I've had in a long time, and that's including the one I had with *her*. No wonder she took our money," JJ says.

I lean forward. "Okay, let's forget about what to call her, or us. We don't have to be a band of brothers, or a band of Jessicas, or anything. But she took something from us. She did. And we should try to get it back."

"What makes you think you'll succeed?"

"I have no idea if I will. But I feel like the three of us together have a better chance than me alone."

JJ looks me in the eye. "She's not going to like this, you know."

"Who cares what she likes or wants."

"You should care."

"Why?"

"Because she doesn't stop at taking your money. If she thinks you're a threat, she'll come for more than that."

"How do you know that?" Jessie asks.

"Because that's what she did to me."

Chapter 18

You Know the Drill

JJ's story has a familiar ring to it. When she got back from Afghanistan and finished her rehab, she decided to pursue her first love, cooking. She did great in chef school despite her disability, but when she graduated, she couldn't get a job. She was receiving a disability pension from the VA, but she was down. A friend of hers hired her to cater a dinner party to try to kick-start a business, and over drinks in the kitchen they were joking about all the silly advice she was getting.

"Stay positive seemed to be the most consistent one," JJ says. She points to her missing arm. "Like, forget this ever happened! Think of your blessings! You are such a lucky person!"

"Sounds annoying," I say.

"I'll say. But it got us thinking. If people buy into that shit, then maybe we should take it to its logical conclusion. Like, you want positive? I'll show you positive. And that's how the relentlessly positive one-armed lady chef was born."

"Is that what you call yourself?" Jessie asks.

"Not overtly. But it's the not-too-subtle subtext of the YouTube channel I started. Anyway, we were right. We started filming videos in my kitchen, inviting other chefs I'd heard of from around town to guest on the show and they'd have to say yes, because who turns down a one-armed army vet?"

"No one," I say.

"Exactly. And then we'd get them to promo it to their customers and on their social, and pretty soon we'd taken off. We got this massive bump when Bourdain retweeted one of my videos, and then everyone wanted in on the action."

"Advertisers?"

She finishes her drink. "Yep. Knives, appliances, you name it. I was getting big ad buys. I bought a house, paid off my debts, things were going well. Being relentlessly positive didn't come so hard for a while."

"And then?"

"The paper did a profile on me. Mentioned the kind of ad revenue I was getting. I got a lot of business from that profile. I even cut it out and had it laminated and hung it on the wall of my kitchen and everything. You've got to laugh."

"More relentless positivity?" I ask.

She grimaces. "You know it. Anyway, a couple months later, I got invited to give a demonstration at a cooking expo in Des Moines."

"You were flattered."

"Course I was. She knows how to get to a person's soft spot."

"Was it made up?" Jessie asks. "The convention?"

"No, it was real."

"Mine was made up."

"That right?" JJ gives her a look of pity. But we've all been taken for fools.

"How do you think she managed it?" I ask.

JJ shrugs. "Never thought much about that part, to be honest. For all I know, she applied for me. It wasn't a real 'invitation,' if I think about it. More like a confirmation that I was attending, with my travel and hotel information."

"Applying on your behalf would be easy for her," I say.

"For anyone, really. It's not like they check ID when you're offering up your money."

A group of girls who are clearly part of a bachelorette party tumble into the bar. The bride's got a toilet paper veil on her head, and her eyes are already moving in separate directions.

"Good point," I say. "When did she contact you?"

"On the way home. There was a group transport to the airport, which meant I got to the airport about four hours before my flight."

"So you went to the bar?" I ask.

"That where *you* met her—an airport bar?"

"Yep," I say. "Not Jessie, but they did go for a drink."

"So, she likes to drink," JJ says. "That's something, I guess."

"Not unique."

"She drank scotch," Jessie says.

"That right? I guess she likes scotch."

"How did she make the connection?" I ask. "About the name."

"As simple as introducing ourselves."

"And then you played the game?"

"Jessica Williams Twenty Questions? Yes."

"And a few days later, you were missing a bunch of money."

"That too."

Jessie pulls a pad of paper out of her purse. "We should get all the details, right? Like you did with me? See what we can match up."

"In a minute," I say. "I'm curious about something else first."

"What's that?" JJ asks. She's almost drowned out by the loud laughter of the bachelorette party two tables over. They've all got pieces of paper in their hands, comparing notes about something they find hilarious.

Sometimes lives intersect at the oddest moments. I don't ever see myself in their position, laughing without care the night before a wedding, especially not my own.

"What else did she do to you?" I ask.

JJ leans back, holding her empty glass against her chest. "She made sure I'd keep my mouth shut. Or that if I didn't, it wouldn't matter."

"How?"

"By destroying my credibility."

"Why would she do that?" Jessie asks.

"Probably because I was trying to track her down."

"How?" I ask.

"I knew this guy in army intelligence, and he was working on tracing the money transfers. She must've gotten an alert."

"What happened then?"

JJ takes out her phone. "It'll be easier to show you than explain." She opens her photo app and scrolls through her photos. "I screenshot it all, so I'd have proof even though I had to delete a bunch of my social accounts."

She passes me the phone. It's a picture of a tweet JJ sent out using some super offensive language about the locals she encountered in Afghanistan, saying that she was happy about what she'd done to them.

"I didn't tweet that," she says.

"Jessica Two?" Jessie says.

"Of course."

"What happened?" I ask.

"What do you think? It blew up. I lost sponsors, cancel culture . . . you know. I had to go in person to each of them and explain what happened to me, not that it made much difference. And then I got this." She takes her phone back and goes to her texts. She hands it to me again and I read it.

Don't try to find me, it says, or this is just the beginning.

Back in another anonymous hotel room, I don't know what my next step should be.

Jessie and I left JJ about an hour ago. We found a cheap motel nearby and booked into two separate rooms. JJ didn't offer to let us stay with her.

"She doesn't want us to know where she lives," Jessie says as we stand in front of our separate doors. We're somewhere near a highway, and the buzz of cars zooming along pavement fills the night.

"Trust no one," I say.

"What's that?"

"Nothing. I'll see you in the morning."

I go through my nightly routine in a desultory way, mulling over the events of the day. At Jessie's urging, JJ told us that Jessica Two had given similar details about her life to the ones she gave to me and to Jessie. JJ's Jessica had blonde beachy waves and green eyes, but she couldn't remember much else. She didn't have any photographs; Jessica Two had been able to do the transfers without going into the bank. JJ said she'd been pretty, friendly, and sympathetic. All the hallmarks of a good grifter.

I change into my pajamas, pull back the cheap sheets, and lie on my back. Another cracked ceiling, though the patterns are different. My body is tired, but my brain's awake—not a good sign for sleeping. My phone buzzes. It's Liam asking how things are going. I start a text, then change my mind and call.

"Hey," he says. His voice sounds worn out—his after-midnight voice—which I know from shadowing him on stakeouts and when I used to help him with late-night sessions with new members of The Twists who needed company to keep the nightmares at bay. We've drifted apart over the last couple of years. It's only now that we're back in regular contact that I realize how much I've missed him.

"Hey."

"Where are you?"

"In Philly."

"You met JJ?"

"Yeah."

"And?"

Liam's voice in my ear is both soothing and, to be frank, stimulating. I turn on my side and press my hand between my legs.

"Jessica Two stole her money."

"How?"

I tell him what JJ said as I press my palm into myself. My breathing is slightly accelerated. This is wrong, to be using Liam this way, but God it feels good.

"What are you doing?" Liam asks.

"Nothing." I pull my hand away and rest it on the outside of the covers. The blanket is old and torn in the corner, and God knows what's occurred under it. "Talking to you."

"You sound out of breath."

"Must be the connection."

"Mmm."

I'm blushing, happy Liam can't see me. "So, what do you think? What should we do next?"

"I think you should come home."

"Just give up?"

"Yes."

"Why?"

"Have you checked Facebook or Twitter today?"

"No, I've been busy."

"You should."

"Why? And how do you know what's happening on Facebook or Twitter?"

He coughs. "Miller told me."

"Miller told you what?"

"There's another story out. About you."

I'm fully awake now, all thoughts of fantasy cast off.

"What about me?"

"Did you . . ." Liam's hesitation does not make me feel better.

"Out with it."

"Did you plagiarize your thesis?"

I sit up. "What? No."

"Are you sure?"

"Of course I'm sure."

I slaved over that final paper for months, barely getting it in on time. I was proud of it.

"Well, then, how do you explain it?"

"What is *it*, exactly?"

My phone buzzes in my hand.

"I sent you a link. Take a look."

I pull the phone away from my ear and put it on speaker while I check out the link. It's to a piece written by my old nemesis at FeedNews, James, who seems to be back, and in my job.

> FeedNews can exclusively reveal that our former reporter, Jessica Williams, has a long history of plagiarism. We've obtained a copy of her senior thesis from Columbia. As you can see from the comparisons below, large passages of the document are copied from various other sources without attribution . . .

"Jess?"

"Yeah?"

"You okay?"

"Not sure."

"Take me off speaker," Liam says.

I comply and put the phone back up to my ear. My heart is skipping.

"You didn't plagiarize?" Liam asks.

"No. I swear to you."

"Is this just James getting back at you?"

"No, it's . . . She did the same thing to JJ."

I tell him about the tweet, the aftermath, and Jessica Two's warnings to JJ.

"You should come home," Liam says again firmly when I finish.

"I will soon."

"Tomorrow."

"Jeez, yes, Dad."

He clears his throat in a way that lets me know I've gone too far.

"She hasn't reached out to you, has she?" he asks after a moment.

"No," I lie. If I tell Liam I've been communicating with her, he'll be on the next plane to Philly, and I need to do this part on my own.

I can hear Liam fretting through the line. Pacing back and forth in his loft in the Meatpacking District that he bought a zillion years ago when the early-morning streets were stained with blood, not booze.

"Jess."

"What?"

"I'm worried about you."

"I know. But I'll be okay."

"Will you?"

"I've made it this far, haven't I?"

"That's true."

"So, give me some credit."

"I give you a lot."

I close my eyes. I wish it could always be like this. That there didn't need to be crises and lies to bring us together.

"Tell me more."

He laughs gently. "Good night, Jessica."

"Good night, Liam."

"I'll see you soon?"

"Yes."

"Good," he says, then hangs up.

I rest the phone on my chest and think about all the things that Jessica Two has done. She doesn't fuck around. But that's okay.

I don't either.

Chapter 19

Planning Committee

After Todd's funeral, the sun came out, like God approved of what we'd done. Kiki and I left the woods and the others behind and sat on the dock and caught up on what we'd missed in each other's lives. I had more to tell, as I'd been out in the world, getting an education, living on my own. She'd been trapped in the Land of Todd, where nothing changed, but everything had, I learned, after I escaped.

"No more visits to town unless you were an elder, no more free time on Saturdays, and all the books were thrown away. A lot of other things." She shivered though the sun was warm. "They cracked down so that no one else would escape."

"But Covington got out," I said.

"Covington?"

"Oh, sorry, that's the name he uses now. Here, I think he was called Terrence."

"Oh."

Kiki was blushing. I couldn't believe it.

"He's five years younger than us," I said.

"So? He was cute."

"Still is. Did something happen between you two?"

"That's forbidden."

"Oh, Kiki."

"What?"

"Do you actually believe in that stuff? Still?"

Kiki looked out at the water. It was a large man-made pond, not a proper lake, though we always called it the lake. It was the only place I'd felt free as a child, those moments when we were allowed to cast off our uniforms and leap from the dock into the water. We were plunged into the cool, and we felt cleansed of our lives. At least one thing Todd said was true.

"I didn't say I believed," Kiki said. "I said it was forbidden."

"Not now, though."

"You think so?"

"Of course. Todd's dead. You're all free."

She turned to look at me. Her eyes were a clear blue, like the sky above. She was always the most beautiful of all of us, inside and out. Was that why Todd chose me instead of her to enact whatever terrible ritual was waiting for me on the other end of the wedding dress? Because he saw something dark inside me?

"Are you free?" Kiki asked, and I didn't know what to say.

"We need another Jessica," I say to JJ and Jessie the next morning in another coffee shop with a view of the river. It's windy out and the river's choppy. I watch a runner try to keep her hat on as she dips her head and pushes into the wind. "We locate another Jessica and use her as bait."

"How are we going to do that?" JJ asks. She's wearing a different army jacket today, one with a flag over her (our) last name. Her short hair looks translucent in the light from the fluorescents above.

"I've got a friend who has some connections."

"Liam, you mean," Jessie says. She ordered a scone and a yogurt, then put the yogurt on the scone as if it's clotted cream. It looks kind of disgusting, but I suspect it might be tasty.

"That's right."

"Is that how you found me?" Jessie asks.

"That and your nosy neighbors."

She bites her lip and looks down into her cup of coffee, milk, and three sugars. She must have one of those bird metabolisms.

"So, we need to find another victim?" JJ asks.

"No, a potential victim. We need to create a good target."

"How are we going to do that?"

"We know how she works, right? One of us does well, gets mentioned in the news, and she gets a Google Alert. So, we find someone who on the surface is a good candidate, and we build up a social profile for her—maybe she has a rich relative die, or something like that, I haven't worked out all the details—and then we set off the alarm."

"Which is?"

"She talks about how she's going on a trip."

"But I thought Jessica Two was the one who reached out to her victims?" Jessie says. "Like what she did to me and JJ."

"Not all the time. She didn't reach out to me. Look, I know it'll take a bit of time to plan to get it right. What I need to know is, are you willing to help?"

"Define *help*," JJ says. She didn't order anything to eat, but then again, she slept in her own bed last night.

"Whatever's needed, and to be there when it goes down."

"Like, actually meet her?" Jessie asks.

"That was always the plan."

She raises her shoulders to her ears. "That sounds dangerous."

"I think it's more dangerous not to do it."

"Why?" JJ asks. "What's happened?"

"She's ruining my life."

"I thought she did that already?"

I shake my head. "No. One plagiarism count . . . it's bad, don't get me wrong, but I could come back from it. I could've laid low and in a year or two when everyone's forgotten about me and moved on to some other scandal, I could've made my way back. People like giving people a second chance, if they're worth it. If they're redeemable."

"And now you're not?"

"Bingo."

"Why?"

The waitress approaches our table with a coffee carafe. I place my hand over my cup. I don't need any more caffeine today. "This guy that I used to work with 'found' my senior thesis from J school, and he says it's plagiarized. It's all over the internet. But I didn't do it this time. That's not the paper I wrote, I mean, not mostly. Someone's gone in and changed it."

"Couldn't you prove that was the case?"

"I don't think I have an original copy anymore." I'd thrown all that stuff out when I moved into my current semicloset. "It's in a digital archive. Who knows if they even kept the paper original. Someone who knows what they're doing could go in and change some key passages, and there wouldn't be any evidence left about what I wrote."

"What about your senior adviser?"

"I doubt she'd remember—it wasn't that good. And imagine how many she's had to read since then. Now I'm a serial cheater. It's a pattern going way back. I am totally fucked."

"So," Jessie says, "what's finding Jessica Two going to do about it?"

"If we catch her, I can write about what happened to all of us. I can redeem myself. Plus, get my money back. Get your money back. That could help you, too, JJ. And you, Jessie."

"How?" JJ takes her coffee black, and the steam's curling over the cup like a witch's cauldron.

"You think those rumors in your town are actually the work of that woman, Leanne?"

Jessie looks struck by the thought.

"It was probably Jessica Two, don't you think?" I press.

"I guess."

"And nothing's changed since you agreed to come with me. She still has our money; she still has to be stopped. No one but us is going to do anything about it."

Jessie looks grim. "You're not going to start quoting Shakespeare again, are you?"

"If that's what it takes."

"Please don't," JJ says. "All this rah-rah-rah is making me feel like I'm back in the army."

"Okay, I won't. But will you help me?"

I reach my hand out to the middle of the table, palm down. JJ gives me a wry smile, then reaches out with her good hand. I meet her eyes across our stacked limbs and smile.

"Jessie?"

"Yeah, okay, fine."

She adds her hand. I feel the extra weight and let it sit there for a minute. Then I dip my hand and raise it, bumping theirs up into the air.

"And, break!"

Chapter 20

New York State of Mind

I'm back in the city and it feels weird. Like when I first got here with Liam, after the Catskills, when he thought it was safe. At first all I could notice was the smell. The *smells*. Garbage and urine and whatever it is that makes the air that comes out of the subway vents smell that way. There were so many people. I'd grown up almost without touch, and now, walking down the street meant being pressed up against any number of strangers. I didn't know what the street signs meant. I didn't know how to hail a cab or read a subway map. I'd never heard the word *bodega*.

I was like one of the characters in a movie who travels through time or gets defrosted after two hundred years. Only, I'd been living in this time all my life, so nobody gave me any quarter.

TV is what saved me. I sat in Liam's loft when I wasn't shadowing him, and I studied sitcoms and reality shows and news programs like they were my high school. I watched movies and music videos, and sometimes I'd have music going at the same time as a show because I was a sponge and I needed to soak up as much as I could in the shortest amount of time possible. I'd repeat the lines I'd heard till the expressions rolled off my tongue easily. I even changed the way I pronounced words from the slightly elongated vowels of the Land of Todd to the shorter ones of the newscaster. I picked up the pace of my speech, too, because New York was always in a hurry: *Hurry up, move it, move it!*

After a year of doing that, I sat down with real books and I got my GED and I wrote a kick-ass essay and scored well on the SAT, and some other doors opened for me. Todd took the power of the pen seriously, so we'd all learned how to write well, even if it was mostly in praise of him. If I was ready to leave the nest and move into a dorm, I could break free of Todd once and for all, make friends, reinvent myself. I could tell the new people I met that I was anyone I wanted to be.

I could've been anything I wanted to be.

I think about that now as I leave the train station and decide to walk back to my apartment. I need to reacclimate myself to the city, even though I've only been gone for less than a week. The first things I notice, like all those years ago, are the smells and the dust and the noise. It's so loud here. There's never a moment of peace.

I walk through the Sunday pedestrian traffic swiftly. It's a humid, bright day, and there are women in bright sundresses and men in shorts. I wish I had sunglasses and that I was wearing a summer dress, but I press on. The blocks fall away. My backpack is cutting into my shoulders and my feet are starting to hurt. I need new running shoes, but I should keep the unnecessary expenses to a minimum. Who knows how much this next phase is going to cost?

A few blocks from the Village, my phone vibrates in my pocket. It's Covington.

You back in town?

Yep.

Drink?

You bet.

Before I can put my phone away, it rings. Liam.

"Hey," I say. "What's up?"

"Where are you?"

An ambulance barrels down the street, its siren deafening. I wait for it to pass.

"I'm a few blocks from my place."

"You just get back?"

"Yeah. I'm going to drop my stuff, then go meet Covington."

"Covington?" His voice rises in surprise.

"He texted for a drink."

"Ah."

"What?"

He clears his throat. "Nothing. Call me tomorrow."

"Wait, why did you call?"

But he's already hung up. I stop walking and some sweaty guy in a suit slams into my shoulder.

"Hey!" he says. "I'm walking here."

I flip him the bird. Maybe when all this is over, I'll move somewhere else. Somewhere less aggressive.

I look at my phone as if it might hold the answers to why Liam called me. And why he suddenly seems to have a problem with Covington. If I didn't know better, I'd say he sounded jealous.

"Ha!" I say out loud.

"What's your problem, lady?" says another red-faced man in a suit.

It's definitely time to leave this city.

The plan is to meet Covington at Fiddlesticks, which gives me enough time to change clothes and take a cooling shower. The train smell clings to my clothes, and I toss them into the dirty-clothes hamper with a grimace. My roommates have reverted back to their natural state in my absence: there are dirty dishes in the sink and fruit flies hovering over some half-finished toast and jam sitting on the counter.

I start to pick it up, then stop. I'll deal with it later.

When I get to the bar, Covington's sitting on the same stool I was on when Liam found me there—was that only a week ago? It seems like forever and a day. His clothing is loose and comfortable and a weird collection of things that don't match. Cargo shorts in a dark-purple color, an orange plaid short-sleeve shirt that could keep someone from getting shot out in the woods in hunting season, and a knit cap slung low on the back of his head.

He pulls me in for a big hug.

"You smell like a pine forest," he says.

"Jeez, thanks. I showered and everything."

I sit on the stool next to him and signal to the bartender for a beer. He gives me a thumbs-up; I guess I've been coming in here more often than I thought.

"You need more than a shower to get the stench of the Land of Todd off you."

My head spins toward him. "How did you . . . Liam told you he took me there, didn't he?"

"Maybe yes, maybe no."

"Stuff it."

"Okay, yes."

"Did he tell you why?"

He shrugs. "Some shit about healing or letting go. You know how Liam is."

"Yeah."

"He wanted me to go up there too. Thought it might do me some good."

"That right? Liam's being a bit weird lately."

"How so?"

I meet Covington's eyes in the mirror. My face is flushed. Cov's a good-looking guy, but I've never thought about him romantically.

"He maybe thinks there's something going on between you and me."

Covington starts to laugh.

"What?" I say. "Hey. It's not that funny."

He shakes his head and composes himself. "No, no, it's not that."

"What, then?"

"Liam doesn't think there's something going on between us."

"How do you know?"

"Because he knows I'm with Daisy."

"Well, maybe he thinks I have a crush on you—he keeps acting funny when you come up."

The bartender comes over with my beer. I'm thinking about downing it in one long gulp like I used to do at frat parties as a party trick.

"Put that on my tab," Cov says.

"No, what? I got it."

"My tab. I insist."

"Fine. Whatever. In that case, I'll take a menu too."

The bartender nods and goes to fetch it for me. I flash back to the other night in the bar with Jessie. That stunt we pulled. Liam would be livid.

"Don't take advantage," Covington says.

I feel a shiver of guilt. "I wasn't planning on it. Like I said, I can pay my own way."

I hold up the menu and point to the calamari plate. It's a thousand million calories, but I feel like I need some fat in my system to cushion the blow. The bartender nods again and punches in the order.

Covington drums his fingers on the bar. "That woman, that other Jessica, she took all your money, right?"

"Pretty much."

"And you haven't gotten another job?"

"True."

"Probably pretty hard to do that with this new plagiarism thing, I bet."

I pick up the beer and start to drink. It slides down easily, but I stop after a few swallows. I couldn't eat that terrible train food, and my stomach is beyond empty.

"I'm guessing."

"Any idea how that happened?"

"I have a few."

"You *are* kind of channeling Liam right now, you know that?"

"Sorry."

"And if Liam's acting weird when you bring me up, it's because he's jealous."

"What? No."

"Oh, come on. Everyone knows he's had a thing for you for years."

"Years?"

I look at myself in the glass behind the bar. It's been a while since I gave myself a good look. I don't see anything special. I never have.

Is what Covington's saying true? How do I even process this?

"Don't worry, it's not like we talk about it on a regular basis or anything."

"That's a relief."

"I mean, Miller thinks it's a bit weird because of the age difference, but Daisy told him to shut it."

Great, they've all been talking about me. "He's not that much older than me."

Twelve years. An impossible gap at eighteen, but now?

"We don't have to discuss it if you don't want," Covington says.

I lean against his arm. "Thanks, Cov." The bartender brings my order and I put some cash on the bar. "See, I can pay for myself."

"I didn't doubt it. You must have some of the settlement money left."

The settlement. We learned after Todd died that he'd amassed massive wealth. All those "dues" he was charging people like my parents to come live in the LOT. The "buy-in" that was required if you wanted to stay permanently. Any money you had, any money you inherited or could scam off concerned family members with promises of coming home if they'd wire the money, went to him. In the end, he was sitting on a gold mine.

I can't remember who first posted the idea in that Facebook group we had, but it caught hold quickly. Somebody knew a lawyer. Somebody wrote a nasty letter to Todd's heirs, family members he hadn't talked to in decades because they weren't "in the Family," and threatened to expose their connection to him. They fought briefly, then caved pretty spectacularly. The money was divided among the children because we were the innocent victims. We each got an equal share.

"I used most of that on my student loans."

"Ah."

"You?"

"That was my seed money for the day-trading."

"And now?"

"I've done all right."

"I'm happy for you."

Covington looks down at his hands. He flips his arm over to show me his brand. "I've looked into getting this removed, you know?"

"Yeah?"

"It's not a tattoo, though, so there isn't anything they can do about it."

"That sucks."

"It does."

I push my plate toward him. "You want some of these?"

"Sure."

We eat silently for a few minutes. The calamari are crisp and fatty, exactly as they should be, a perfect accompaniment to the beer. We each order another round as the music thrums, encasing us. I listen to the snatches of conversation that reach me from the other patrons. Someone wants to form a union. Someone's asking if they can live with no money for a while.

"What was it like?" Covington asks eventually as he licks some aioli sauce from his fingers.

"What was *what* like?"

"Come on, Jess."

I finish the second beer. I want another, but I need to keep my wits about me.

"About how you'd expect, probably. It smelled the same, you know? But all the buildings looked smaller."

"I can't believe our parents raised us there."

"I know."

"You ever forgive them?"

"Nope. You?"

"Not a fucking chance."

Chapter 21

Replacements

After the funeral and the conversation on the dock with Kiki, I was feeling down. Not because Todd was dead, but because of everything that Todd had done. Kiki was right. I was as stuck as the rest of them. I might've left, but I hadn't moved on. Besides Liam and The Twists, I didn't have any close friends. My life didn't feel permanent, and despite all my studying, I didn't fit in at college like everyone else did. I had a fake backstory ready for when people asked: I'd grown up in a small town that no one had ever heard of, been homeschooled, moved to the big city, and that was it. Nothing to see here, folks! I never mentioned Todd. I never used the word *cult*. The scar on my wrist was hidden most of the time and was from an accident, if someone happened to see it. My parents were dead.

Only they weren't. My mother, Therese, was standing right there in front of me as I walked back to the Gathering Place. She was dressed in white—Todd hated black, and I'd worn a black dress to the funeral out of spite rather than mourning—and her hair had gone completely gray. She'd cut it short, and with her thinness and the hard planes of her face, she might've been a man. She still had that light in her eyes, though, this clear certainty that dissuaded me from asking too many questions.

I'd avoided eye contact with her and my father during the funeral, but I couldn't help but notice that there was a child standing with them. She looked to be about four, though it was hard to tell, as children in the Land of Todd were often small for their age. She was dressed in one of the Scout uniforms I used to wear, and her blonde hair was in two braids. She looked enough like me at that age that it was disconcerting. Who was she? Had my parents had a replacement child after I'd left? No, that was impossible—they were too old. Did they kidnap her from somewhere? I wouldn't put it past them. Why was my mother holding her hand? Why was this little girl leaning against my mother as if she was someone who could provide comfort?

What the hell was happening?

"Hello, Jessica," my mother said when I'd gotten to within ten feet of her.

"Therese."

She flinched. "I wish you'd call me Mom."

"You must be joking. 'There are no mothers or fathers. Only citizens. We all belong to one another—'"

"Stop."

"What? You don't want to hear the words of your precious Todd anymore?"

My father came out of the lodge with my aunt Tanya. He went by the name Trevor, a *T* name like the rest of them. I was supposed to change my name to one when I turned eighteen, but that had never happened. I wondered what Kiki's name was now, but I also didn't want to know.

My father wasn't wearing white. Just a pair of jeans and a sweatshirt that had a faded college logo on it. His hair was gray, too, and I wondered how old my parents were. One more thing Todd had stolen from me—the basic details of the members of my family were lost to me.

"Jessica, don't talk to your mother like that."

"My *mother*. Ha. Right, sure, Trevor. Whatever."

My mother's lips were trembling, and she was doing what I did when I was nervous: rubbing the scar on her wrist over and over like it was a magic talisman.

"I'm sorry," she said. "I didn't mean—"

"You didn't mean to what? Ruin my life? Ruin the lives of the rest of our family?"

Kiki was standing next to me now. She rested a hand on my shoulder. I shrugged it off.

"Honestly, *Therese*, how could you? I mean, if you wanted to come here and live with that monster, so be it. But then you had a child. You had *me*. And you stayed anyway. Even when Todd made us move up the hill and told us to sit this way and talk that way. You had to know that was wrong. You had to."

"I didn't . . . I couldn't . . ."

"Right. Sure. And what was supposed to happen on my eighteenth birthday? What was supposed to happen in that cabin right over there?"

I pointed to the cabin that I'd built all by myself the year I was seventeen. Maybe someone else lived there now. One of Todd's other playthings.

My mother was as white as her clothing. Tanya and Trevor stood on the porch, looking down at us. Then that girl came out. The one who'd been standing near my mother at the funeral.

"You couldn't protect me from whatever was supposed to happen. So, I had to leave. And the only thing I feel bad about is that I didn't drag Kiki with me and burn this motherfucking place to the ground as we left."

"Jessica! Don't speak that way."

"Why? Because you can't take it? Because that little girl is standing there? Who the hell is she, anyway?"

My mother looked at the ground, and I knew. Wherever she came from, she was my replacement.

I felt manic and unhinged. I couldn't control my shaking body or the words flying out of my mouth.

"Where are her parents? Why the fuck is she treating you like you're her mother? I want some fucking answers."

"Jessica." It was Kiki, speaking low, her voice shaking. "Leave it."

"Leave it?"

I looked at her. Her eyes were filled with tears. "Please?"

I felt as if I were going to shatter. "Yeah, fine, fuck it. But there's one thing I'm not going to do."

"What?"

"I'm not leaving you behind, not this time, even if I have to take you out of here kicking and screaming."

Kiki smiled at me for the first time that day. "I'd kick and scream if you left me here."

Many, many beers later with Covington, I do something I'm going to end up regretting.

I go see Liam.

I do not give him a heads-up. No text. No call. I settle up my tab and tell Covington I have to head out. I do this because with each beer I drink, my anger with Liam for taking me back to the LOT grows. I know this isn't rational. I asked him to go with me to see Jessie, which brought us near Schroon, and the rest, well, the rest was predictable. But, still. He didn't have to stir all that up again. He knows how hard I've worked to put it behind me. To lead a seminormal life.

Yeah, Liam. You hear me? That was not okay.

I need to tell him. Not in a text, not over the phone, but in person.

So that's what I'm doing. I'm on the subway heading in his direction, keenly aware that I'm one of those drunk people on the subway, weaving slightly, maybe even muttering aloud to herself.

But who cares? Who cares, Preppy Boy with the large headphones that I can still hear music through who's staring at me? I have something to say and I will not be denied.

So long as I don't pass out before I get there.

I wait outside Liam's apartment building until someone leaves. I don't want to ring his bell and be denied entry. Not that he's ever done that before, but I have a feeling tonight might be different. Maybe because I feel different. For once, there's nothing about Liam that's intimidating me. Alcohol is a wonderful thing.

I walk up the three flights of stairs to the top floor. The entrance to Liam's apartment is a heavy metal sliding door on a track that's almost too much for me to open. One of his many security precautions. Plus, it won't be unlocked. It's never unlocked. And no key to find lying around somewhere. Nope. So, I have to knock. I have to knock.

I am knocking.

As I'm knocking, I hear a sound. A laugh. A woman's laughter. Oh my God. Liam has a woman in there. What am I doing? I should get the hell out of here.

I turn to leave but it's too late. The heavy door slides open and Liam's standing there. He's wearing his usual dark jeans and a gray button-down shirt with the sleeves rolled up. A blast of cold air hits me in the face; Liam likes to keep his apartment frigid.

"Jess? What's going on?"

"It's nothing. You have . . . company."

"What? Oh no, that's just Diane."

He steps back, and I see "just Diane" standing by the kitchen counter. She doesn't look too pleased at the interruption or the way that

Liam referred to her. She's a tall, thin brunette wearing slacks and a cashmere sweater, and the way she's holding herself is so assured that it reminds me of Jessica Two. I need to get the fuck out of here.

"Hi," I say lamely, waving hello at this woman. She's about thirty-five, maybe even forty. Closer to Liam's age.

"Hi," she says. Her voice is cultured and smart. Adult. *Oh, stop it, Jess. If you keep going, you're going to fall in love with her.*

"What's going on?" Liam asks again.

"I wanted to ask you something."

"Yes?"

"Do you think . . . Could we have a minute alone?"

"That's my cue to go," Diane says.

"You don't have to," I say.

Please go, please go, please go. There's a wineglass on the kitchen counter and evidence of dinner. No candles, though. Not that I think that Liam would ever prepare a candlelit dinner for someone, but it still looks intimate.

"It's all right. I've got an early meeting in the morning."

She picks up this beautiful white linen blazer that's hanging on the back of one of Liam's bar chairs. Then she grabs a kind of attaché case, which also makes me feel better, like the lack of candles. And also the fact that it's Sunday. People don't have dates on Sundays, right?

Liam watches her gather her things without saying anything. I can't tell if he's pissed, but he probably is. I would be if I were interrupted by a drunk guy while I was having dinner with this nice lady or her male equivalent.

"I'll talk to you tomorrow?" she asks Liam.

"Sure," he says.

She hesitates. Is she waiting for a kiss? A handshake? Whatever it is, she decides she isn't getting it. "Night, Liam." She stops in front of me and holds out her hand. "We didn't meet."

"I'm Jess."

We shake briefly, and though I'm hoping she has one of those lame handshakes, she doesn't. It's dry and firm and professional because this lady is perfect, and I am drunk.

"Nice to meet you, Jess."

She actually sounds like she means it.

"You too," I say.

She walks past me, and Liam follows her out. He walks her to the stairs, but I don't turn around to see if he kisses her goodbye. He says *something*, but I can't hear what.

He comes back into the apartment and closes the door behind him. It slides into place on its track with a heavy *click*. The walls of the apartment are still builder's white and unadorned, but this place feels like home to me. It was my home. But that was a long time ago.

"Hey," I say.

"Hey."

He walks past me to the kitchen counter—a large slab of dark concrete—and picks up his half-full glass of red wine. The bottle it comes from is his favorite, I notice. This was a date. I broke up a date.

"What's going on?" he asks. His face is clean shaven even though it's late. Definitely a date. My God.

"I shouldn't have come," I say.

"But you did."

"Yeah."

"So?"

I turn my palms out to face him. There's nothing in my hands. Should there be? I'm too drunk to have this conversation, but I need to do it anyway.

"I wanted to tell you something."

"What?"

"I'm not sure now."

"Not sure you want to tell me or not sure what it was?"

"Both. Either."

He shakes his head and takes another sip of his wine. Was I mad at this man? Is that why I came? I don't feel mad now. Not even a little bit.

"You were on a date," I say. "She was a date."

"She's a colleague. We were discussing a case."

"You don't have to lie to me."

"I'm not lying."

I've made him mad now. He hates being accused of being untruthful. "It looks like a date."

"Not that it's any of your business."

"It feels like it is."

"Why?"

"Covington said—"

"What did he say?"

"Why do you use that tone of voice when I talk about Covington?"

"What tone?"

"That one. That one right there."

He finishes his glass of wine and reaches for the bottle. "You want?"

"Sure."

He moves to the cupboard and takes out a glass, then fills it. Our fingers brush as he hands it to me.

"Covington thinks it's jealousy," I say, because *fuck it.*

Liam's looking at me with an expression on his face that I don't recognize. He might also be a bit drunk, but it feels like something else.

I take a gulp of wine for courage. "Is he right?"

"Is something going on between you and Covington?"

"I'd never do that to Daisy."

"So, no?"

"No. But why do you care?"

He drinks some more of his wine and shakes his head at me.

"What?" I ask.

"Don't do this."

"Do what?"

"Play with me."

"I'm not."

"Sure, Jess, if you say so." He puts his glass down on the counter.

"Liam . . ."

"What?"

"Come on, you know . . . You must know."

I take a step toward him. The room's cold, but the air between us feels warm. Inviting.

"I know?"

"Yes," I say.

He gives me that look again. "What did you come to tell me?" he asks, but gentler this time, the words low and slow, like a caress.

"This," I say, reaching for his hand.

He watches me take it. He looks surprised, but he doesn't pull away, and this is enough for me. I take another step toward him and now we're almost in an embrace.

I tip my head up. He's looking down at me, his face slack.

"There's no music," I say.

"Why would there be music?"

"Because we're dancing, aren't we?"

"Is that what we're doing?"

"Why not?"

He takes my glass from me and puts it next to his, then slips his free hand around my waist. He tilts me slightly and we start to sway. I haven't taken my eyes off him. I think we're supposed to kiss now, but I don't know how to make that happen. I can't believe what's already happened, I—

"What's going on up here, kid?" Liam asks, resting his forehead against mine. His breath smells like wine, spicy and delicious.

"I'm not a kid."

"No, you're not. I'm not sure I know how to do this."

"Do what?"

"You know," he says. He brings his chin down so his lips are an inch from mine. "Is this what you wanted to tell me?"

"Yes."

He closes the gap.

Chapter 22

Afterglow

Two months later, I'm camped out in Grand Teton National Park in Jackson, Wyoming.

I'm here because this is where the fifth Jessica Williams lives, the one Liam helped me find. The one I need for the next phase of the plan.

I asked him to help me locate her the morning after I woke up in his bed.

That was a strange wake-up. Although my eyes were closed, it felt as if the room were flooded with that white light you see in TV shows where the person is dead or dreaming. Only I wasn't dead, and it wasn't a dream. At least, I didn't think I was. I'd dreamed about waking up in Liam's arms so many times that waking up to the reality of it felt disorienting. It's possible I even pinched myself to make sure.

"What are you doing?" Liam asked, lifting up the covers to look at me. I'd drawn myself down under them because it felt safer to be hidden by his black duvet than it did to have the morning sunshine on my face.

I opened my eyes. There was Liam, inches from my face, with his hair askew and tired eyes. Were they tired because he was regretting what had happened? Or had I worn him out? We'd taken our time with it, with each other, but I didn't feel tired. I felt like I could run a marathon. Like I had superpowers.

"Jess?"

"I was pinching myself."

Liam brushed his thumb against my arm. "I see that."

I lowered my hand. I could feel the bruise I'd given myself starting to form. But there was also the warmth from Liam's hand, and an answering response in my body.

"It hurt," I said.

"Don't do that again, then." His voice was gravelly in the morning. I liked it.

"I won't," I said as I tucked my head down.

"What?"

"There was something I wanted to do again."

He smiled slowly. "That right?"

This time I was the one who kissed him. It was even better sober.

It was midmorning when I told him the details of the plan for drawing Jessica Two out and asked him to help. He was reluctant at first, but I knew he'd agree eventually. When he did, I rewarded him.

It took him a while to find a good candidate, though. Another July 10, 1990, baby whose life we could co-opt, though I didn't put it that way. Instead, I promised him that we wouldn't do anything to harm this innocent person we were using as bait and that I'd get her consent to participate once, if, he located her.

I didn't mind the wait. When I wasn't refining the plan, or messaging with JJ and Jessie, I kept myself occupied with Liam. I'd never been in a real relationship before, if that's what this was. Not one of those immediately settled, we see each other at the end of the day without discussion unless there's a reason not to kinds of things. It was amazing. No fuss, no muss, no anxiety of whether he'd call or return my text. He always did. He was always there when I needed him or even when I just wanted to hear his voice.

It was different in other ways too. We'd known each other so long that we didn't have to get to know one another. Not like with a stranger. But then again, we didn't know each other this way, romantically, intimately, even though I lived with him that first year after I left the Land of Todd. That was twelve years ago, though. Then, I stuck to the outskirts of the apartment, the places I didn't think Liam cared about. The guest room. The crappy chair in the corner of the living room. I took the second shower to make sure he had enough warm water.

This time I was front and center. It was surprising how easily I fit into his life again. Could I have had this all along, I wondered, if I'd had the courage to speak up? No. I'd tried, and he'd pushed me away. He was right to do that. I was far too young then, and how could he tell whether I wanted him for real or simply out of gratitude? But something had shifted over time, and I wasn't sure how I'd missed it. What else was I missing?

I tried not to torture myself too much, or pepper Liam with questions. He didn't want to analyze; he wanted to be. Mostly, I was happy to do this, even though I kept telling myself it wasn't going to last, that I'd fuck it up somehow, that I should end it while we could still be friends. But I didn't want to. I wanted to live in this contented place as long as I could.

So I did.

And then Liam found Jessica Five.

He told me about her over the birthday dinner we shared at his place. Turns out, Liam does have candles. I found them at the back of a drawer and lit them, letting the wax drip onto a plate so they'd stand upright. It was another sweltering day after weeks of heat. The trees outside looked like they were dying, but inside his apartment, it was pleasant and cool. I'd decided to try to cook something, a simple pasta sauce over fresh pasta. I'd never had the time to learn how to cook, so I watched a YouTube video—one of JJ's—and followed the instructions.

The kitchen was a disaster, but the smells alone were worth it. I texted her a photo. She sent me a middle-finger emoji in response, which I took to mean *Leave me alone until you have something to tell me about the plan.* I sent her back a thumbs-up. Then I put my phone away and concentrated on Liam.

We'd finished eating, and I was trying to summon the will to get up and start washing the dishes when Liam pushed an envelope across the table.

"What's this?" I asked, taking it. It felt thick inside.

"What you asked for. Sorry it took so long to find it."

I opened the envelope. There was a sheaf of papers inside, and also a photo—more of a headshot—of a woman about my age. I knew who she must be. Even though I wanted this, I felt the start of dread.

"Another Jessica Williams?"

Liam relaxed into his chair. "That's right."

"Ah."

"You're disappointed?"

"No, it's . . ."

"Not what you were expecting for your birthday?"

"Not exactly."

He grinned. "There's something else for later."

"I sure hope so." I tossed him a napkin. "You have some sauce on your face."

"Nice way to thank me for finding something I didn't even want to find."

"Oh, I'll thank you."

And I did.

So here I am in Jackson, Wyoming, 2,164 miles from New York. Elevation, 6,237 feet. Population, 10,532. It's the middle of August, and the weather is perfect. Eighty degrees and sunny with that wide-open sky you only get at elevation. Big Sky Country, I think they call it. Or maybe that's in Montana. Whatever. I'm not here as a tourist, but I see the appeal.

This is where Jessica Five lives. Thanks to Liam, I know a lot about her. She was born to former ski bums who now own a brewpub. Her parents have a house up the side of Snow King, the town hill, which has amazing views of the Tetons. She lives in a small house that looks like it isn't insulated properly on one of the flat streets in the valley. She went to college in Colorado and now works as a photographer. Lots of black-and-white landscapes of the Tetons. Those sharp peaks, snow-topped, with flowers in the valleys below dancing merrily in the wind.

I've spent the last week tailing her, so I know a lot more than what was in Liam's packet, like where she goes for her morning coffee and what her favorite restaurant is. She's a happy person who starts her day with a run up Snow King. I walked the same switchback path one day, and it felt like my heart might explode. She has a small group of friends that she hangs out with most nights. She takes Fridays off to hike.

It didn't take long to complete the plan. JJ proposed setting up a fake photography prize and awarding it to her, after we created some online profiles for her. Before us, she only had a work website. What kind of millennial has no social? The kind who lives in Jackson. After we were done with her, she was on Facebook and Instagram. She even tweeted once in a while. Impersonating her made me nervous. What if she noticed? What if one of her real friends told her about it? What, then? But none of that happened. She carried on, obliviously living her fabulous life.

It had been a while since I followed someone, working with Liam or even in my early days trying to make a name for myself at FeedNews. It was hard in the city, even harder in a small town. I had to change my wardrobe. My New York uniform of black T-shirts and dark jeans made me stand out in this land of blond, tanned Amazonians. I spent too much money pulling things from the sale rack at Skinny Skis, and now I had hiking pants and shorts and colorful T-shirts in a wicking fabric, and a puffy jacket for the cool nights.

Surveillance is always an odd, voyeuristic experience, but trailing Five was even more so. She didn't feel like a stranger, more like a *Russian Dolls* version of me. Same name, same birthday. I could've had this life. Easy money and outdoor healthfulness instead of Todd and discipline. If my parents had only made better choices.

Once I thought she made me. We were sitting at Thai Me Up—all the Thai restaurants in town have punny names for some reason—me a couple of tables away from her, and she was looking at me like she knew me from somewhere. I smiled at her in a friendly way, nothing to be nervous about, and she smiled back. Then her food came, and she lost interest in me and went back to reading her book. But I was more careful after that. I didn't need to be there for everything. I already had enough.

I was there when Five got the notice that she'd won the contest we'd created, though. A UPS package left on her doorstep. I was sitting at the bus stop across the street, a Jackson Hole ball cap pulled down low. I watched her bend to pick it up, then open the package. She squealed when she read what was inside and almost skipped into her house. Who could blame her? An all-expense-paid trip to New York. A hotel room at the Parker. A $25,000 cash prize would be awarded to her there so she could travel to wherever she wanted and advance her art.

When she was inside, I took out my phone and called the local paper. I'd checked them out too. They did a great job covering local events, but they weren't a crack team of investigative journalists. I let them know that one of their local citizens had won a prize for her photography and that a press release would follow shortly. When they received it, the contact person to call was Jessie. JJ had designed a website for the prize—an anonymous philanthropist who enjoyed finding new talent and rewarding it—had set it up five years ago. His team of volunteers scoured the internet to find the year's best photos. We'd worked hard to make it good enough to fool anyone, including Jessica Two.

If Five, or anyone else, called the Parker, she had a reservation. A few days later, I was the one who called her to book her flight. When my own Google Alert picked up the story, I knew everything was in place.

Now we had to wait and see if Jessica would take the bait.

Chapter 23

We Few, We Happy Few

It's August 15. JJ's flying into Jackson this morning; Jessie comes tomorrow. Five's flight is set for the day after that.

I crawl out of my tent and work the kinks out of my body that have accumulated overnight. I've been camping in the park in the campground near Jackson Lake. It's about forty-five minutes outside of Jackson, which is deliberate. I didn't want to get known by a hotel, which would have been inevitable if I stayed there for weeks. The campground has the added benefit of being cheap and full of a transient population. It's rare for the sites surrounding mine to be occupied by the same group two nights in a row. I bought a tent, sleeping bags, camp stove, and pans in town. I use a headlamp to read at night. I shower in the communal camp showers every other day so the attendants don't get too used to seeing me. I talk to no one but Liam.

It's not the same between us as it was in New York. That idyll we created, where our differences and our pasts didn't matter—that's all slipping away. Liam doesn't want me doing this, so he says on a regular basis, and yet he's the reason I've been able to get this far. What am I supposed to do with that information?

I try not to let thoughts of him consume me. I need to focus on what's ahead. I need to shower, get dressed, and go pick up JJ. In forty-eight hours, this is all coming to a head.

I start the clock in my mind and get to work.

"Never thought I'd stay in one of these again," JJ says as she stoops and peers into the tent. "You think we're all going to fit in here?"

"I bought two. Jessie likes to sleep alone."

She gives a look over her shoulder and stands up. She walks over to the paddleboards I rented. I've been taking one out most mornings, and I got two more yesterday for JJ and Jessie. When you get away from shore, the lake looks the way it must have before anyone got here and decided to erect a campground. Each morning I paddle farther, my arms straining until the effort seems less.

"The tent's not too bad with an air mattress," I say.

"Air mattress!" JJ says. "Ha."

"You didn't have those in Afghanistan?"

"Not so much."

She turns around to face me. She looks focused and far away at the same time.

"Why did you pick here?" she asks.

"It's out of the way. No one stays here long. Easier to stay anonymous."

"Makes sense."

"You did a great job with that online stuff," I say. "I felt like you captured Five's authentic voice."

She smiles. She's wearing a Killers T-shirt and cargo shorts. "Yeah, right. Whatever. You think it's going to work?"

"Five bought it."

"Sure. Who wouldn't want a free trip to New York? But will *she*?"

"Jessica will play along."

"Why are you so sure?"

"She can't stop now. She's come too far."

"I hope you're right." JJ shakes her head. "If there's a God up there, and he sees all of us in the same place, do you think he might open a rift in the time-space continuum?"

"Like the intersection of religion and science fiction?"

"Sure."

"I don't believe in either."

"You would if you'd been to the places I have."

I walk away from the tent and sit on the top of the picnic table. The wood is perma-damp and a bit soft. "War made you believe in God?"

"It did."

"Why?"

"Because if there wasn't a purpose bigger than me, or the government, to being there, then what the fuck was I doing?"

"I guess that makes a certain sort of sense."

"What made you lose faith?"

"Assuming I had it in the first place." I rub at the scar on my arm. "It was forced out of me. You might even say burned."

"That's pretty bleak."

"Sorry."

"It's fine. I'm not here to sing songs around a campfire."

"Damn, and I've been practicing and everything."

JJ smiles. "That, I might like to see." She looks at her watch. It's around noon. "I'm hungry."

"I can make some pasta."

"Nah, let's go into town. I'd like some of that punny Thai food you told me about."

I hop off the table. "That does sound good right about now." I look around the campsite to make sure that everything is squared away, then walk over to the Jeep I rented when I got here. JJ and I climb in. I turn on the engine and put it in reverse. "You know what?"

"What?"

"I don't think the time-space continuum is going to rip apart."

"Why not?"

"Because Jessica's not one of us."

"How do you figure?"

"I don't care what her name is. She's not a Jessica Williams."

The Thai place I like was full with its lunch rush, but the sushi place down the road wasn't. Who eats sushi in landlocked Jackson? These girls, apparently. The decor is black lacquer and bamboo, and there's a large fish tank near the bar that's devoid of fish.

JJ ordered a plate of spicy tuna, then mixed a boatload of wasabi into some soy sauce and proceeded to dunk each piece until it was almost drowning. Now I think she might be regretting it. She's downed two large glasses of water, and she's sweating like she's in the desert when Five walks in with one of her girlfriends.

She's cute, Five. A head of curly hair that she must've hated when she was a kid but looks great on her now. Tall and athletic, she fits right in. She's got her camera slung around her neck and is carrying her camera bag. She looks happy, lit up, and I feel a bit bad for the disappointment she's going to feel when she gets to New York and learns that there isn't any conference or prize. She'll have a free weekend in the city, though. And she'll still have all her money, et cetera, so it won't be a total loss. I thought about asking Covington to look out for her once she gets there, but that would've required more explanation than is prudent.

"What are you looking at?" JJ asks between coughs.

"Five is on your six."

"You proud of yourself for the military terms?"

"A little bit, yes."

"You are having too much fun with this." JJ looks over her shoulder. "She's taller in person. Who's the girl?"

"A friend."

"How closely have you been tailing her?"

"Pretty closely."

"Was that a good idea?"

She dips the last piece of sushi into her wasabi float and pops it into her mouth.

"About as much as that was."

"Right." She pushes her plate away from her.

"We should leave."

"Why?"

"Because she's seen me one too many times already."

JJ taps her fake arm on the table twice. I suggested she bring it with her instead of the hook to make her less conspicuous. "Great, good work."

"You try tailing someone in a small town."

"But why was the tailing even necessary, though?"

"The more we know, the better."

"Funny," JJ says. "I already feel like I know too much."

I push my plate away. I ordered the spider, deep-fried soft-shelled crab. It was delicious, but it's roiling in my stomach right now.

"Has she been in touch with you?" I ask.

"Who, Jessica?"

"Yeah."

"Nothing recently. You?"

"No."

"That worry you?"

"It's hard to know what to think."

"I guess we don't have any choice about going through with it."

"You having second thoughts?" I ask.

"Always, but I think we should stick with the plan."

"We don't have a choice, I guess."

The only choice is us. That's what Todd used to say.

I'm about to find out if that's true, after all.

Chapter 24

Never Get Involved in a Land War in Asia

After lunch, we explore Jackson a bit, then get back to camp around six. We're still both full from lunch, so JJ suggests we go out for a paddle. The lake is crystal clear and flat, it'll be light till ten, and I'm keyed up and awake, so I agree.

We walk the paddleboards down to the lake and climb on. The cold water laps at my toes as I splash myself with my paddle. I start to lose my balance, then right myself.

"Careful," JJ says.

"I got it."

"Don't drink and paddle."

"It was your idea."

Despite my recent excursions, JJ is more efficient than I am on the water. She leaves her replacement arm behind, tucks the end of the paddle into her armpit, and uses her good arm on the shaft. We stop when we get to the middle of the lake.

"It's so beautiful here," she says when I get close to her.

"You could do a whole relentlessly positive segment. Live from the Tetons!"

"That's not a terrible idea. I mean, look at this."

She sweeps her arm away from her. The water is a clear blue, and the Tetons' snowy peaks are sharp and close. The sky contains a few puffy clouds. There's land across from us, thick pine forest that looks like the perfect home for moose and bears. We're alone out here, not another person in sight, though I can hear an occasional echo coming from back at the campground.

"It's pretty amazing," I say flatly.

JJ shakes her head at me. "Don't you get excited about anything?"

"I'm just preoccupied."

"About the operation?"

"Is that so odd?"

"Nah. I always got that way before missions."

A shiver passes through me. It's so tranquil here, so different from where she's been. "Was it tough, over there?"

"Tough?"

"Yeah. You know, I mean, was it . . . Ah hell, I don't know what I'm asking."

"It's fine. We don't learn how to talk about that stuff."

"We don't have to."

JJ looks ahead. "Have you been over to the other side?"

"Not yet."

"Looks pretty isolated."

"It is."

"Is it too far away?" she asks.

"We'll only know if we try."

"True. Shall we paddle?"

"Let's do it."

Jessie arrives the next day in the midafternoon.

JJ and I have spent the morning going over the plan again, then lazing around camp, soaking in the sunshine and clean mountain air. Liam's called twice, but I texted him back that I have bad cell reception and that I'll call him when I can. The longer I spend here, and the closer

I get to tomorrow, the farther away I feel from him, my life in New York, even the person I usually am.

Jessie's driving a nondescript sedan that she rented at the airport. She's taken my advice and is dressed in hiking pants and a light cotton T-shirt. She's got sturdy-looking shoes on her feet, and with her hair in a high ponytail and a pair of Oakleys pushed up onto her head, she looks like a local.

I spent some of the time this morning setting up Jessie's tent. She looks satisfied when I show it to her, then crawls inside and deposits her bags. When she comes out, she's changed into shorts and a tank top.

"Who knew it could be so hot in Wyoming," she says. She fans herself, then swats at a fly.

"Right?"

I give her a brief tour of the campsite—pointing out the bathrooms and where I've stashed the cooler under a tree to keep it out of the sun. It's next to the stack of paddleboards.

"What are these?" Jessie asks.

"Paddleboards. I rented them."

"You been having a good vacation?" she asks a bit aggressively.

"I couldn't tail Five twenty-four seven."

"I guess."

"Are we fighting for some reason?" I ask.

Jessie blows out a long breath. "Sorry. It's been a long day. And that landing. You should've warned me."

The Jackson Hole Airport is in the Teton National Park, and you fly right over the Tetons before dropping down into the valley. I'd found it nerve-racking, but the local sitting next to me on my flight told me that I should've seen what it was like before they lengthened the runway.

"Bumpy?" I ask Jessie.

"Three people puked."

"It was smooth sailing for me," JJ says.

"That right?"

"We are pissy today," I say. "All of us, I mean."

"We should talk about tomorrow," JJ says.

"Will that help?"

"Never know until we do it." She sits at the picnic table and pats the seat next to her. "Come on, now. I don't bite unless asked."

It's dark now, and we've eaten dinner and talked everything over. Our plan is as simple as we can make it. We go to the airport tomorrow. I set up shop inside and look out for Jessica Two. When she approaches Five, I watch from a safe distance. She's most likely to leave the airport and head for town so she can get to Five's bank and liquidate her assets. Jessie and JJ will be there to follow her if she does until I can catch up with them and we can confront her. But if it looks like she's going to get on a plane, then I call in security.

JJ left a few moments ago to go to the bathroom. Jessie's inside her tent, shuffling around. I look up at the sky, the stars scattered like snow in a globe. Despite the heat of the day, there's a frost warning in effect. I can see the beginnings of my breath, or its end.

I should call Liam, check in for the night. But it's midnight in New York. He's probably asleep. He texted me while we were planning earlier, but Jessie gave me a look when I glanced at my phone, so I put it down without answering.

I can hear other campers moving around the campground. The slam of a camper door, then a car. A group of kids laughing. Teenagers, by the sound of it, in their loud, self-involved way. It's so hard to tell the direction of sound, especially at night. The world is both quiet and loud all at once. One of the teenagers barks with laughter, only it's a cruel sound, angry and mean. The zipper on Jessie's tent slides down and she pokes her head out.

"What's going on?" she asks.

"Just some kids."

"Sounds like something different. Where's JJ?"

"She went to the bathroom."

"That's where those kids are."

"How can you tell?"

Jessie puts her hands on the ground and hops out of the tent, landing on her hands and feet. Her shirt rides up her back, revealing her bony back. She's much thinner than she looks in clothes. She stands up and straightens her sweater.

"How can you not?"

"Not what?"

"Tell where the—"

"*You do not want to do that . . .*"

I spin my head around. "That was JJ's voice."

We both take off running. The bathroom is two hundred yards away, and we're there in thirty seconds. There's a small crowd standing in a circle. People in pajama bottoms and puffy jackets, clutching their toilet bags to their chests. I can't see JJ. I push past someone encased in fleece. JJ's got a gangly teenager on the ground, her fake hand against his throat.

"Get off," he says in a squeaky voice. "I didn't mean it."

"Please, miss? Please," a girl with a rash of acne across her forehead says. "You're hurting him."

"What's going on?" I ask. "JJ?"

She looks up at me. Her eyes are dark. "This little shit thought it would be fun to pick on a . . ." She turns back to him. "What was it you said? Go on, say it again."

He shakes his head vigorously. "No, ma'am, I'm sorry, please."

"Let him up," Jessie says. Her voice is firm and as dark as JJ's eyes. "Let him up now."

"Let's give it a minute, shall we? Till the lesson sinks in?"

"I think you've made enough of an impression." Jessie emphasizes the last word, making it low and harsh. It gets through to JJ. She's already called too much attention to us, even in this transitory place.

She springs to her feet in an elegant move and slaps one of her relentlessly positive grins on her face. She extends her hand to the ground.

"Little Timmy here is all right, isn't he?"

Timmy, or whatever his name is, is probably not all right. But JJ's grin is infectious, so he reaches out his hand and she pulls him up.

And maybe it's only me that sees the menace in her smile.

Chapter 25

Game Day

It's game day.

That's what I've taken to calling it in my head.

I'm seated at a high-top table in the Jackson Hole Airport in the only restaurant in the place. It sells big burgers and salty, thick-cut french fries and looks out over the tarmac, which is the second-best view of the Tetons I've seen since I've been here. There are several large-screen TVs mounted on the walls, which are all tuned into sports. My fellow patrons look longingly at the view they'll soon be leaving. It's a bluebird day. Only, I'm not looking at the TV or the view. Instead, I've positioned myself so I can see the departure lounge.

I've been here for two hours already. JJ and Jessie are in position in the parking lot.

The airport website says to get to the terminal three hours before your flight during tourist season. The town's a gateway to Yellowstone, so a million tourists come through it in a good summer. I just hope that Five is one of those people who follows instructions and not one of those last-minute airport people who rush up to the gate right before it's supposed to close. The kind of person Jessica Two turned me into.

I needn't have worried. I see her enter the lounge—one large room with plenty of comfy dark-leather chairs and a massive stone fireplace in the middle where the fire is roaring despite the weather—an hour and a half before her flight's supposed to leave. She looks around for an empty spot. A woman about our age motions that there's room for her on the couch she's sitting on. Five walks toward her gratefully. Maybe they know one another? No. They're not talking to each other like friends. Instead, Five pulls out an iPad and starts to read.

I survey the woman. She's in her late twenties or early thirties. A nondescript brunette dressed in a plaid shirt with her hair in a messy ponytail. She could be anyone, but in this moment, she looks like she's searching for an opportunity to engage Five in conversation.

I tap my foot nervously. It's go time.

I take out my phone and text Jessie and JJ in the group thread we created earlier.

I think she might be here, I write.

For sure? Jessie types back.

Strong possibility. I'll keep an eye out.

I should come in.

No. We agreed. Stay in the car so you can follow her when she leaves the terminal.

I put my phone in my pocket and leave cash for my check and go up to the information desk. A pretty young blonde woman is working there.

"Hi, um, I've lost my friend and this is ridiculous because, look at this place, it's tiny, but I can't find her. Do you mind paging her?"

The blonde tilts her head to the side. "Sure. It happens all the time."

"Oh, thank you. I feel so silly."

"What's her name?"

"Jessica Williams."

"Gotcha."

She picks up her microphone. I can tell she's relishing using it in this TV-like way. "Jessica Williams to the information podium. Jessica Williams to the information podium."

"Thanks," I say, then walk a few feet away to look out at the room full of crowded travelers. I watch Five. She stands, puts her backpack on the seat, and asks the woman next to her to watch it while she finds out what's going on. This happens in hand gestures, but it's easy enough to understand.

Five walks toward me. I'm wearing a dark wig I brought with me, but I take out the cheap glasses I bought in the pharmacy in town a few days ago and put them on. My clothes are a size too big, and I'm barely recognizable even to myself. I turn around and arrive at the kiosk at the same time as Five.

I wait for her to speak, then say with her, "I'm Jessica Williams."

Five turns toward me with what must be a duplicate of the look I gave Jessica Two a few months ago. "What?" She turns back to the girl behind the counter. "What's going on?"

The girl behind the counter gives me a funny look. "She was looking for you . . ."

"Me?" I say. "Was it my sister? We look alike."

"Oh, maybe . . ."

"Excuse me?" Five says. "Were you looking for me?"

The girl's confusion deepens. "Are you Jessica Williams?"

"I am."

"Wait, whoa," I say. "Me too."

"You are?"

"Yeah."

"So, which one of us was paged?"

I raise my shoulders. "Not sure. Maybe it was my sister looking for me? I'm not sure where she's gotten to."

I feign looking over my shoulder to try to find my imaginary sister.

"I could page her," the girl says helpfully.

"Oh, don't bother. She's probably in the bar. Speaking of which." I loop my arm through Jessica's.

She pulls back. "What are you doing?"

"Don't you think we should have a drink?"

"Um . . ."

"Come on, it's not every day that you meet another Jessica Williams, is it?"

She hesitates, but my smile is so wide open, and this place is so trusting, that she caves.

"I guess not."

"What time's your flight?"

"Not till two."

"Plenty of time, then."

"Yeah, I should get some lunch, I guess."

"Perfect. I even have a table."

I can tell that Five is still hesitant, but she's surrounded by a familiar environment, and she's still giddy from winning the trip. What can a drink with a stranger with the same name as her do? Nothing, she thinks.

Ha.

The table I left earlier is still empty but for the twenty I secured under the salt and pepper shakers.

I catch the server's eye, and he walks over looking resigned. He's got a mustard stain on his black apron, which blots out the *J* in Jedediah's.

"Back?" he says.

"Yep."

"What can I get for you?"

I look at Jessica. "What do you like? They have that local IPA here, right?"

"Pako's. Sure, that sounds good."

"Two Pako's." The waiter writes it down.

"Two Pako's. Two Jessicas," I say.

Five looks nervous. "It's weird."

"Yep."

She's very pretty up close, this Jessica. Much prettier than the rest of us. Not that we're unattractive, just that this girl could be a model. In fact, she was for a while, which is how she got into photography. Tall and willowy in a way that isn't achieved through the gym but through genetics. Also, probably, *not* growing up in a cult doesn't hurt.

The waiter brings our pint glasses.

I raise my glass to hers. "What should we toast to?"

Before Five can answer, a voice says, "There you are!"

It's Jessie. She's wearing a tight smile that's meant to look friendly, but she's clearly pissed. I'm off book, and she wants to know why.

"Who's this?" Five asks.

"My sister," I say before Jessie can speak. "The one who was looking for me. You paged me, right?"

Jessie's confusion disappears quickly. "How come you didn't come to the counter?"

"I did, but I met her and forgot all about it." I turn to Five to include her in the conversation. "Can you believe it, J . . . Julie? She's *another* Jessica Williams!"

"No *way*."

"Yeah, weird, right?"

"Totally." Jessie pulls a seat over from the table next door and sits down. I want to find a way to ask her what she's doing in the airport, but I hold it. There's no way to have that conversation right now.

"So," Jessie says to me, "have you done it?"

"Done what?"

"You know, played the game."

"The . . ." I stop and give Jessie a look.

"What game?" Five asks.

"It's nothing," I say quickly, trying to kick Jessie under the table.

Five puts her hands on the table and pushes her chair back. "I think I'm going to go."

"No," Jessie and I say in unison. "Stay."

"Then tell me what's going on." Her eyes wander around the restaurant and come to rest on the security guard standing near gate three. One yell from her and we'll all be in some trouble.

"I'm Jessica Williams," I say.

"Yeah, you said that already."

"And she's Jessica Williams too." I point to Jessie. Jessie's face reddens. We are way, way, way off book now.

Five frowns. "I thought you said her name was Julie? And that she was your sister."

"She's not."

"And you're both called Jessica Williams?"

"Yes. And we were all born on the same day."

Five's hands start to shake in fear. "How the fuck do you know that?"

"That's a long story."

She checks her watch. "I've got an hour. That long enough for you?"

It only takes half an hour to tell her the condensed version of what's happened up to now. All the "chance" meetings, the cons, how I'd hatched this plan to finally catch Jessica Two.

"Why did you think this was going to work?" Five asks. She hasn't touched the burger she ordered, though I've already finished mine, eating it greedily between snippets of explanation. Jessie didn't say much as I talked, just steadily ate a plate of fries, dipping each one into a mound of ketchup with the precision of a surgeon.

"Because this is how each of us got taken in."

"But no one approached me."

"There was that woman you were sitting next to earlier."

"What woman?"

"The one over there." I point to where she was sitting before.

"Shit, my bag," Five says. "I should go get it."

I stop her. "It's still there. Which doesn't say much for security, but I've been checking."

"Is she Jessica Two?"

"Hard to be sure. She's good at disguises." I take the pictures I have of Jessica Two out of my bag. I lay them on the table in front of Five. "Have you ever seen this woman?"

She picks each one up individually, then puts it back down. "This is the same person?"

"Yes."

"She's smart to cover her ears and forehead."

"That's what Liam said."

Jessie rolls her eyes. "How did you know that? About the ears?"

"I did portraits for a long time. You learn pretty quickly how to make someone look different, especially in photographs."

"So," I say, "that woman could be her."

"Yeah, I guess. So why did you call for me on the intercom?"

"I wanted to flush her out. If she was here, she would've reacted to me calling her name."

"Or, she saw what you were doing and beat it," Jessie says, staring down into her endless glass of Coke.

"I made a snap decision."

Jessie looks up. She's furious. "It was a stupid decision. And now we're left with nothing."

"We'll think of something."

"You should go to the police," Five says.

"No," Jessie says. "We've tried that. Useless. Besides, what's the crime right now? We're the ones who set up a fake event. We could be in trouble."

A voice speaks through the loudspeaker. The flight to New York will begin boarding in ten minutes.

Five stands. "This is where I leave you."

"You're still going?" I ask.

"Damn straight. Free weekend in New York. Why not?"

"Makes sense," I say. "Only . . ."

"What?"

"Be careful, okay?"

"Don't speak to any other Jessicas?"

"Definitely not."

She stands and picks up her cell phone. "Let me know how this all turns out. I'm curious."

"Sure, give me your number."

"What's yours?" she says. I give it to her and she texts me. This is Five.

I smile. "Sorry about all this."

"It's fine. Maybe you even saved me from a world of trouble."

"Maybe."

"What are you guys going to do now?"

Jessie hops off her chair. "First, we're going to have to explain this all to JJ."

"Worried?" Five asks.

"Nah, that's going to be *her* job." Jessie presses a finger into my chest too aggressively.

"It'll be fine."

Jessie doesn't answer me. Instead, she reaches her hand out to Five. "Nice to meet you."

"You too. I think." Five turns and walks toward where she left her bag.

When she's out of earshot, I say, "How did you get in here?"

"Forget about that. We are in so much shit."

"What do you mean?"

"She was here." Jessie pulls her phone from her pocket. There's a text on the screen.

Nice try, it says from a number I recognize.

Shit.

Chapter 26

Incomplete Pass

One of my biggest regrets in life is that when I took Kiki out of the Land of Todd, I didn't bring her right to Liam. I don't know why. Probably I wanted to prove something. That I could do it on my own. That I could succeed at life without Liam being there to steer me in the right direction. And because I'd never told Liam about her, I didn't want to have to explain why I'd kept her from him for so long. Besides, I knew Kiki. I knew her like I knew myself, and myself had made it out of the Land of Todd and through to something better. It was better, whatever Kiki thought. I'd show her.

I'd show her.

So I followed Liam's plan without involving Liam. I took Kiki to the same run-down hotel in the Catskills even though I was supposed to be starting my job at FeedNews. I told them there'd been a death in the family and that I needed a couple of weeks off to process it. That was close enough to true to pass, even though it felt gross using Todd's death for anything. He wasn't my family; he'd ruined my family. I guess that's a kind of death.

It was weird being back in that hotel. Not Land-of-Todd weird, but weird just the same. The place had continued to decay. The paint was chipping away. Leaves were left unraked. There was an abandoned look to the swimming pool. The random collection of guests made it feel as if we were on the set of a horror movie, or in a locked-room murder mystery. Was that man that little girl's father, or was this some stopping place along a kidnapping route? I was suspicious of everyone, jumpy. Scared.

Kiki didn't say much on the drive there. She was too used to following directions. When we got to our room, she walked to the bed closest to the door, kicked off her shoes, and lay down as if she were waiting to be examined. That scared me more than the silence, but after a night where we both slept more than twelve hours, I forged ahead. I started her on the deprogramming/relearning right away—showing her all the classic movies I could find on the movie channel the hotel got, only stopping for food and sleep. We ate on our respective beds, watching the screen, and I'd provide additional narration to explain what I knew she didn't understand, something Liam never did for me.

"So, like, in this scene we're learning that they have to come to school on a Saturday for detention. That's, like, extra punishment. Not Back Forest or anything, but—"

"I got it," Kiki said, pushing away her half-eaten pizza. "This is kind of gross."

"It is. That's the whole point."

"Why?"

We were wearing matching pajamas that I'd gotten at the nearest Walmart. "Because sometimes you need to eat something that's bad for you."

"But Todd says—"

"Yeah, I know, but he's wrong. I mean, not totally wrong about this one thing, because, ultimately, it is better to eat healthy most of the time, but you know, in the grander scheme of things . . ."

Kiki lowered her head onto her knees, stretching her back out. "I get it."

"How can you?"

"We had books."

"Crappy romance novels from the seventies."

She turned her face toward me. "No, after you left, someone started smuggling in better stuff."

"Covington? I mean, Terrence?"

His real name felt weird in my mouth. I thought about calling him, letting him know where we were. He'd let me take the car we'd rented to go to the funeral and told me he'd make his own way back, not to worry about it.

"Yeah," she said.

"How?"

She sat up and turned her head back to the screen. "He found this way out of the back of the property. There's a town over there. I never knew its name. But they had this used bookstore, and they'd sell books to him for a quarter. So, we'd all scrounge around to find whatever change we could and give it to him."

"He didn't tell me about that."

"Do you guys hang out a lot?"

I watched Kiki's bony shoulders rise and fall. She was so thin under her pajamas. She needed more pizza. "Not that much."

"Did he mention me?"

He never had, but she didn't need to hear that. Covington and I didn't talk about those sorts of things.

"A couple of times. Do you want . . . Would you like me to call him for you?"

"No, that's okay. Everything in its time."

Another Toddism, but I let it be. It felt so hopeful, you see. So normal. To be talking about a boy with Kiki like we should've been when we were growing up instead of learning how to prepare ourselves for the end of civilization.

I thought that we were making progress. I thought we were past the worst of it.

I was wrong.

"What the fuck was that back there?" I ask Jessie once we're in my rented Jeep, heading back to the campsite. I'm driving. JJ's next to me, and Jessie's in the back seat.

"I could ask you the same," Jessie says.

"Will someone tell me what the fuck is going on?" JJ says.

I turn onto the highway toward the campground. There's a steady flow of traffic ahead, though a continuous stream of cars is peeling off the road onto one of the turnouts where you can get great shots of the Tetons.

"She didn't show," I say to JJ.

"That's not true," Jessie says. "She was there. But Jess screwed everything up."

"I did not."

"You didn't stick to the plan."

"Neither did you."

"Pull the fucking car over," JJ commands.

She means business, and I do what she asks at the next pullout. We're not alone, but the occupants of the other cars are too busy with their camera phones to take any notice of us.

JJ climbs out of the Jeep. We follow suit. She stands in front of us.

"Okay, spill."

She's looking at me, so I start. "I was in position, like we agreed. Five came in and sat down. There was a woman talking to her. I thought it might be Jessica Two."

"Why?"

"Right age, right build. But I wasn't sure. There wasn't any way for me to get close to them without potential Jessica Two spotting me. So, I decided to try and flush her out. Use a page from her own book."

"That wasn't the plan," Jessie says.

"What did you do?" JJ asks.

"I got them to page Jessica Williams."

"And you figured, what?" Jessie says. "That she'd be stupid enough to fall for that? She's not an idiot."

"I know that. But I had to think fast. I thought that she'd at least react if that name was called, and then I'd know it was her for sure."

"But she didn't, did she? And then you blew your cover by going up to the counter with Five."

"That's right. And then you showed up."

Jessie looks across the road. There's a bison ambling slowly along the fence line. A car stops suddenly with a screech of tires, and the car behind it almost hits it.

"Bison jam," I say.

"What?"

"Never mind. What were you doing in the airport?" I ask Jessie.

"I went in to use the bathroom."

I look at JJ. She nods.

"When I was in there, I got your text saying you thought she might be there."

"And?"

"Then I heard our name being called on the PA. I assumed it was Jessica Two who did it, so I bought a ticket to Salt Lake City so I could get through security."

"Just like that?"

She grits her teeth. "I thought you might need help."

"Well, I didn't."

"So, now what?" JJ says.

"She's here," Jessie says. "Jessica Two is here."

"How do you know that?"

"Show her the text," I say to Jessie.

Jessie takes out her phone and gives it to JJ.

"Why didn't you tell me this back at the airport?"

"It wouldn't have mattered."

"Of course it might've mattered. She was there. She was right there."

"She wouldn't have sent that text if she was findable," Jessie says. "She probably sent it from the plane."

"What plane?"

"The flight that Five's on," Jessie says. "I bet she's on it."

"Fuck," JJ says. "We have to warn her."

"We told Five about Jessica Two," I say. "She knows to be on the lookout."

"That's not sufficient," JJ says. "Goddammit, we are so fucking dumb. We teed her up for Jessica, and now we're here and they're going to be in New York for the weekend together."

"It's not like she's actually rich, though."

"She's not a pauper. Jessica will take her for whatever she can. Just to punish us. Just to show us she can."

"What can we do about it?"

"You could ask Liam for help," JJ says. "That's his name, right?"

"That's his name," Jessie says.

"What's that supposed to mean?"

She doesn't say anything, just watches the line of cars that has piled up to get a photo of the bison, who's chewing, unconcerned, on the side of the road.

"Jessie?"

"Just call him."

"And say what?"

She turns toward me. "Why are you asking me? He's *your* boyfriend."

Chapter 27

Aha

The lawsuit was the beginning of the end. Or the beginning of the beginning. I might write other people's stories for a living, but I have trouble with figuring out where to start, and where to end too. But I've had a lot of time to think about this one, and that lawsuit was definitely the start of something.

And the end of Kiki.

I don't blame the people who suggested bringing it, or those in the Not in Todd Anymore Facebook group who jumped on it. When we learned how much money Todd had accumulated, it was the natural thing to do. That was our families' money. My parents' and Kiki's parents' and Covington's. All of us, those who escaped, and the ones who never wanted to leave but were forced to when Todd died, and everything fell apart. We didn't have the lives we were supposed to, the version we would've had if Todd had never existed. And though money doesn't solve anything, it can feel like it does. If you don't have to worry about where your next meal is coming from, or how you're going to pay for school, that's one less thing to weigh you down.

So, I was all for it. We all were.

Todd's family caved pretty quickly. His real relatives he'd disowned in life but who were the ones who got it all after his death. The many millions of ill-gotten gain, mostly invested in the market in blue-chip stocks. All the companies that Todd had railed against, that he'd told us we'd be taking down *when the day came*, they were the backbone of Todd's wealth. I think that was the actual final nail in the coffin for the LOT; the rank hypocrisy finally penetrating through to even the diehards.

Nothing went to the adults who'd chosen to live with Todd. Everything went to the kids in equal portions, right down to the smallest one, the girl who was with my parents at the funeral. There was one helluva party, but then we pulled apart. We'd won, achieved our purpose, and now we could move on. Only, someone should've done some research. Looked at the data on lottery winners, for instance, who often end up bankrupt, addicted, or right back where they started only a few years later. We were no different from the statistics. Some of us were prudent. I paid off my student loans and socked the rest of it away for a rainy day. Others bought a boat and sailed around the world, skipping from beach town to beach town as their livers slowly disintegrated under the constant pressure of cheap liquor and sugary mixers. Et cetera.

And Kiki. Kiki used her money to educate herself. Her plan was to become a teacher. But that's not how it turned out. And when it all fell apart, she didn't have the tools to cope. My John Hughes–inspired education wasn't a substitute for the real help I should've found her. The therapy Liam helped others get, which I'd always turned down because I thought I didn't need it.

She sank.

And sank.

And it wasn't until she turned up dead that I even knew she was drowning.

I tell Jessie and JJ that I'll call Liam once we're back at camp. I don't want to talk to him while they're watching me. Things are shifting between Liam and me, but whatever there is, it's still private.

When we get to our tents, I park the car and we get out.

"What should we do now?" Jessie asks. It's midafternoon, and hot. The air is full of buzzing insects. "While you talk to lover boy?"

"We need a new plan," JJ says.

"No shit," says Jessie.

"Guys, Jesus. This is exactly what she wants," I say. "To divide us."

"Looks like it's working."

"Enough!" JJ says. "This is not helping."

I take a deep breath. "You're right. This isn't the way."

"What is, then?" Jessie asks.

"We need to work together."

"That hasn't gotten us anywhere to date."

"Come on, Jessie," I say, reaching out my hand. "Truce?"

She hesitates, then reaches out. Her hand is cold, like it's been dipped in ice. "Truce."

Because we're playing nice now as we try to think up our next move, Jessie agrees to go for a paddle. JJ needs time to think, she says, and we can bring some food and regroup on the other side of the lake.

"You guys get changed," I say after we've settled this. "And I'll call Liam."

They agree, and I take my phone out and start walking to where I can get a clear signal. The Tetons are beautiful, but they aren't great for cell service. Liam picks up before the first ring is through.

"Hey, there," he says.

I can't help but smile. "Hey."

"How did it go today?"

"Not great."

"She didn't show?" he says with resignation.

"No, she did. Listen." I sit down on a pine bench on the side of the road and fill him in. "So, can you do it?"

"Watch out for another Jessica Williams? Of course."

"Don't watch her too closely."

"Is that jealousy I hear?"

"Maybe."

Liam goes silent.

"What?"

"That was weird that Jessie came into the airport."

"Yeah. Wait, do you know something?"

"Sometimes the absence of something is something."

Classic Liamism.

"What did you not find?" I ask.

"I can't find any record of her going back more than four years."

"Why didn't you tell me this before?"

"Mario just got in touch. He's the guy who helped me find Jackson Jessica."

"We call her Five."

"I'm sure she loves that."

"Yeah, yeah. So why was he looking into Jessie?"

"I told him to look into both of them."

"Jessie and JJ?"

"Yes."

"Why?"

"Because I worry about you. You're putting yourself in vulnerable positions with people you don't even know."

"Please don't raise your voice at me."

"I'm sorry."

My brain is whirring. "So, he found something?"

"Like I said, he didn't find anything. No record of her until four years ago. That's when she started working at that high school in Illinois."

"There could be lots of explanations for that."

"Not that many."

"There weren't any records of me until I left the Land of Todd."

"Was she in the Land of Todd?"

"No."

"So . . ."

"Okay. It's weird."

"You should go to the police."

"So you're always saying."

"And you never listen."

"Go to the police with what? We don't know anything."

"Come home, then," Liam says.

A mosquito bites me. I crush it against my arm, my own blood oozing onto my hand.

"I will. Tomorrow."

"And until then?"

"I'll be careful." JJ appears across the road. She's waving at me. "I've got to go."

"Call me later?"

"Of course."

I hang up the call and stand. I wipe my sticky hand on my pants as I cross the road.

"What's up?" I ask.

"We're ready to go."

"I need a few minutes. Why don't you take your boards down to the lake and I'll catch up."

"You okay?"

"Just trying to figure this all out."

JJ gives me a look, then decides to let it go.

When we get back to the tent, Jessie's dressed in a pair of dark-blue shorts, a white T-shirt, and flip-flops.

"I have to get changed. I'll meet you on the beach."

I watch them pick up their boards and paddles and start down the path. Then I go into Jessie's tent and zip the door behind me. Her suitcase is closed. I pull it toward me. I spread out her sleeping bag and dump out its contents. Clean clothes. The jeans and underclothes she was wearing earlier today. I check the pockets. There's a folded piece of stiff paper in one of them. I pull it out. It's the boarding pass for the ticket she bought to get through security.

It's not in the name of Jessica Williams. Instead, it says Molly Carter.

PART III

Chapter 28

The Final Countdown

One of my clearest memories of Kiki post-LOT was the first and only New Year's Eve we went out and celebrated together.

It was at a huge loft party in the Meatpacking District, not that far from Liam's apartment, though he didn't attend. It was one of those parties with hundreds of guests and cheap alcohol and people dressed up even though it wasn't a dressy party. It cost fifty dollars a head, and they gave you a gift bag at the door with a bowler hat or a sparkly headband, and a necklace made out of letters that created the phrase NEW YEAR'S EVE over and over. There were noisemakers, too, those plastic horns that make obnoxious sounds that only children enjoy, or adults at a year-end party. And there were drinks included: a glass of "champagne" at midnight, and a strong punch for the rest of the evening.

Kiki didn't want to go when I first brought it up, but I persuaded her. That felt like a metaphor for what our relationship had become since Todd died. Me persuading Kiki eventually. It was as if she'd used up whatever will she had by agreeing to leave the LOT in the first place. Anything else simply took too much effort. So, I had to persuade her, cajole her, threaten her, even, sometimes.

"You should learn how to live on your own," I said to her six months after I'd brought her back from the Catskills. After years of having to share a room with another student at college, and now Kiki, I was ready for a room of my own, even if it was a tiny closet. But I didn't tell Kiki that. No. I made it about her, her development, her progress.

She needed to go to real school, like I had, and live in a dorm and meet people. She needed to get her life into gear and do all the things I'd done, but without the year at Liam's. I had Kiki on a faster timeline, and I'd been keeping Liam at a distance. I still hadn't told him about Kiki. He had a few new escapees he was working with, not to mention his usual private detective business. It was a good thing, I thought then. I was growing up along with Kiki, leaving the nest, spreading my wings.

We were about to get the money from the settlement, and it eased our path and our plans. Slowly, slowly, Kiki came out of her shell. After I signed her up and helped her prep for the tests, she got her GED on the first try; she was always the smartest of all of us. She started looking into college programs, and eventually decided she wanted to teach kids—kindergarten, specifically. And though I thought she made that choice partly out of fear, I understood it. Five-year-olds could be monsters, but not the kind of monsters we'd grown up with. I helped her write her college essay, and she got into Columbia and NYU.

She chose NYU and enrolled in their early-childhood-education program. By the time New Year's had rolled around, she'd completed her first semester and had even made a few friends among the girls she dormed with. To be honest, they were mostly washed-out girls who'd lived on the fringes of their high schools, but they were kind enough. Safe. Safe. Kiki always wanted to be safe.

Who could blame her?

Not me. But I could cajole her. Get her out of her comfort zone.

Which is why I pushed so hard about the party.

I didn't even know the people throwing it, but a few people from FeedNews were going to be there, and I thought the anonymity of the crowd would be a good thing. Better than standing in the cold among the drunks in Times Square, or curling up in bed with a book, which is what Kiki wanted to do. A party full of possibilities seemed like the right thing for both of us.

I picked Kiki up in an almost-impossible-to-find cab in front of her building. When we got to the party, we climbed the metal stairs to the top floor, the bass notes of a club song pushing the party out into the street. They had a coat check, and with trepidation, I handed over my black coat that looked like hundreds of others. I shook out my hair and turned to Kiki. She looked especially beautiful that night, her hair golden and straight, wearing an empire-waisted dress that sparkled with sequins.

"Where did you find that?" I asked as she fished a party hat out of her favor bag and stuck it on her head.

"At a thrift shop near my apartment."

I touched the fabric. It was a soft velvet. "It looks fantastic."

She blushed. "Thanks."

I slipped the New Year's necklace around my neck and the headband on my head. I knew I looked kind of ridiculous, but I didn't care.

We entered the party. It was after nine and there were already hundreds of people there. An informal dance floor was going on in the middle of the room where a crowd of girls were *werk, werk, werk*-ing it.

I leaned close to Kiki so she could hear me. "Should I get us a drink?"

"Sure."

I went to the open kitchen—long concrete countertops and glossy black cabinets—to get us some of the high-octane punch we'd been promised. I ran into some of the FeedNews crew there and lost track of time. When I went looking for Kiki half an hour later, I couldn't find her.

I wove through the crowd like a panicked mother looking for a wayward child in the mall until I found her. She was sitting on the interior balcony that overlooked the loft, her feet through the railings, dangling over us. I climbed up the metal, fire-escape-like stairs, and sat down next to her, handing her the drink I was still clutching. It was less loud up there, and the DJ had decided to mellow out the tunes for a bit, maybe encourage some romance. Everyone had to have someone to kiss at midnight, after all. Maybe I'd end up kissing Kiki.

"I thought I'd lost you," I said.

"I didn't go anywhere." She took a hesitant sip of her drink, then made a face. "What's in this?"

"Swamp juice."

"What's that?"

"One of everything in the bar."

"Ugh." She put the glass down next to her. She looked down at the crowd. "There's a lot of people here."

"It's a party."

"You know all these people?"

"Only a couple."

"Why did you want to come, then?"

"I like big parties."

Her shoulders rose and fell. "I don't."

I reached around her to pick up her glass. I drained it. "I've screwed all this up, haven't I?"

"What up?"

"You? This. Reintroducing you to society. I'm failing."

"I'm not a class."

"I didn't mean it like that."

"Didn't you?"

"No, of course not. Fucking Todd."

I felt her tense next to me. How long would it take until she didn't react when I spoke badly of Todd? I'd never been so glad he was dead.

"I'm going to write about him," I said.

"You are?"

"I had the idea a couple of weeks ago. I pitched it to my editor and he loved it. It's going to be my first big piece."

"Do you think that's a good idea?"

"Why not?"

Kiki played with the ends of her hair. "Something about it feels dangerous. And wouldn't you have to disclose your connection? Do you think you could even be objective?"

My cheeks flamed. "The piece isn't going to be about me."

"But, oh—"

"What?"

She turned away from me. "Nothing, it's, um . . . Covington is here."

I looked down at the crowd. There he was, all tall and gangly, with a knit cap resting far back on his head. He was searching the room, looking for someone.

"Did you invite him?"

She nodded. They'd been in touch, obviously, but for how long? Why hadn't she ever mentioned it? Why hadn't he? Were they dating?

I stopped my spinning brain. I didn't care if Kiki dated Covington. He was a good guy, but I had zero romantic interest in him. It was the lack of input that was bugging me. I could hear Liam's admonishment: *You can't control for all outcomes.*

Oh, but I wanted to.

I forced a smile onto my face. "That's great, Kiki. Good for you."

She looked away. "It's stupid."

"Why?"

"Because I'm doing that exchange thing next year. It can't go anywhere."

What the hell? "What exchange thing?"

"I told you. I'm doing a year at Ohio State."

I felt queasy, though I hadn't yet had that much to drink. I had zero memory of Kiki telling me about it. But that didn't surprise me, in some way. We'd learned in the LOT that it was easier to blame the other person for something than tell them the truth. *You just weren't listening to me* was a frequent ploy used in the Upper Camp to get away with minor infractions, right along with *But you said yes when I asked you.* Lying was so ingrained as forbidden, and the punishment for being caught so severe, that the adults mostly chose to believe that they'd forgotten over the possibility that we'd disobey them deliberately.

Or Kiki actually had told me, and I'd been so wrapped up in my own shit that I hadn't listened. That was a possibility too.

"You're leaving for real?" I said.

"Just for a bit. And not until the fall."

I pulled her to me. She still smelled like our childhood, as if she were carrying the Land of Todd around with her wherever she went. And maybe she was. "I'll miss you."

"I'll miss you too."

"What am I going to do without you? I just got you back."

"I won't be far. And I'll be back."

"You better," I said, then pulled away. "Now go find Covington."

After I've finished looking around and collected everything there is to find in Jessie's tent, including a cell phone I've never seen, I leave the tent, dip into mine, and quickly fill my backpack with some necessities. Then I climb out and hoist the bag onto my back. I pick up the third paddleboard, loop the life vest around my neck, and tuck the paddle under my arm. The board is heavy, and I hate carrying things long distances, but it's only about a quarter of a mile to the beach. The path is an old ski trail, not properly tended, and there are downed trees across it every hundred feet or so. I walk into the woods to go around them, breathing in through my nose as the weight starts to pull at me. The last part of the path is a hill. I drop the board and hurry up it, leaving my pack and paddle at the top, then return down to retrieve the board.

I continue past my stuff and reach the beach just as JJ and Jessie are ready to push off. I was worried about being too far behind them, but the adrenaline coursing through me made swift work of the path.

"I need to go back for my paddle and pack," I say, motioning to the trees behind us.

"Should we wait?" Jessie asks.

"Start. I'll catch up."

JJ gives me a look. "You okay?"

My face feels red, like I've been drinking or caught a bad sunburn. "Yeah, of course. I just hate carrying stuff. Plus, it's hot."

"It'll be cooler out on the lake."

"Get going, then."

I watch them for a minute as they leave. JJ explains how to paddle to Jessie, and they soon have a good rhythm going. The lake is glass, like it gets most afternoons. There's no one on the beach, and though I can hear the faraway buzz of a motorboat, I can't see it. The scene looks like one of the postcards you can buy in the gift shop.

I hustle back to the trees to recover my pack and paddle, then rush down to the water once more. Beads of sweat are running down my back, and my hands are slick as I put the board in the water. I drop it, splashing myself, then almost lose my balance as I scramble onto it. When I'm finally situated, kneeling in the center of the board, I push off, using the paddle to get past the rocks before I stand up.

JJ and Jessie are not that far ahead of me, and once I stand, it only takes a few minutes of hard paddling to reach them, my shoulder initially protesting, then warming up and settling in. I slide in between JJ and Jessie.

Or should I call her Molly?

She doesn't look like a Molly. As I watch her paddle, I wonder how often she goes by that name. Are names part of the game for her? And what does she call *this* game? This finding and frauding of Jessicas? What made her like this? Did she belong to a family of grifters? Was she simply the bad seed in an ordinary house? Did something happen to her when she was a child? I'm old enough to admit that I'm the way I am because of Todd. And what has she been doing with us all this time? I have my theories, but that's all they are.

"We're going all the way across, yes?" JJ says.

"Huh?"

"The lake? We're going to the other side, right?"

I turn toward her. She's got a compact motion with her paddle. It breaks the surface without a splash and leaves little eddies in its wake.

"I'd like to," I say. "You up for it?"

She nods, her eyes hidden by her sunglasses. "Sure, if you think it's safe."

"What's that supposed to mean?" Jessie asks, sounding nervous.

JJ raises her eyebrows, mocking her. "Lions and tigers and bears, oh my!"

"Surely not."

"Bears, probably."

"Maybe we should go back?"

"What are you, chicken?" I flash Jessie a smile that's a challenge. "First person to the other side gets a prize!" I shout for good measure.

"What's the prize?" JJ asks.

"You'll have to paddle to the other side to find out."

"Fair's fair, though. Let's line up."

I miss a stroke and wait for us to re-form our line. Three Jessicas in a row. *Ashes, Ashes, we all fall down.*

JJ leans forward, ready to take me on.

I look at Jessie. "You in?"

She squares her shoulders. "Bring it."

"Three, two, one . . . go!"

Chapter 29

End of the Line

It's hard to tell how long it takes us to get to the other side of the lake. All I know is that my lungs are screaming, and the buildup of lactic acid in my arms almost makes me stop, but I don't. I think about everything that Jessie has done, and this propels me. I can look past the pain and focus on the shore as it gets closer, closer, closer, we're here.

My arms feel like lead, and I'm worried about the paddle back, but it's too late for that now. I paddle right to the shore, the bottom of the board scraping against the rocks. I walk off the end, teetering slightly, and pull it up so it won't float away. Then I fall to the rocky beach. I lie there on my back for a minute, trying to catch my breath. JJ got here first, winning the race, and Jessie's somewhere behind us.

I prop myself up and sit on my bum. I look up at the blue sky. It feels so impossibly far away even though we're actually closer to it than back in New York. I check the lake as I take off my pack. Jessie's a couple hundred feet away. My pack clangs and sloshes as I put it down.

"What you got in there?" JJ asks.

"Your prize."

She pulls a piece of driftwood toward me and sits down on it, grinning. I haul myself up beside her, my feet curling into a cramp. I kick off the cheap water shoes I bought a week ago at the convenience store near the park entrance and flex my toes against the rocks. I look around to distract myself. The forest is thick on this side, though there's evidence of people. A fire ring. A picnic table. A few discarded cigarette butts.

"You bring anything to drink?" JJ asks.

"You bet."

I reach into my pack and take out a canteen. I take a long drink of water; it's still cool, well insulated from the sun. I pass it to JJ.

Jessie's board scrapes against the rocks, announcing her arrival.

"You made it," JJ says.

"Barely." She stumbles off the board like I did a few minutes earlier. She's very red in the face, both from sunburn and from the exertion. "Dead last," she says.

"You'll still get a reward," I say.

"Lucky me."

"There's water." I motion to the canteen in JJ's hand. "And also . . ." I reach into the backpack and pull out the cans of beer I stashed in there. "How about a real beverage?"

JJ puts the canteen down on the gravel at her feet. "Now you're talking."

I pull a beer off the tab and toss it to her. She cracks it open and drains it like we're at a kegger. She crushes it under her arm and wipes her hand across her mouth. "That hit the spot."

"You want one, Jessie?"

"Sure."

She takes a seat next to me gingerly and I hand her the beer. I put the six-pack back in my bag.

"You're not having one?" she asks.

"In a minute."

Jessie nods as she opens her beer. I look out at the lake again. There's no one in sight. The only thing I can hear is the soft lap of the water against the shore and the buzz of insects in the trees.

JJ stands. "I'll be right back."

"Where are you going?"

"I've got a date with a tree."

Jessie takes a sip of her beer. "Don't let a bear get you."

"I can defend myself."

JJ walks into the woods.

"What else you got in there?" Jessie asks, nudging the pack with her foot. She's wearing an old pair of Adidas, gray with grime.

My heart thuds. "What?"

"In your pack. You wouldn't happen to have any snacks in there, would you?"

"Oh yes. Of course." I put it between my legs and root around inside. I pull out a package of beef jerky and another of trail mix. "Which do you want?"

"I'll take the jerky. And water, if you've got it."

I toss the jerky to her. She catches it easily.

"The water's in the canteen."

"Can you hand it to me?"

"Oh, sure." I keep one hand on my pack while I reach for the canteen. I take a sip of water to quell my dry mouth, then hand it to her.

I can feel her eyes on me. Am I behaving strangely? I can't tell. Is Jessie looking at me oddly? Maybe, maybe she is.

"Well, this is a party," JJ says, reappearing with her arms full of wood. She dumps it into the firepit, bends down, and makes short work of starting it with a lighter that she pulls from her pocket.

"What's the fire for?" Jessie asks.

She shrugs. "Felt like making it. Who knows how long we'll be here?"

"It doesn't get dark till late, though." Jessie looks at her watch. "It's only four. We have plenty of time to rest, then get back."

"Who doesn't like a campfire?" JJ says by way of explanation, then walks over and sits next to me. She reaches into the pack and emerges with a beer. The pop of the tab opening sounds loud. Everything seems loud.

I think I'm losing my mind.

"What's wrong with you two?" JJ asks.

Jessie rips open the beef jerky package with her teeth. "Nothing."

"Yeah, nothing," I say.

"Bullshit. You guys have a fight when I was gone?"

"Nope," Jessie says, putting some beef jerky in her mouth. "But Jess doesn't feel like talking."

"It's nothing," I say. "I'm tired."

I take one of the beers and open it. It's lukewarm, but I need something to calm my nerves.

"So, that was a shitshow today," JJ says, crushing up her beer can and tucking it into the pack. "Ooh, trail mix." She pulls it out.

"You don't say," I answer, trying to keep my tone even.

"We should go home," Jessie says.

"You sound like Liam," I say, and Jessie makes a face.

"And what, give up?" JJ says.

"I guess."

I take a long drink of the bitter beer and listen to the fire pop. Going home would be the easy thing to do. It would be the sensible thing to do. But it's not what I'm going to do. Because I came here to catch a Jessica, and here she is, sitting next to me, like she's been all along.

"No," I say.

"What's that?" Jessie says.

"I said no."

"Why not?"

"You know why."

I haven't been looking at her directly. But now I do. I gather my courage and remember everything she's done to me, and JJ, and the others. And then I imagine that she's Todd, and I look her right in the eye like I wanted to look at him all those years. Like I did when I was twelve and we got sent to the Back Forest.

"What's that?" she says again.

"I said, you know why." I pause. "Molly."

The beer can slips from her hand and splashes against the rocks.

"What did you just say?"

"I called you Molly."

Jessie scrambles to her feet. JJ and I are not far behind.

"Catch me up," JJ says.

"I went through her stuff while you guys were going to the beach."

"You what?" Jessie says, her voice shaking.

"Shut it," JJ says.

"I found her other ID." I bend at the knees so I can keep my eyes on Jessie. I put my hand in my pack and pull out Jessie's wallet. Her eyes narrow. "Here." I stand and toss it to JJ. "Check the inner compartment."

JJ opens the wallet and finds a second driver's license with Jessie's photo on it.

"There's a boarding pass in there too," I say. "The one she used to get into the airport today. She also had a bunch of other IDs in a pouch, bank cards, a few passports. Who knows which are real and which are fake."

I'm explaining to JJ, but my eyes haven't left Jessie. She hasn't reacted beyond the first blip. She's standing there, a stone. Only her eyes are moving slightly, as if she's calculating the distance to the door. But there isn't any door. There's nowhere to go but the lake.

"I can explain," Jessie says finally, her voice a squeak.

"I'm listening," JJ says, but she takes a step toward Jessie. JJ's body is tense, like it was last night at the washstand. As if violence isn't far behind.

"It's not what it looks like."

"Of course it is," I say as JJ takes another step.

"It's not. I swear. Jess, come on. We've been together off and on all summer. I'm not . . . I'm not her."

"You are."

"No. I only have those IDs *because* of her. I needed to be someone else for a while. Someone she didn't have a hold over, a connection to. You understand, don't you, JJ? After everything she did to you, wouldn't it be nice to be anonymous?"

"That's a good story," I say. "Tell me, have you had that ready for a while, or did you make it up on the spot?"

"It's not a story."

"It is, though. And I can prove it." I reach into my pocket and take out my cell. I scroll through my texts until I find it. The thread with Jessica Two. The threats she's sent me, including the one from today.

I type something and hit "Send."

Then I take out the other cell phone that I found in Jessie's tent and hold it in my left hand. An unmistakable sound goes off as it receives my text.

Ping!

She got the message.

Chapter 30

Ollie, Ollie, Oxen Free

Seconds later, JJ and I are chasing Jessie through the woods. I stopped long enough to shove my feet back into my water shoes, but part of me regrets it as the wet fabric rubs against my skin.

Jessie's faster than I expected, weaving in and out of the trees, not looking back. But then I think back to that first time I saw her, at the end of her run back in Wilmington. Who knows how long she'd been out there that day, or how fast she could go?

I drop my head to avoid the branch of a conifer but not fast enough. I feel the skin on my cheek slice open, but I can't stop to tend it. It's easy to see Jessie; she's still wearing her bright-yellow life jacket, jumping over logs like a deer. JJ's to the right of me, just ahead, also faster than I am, her arms pumping. I'm having trouble catching my breath, and my legs feel like they're moving through molasses.

I stop and cup my hands around my mouth. "Jessie! There's no use running! Stop!"

She keeps going, so I start to run again. JJ's gaining on her but still hasn't caught her.

Wham!

I slam into the forest floor so fast I don't even have time to get my hands out in front of me. My chin hits first, clicking my teeth into my tongue. My mouth fills with the metallic taste of blood as I lie facedown, stunned, unsure of how badly I've hurt myself. I can feel my heart thudding, the blood rushing to the various scrapes and bruises that I've collected today. I hear a shout up ahead, indistinct. Was that JJ?

I pull my arms out from under me; nothing's broken. I place my hands on the ground and start to push myself up gently. Everything hurts, but it all seems to be working.

"No!"

The voice seems closer now, and scared. A new jolt of adrenaline brings me to my feet. I grab a rock off the ground, then spin around in a circle, looking, looking. Dammit, where are they?

"Stop!"

There! A flash of yellow. I start to run, my left leg dragging with a sprain that might be more serious than I can absorb right now. I break through the trees and there they are, in a small clearing. Jessie's on her back on the ground, her hands up, trying to protect her face. JJ's standing over her with a heavy piece of wood in her hand, ready to go in for the kill.

"Stop!" I scream as JJ pulls her arm back.

"You stupid bitch," JJ says to her.

"JJ, no," I say. "Not like . . . Stop! Back away."

"Please, JJ, please." Jessie's crying, but it sounds fake to me.

I walk toward them gingerly. Jessie has a gash across her forehead. Her arms and legs are scratched up like mine. Only JJ seems unfazed and uninjured.

"Please, Jess, don't let her—"

"Shut up, Jessie!" I say. "You're not helping."

I put my hand on JJ's shoulder. She rounds on me quickly, and I duck out of the way of the log.

"Hey! Watch it."

"Sorry, man, I—"

Jessie uses the moment of inattention to jump to her feet. "She almost killed me," she says to me.

"Drop the act, Molly."

Her face relaxes and it's easier to see her now: Jessica Two. Like a painting that was there all the time, only a bit of linseed oil needed to reveal the image underneath the mask.

"Fine," she says. "Whatever you like."

"There's nothing about this I like."

"Bullshit."

"Stay there." I point to her. "What do you want to do?" I ask JJ.

She thinks about it. "Nice secluded spot. No one will find the body before the bears get to her."

I watch Jessie as JJ speaks. She's calculating the odds that JJ's actually going to hurt her. Maybe she's remembering back to last night at the washstand. We both saw the look in JJ's eyes. The casualness. She's killed someone before, maybe at close hand.

"We've left our DNA all over, though," I say, as I wipe my hand across my cheek. It comes away full of blood. "Plus, the mess we've made of the forest."

"You think they're going to get all CSI out here if this piece of shit goes missing?"

"Not sure. It's possible, though, isn't it?"

"They'll definitely do it," Jessie says.

"Shut up!" JJ and I say together.

I get closer to JJ without taking my eyes off Jessie. She smells earthy, sweat and dirt mixed with a tinge of blood.

"Let's get the money first."

"First? What's—"

JJ turns and thrusts her hand out in a chopping motion against Jessie's throat. Jessie falls to the ground, gasping, clutching her neck.

"Shit, JJ. How's she going to talk now?"

"Don't worry, I didn't do anything permanent. That'll keep her quiet for a minute. I couldn't stand her talking anymore."

I watch Jessie rolling around on the ground, clutching her throat. I have to admit, it feels good to see her suffer.

"You think we can get her to talk?" JJ says. "Tell us where the money is?"

"I think so."

I walk to Jessie. I crouch down so I'm closer to her. She's stopped struggling, but she's still rubbing at her throat like she swallowed a pill down the wrong tube. The gash on her forehead is oozing and looks like the kind of thing that could get easily infected.

"Where is it?"

She coughs. Tries to speak. Coughs again. "Where's what?" she finally gets out in a scratchy voice.

"The money, moron. Our money."

"I've spent it."

"Come on. All of it?"

"Most, anyway."

"I don't believe you."

"Well, I have."

"Living in the middle of nowhere, working in an elementary school? Nope, I'm not buying it. You, JJ?"

"Not a fucking chance."

I shove the rock I'm still holding into the large pocket of my board shorts and reach out my hand. "Give me your phone."

"Why?"

"Just do it."

She takes it out of her pocket and gives it to me. It's encased in one of those waterproof housing units, which is why I assume she was willing to bring it out on the water. While the cell reception on the other side of the lake is spotty, here her phone has four bars of service, something I'd noticed when JJ and I came over here two days ago. I hit the home button, and the lock screen appears.

"What's the password?"

"123456."

JJ's next to her in an instant. "You think this is funny?" She grabs one of Jessie's arms and twists it behind her back. "Some kind of joke?"

"Ow, no, no."

"Then what's the fucking password?"

"071090."

I shake my head as I enter my birthday. "You have no fucking respect, do you?"

The screen clears. I flip through several screens till I come to a folder called "Bank." I open it. There are several banking apps inside.

"Which bank?"

"Guess," she says.

JJ pulls her arm tighter. "Don't think I won't break it."

"Okay, okay, it's the Wells Fargo one."

I open the app and enter in the same passcode. Nothing happens.

"It's not working. Is there a different password?"

"No."

JJ tugs again.

"I swear, it's the same password."

I try it again and get the same error message.

"Hand me the phone," JJ says.

I put it in her outstretched hand. She untwists Jessie's arm and puts the phone in Jessie's hand, then moves her thumb over the home button.

"Two-factor ID," she explains, then hands it back to me.

The app is open. I check her account. She's got less than $5,000 in it.

"Is this all of it?"

"Yes, I swear."

"What about these other bank apps?"

"I just use those to . . . you know . . ."

"Take other people's money?"

"Yeah."

"That's what you were trying to do today in the airport with Five, right? Trying to get her to play the game, right in front of me. How fucking stupid do you think I am?"

"I wasn't, I swear, I—"

"Enough! God, you're such a liar."

JJ looks at me. "What are you thinking?"

"She wired the money from my account to some account offshore. But these are domestic banks. I bet she did the same with your money. And the others."

"Right." JJ turns back to Jessie. "Where's the fucking money? And don't even try to tell me that you've spent it. You only took Jess's money a couple of months ago, right, Jess?"

"That's right. Two hundred and fifty thousand dollars."

"So, there's no way that's gone."

Jessie tries a different angle. "It's not that simple. I can't transfer it by phone. I have to make some calls and answer security questions and—"

"Then you're going to tell us how to get it."

"And if I do? What happens to me?"

"We're not killers," I say.

She looks at me. "*You* might not be. I'm not so sure about her."

JJ tilts her head as if she's proud. "If we say we'll let you go, we'll let you go."

"What assurance do I have?"

"You're going to have to trust us," I say. "You have no other choice."

"At least let go of my arm. It hurts."

JJ looks to me for my opinion.

"Do it," I say.

She lets go. Jessie moves a foot away and pulls her arm to her chest, rubbing it.

"Tell us how to get the money," I say.

"Not here, okay? When we get back to camp. We can go to the lodge where there's good Wi-Fi, and I'll walk you through the whole process."

"No, tell us now."

"Or what?"

JJ gives her a hard stare.

"More arm twisting, for starters, I'd imagine," I say. "Unless you start answering some questions."

"Like what?"

"Like what are you even doing here? Why didn't you just tell me to go stuff it when I found you with Liam? Or throw me into the Ausable River?"

"I tried."

"You what?"

"I did try to push you into the river. Then those people came along."

"She's shitting you," JJ says.

"You think?"

"Course. Why would she admit that if she's trying to live?"

"Good point." I crouch down in front of Jessie. "So, what are you doing here?"

"Who cares?" JJ says.

"I want to know. Why did you do it? Why play along?"

I hold Jessie's gaze. She gives a shrug. "Couldn't pass it up."

"What's that?"

She smiles in a way that reminds me of Todd. "The fun. Watching you flail around. Trying these desperate plans. It's been . . . fun."

Her words have a ring of truth to them. And so there you have it. We've been amusing her. We've been sport.

"Tell me something," Jessie says.

"What?"

"What made you go looking? Why did you go through my bag?"

"Liam was suspicious."

She makes a face. The face she always makes when Liam comes up.

"Liam."

"Yeah, Liam. What about it? Why are you always so down on him? He frightens you, right? You knew he didn't trust you."

Jessie shakes her head. "He doesn't love you, you know. You're just . . . a distraction."

"You don't know what you're fucking talking about."

"Of course I do. Don't you get it? I've studied you for a long time. And you, too, JJ. That's what I do. You're not the first of his little foundlings that he's been with, did you know that? I bet you didn't, I bet you—"

"How many times do I have to tell you to shut up!"

She stops talking. Maybe she knows she's pushed me too far.

"Now, for the last time, tell us how to get the money back."

"We mean it, Jessie," JJ says. "Last chance to cooperate."

She stands there, her eyes roving between us, weighing her options, and I can see her choosing the wrong thing as she does it.

She runs.

Chapter 31

Fugue State

"Everyone dies," Todd always used to say, "except me."

It was how he started off his weekly meetings, those interminable Sundays where we had to make extra sure we were sitting the way he wanted and that we kept the younger children away. Once, a boy of about three fell off his chair, and we got half rations for a week. We made sure to pay attention as best we could even though none of it made any sense. Was Todd saying he was immortal? A god? Or was he being more figurative, that he'd be someone remembered by history long after he was gone, but we'd be the dust under his feet that no one remembered? I didn't spend too much time thinking about it; it made about as much sense as anything Todd ever said. Besides, why couldn't it be true? He'd convinced all these seemingly rational people to leave their lives and sign over their money and their children to his experiment. Maybe he had found the secret to eternal life?

Only he did die. He did die, and I had questions.

Not right away. Not when I was living with Kiki and acting like I was as wise as Liam. But after I failed, after I was left with my guilt and my regrets, I wanted answers. I wanted answers, finally, to all the questions I'd left behind, what had happened after I left, and what it meant for me and the people in my life who were still being affected by all of it on a daily basis.

I only knew one place to get those kinds of answers.

It was, unfortunately, the last place I wanted to go. But I was so angry that it overcame any rational objections. I was keeping to myself those days. I hadn't seen Liam or The Twists in months. The guy I was seeing off and on wasn't someone I could tell any of this to. And my work friends at FeedNews tended to give advice like: *You don't need negativity in your life, Jess. Light a candle and let it go.*

Fat fucking chance I was doing that, even if I was able to.

So, I made my plans and took a few days off. I rented a car and navigated cautiously out of the city. Having only learned to drive as an adult—from Liam, of course—I still didn't feel the confidence that I imagined came with learning at sixteen like a normal kid. It was one more thing that Kiki and I had bonded over. She'd learned to drive during her year in Ohio. She'd called me all excited about it, and the roommate who'd pushed her to do it. "I finally feel free," she'd said, and I'd felt so fucking *smug*.

And now she was gone, and my parents—who were not dead, despite what I'd told everyone—had settled on an old horse farm in Connecticut with some of the remnants from the Land of Todd. They didn't get any money in the settlement, but one of the women had an inheritance she'd kept from Todd, this run-down property in the middle of nowhere. About twenty of them had gathered there after the LOT was closed down. My parents. Kiki's parents, most of the originals who'd spent too much time living communally to go back out into the regular world.

My mother had, bizarrely, sent me a Christmas card with the address a year after that New Year's Eve party with Kiki. I didn't know who it was from when I got it; I'd never seen my mother's handwriting. The return address was for someone named Charlotte Williams, which I honest to God had forgotten was my mother's actual name. I thought it might be some long-lost cousin reaching out after having read the piece in FeedNews. It had come out in September and had garnered a ton of attention, both for me and the cult itself. I'd gotten a steady stream of emails from people I barely remembered. Some of them were thanking me. Others wished I'd left well enough alone. I didn't care about them, though. What mattered to me was Kiki's reaction, and the leg up the article had given me at work.

I'd made Kiki the protagonist of the story. She'd started her year away in Ohio. I'd included that detail in the story too. Her happy ending, turning all the bad she'd suffered into something better for a new generation.

"I don't want people to know my business," she'd said to me in a phone call after it had come out.

"I hid your identity." I'd called her Katherine in the story, her middle name.

"That doesn't change anything."

I felt like shit. I'd made the usually placid Kiki angry. All to advance my career. "I mean, I hoped that the story would get a lot of reads, and I told you I was writing it."

"You didn't say it would be about me. You didn't ask my permission."

"You're right. I suck. Forgive me?"

The line went staticky.

"Kiki?"

"I wanted to start over."

"I know. Me too." I looked at the picture she'd painted for me for Christmas, which I'd hung on my wall. "No one will figure it out. And if they do, you can use it to your advantage. Like, I grew up in a cult! Isn't that cool?"

"I'm not cool; I'm going to be a kindergarten teacher."

"You're the coolest person there ever was," I said, and she laughed. "Besides, this story will be yesterday's news tomorrow, and you can go on living your elementary schoolteacher dream in peace."

Those words have haunted me.

So, there I was, on a hot June day four years ago, driving down a dusty road searching for an address that had been a bit blurry on the

Christmas card my mother sent me. Inside was a premade Christmas message, but below that she'd written: *We love you.* And that was it. Nothing asking to see me. Nothing saying she was sorry. Just a declaration of love that I had trouble believing.

I found the right road and turned left. From a distance, the house looked impressive—a large white farmhouse surrounded by pastures. Up close, though, the house screamed of neglect. The paint was flaking off, the garden was overgrown, and several rusted-out trucks were parked near the garage.

It seemed almost abandoned, except for the little girl swinging in a tire hanging from a tree. It was the girl I'd seen with my parents at Todd's funeral, the one who looked enough like me to be my sister. She was about seven then, and her yellow hair was in two pigtails caught at the end with red barrettes. She was wearing a pair of blue coveralls, and she looked so innocent and perfect that it occurred to me that she'd been placed there to lure people in.

Nothing to see here, folks! Look, we have cute little girls in pigtails!

I hadn't given her much thought since the funeral, and I wasn't expecting to see her. What I was expecting, I didn't rightly know. Just not her.

"I know who you are," she said to me after I got out of the car and started walking to the house.

"That right?"

"Yeah. You're the girl who left."

"My name is Jessica."

She cocked her head to the side. "I didn't know that."

"No?"

She popped her fingers into her mouth, sucking them. "Nah, they don't use your name."

I wanted to vomit. My parents didn't use my name? They just referred to me as what? *The Girl Who Left?* What the fuck was this? Why the hell was I here?

I almost turned around and got back in my car, but I could see my mother peeking through the window, and I didn't want to give her the satisfaction of seeing me turn tail and leave.

"What's your name?"

"Serene."

"That right?"

"Yes."

She had a slight lisp, which must have put her on Todd's shit list. Any imperfection was the fault of the imperfect person. He nearly lost his mind once when he noticed that one of the boys had a large zit on his chin. Clean living, you see, should've kept the downsides of puberty away. God, he was an asshole.

"What's your last name?" I asked her.

"Blakemore."

I clenched my fist so hard my nails almost broke skin. "That's not your last name."

"Yes, it is. Mom says."

Fuck, fuck, fuck. We were all Blakemores when we lived in the LOT. Todd's last name was given to all of us—we were all his children, apparently, belonging to him. But he didn't have any actual children, not that we knew of. There were rumors—an occasional woman who gave birth to a child who people whispered about and then watched for signs of particular favor from Todd. Liam's nephew, Aaron, was one of those kids, but it's also just as likely that the other kids were simply jealous and looking for a reason why he didn't have to spend as much time as we did learning how to dig the perfect ditch and tricking out end-of-the-world shelters.

"She's not your mom."

"Jessica!"

My head snapped to the left. My mother stood there, wearing coveralls similar to Serene's. Had they traded one uniform in for another? Why couldn't these people be free of each other?

"Therese."

She looked stern. "You don't . . ." My mother's hands fluttered at her side. She looked tired, and old.

"Don't what?"

"You can call me Mom. Or Charlotte. I don't go by Therese anymore."

"Can I?"

I could feel Serene's eyes on us. I didn't want to have this conversation in front of this girl who looked too much like me, too much like memories. I didn't want to be having this conversation at all.

"Of course you can, honey, I—"

"Is Tanya here?"

"She's in the kitchen. Why?"

"Because she's the person I came to see."

"I don't understand."

"You don't have a phone," I said. Serene's swing squeaked. I turned to look at her. She was pumping her legs methodically, pushing the tire higher into the air. Was she going to jump? Should someone tell her to stop and consider the consequences? Todd didn't believe in that. *Let the children fall where they may*, he used to say. *They'll find a way to get back up again if they're meant to.*

"What?" my mother said.

"You don't have a phone," I said again, turning back to her. "That's why I had to come."

"You didn't come to see me and your father?"

"No."

"Why are you here, then?"

My mother shrank into herself as she asked that question. And if I'm being honest, I took some pleasure in that. It made me feel bigger, powerful somehow, to know I could injure her without even lifting a hand. And I hadn't even said the worst part yet.

Because the worst part was why I was there.

The worst part was, "Kiki's dead."

Chapter 32

The Consequence

My ankle protests at the renewed run through the woods, but JJ doesn't seem to feel any strain. She yells after Jessie, "There's nowhere for you to go!"

But she's wrong about that. Jessie's running back to the water, where there are paddleboards and potentially other people if she makes it out into the lake, and we have to stop her before she gets away.

"Don't let her get to the water," I yell to JJ, and she kicks herself into another gear as she dodges and weaves through the thick stand of trees.

My lungs are screaming at me to stop, but I can't. I count out the seconds in my head. How long did we run last time? How long till she makes it to the shore? We haven't seen anyone all day, but there's no guarantee of that continuing.

I dig as deep as I've ever had to in my entire life, knowing how important it is to get to Jessie before she reaches the beach. At some point, Jessie's flung off her life jacket, and I can see her shoulders flagging, her steps a bit more cautious. She seems to be limping slightly; maybe she hurt herself in the tussle with JJ. I lengthen my stride, getting closer with every step, and finally she's right in front of me. I can see water up ahead through the trees, but we're still two hundred yards from the beach. Jessie trips on a root, her arms flailing in front of her as she loses speed trying to keep her balance.

Now. I have to strike now.

I reach into my pocket and take out the rock I stashed there earlier, then take a few running steps like I'm doing the long jump and catch her around the middle, knocking her down.

We tumble together to the ground. She screams, and then there's a loud *crack*, a horrible wet sound. Jessie goes limp beneath me and I skid past her, ending up back on the forest floor with knees that feel like the skin's been ripped off them. I drop the rock still tight in my hand, bring myself to a standing position, then turn around and look down. She's lying perfectly still, silent and gray. Her head is at a weird angle, like her neck's been snapped, and there's blood oozing from her forehead and mouth.

I heave once, but hold it in, bringing my hand to my mouth.

JJ slaps through the trees and stops next to me. I can smell the sweat coming off her; we're both a mix of blood and exertion.

JJ looks down at Jessie, then rears back her leg and kicks Jessie in the shin.

"Get up!"

I drop my hand. "JJ!"

"What?"

"She's not . . ."

I point to Jessie, motionless on the ground. The blood is more obvious now, a wet streak on her chin, and there's a sharp rock with a terrible stain on it inches away from her head.

JJ understands in the same moment that it sinks in.

Jessie's dead.

I've killed her.

I'm struggling for breath, and all I can think is, *Don't throw up, don't throw up, don't throw up.*

I've killed someone.

Don't throw up.

"Stupid bitch," JJ says. "She got what she deserved."

"We need to clean up," I say a few minutes later after my heartbeat has returned to a more normal rhythm and the dry heaves have passed.

JJ agrees, and so we spend the next hour clearing the scene. I pull a tarp from my pack, and we put Jessie on it so her blood stops oozing into the ground. JJ takes the latrine shovel I also brought to dig up the earth around Jessie's head and walks it into the lake to let it disappear. Then we repeat the scene at the clearing in the woods where Jessie fell the first time. It takes a while to locate the spots of blood, and we can't be sure we've gotten all of them, but it's the best we can do under the circumstances.

We don't talk much. JJ dumps the dirt in the water, letting it darken and then dissolve, and I toss the stone I was holding and the one that she struck her head on as far away as possible. Then we both take a swim, scrubbing the dirt and blood from our bodies and cleaning out the scrapes we've collected as best we can with a tube of biodegradable soap, using up every drop. My fingernails are caked with dirt, and maybe more, so I find some sand to use as a scrub and work them until they're clean and my fingers start to prune. The water is cold, and by the time I'm satisfied that I've gotten myself as clean as possible, I'm shivering.

When I head back onto the beach, JJ's got her shirt wrapped around her waist, and the rest of her clothes are drying on a log near the fire that she's built up again. Her prosthetic arm is resting next to it. Her hair is spiked and her breasts are lying flat against her chest. I can see the ridgelines of her stomach muscles. She looks like an Amazon—not someone to be trifled with.

I guess we both look like that now.

I wrap the other towel around me and sit on the log. The fire is hot and starts to warm me quickly. JJ takes a seat next to me and I check my watch. It's six thirty.

"We need to get going so we have enough time to get back while it's still light out," JJ says.

"How long did it take us to get here?" I look across the lake. Our beach seems far away and deserted.

"About an hour. But we were also racing. And I don't know about you, but I'm worn out. I think we should leave at least an hour and a half to get back. Especially since we're also going to have to tow the extra paddleboard."

"We could leave the body here," I say.

"I think that's a bad idea. The animals might dig her up, and people come over here."

I put my feet out in front of me. They're full of scratches. My whole body is. "The lake it is, then."

"Agreed."

"Then tomorrow, we go to the local cops to tell them that Jessie ran away."

"And say what, exactly?"

"We tell them the truth. Not all of it, of course, but enough of it that our story will check out. I lost my money, I went searching for the bad guy, met Jessie who presented as another victim, we teamed up, found you, and then came here because there's another Jessica living here. Turns out, Jessie was the bad guy all along, which we figured out when we found her Molly ID and the other stuff in her bag. When we confronted her about it, she ran away."

"You think it will work?"

"It's taking a page out of her book, right? How she was hiding in plain sight the whole time. How hard are they going to look for her?"

"We could try telling them it was self-defense," JJ says.

"Too risky," I say. "If they don't buy that, then I'm going away for a long time. You too."

"You're right. I want to get our money back, though. How are we going to do that?"

I face a grim thought. "We're going to have to use her fingerprint to get back into her accounts and then change the password to give us time to figure it out."

"We need to keep this as simple as possible," JJ says. "A lot could go wrong."

"Yes. And then we need to pray that no one ever finds the body."

Chapter 33

Someone Always Has to Do the Dirty Work

We decide to wait till twilight to do the deed. There'll be less chance of us being seen then, when we dump her body in the lake.

"We'll have to weigh her down," JJ says.

"À la Virginia Woolf?"

"Who?"

"An author who killed herself by filling her pockets with stones. She wasn't found for almost a month. And then her husband buried her body under her favorite tree or something."

"People believed that story?"

I shrug. "She suffered from depression."

"Sounds like her husband killed her, then covered it up."

"I guess that's possible. Regardless, that was in a river. Think about how deep this lake is. Plus, there must be lots of fish in there."

"Do fish eat humans?"

"Some must."

"All right, let's go find some rocks."

The shore is full of them. I dump out the backpack and we fill it with rocks. JJ hauls it to where we've left Jessie, about two hundred yards from the beach in the woods where she can't be seen from the water in case someone goes by, and dumps it out. Jessie's board shorts have deep pockets, as does her sweatshirt. We fill them both with the heaviest rocks we can fit inside. Then we wrap the tarp around her and tie it off with the rope from the ankle leash from her paddleboard. We bring her board into the woods, then work together to lift her onto it so we can use it as a stretcher.

When we get her down to the lake, the light is murky as the sun sets, and there's a kind of steam coming off the water as the colder air meets it. It's the perfect cover for what we're doing, thank God, even assuming there's anyone around. But the lake is bare. The pattern I've noticed over the last week is the same: people pack up shop around five and then stay close to their campsites. In fact, the only thing I've seen more than a couple hundred feet from the tents after dark was a moose.

I felt sick the entire time we were working and was glad I'd only had a couple of sips of beer, but as soon as we're back, JJ picks up the trail mix I'd offered Jessie earlier and eats it quickly, washing it down with one of the remaining beers.

"How can you eat?" I ask.

"You should too. We have a long paddle ahead."

"Can't."

"Suit yourself."

When she's finished, we clean up the camp, returning everything we brought to my backpack and JJ's. I add Jessie's phone wrapped in a plastic bag along with her wallet and ID to mine. Unlocking her phone had been the worst task. Jessie's hand felt cold, though that was probably my imagination. But we need that phone unlocked to change the password, and now it works with my fingerprint. Everything in it is mine.

We each do a last survey of the campsite. The fire has died way down, but JJ insists on dumping the remaining beer on it to put it out, and when that isn't enough, we fill and dump our canteens time and again until it's all runny ash.

"The last thing we need," JJ says, "is to start a forest fire."

"We've done enough damage today."

We carry Jessie's paddleboard to the water. JJ takes her own ankle leash and attaches it to Jessie's board as a tow rope. I hold the board steady while she climbs on, then help her push off with Jessie trailing behind. She needs to paddle slow and steady, so Jessie doesn't roll off her board too early, and the rocks help with that, keeping her firmly in place.

I get on my own board and paddle softly behind JJ. I wish I'd brought headlamps, but we'd have to keep them off, anyway. The moon's not out yet, but it will be soon. We have maybe thirty minutes to get this done.

JJ keeps a steady rhythm, and the water's still flat, easing our path, though I feel a trickle of a breeze on my neck. That's all we need, for a storm to start up. The weather can change in an instant in these mountains. Just last week, eight people had been blasted off the Grand Teton by unexpected lightning. That mountain is behind us, looming large and sharp. I've marveled every morning at the view, but now it seems sinister.

"We should do it here," JJ says.

We're still closer to the beach we just left than the beach we're going to, but already my arms are killing me. "You sure?"

"Yeah. Wouldn't want to risk getting any closer."

"All right."

I paddle up to her so we can raft up. Jessie's bobbing behind us, almost peaceful under the tarp. Until I notice the stain seeping through, dark red, almost black. Ugh. I thought these things were supposed to be waterproof.

"What do we do?" I ask.

"Push her off gently, I think. Let's not make a splash."

I pull on the ankle leash to bring the board in between ours. The moon is rising. We have to do this now. The board is between us. "I think we should tilt it."

"Toward you or me?"

"You. Okay?"

She nods and leans her weight on her side of Jessie's board, while I lift with all my might. It doesn't budge at all at first, but then slowly, slowly, it rises, and she starts to slide off. I heave even harder to bring the board up as JJ pushes down, and then she's off the board and into the water. The body floats there for a moment and I despair that we've fucked it up, but then the tarp takes on water, and I guess Jessie does, too, and she starts to sink slowly beneath the glacial water in a rush of bubbles.

"We return thee to the earth from whence all things came," I find myself saying, an old incantation the kids used to chant in imitation of Todd when our pet mouse or cat would die, and we'd sneak away to bury it. "Find peace there, and know that ye will be remembered."

The moon has risen like a flashlight on our sins by the time we get back to shore. I can barely paddle, and I've gotten down on my knees to make the strokes shorter because I'm so woozy from lack of food and everything else that's happened today that I'm worried I might fall off.

I realize I was half-asleep when my board scrapes against rocks.

We've made it. We're here.

JJ hops into the water, her prosthetic arm held high. "Come help me."

I follow her command again. She motions what she wants me to do—clean off Jessie's paddleboard. I reach down and scoop up handfuls of sand and rocks and sluice the board. There's a small dark stain near where her head was resting that's visible in the moonlight. Nausea overtakes me again, but we can't stop now, so I renew my scrubbing until the stain is gone and the board looks like it did before any of this happened.

"What should we do with the boards?" I ask, speaking low.

"Bring them back to camp, then return them to the rental place tomorrow."

"Okay."

We're both whispering, but our voices seem loud to me. There's no one around to hear us, but we can't take the risk our voices carry.

"One of us will come back for hers, I guess," I say.

"If you take my paddle, I can carry both."

We climb out of the water. I help JJ put a board under each arm, then pick up my own board and our paddles. I can barely carry one board; I don't know how she handles two.

"You got all that?" she asks. "We can make two trips."

"I think I'm okay."

I start to walk up the hill. This is the worst part, but I grit it out. I get to the top and find the path as my eyes adjust to the dark. I can see lights up ahead: car headlights, or maybe it's from camper vans. I can smell the smoke from a campfire and the most amazing smell of frying meat. It makes me woozy, but I keep walking. It's about five hundred steps, and I start counting down— five hundred steps. I can do this.

I get to the first felled tree and almost start to weep. I forgot about the trees. I cut into the woods to get around it and get snagged on a branch. I tug myself free and find the path again. 450 steps now. 449. 448. 447 . . . My foot snags on a root, and I fall to the ground with a great clatter. Equipment splays out around me. I can't even tell if I'm injured. I simply feel broken.

"You okay?" JJ asks quietly.

"I'm okay," I say, but I'm not. The day has finally caught up to me. Everything that happened. Everything we did.

Jessie is dead, she's dead, and I killed her.

My God, I actually killed her.

I let out a great choking sob, and I hear a clatter and JJ's on the ground next to me, her arms around me, one warm and one steel. I sob into her shoulder.

"We did it," I say. "We did it."

"Shhh, come on, don't lose the plot now."

"It feels like I'm falling apart."

She leans back and looks me in the eye. "That's a normal reaction. But we've got a long way to go yet tonight. So, I'm going to need you to buck up, take a deep breath, and dig in."

"Does that work in combat situations?" I say through something between a sob and a laugh.

"Sometimes. A lot of people in my unit have some pretty serious problems."

"PTSD?"

"For starters. I lost an arm, but they've never gotten back to normal."

I almost sob again. "What's normal?"

"Fuck if I know. But that doesn't change the fact that we've got to get up and get back to camp." She stands but I don't move. She reaches out a hand to me. "On your feet, soldier."

I slap my hand into hers, and together we get me up to a standing position.

"I think you might want to take less equipment this time," JJ says. "And come back for the rest."

"Good idea."

I reach down and pick up the paddles. There's blood oozing from the wounds on my knees.

"Don't look," JJ says. "Eyes front."

I obey.

"Now, march!"

Chapter 34

The Greatest Sin

Tanya didn't take the news of Kiki's death well. They'd kept in touch sporadically since Kiki had left the LOT. I hadn't realized, but that wasn't the biggest secret I'd learn that day.

I told them all in the kitchen. My parents, my aunt and uncle, the other adults who'd joined them in this splinter cell, and Serene. The kitchen was painted a faded yellow, and the white paint on the ceiling was peeling and cracked. This was quite some paradise they'd built for themselves.

Before I spoke, the kitchen was full of buzzy energy, everyone talking and asking questions and muttering. Everyone except for Serene. Like her name, she was a calm little girl; she might've looked like me, but she resembled Kiki in temperament.

After I gave them the news, Tanya sat there in shock, her face white, then buried her head in her hands on the battered kitchen table. My uncle Tom placed his hand on her back, rubbing at her neck while large tears ran slowly down his face. No one else said anything. They all just stared at me as if keeping silent would contain the truth to that room and make it reversible. Then I realized that they were simply reverting to their original programming, performing the Silence Ritual, which was how you honored the dead, according to Todd. You didn't speak about them or remember their life or toast and tell stories. You held your tongue, sometimes for days, and when you could speak again it was as if they were never there. Only Todd got the special treatment of a funeral, I realized.

Only Todd was allowed to be treated like a regular human being.

"What's wrong with you people?" I yelled. "Todd's been dead for years, and you're still, what? Living the life? This is so pathetic. I mean, how many days of silence is Kiki going to get? Or will it only be hours? And then it'll be lunchtime, and someone will be hungry, and you'll make a sandwich, right, Tom? That was always your job, and you'll ask about wheat or rye and that will be it. She'll be gone. She'll be gone forever."

I broke down then. I didn't want these people to see my weakness, but there wasn't any helping it. Kiki was dead and it was my fault, and sitting there in that small re-creation of the LOT was my punishment for all of it. How long was I going to have to sit there, I wanted to know, until it was okay for me to leave and never look back?

Then a strange thing happened. Serene came and stood next to me, slipping her small hand into mine, and patting me on the back the way Tom was caressing Tanya. I was both repulsed and comforted by it, but I didn't know how to make it stop.

And then my mother spoke.

"Was it in Ohio?" she asked, breaking the spell.

I pulled my hand gently from Serene's and patted her on the head. She smiled at me and ran back to my mother.

"Jessica?" my mother prompted.

"Yes."

"Why did she go there? She never said."

"She was taking a year away. I think she found New York overwhelming."

"You never should've brought her there," Tanya said, raising her head and speaking through clenched teeth. They were yellowed and crooked from years of no dental care, but she still resembled Kiki enough to make looking at her hurt. They had the same eyes, the same innate wish to please.

I rocked back on the creaky wooden chair I was sitting on.

"You don't think I feel guilty enough already? But honestly, you've got some nerve pointing fingers. She would've been fine there if it weren't for all of you."

Tanya looked down at her hands. There was dirt caked under her fingernails. She'd been weeding the garden that morning, she'd said when I first arrived, and had just made tea. The pot had gone cool now.

I banged my hand on the table. "I mean it. How can any of you stand to live with what you did?"

"Jess . . . ," my father warned. He, of all of them, was the most like a stranger to me. He'd been Todd's right-hand financial man, always tucked away in Todd's study in the big house with the only computer on the property. We learned after Todd died that he was managing Todd's investments, and he was good at it. Very good. It was mainly because of him that there'd been so much money to distribute to the survivors. My dad had a knack for making well-timed stock purchases in all the companies Todd used to rail against, Apple and Microsoft and Shell and Monsanto—names we didn't even understand most of the time. I never saw a Mac or an iPhone or any kind of technology at all except for the brief moments we spent in town, until Liam rescued me. But my dad knew. While Todd was predicting the downfall of civilization, that moment we were planning and digging for, my dad was making Todd rich. For what, was never clear.

"Don't speak to me," I said to him. "Not now. Not when you never bothered to before."

"I don't think that's fair," my mother said. "We—"

"You did your best? No. No, no, no, no, no. Do not even fucking start with that today. Your best would've been not to join up with Todd in the first place. Your best would've been to leave when you had a kid or when Todd decided that we all had to live away from our parents and become little soldiers of the apocalypse. Your best would've been to tell Todd *no* when he decided I was going to build that cabin on my own where he was going to—"

"Stop!" my mother yelled. "Not in front of Serene."

I looked away from my mother and at Serene. She was pressed against my mother's side, and she had a small smirk on her face, like she was enjoying the drama. I felt a bolt of rage go through me. Why the hell did she get the innocent childhood? Why did she have to be shielded? But no, that was jealousy. My parents suddenly caring about the welfare of a child who wasn't me. It wasn't her fault they chose her over their own flesh and blood. It wasn't my fault, either, but there wasn't anything I could do about it now. There was no way to turn back the clock and bring my childhood back.

So instead, I stood, turned on my heel, and stormed out of the kitchen.

At least I could leave on my terms, if nothing else.

The rest of the night in Jackson is a bit of a blur. When you're done in with exhaustion, it's easy to lose track of time. Thank God JJ's there to keep me on track.

The first thing we do when we get back to camp is eat. I don't think I can, but JJ makes some pasta and sauce and orders me to eat it, and I do. I also down two glasses of water, only then realizing how dehydrated I am.

"What now?" I ask after I finish a second bowl of pasta. My stomach's still unstable, but I feel more focused.

JJ keeps her voice low. There isn't anyone in the campsites on either side of us, but voices carry in the night. "Get some of her clothes out of her tent, take them up to the showers with you, and get cleaned up."

"But I have to pay the attendant. What if she remembers me?"

"We're not hiding that we're here, remember? And you've got to get cleaned up, dress in her clothes, et cetera, so you can take her car back to the airport."

The thought of putting on Jessie's clothes almost makes the pasta come up. "Yeah, okay. What are you going to do?"

"I'll clean up and then get some stuff together here. When you get back, you'll drive her car to the airport." She hands me her laptop bag.

"What's this for?"

"Use the Wi-Fi up at the showers to book her on one of the morning flights. Whatever you can get. Use her Molly credit cards and ID."

"But they'll know she didn't take the flight. They can check the manifest."

"It will look like she's trying to hide where she's going. That's what's important."

"When do we have the fight?"

"When you get back."

I breathe in and out slowly. I'm bone weary.

"You up for this?" JJ asks.

"I wish we could do this tomorrow."

"I know. Too risky. Go now, you'll feel better after a shower."

I go into Jessie's tent and riffle through her clothes until I find something that will fit me. I'm not going to wear her underwear or bra; that's too gross. But there's a sweatshirt and jeans that look like I can wear. And when I reach right to the bottom of her bag, I come up with something else.

I leave the tent.

"Hey, check this out." I hold it up. It's a black wig, probably the same one she wore when she met me.

"Perfect."

"She has a ton of makeup in there too. And what looks like colored contacts."

"Stands to reason."

"I'm not going to fool anyone, though."

"You don't have to. You just have to look enough the part for the cursory look the tape from the airport cameras is going to get, if any."

"Right."

"We can do this."

"We are doing this."

JJ nods. I put everything I found in a pack and sling JJ's laptop bag over my shoulder. I decide to drive to the showers, which are near the entrance to the park, a ten-minute walk away; they're closing in twenty minutes and I don't want to miss my shot.

When I get there, I hand the sleepy woman behind the counter six bucks and ask for two towels. There's no one else in there except for a young girl watching her laundry spin in the laundry room.

I go into one of the shower stalls and peel my clothes off, then step into the spray. Everything stings, but I make sure to wash my cuts and bruises carefully with soap and shampoo my hair twice. I would love to stay in there forever, but we're on the clock.

I get out and dry myself, then slip into Jessie's clothes. I catch a whiff of her perfume, a distant echo of something expensive. I comb my hair and tie it back in a tight bun like a ballerina, then slip the wig on. When I emerge from the enclosure and check myself in the mirror, I look like someone else. Something about the cut of the wig transforms my face from its normal rounded proportions to one with angles. I'm not Jessie, but I'm not me either.

After checking for cameras, I stuff my clothes in the large garbage can in the bathroom, then sit on the bench outside so I can use the Wi-Fi on JJ's computer. There's a selection of morning flights with seats. One to LA. One to Salt Lake City. One to Minneapolis. I choose the last one. I enter her Molly information. I check her into her flight, then close everything up. When I pull back into our camping spot, JJ's sitting at the picnic table. She's packed Jessie's suitcase and it's sitting next to her. She's changed into all black, including a knit cap. She's almost invisible.

"Where's the phone?" she asks.

"I've got it. She had two. That's how she sent herself that text in the airport, pretending to be Jessica Two."

"You should take the SIM card out now on the one with her banking info. Give the other one to the police."

"I've got to back it up to my laptop first. So we don't lose access."

"How long will that take?"

"A few minutes."

I get my computer out of my tent. One of Liam's seminefarious contacts/friends showed me how to clone a phone's contents a few years ago. You never know when you're going to need to know how to do that, apparently.

I boot up the program he installed for me and connect her phone to the laptop. I put in her password to unlock it. The transfer happens quickly.

"We might as well fight while we do this," JJ says.

I touch my hair. "How do you like the look?"

"It'll do."

"Well, fuck you!" I say loudly. JJ starts, then realizes I've slipped into character. "I don't owe you any explanations for anything!"

"Don't talk to me like that."

"I can talk however I want. What I don't have to do is sit around and listen to your baseless accusations!"

"Hey!" someone yells from a tent a few spaces over. "Some of us are trying to sleep here!"

"And some of us have young children!" comes from the other side of the road.

I try not to laugh.

"Aw, fuck off or I'll make you regret it," JJ says.

I shake my head and whisper, "We don't want them coming out of the tent."

"Don't worry, they won't."

My computer beeps; the transfer's complete. I untether it and take the SIM card out of the phone.

"You should just shut your mouth, JJ! And you, too, Jessica! I was better off before I met either of you!"

"That's a laugh! You fucking thief."

"I don't need to stand around and take this."

"Oh yeah? What are you going to do about it?"

"You'll see."

I stand and stomp over to the car, grabbing the suitcase from the table.

"Where are you going?"

"None of your business! Just leave me alone!"

"Yeah," shouts one of the tent dwellers. "Leave her alone!"

I get into Jessie's rental and start up the engine. I rev it once, loudly, then drive off down the road.

I roll down the windows and jack up the radio. George Michael's "Freedom! '90" is playing.

It seems fitting somehow.

Chapter 35

Lies and the Lying Liars Who Tell Them

The next morning, I rectify something I forgot to do last night as soon as possible. I call Liam.

It's seven mountain time when I call, which makes it nine in New York. I've had about an hour of broken sleep. Though the airport isn't far, I almost drove off the road on the way there last night because I thought there was a bison in front of me. I was imagining it; it was only a shadow. But, after that, I drove slowly until I got to the airport, parking Jessie's car in the lot and leaving her suitcase in the back. I left the keys inside, wiping them and the steering wheel off as best I could with a piece of cloth and some rubbing alcohol I got out of the first-aid kit. It didn't matter if I left some traces of me in the car; I'd been in it for legitimate reasons. We wanted to give the impression that she was covering her tracks in a hurry, not actually erase any sign of her.

Although there was a place to drop off keys when you returned a car off-hours, I didn't want to get too close to the terminal, or to the cameras I knew were hanging from the ceiling above every entrance. So, I left the keys on the seat in plain sight; maybe some kid would get a joyride. More likely, in this honest western town, someone would report it before we went to the cops. I left her suitcase in the trunk.

Then I turned and started to walk out of the deserted parking lot. There were no flights coming in or out at that hour, nearly midnight, and with the moonlit mountains behind it, the airport looked like a film set.

The airport road was similarly deserted, and way creepier. On either side was a split rail fence and pastures. I could see the outline of some large animals and hear them as they expelled their breath and called to one another gently. I was hoping for cows, but these probably were the bison I thought I was going to hit on the road. The fence looked more like a suggestion than a real barrier, and every step I took sounded like thunder. I was thoroughly freaked out and almost running by the time I got to the main road where JJ was waiting for me in the Jeep. We drove in silence back to the camp, and though I was exhausted beyond anything I'd ever felt before, I couldn't settle into sleep once we crawled into the tent.

Liam picks up on the third ring. Uncharacteristic for him to wait so long, but maybe he's pissed at me. I have two missed calls from him and a text that says simply ?. I'd like to think it's love-fueled worry, but it's probably just worry.

"Hey," he says.

"Hey, yourself."

I'm lying in my sleeping bag in the tent. JJ left a couple of minutes ago to take a walk. I suspect she's gone down to the beach to make sure we didn't leave anything behind. Or that there's not a blue-shrouded body floating in plain sight on the lake. I shiver and close my eyes.

"Where'd you get to last night?" Liam asks.

"Sorry, there was some major drama."

"Oh?"

"So it turns out you were right to be suspicious of Jessie. Or whoever she is."

Liam's voice tightens. "What happened?"

"I, um, tried to get some information out of her while we went on this epic paddle, but she stuck to her story. So, when she went to take a shower, I went through her stuff in her tent."

"That's my girl," Liam says in a way that should be accompanied by a chuckle but isn't.

"Aren't you the one who taught me to do such things?"

"I wasn't scolding."

"Oh. Okay, then."

There's a mosquito buzzing around inside the tent. Its buzz gets closer, closer, and then stops. I slap it dead against my neck right as I feel it pierce my skin.

"What did you find?" Liam asks.

"She had another set of IDs. Someone named Molly Carter. That was the name she used to buy the ticket to get into the terminal yesterday."

"Give me the details. I'll check."

I wipe the blood from my neck with the edge of my shirt as I rattle off the information I memorized last night when I was buying her plane ticket.

"What happened after you found the IDs?" Liam asks.

"We confronted her."

"Jess . . ."

"What? What was I supposed to do?"

"You could've called me. You could've left. You could've gone to the police."

"She would've just taken off before you or the police got here. Plus, JJ was here, so it was two against one. I mean, I wasn't worried she was dangerous or anything."

"What if she had a weapon?"

"I'd searched her tent and didn't find anything. We wanted to confront her and get it over with. After all this time . . ."

"What did she say?"

"She denied it at first, but then I remembered that she'd been sending me these threatening texts."

"What?"

"Oh, right, I haven't told you about that."

The sky's lightening, turning the tent a rosy orange. I can hear JJ shuffling around outside.

"No, you didn't."

"Sorry."

"She was texting you?"

"Well, I started it, out of frustration—telling her I was coming for her, that sort of thing—but then she answered a couple of times, warning me to stay away. It felt like, I don't know, a game or something."

Liam sighs. "Continue."

"Anyway, I sent her a text—to Jessica Two, I mean—and it dinged on Jessie's phone, so she admitted it then."

"What? The whole thing?"

"Not the details. It wasn't like those times in the movies where the bad guy spills the whole scheme. It was more like a lot of yelling, and us asking for our money back, and her refusing, and saying she'd spent it all, et cetera."

"That et cetera's doing a lot of work."

"I'll give you the blow-by-blow when we see each other."

"Where is she now?"

"Dunno. She packed a bag and took off."

Liam sounds tense. "Took off where?"

"JJ thinks maybe Salt Lake City."

"When did this happen?"

"Last night. It was late, so we decided to wait to go to the police until this morning."

"They should take it seriously now."

"They didn't before."

Liam sighs again. A double-sigh conversation. This is not looking good for our romantic future. What with me being a killer and the lies growing between us.

"Do it anyway," Liam says.

"Are you worried she's going to come back?"

"I don't know what she might do, and neither do you. You know her secret and the name she's been using. You know where she lives. Going to the cops is as much protection for you as anything."

"I see your point."

"I mean it, Jess. She's smart. She made it so she could live in plain sight this whole time, created this whole cover story where she was a victim too. She thinks ahead. She knew you were onto her."

"And yet, she came along for the ride."

"She probably couldn't help herself."

"That's what she said. Also, she could monitor our progress. Plus, I think she tried to steal money from Five right in front of me at the airport yesterday."

"That's very reckless."

"Dangerous, you mean."

"Yes. She's going to be very dangerous now. Please go to the police immediately."

She isn't going to hurt anyone anymore, but Liam can never know that.

"Okay, okay, we will."

His voice softens. "And then come home."

"Yes."

"When?"

"Tomorrow, if I can. I promise."

We say our goodbyes and I lie in the cocoon of the tent for a minute, wishing I could close my eyes and fall back to sleep. But my bladder is full, and my brain is whirring, and I can sense JJ waiting for me to emerge.

I unfurl myself from my sleeping bag and climb out of the tent. It's a cold morning, and my breath clouds around me as I stuff my feet into my running shoes.

JJ's sitting on the picnic table cradling a cup of coffee. She's dressed in a puffy jacket and her wool cap from last night.

"How much of that did you hear?" I ask.

She makes a face. "Your boyfriend talks loud."

"Everyone has a flaw. Besides, there's no one camped close to us." The nearest tent is two sites over.

"You think he's right about going to the police today?"

"Yeah, we probably should." I sit down next to her. The wood seat is damp. "Everything's in place, right?"

"I guess we'll find out."

We're somber on the drive into town. We spent a bit of time vacillating over who we should tell—the Teton County Sheriff's Department or the Jackson Police. Or I did, anyway. Stalling. While I was googling, I came across a news story about a woman, a girl, who'd been in the park as part of an outdoor initiative. She was from Ohio, like Jessie said she was at the airport. It was an eight-week program with twenty other kids. Cleaning up, mending fences, that sort of thing. On her last day there, she'd posted a picture of herself on Instagram in Jackson, under one of those signs they have in the town square made out of antlers, saying how much she'd learned and how much she was looking forward to going home. Only, she didn't make the flight. Instead, on the last hike, she peeled off into the woods and disappeared.

There was a massive search. FBI, local police, the Park Service. Friends reminded one another that she'd had wilderness training, that she knew how to survive in the woods if she needed to. She'd be okay. Her Instagram post gathered hundreds of comments, and her parents were understandably frantic. The searchers found no signs of her. People began to despair. And then, three days later, they found her on a side road. Her hair had been cut and dyed a different color. She was wearing new clothes. She tried to run from the police, but they caught her. She was brought to the hospital for a psych evaluation, and someone wrote on her Instagram that she'd done something like this before when she was fourteen.

"And that was it. That was the last thing the story said," I told JJ as we slowed in the morning traffic on Broadway.

"She probably had a psychotic break."

"Maybe she was joining a cult."

"That seems unlikely."

"Why? My parents did."

JJ was driving and I could tell that the traffic frustrated her. "Right, but not like that."

"I'm sure it seemed like that to my grandparents. One day, normal kids. Next day, poof, gone into the Land of Todd."

"Okay, good point."

I look out the window. We're passing Persephone, this great pastry shop. "Hey, park the car over there."

"Shouldn't we be getting to the police station?"

"I need something to eat. We might be a long time with them."

"True."

JJ turns the wheel and parks the car in a spot down the road. The day has warmed up some, and there's a line of people waiting out the door.

We get to the end of the line, and JJ says, "Can't we go somewhere else? Isn't there a Starbucks over there?"

The person in front of us turns around in horror. "Dude, you do not want to choose Starbucks over Persephone."

"Okay, sorry. Jeez."

"It's pretty good," I say by way of explanation. Persephone was part of my routine when I was following Five— "Oh, shit."

"What?"

I lower my voice. "Five. Goddammit. *Five.* We forgot about her."

"What's the problem? Liam said she was okay, right? Plus—"

"He didn't say. She only got there yesterday . . ."

"Right. I lost track of time."

I had too. Yesterday feels like a week ago.

"So, what's the issue?" JJ asks.

I hold up a hand. "Let's get some food. Then I'll explain."

We stay silent as the line moves quickly. When we get inside, I feel ravenous. The air smells like butter and frying bacon and fresh-brewed coffee. There's an assortment of tables on either side, with a long glass counter at the back that displays the best pastries I've ever seen, including in New York. When I get to the cash register, I order a ham-and-cheese croissant, guaranteed to have enough calories for an entire day, and a latte to go. JJ gets the same, and we take our food out onto the patio. There's an open table in the corner where we can talk in relative privacy.

JJ unwraps her croissant and takes a bite. "Now I get what that guy was talking about."

"Right?"

"So, what's all this with Five?"

I open the paper around my croissant and take a large bite. The fats rush into my bloodstream like an opioid. "If we tell the police what we did with her, we're going to be in trouble."

"What part, specifically?"

"Tricking Five like that. That was a crime, wasn't it?"

"Tricking her into a free trip to New York?"

"Not so much that, but all the other stuff. Impersonating her online. Luring her to the airport. It could look like we were trying to scam her *with* Jessie."

"Shit. I didn't think about that."

"Me neither until just now. She used to come here every morning . . . that's what made me think of it."

"So, what do we do? Leave it? Go home and forget this ever happened?"

"No, we need to stick to the plan and go to the police."

She takes another bite of her croissant. "I never mastered how to make these things. They're so finicky, and you would not believe the amount of butter—"

"JJ, focus. Come on."

"Sorry, I'm tired."

"Me too."

JJ puts down her croissant and brushes the crumbly bits off her fingers with a napkin. "So, we're fucked is basically what you're saying."

"There must be a solution."

I look around at the other patrons. Everyone looks so healthy here, like they just went on a ten-mile hike at sunrise and are running a marathon this afternoon.

"You want to ask those people for some input?" JJ asks.

"What? No."

"What are you staring at, then?"

I look away. "Todd always told us that clean living would make us beautiful. That wasn't true in Upstate New York, but out here—have you noticed what everyone looks like?"

"You mean the whole Germanic-pod-people thing?"

"I think it might be more Scandinavian, but yeah."

"I've noticed."

"Do you think they'll put us in a local jail? That might not be too bad."

JJ finishes her croissant. "Stop being so melodramatic. You have Five's number? Call her and ask for help."

"You think that's a good idea?"

"Better than the alternative."

I take out my phone and find Five's number. She picks up quickly.

"Hey, it's Jessica."

"Which one?"

"The OG. How's New York?"

"Good so far. What's up."

"Well . . . Jessie's gone."

"What does that mean?"

"We figured out she was the bad Jessica yesterday."

"What?"

"Yeah . . ."

"Is she coming after me?"

"I don't think so. But I'll text you my friend Liam's number. He'll keep an eye out."

"Is that why you called?"

"No, um, we're going to the police."

"That sounds like a good idea," she says.

"Yeah, but do you mind if we keep all that stuff we did with you out of it?"

"The fake contest, you mean?"

"Yes."

"Why? Because it will make you look bad?"

"Of course."

"Why should I?"

"You probably shouldn't, actually, but I'm going to ask you to do it anyway."

She laughs. "Did you get it?"

"What?"

"Your money back."

"No. Not yet."

"Okay, I'll do it. But if you do, you have to promise to do a scholarship for real this time. Like a local kids' thing in Jackson or something."

"I'll do that. Thank you."

"No sweat. You think Liam can show me where to get good sushi?"

I shove down the pang of jealousy I have. "Definitely."

We say goodbye and I walk back to JJ. "We're all set."

"She'll play along?"

"Yes."

"So . . ." She picks up the remnants of her breakfast and crushes it into a ball. "Time to face the music."

"Let's hope we both can dance."

Chapter 36

Perfect Circle

My mother caught up to me in the cornfield. I never knew there were farms in Connecticut. I always thought of it as the preserve of rich family compounds. But I guess there are farms everywhere, of one kind or another. Regardless, it was a cornfield, and who cared about my stupid misconceptions about Connecticut?

My brain is a prison I have trouble escaping sometimes.

It was early summer, and the stalks were low and bright green. They hadn't cleared out last year's crops properly, so there were dead, brittle canes in among the new growth. The property must've been a couple hundred acres, and part of me wondered why the lawyers hadn't gone after this, too, even though it wasn't part of Todd's estate. If I told Covington about it, he'd be pissed. But I hadn't even told him about Kiki yet. I didn't know if they'd kept in touch while Kiki was away, or what had even happened to them after I saw them exchange a tender kiss on New Year's. I tried to ask her the next morning, but she just blushed and changed the subject. I knew how hard-won her privacy was, so I let it go.

But I was going to have to tell him, and it was a conversation I wasn't looking forward to, like the one I was waiting to have there, on the edge of a cornfield in Connecticut.

The lawsuit, the settlement—they were supposed to make things better. But money wasn't going to bring Kiki back. Money was the root of all evil, Todd used to say, though we didn't know that wasn't an original thought when he said it. I didn't, anyway. My parents surely did, the idiots.

I hate to agree with Todd about anything, but he might've been onto something there.

The sky was a slate gray and the air smelled like rain. The sweater I was wearing wasn't quite warm enough for the day. I wanted to get back into my car and drive away from that place, and let the only proof that I'd been there be the dust my car kicked up, but something held me back. I had so many questions about my life, my childhood, my parents' choices. If I didn't ask for answers now, it felt like I might never get them. So, I waited out in the yard, on the edge of the cornfield, knowing that she'd come speak to me eventually.

And she did.

"You're right, you know," my mother said, coming up next to me so silently that I started when she spoke. I wasn't sure how old she was. Sixty? Sixty-five? No, not that old; she hadn't been forty when she'd had me. But it was one more thing I didn't know about my mother, because Todd forbade all birthdays except the eighteenth and his own, of course, where he turned thirty-three over and over, the age of Christ at his crucifixion.

"Right about what?" I said, making an effort to keep my voice unconcerned.

My mother shifted from one foot to another and then settled back into stillness. One thing I always noticed about us growing up was that she and I had the same posture. It wasn't Todd-imposed either. It was simply the way we both naturally stood when we weren't paying attention, one shoulder lower than the other, a hand on a hip. There's a kinship in these things, a reminder of the blood ties that bind. However much I might try to pretend or forget, she was my mother. And I was her daughter.

"All of it. Todd especially. You don't know what he was like then."

"Tell me."

"You want to know?"

I shrugged, and that was enough for her to begin.

"We were so young, your father and me, when we got married. We were so naive. We'd been sheltered growing up in Provo. No alcohol. No music other than what we sang on Sundays. You never met your grandparents, but they were so, so strict. Everything I wore, everything I did, everyone I knew, they controlled all of it. If they hadn't decided your father and I were going to get married long before we even knew one another . . ." She shook her shoulders. "But that was the one thing they got right. Your dad was different. He's so smart, and even then, he could see around corners."

I nodded in agreement, but I didn't know anything about my father or my parents' religion, whether they were regular Mormons or in one of those splinter sects. Even when I was little and allowed to live with them, it was my mother who'd been the caretaker. If I had to guess, he agreed to have me to please her. Or I was an accident. More questions I couldn't ask.

"Anyway, our parents decided we'd get married right away, at twenty, after your dad got back from his mission, Lord knows why, but it was such a blessing. Once we had our own home, we could make our own rules. We could sleep in, or watch TV, or sing along to songs on the radio. The one thing they believed in, our parents, was an education. They thought we were going to Brigham Young—your dad, anyway—and they gave him the money for it. But we'd applied to colleges in the East without them knowing, and we both got into Connecticut College with some scholarship money, and we decided to go for it."

"They must've been upset."

"They were livid. But we did it anyway. We moved away, went to college, met other kids."

"And Todd."

She nodded. "He was a philosophy professor. But he wasn't like the other teachers. He wasn't teaching from books; he was teaching from life. For life. Everything he said made so much sense to both of us."

"If he was teaching anything resembling what I've heard, he should've been fired."

My mother cleared her throat. "Well, he was. Fired. There was an . . . incident. But it was never clear what had happened. That girl was always throwing herself at him, and we were already in his thrall, and when he told us it was all made-up lies by the patriarchy to keep us asleep, well, we believed him. Without question. That's when he came up with the idea of going to Schroon."

"Why there?"

"He grew up there. That was his family's land."

A flock of birds crossed overhead. I wondered if they were still migrating back from wherever they went to in winter, or if they were local. Were these birds in my mother's life, or only temporary visitors, like me?

"And you decided to follow him."

"I know it sounds nuts, and it was, in a way, but after the way I was brought up . . . freedom was great for a while, but then I saw all the things that people did when they were free. We were learning about life for the first time. Seeing what all the possibilities were, but all the bad stuff too."

I wanted to scream, and maybe the birds heard my thoughts because they suddenly wheeled away in a shriek of their own.

"You think I don't know what it's like to leave a cloistered life and get out into the real world?"

"I didn't mean—"

"Right. Whatever. You never do."

I crossed my arms, hugging myself like I used to do when I was a child and I wanted to sleep. When I needed comfort. I was falling to pieces right there in that cornfield. It had to stop.

"This isn't helping," I said.

"What do you mean?"

"You telling me how you ended up under Todd's spell, it isn't helping. Kiki's still dead and it hurts, Mom. It fucking hurts."

She put her hand on my arm. I shrugged it away. "Don't touch me!"

"Jessica, please—"

"No, you can't make it better, Mother, okay? You didn't even try. How could you not have even tried?"

She was crying, and I was fine with that. "I did try, I did."

"Oh, please. No, you didn't."

"But I did," she said, taking in a deep breath and letting it out through her nose the way Todd had taught us to when we were losing control. She did it again and I watched the tears stop. When she spoke, her voice was calmer, almost trancelike. "I let you go up that hill even though Todd offered to let you stay with us because I knew it would be better for you up there than with us. With him. And I did do something for Kiki. It was too late, too late for all of us, as it turns out, but I did try."

"What the hell are you talking about?"

She turned to me with an expression I'd seen once too often growing up. The light of certainty even as the worst offense was being committed.

"This is bullshit," I said. "What did you do? Nothing, just like always."

She reached out her hand as if she hadn't heard me, placing it gently on my arm. "Tell me, dear. Are you still under the impression that Todd died of natural causes?"

JJ and I drive through town to the police station. It's not far, but sometimes short journeys can feel momentous. We park the car, then stand outside the building. Its base is made of the same stone they seem to use for a lot of buildings in town, a local granite, perhaps, though it hasn't got a shine to it. It doesn't look big, but there are jail cells inside and so many lies to tell if we're going to avoid ending up in one of them.

"Are we doing the right thing?" I ask JJ as we stand on the walkway.

"You're asking me that now?"

"I know, right? But seriously. We could . . ."

"Run?"

"We have her money."

"Not yet."

"No, but we can get it. And then we could be free."

JJ shakes her head. "I don't think any of this was about freedom, was it?"

"No."

"Besides, living her life, being on the run . . . that's not something I want to do."

"We wouldn't have to live her life."

She looks at me. "It would be, though, in some way, wouldn't it? You'd never get to be yourself again."

"I guess." That doesn't sound that bad to me, if I'm being honest. What's so special about my current life?

A carload of teenagers drives by with their windows down. They're blasting a Kanye song, singing along to the lyrics.

"You're not going to give me some crap about how we're never ourselves, are you?" JJ says.

"Ha! I was thinking of it."

"That something Todd used to say?"

"No, I thought of that one all on my own."

"Well, it's crap. We're always ourselves. Every God damn day. And you know what? Before Jessie came along, or whoever the fuck she was,

I was happy. I had a good thing going. It wasn't perfect, but that whole relentlessly positive thing wasn't a total act."

"So, you'll go back to that?"

"That's the plan."

"I don't know if I can go back."

"Why not? Isn't Liam waiting for you?"

"Yeah, but who knows if that's going to work out. Plus, my career's in tatters."

"So, start over."

"Easy to say, hard to do."

She rubs at the spot where her prosthetic arm meets what's left of her real arm. I've never heard her refer to it as a stump, and so I don't feel like I can, even in my thoughts.

"Yeah, it is hard. But that's okay. We're still young. And soon, if you're right, we'll have our capital back. The world's our oyster, I say."

"You do have a positive attitude."

She flashes me a smile. "I've got an idea for a new show."

"Oh yeah?"

"Turning around the lives of depressed people through teaching them how to cook for others."

"That's pretty good."

"You want to be the first guest?"

"That's sweet of you, but I think I've had enough exposure for a while."

"Understood. But do something, okay? Don't just sit around and brood."

"I won't."

I look at the building again. A patrol officer is leaving. He stops when he sees us.

"Can I help you, ladies?"

We glance at one another, and then I say, "We're here to report a crime."

Chapter 37

Home Again, Home Again

Three days later, we're at the airport saying goodbye.

It turned out that we had nothing to fear in reporting Jessie, not in the short term, anyway. But once we did, it seemed weird for us to leave immediately. Even though we made it clear that she wasn't our friend, it felt as if we had to show some concern for her well-being, and the well-being of the others she might be trying to scam. So, we stayed, and cooperated, and asked for details on the investigation like we cared whether they found her when we both very much hoped they wouldn't.

After a few go-rounds with the initial officer we spoke to, we ended up in the investigative unit of the Teton County Sheriff's Department. Sergeant Axel Johansson, the head of investigations, was about forty-five and as fit and tall as the citizens he was sworn to protect. He wore a tan uniform, with a crest that had a moose's head in profile on its breast. He had an open and friendly air about him that we feared hid a keen investigative mind. And perhaps it did. He asked all the questions we thought of and many, many more, listening for the full two hours it took us to go through everything that had happened to JJ and me, and then all of us together.

We'd done the right thing in telling him, he said. She might still be in the vicinity, and she sounded like a highly dangerous person. That's what he called her, a "highly dangerous person."

I tried not to laugh as I agreed with him. Besides, he wasn't wrong. She was still highly dangerous to both of us.

We stuck to our story. They issued an APB. They uncovered her plane ticket and took JJ's computer to analyze it. They checked in with the officer I'd reported the theft to in New York, and JJ's one in Chicago. They were thorough.

In some ways, the investigation that Liam was conducting on the other end of things was the harder one to get through. He kept texting me with questions, like what she was wearing the last time we saw her, what exactly her last words were, and how she'd gotten her hands on JJ's computer to book her ticket. What had we asked her on the paddle? Why had we even gone on that paddle in the first place, knowing who she probably was?

I called him when I got the paddle text.

"I thought maybe she'd loosen up. I didn't have a lot of time to think about it. You'd just told me that her backstory was probably made up. I was trying to think of what to do."

I stopped talking. I was saying too much, sounding defensive.

I was sitting in the town square eating an ice cream. It was the only thing I could get down these days, its cool creaminess slipping past the permanent lump in my throat. There was a family sitting on the grass having a picnic, their two little kids running around in circles chasing one another and laughing.

"I kept telling you she was dangerous," Liam says.

This was a theme I was getting tired of, but I couldn't lose my temper with him. "And I kept telling you I was with JJ. Plus, she wasn't dangerous in the end, was she? She just left."

"But did she? She didn't take the flight."

"You been hacking again?"

He coughs. He doesn't like it when I say words like *hacking* on a cell phone. Who knows who was listening in?

"Didn't the police tell you that?" he says.

"They might've mentioned something."

"It's odd, isn't it?"

I reach the cone part of the ice cream and stop eating. It's sweet and delicious, but I can't handle those sharp edges; they make me want to vomit.

"Maybe she had other ID," I say.

"I thought you searched her bag?"

"I did, but not that thoroughly. I didn't have much time. Maybe there were secret compartments, or she had . . . what's that called? A go-bag? She probably had one of those. Maybe she stashed it at the airport."

"Have they confirmed that she went into the airport?"

"Her car was found there."

"But did she go inside?"

"I don't know, Liam. They don't tell me everything. I assume she did at some point."

A shadow crosses over me. It's JJ. I mouth to her *Liam*, and she nods.

"What are you so worried about?" I ask.

"I think she's still in Jackson."

"Why would you think that?"

"Because there's no sign of her leaving."

"There's a zillion ways she could have left. Maybe she took the town bus to the ski hill and stole a car. Maybe she stole one in Jackson. Maybe she hitched a ride. Or took a Greyhound, or . . ."

"Okay, okay, I got it. You know it's only because—"

"You worry. I know."

I look up at JJ and roll my eyes. I make a crazy motion with a finger next to my temple, then turn it into a gun and pull the trigger.

"JJ's here. I've got to go."

"You're coming home tomorrow?"

"Yes, tomorrow. Will you pick me up?"

"Text me your flight info."

"I will."

"And be—"

"Careful, I know. I will, I promise."

He sighs again and it feels like a transition. I've moved away from being his girlfriend and back to being his . . . *daughter* isn't the right word, but sometimes it feels like that.

"See you tomorrow," I say, and hang up before I say something I'll regret. "You ready for the shoot-out?" I say to JJ. Every day at six, there's a fake shoot-out in the town square. JJ's become a little obsessed with it.

"You know it."

She's picked up a cowboy hat at one of the stores along Broadway. It's sitting on her head at a jaunty angle. If I didn't know better, I'd say she looked happy. And maybe she is.

"You're turning into one of them," I say.

"Who?"

"The tourists."

"All part of the facade."

"If you say so."

She tips her hat at me. "You could start running up Snow King every morning. And wearing more fleece."

"I'm already at maximum fleece, thank you."

She smiles. "Liam going to be a problem?"

"He'll let it go eventually."

"Hope so."

"Me too."

We check in with Sergeant Johansson before we leave and make sure he has all our numbers and emails and that he'll let us know if he finds anything.

"This is a puzzler you've left me," he says, tapping a pencil on his desk in time to some rhythm I can't make out.

"Sorry," I say.

"Not at all, not at all. I suspect she'll turn up in some other jurisdiction soon enough."

"What, then?"

"That depends on what she's done in the meantime, but I reckon she's in for a long haul in prison. She's committed dozens of crimes."

"So, there'd be a trial?" JJ asks. "Or more than one?"

"That's right. Unless she pleads guilty. But let's not get ahead of yourself. We have to find her first."

"Thank you for looking," I say.

"No trouble at all. It's my job."

We shake hands all around, and then JJ and I leave and drive out to the airport. Despite everything that's happened, I've grown pretty fond of the place. As we drive past the marsh and the vast expanse of the Elk Refuge, I try to take it all in. The big sky, the rolling hills covered in scrub pines, and that incredible view of the Tetons as we turn down the airport road. I don't think I'll ever be able to bring myself to come here again, but I wish I could. I wish I could show Liam Jackson Lake without thinking about what lies below its cold blue surface. Or climb up to the saddle of the Grand and take in the view of the valley and the dotted cars along the highway. I never made it to Yellowstone or saw half the wildlife there is to see; I mourn for these last things that Jessie took from me.

We drop off the Jeep near where I left Jessie's the other night, check into our separate flights, and go through security. As I place my pack on the conveyor, I start to feel a bit lighter. Maybe we can put all this behind us, let it all be scanned out of us.

But then I hear the TSA agent say something to JJ behind me, and there's a tap on my shoulder and a voice saying that I need to come with him, and the feeling slips away.

The TSA holding room is small and windowless, and we're in here because we're idiots who, after all our careful planning, forgot that going through TSA at the same time with the same name and birth date might set off some alarm bells.

Compared to the interrogations I've been through with Liam, this one is gentle. The TSA agent, a balding black man in his midfifties, runs our IDs through the system and confirms that we're two separate individuals. He tells us that the agent out front didn't have any choice but to bring us back once the flag had been raised, and that he's sorry for the inconvenience. He assures us that we're unlikely to miss our flights. Then he asks us if we know that there's an APB out for a third woman with the same name? "Yes," we say together. I can see Jessie's face on his screen, and I wonder if this is part of my life now. Getting pulled out of line every single time I travel forever because of Jessie. Being reminded of her everywhere I go. I'm sure it's something I deserve, given everything, but I don't relish the thought.

JJ hands the TSA agent Sergeant Johansson's card. "If you call him, he can vouch for us."

He takes it and places the call and returns a few minutes later with the all clear.

"Might be best if you don't travel together for a while," he says. "And keep that card handy."

"Understood," JJ says, though I hope never to speak to the sergeant again. If that means sticking to land transportation in the continental United States, so be it.

We leave the room, go through the metal detectors without any further issue, and retrieve our bags. JJ's flight is leaving first. It feels weird to be saying goodbye, dangerous and sad. Together, we could face whatever's coming, but apart . . .

"Keep in touch," she says.

"Of course."

"Also, start eating solid food?"

"I'll try."

"Don't make me make you be the first guest on my show."

"I won't."

She swoops in for a hug. Her arms are powerful around me, but mine still ache from the paddle. I have trouble reaching above my head, and getting dressed is a chore.

She releases me. "See someone if you need to. You've been sleeping badly. It's normal."

"That's risky, isn't it?"

"They'd be bound by confidentiality."

I'm not sure that's right, but I nod anyway. "We'll see. I'll be okay once I'm back in New York."

"With Liam?"

"Maybe."

"Get back to writing."

"Journalism? No, that's over for me, I think."

"People love a comeback story."

"Is that what this is?"

"If you leave out a detail or two, I think so."

"You might have something there."

She laughs. "See? Glass half-full."

"Thanks, JJ."

"You betcha."

She slings her backpack over her shoulder and gets in line for her flight. Veterans board first, and she's taking advantage of it, as she should. My flight's leaving in thirty minutes. Maybe I'll be able to get some sleep. I should eat something before it leaves, but the lump is still there in my throat.

It's always there, reminding me.

I killed someone.

I'm not sure I'll ever be able to forget.

Chapter 38

A Warm Embrace

Liam picks me up at the airport. This makes me so happy that I burst into tears when I see him, which also makes me *that girl* making a scene at the airport. Liam clearly thinks it's the stress of everything that's happened, and it is, but I'm having trouble stopping the blubbering, even once we're in his car and stuck in traffic.

Part of the reason is the wedge I feel between us now. A wedge made of deceit. I was always keeping things from him; there was so much that had happened in my life that I'd never told anyone, but I used to be able to keep those things in a separate compartment. I was a need-to-know kind of person, and I had it under control. But the techniques I once used don't seem to be working now. I need to find a way to get back to that person, pronto.

Liam takes me back to his apartment, where he's decided to make me dinner, he says. This is so sweet I almost start crying again, but I hold back. He's trying to impose a bit of normalcy, I'm guessing, because he hasn't asked me one question about Jessie since I got here.

I bring this up over the poached salmon paired with a dry Australian wine that we're eating at his kitchen island.

He puts some salad onto my plate. "I thought I'd probably asked you enough questions."

"You were worried I'd start crying again."

"Maybe."

He smiles and I feel close to the brink. I don't know if I'm going to be able to take his kindness or convince myself I deserve it. He looks so *Liam* sitting across from me, in a dark button-down shirt that he's rolled up to his elbows and a five-o'clock shadow across his chin.

He's watching me, though, so I take a small bite of the fish. It's delicious, cooked in a mix of wine, lemon, capers, and dill, but I can't get it past that ever-present lump, not even with a large gulp of wine.

"You're not eating," Liam says as I put down my fork.

"I'm sorry."

"You don't have to apologize."

"I haven't been eating well these last couple of days."

He frowns. I like the way his forehead crinkles and then relaxes. When I was younger, I used to say things to make him frown on purpose. It was easy to do. What a punk I was. He should've remembered that. People don't change; they just get better at hiding who they are.

"I'm sure it's just the . . . stress," I say. "Like the tears earlier. It's all catching up with me."

"You've been through a lot."

"Have I?"

He stares down at his plate. "I shouldn't have let you go after her alone."

"Let me?"

I say it with a challenge, which he hears.

"You know what I meant."

I reach my hand across the table and place it on top of his. We lock eyes for a moment, his gaze intense and probing. "Liam, let's not fight my first day back."

"Okay."

I let go, then try another bite of food. The wine goes down easily, which I should watch because drunk Jess is not a good idea right now, if she ever was.

"Thank you for making this," I say. "Maybe I'll be able to eat it for lunch tomorrow."

"Whatever you need."

"I missed you."

He smiles again, less intense this time. "I'm glad to hear it."

He is so far away from me even though there's only two feet of concrete between us. I need to see if I can bring him close again. I need to feel something other than this.

"Are you going to stay on the other side of the counter all night?" I ask.

He puts his fork down deliberately and stands. He walks around the edge of the counter until he's in front of me. I turn on the stool and raise my arms up to him. He steps into them, and I wrap my legs around his and bury my head in his chest.

I breathe him in. He kisses the top of my head and I look up. There are so many reasons why this shouldn't work, whatever there is between us, but it does work in moments like this. Because now he's kissing me gently with his soft lips, his stubble grazing my chin, and I can push the thoughts away.

I can bury them in him.

I wake up two hours later shaking and naked in Liam's bed.

"Jess! Wake up! Jess."

"What? Where am I?"

"You're here," Liam says. "With me."

I feel like I've been drowning. Like I can't get enough air. The room is pitch-black, Liam's blackout curtains doing too good a job at keeping out the light from the streetlamps.

"You were yelling," Liam says.

Oh God. "What was I saying?"

"Nothing, just *no*, over and over again."

He snaps on the light on his side of the bed. I pull the covers over my face.

"What's going on, Jess?"

"I was having a bad dream." The blankets muffle my voice. I sound like a child.

"Clearly, but—"

"Can you turn off the light?"

It turns off with a snap and I feel safer again. Why do I feel safer in the dark?

I lower the covers and Liam is there. I can see his profile. I reach up and stroke his face.

"Will you talk to me?" he asks.

"I had a bad dream. It happens."

He rolls onto his back. "When I first helped you escape, you used to have bad dreams all the time."

"I did?"

"You don't remember?"

"No, tell me."

I reach out for his hand. Our fingers interlock, and he moves his thumb over my knuckles in a circular pattern. "Not much to tell; you'd start thrashing in the middle of the night until I soothed you."

"How would you soothe me?" I ask teasingly.

"I'd rub your head and tell you everything was going to be okay."

I prop myself up on my elbow and reach out to Liam's head. I run my hands through his close-cropped hair; I've always loved the silky thickness of it. "Like this?"

"Well, not exactly like that. That would've got me arrested."

"I was eighteen."

"That doesn't make it okay."

"It wouldn't have been illegal, though."

"Maybe not. But not right."

"That was a long time ago."

"It was."

He turns over and kisses me, then breaks away. "What's brought the nightmares back?"

It's Jessie, but I can't tell him that. But I feel like I have to tell him something. If we have any chance of surviving this, I need to open up to him.

Lucky me, I have so many stories to choose from.

"Has Covington ever told you his theory about how Todd died?"

Liam stiffens next to me. "No. What?"

"I just wondered because he mentioned it to me a while back. Anyway, he has this whole theory that someone poisoned Todd's IV solution, because Todd was an exercise freak, and he died of a heart attack."

"What are you talking about?"

"Shhh. Listen."

He settles against the pillows, and I reach down and take his hand again. This time, I'm the one making slow circles with my thumb.

"Covington's right. Todd didn't die a natural death. My mother killed him."

Liam grips my hand tightly. "That's not funny, Jess."

"I'm not joking. I should've told you this forever ago, when I learned about it, but I didn't know how. But I want to tell you now, okay? Will you let me?"

He squeezes my hand in answer.

"But not a cross-examination, all right? Let me tell it my way."

"No questions, got it."

"Are you mad?"

"Just tell me about Todd, Jessica."

So I do.

Chapter 39

A Note to Follow So

This is what my mother told me in the cornfield. She'd been having doubts about Todd for years. Things he said, preached, and commanded that she didn't agree with and didn't see the point of. Then there were other things that she closed her eyes to. How he favored some children, especially Aaron. The eighteenth birthdays and his "special" celebrations with certain girls. Too many things to name. She'd thought about leaving, but everything they had was with Todd. They had never held jobs, had no money, and their families had disowned them. They had no idea how to live outside the LOT. And when she tried to talk to my father about it, which was almost impossible to do given the strictures they lived under, he'd always have some rationale to stay. He had access to the real world because of the work he did for Todd, and he'd tell her enough—about the war in Kosovo, for example, or all the Iraqi children who died in the bombing during the Iraq War, some famine in Africa, whatever news horror of the day—and then she'd look around her, and everything seemed so much better in comparison.

"He never showed you the good parts," I said. "He wanted to stay. Your families would have taken you back."

"I guess I didn't want to leave either. All the things that drove me there, that drove both of us, they were so ingrained that I thought there was a good possibility that I'd die if I left."

A large black crow landed next to one of the cornstalks and started picking at it. They needed a scarecrow or they were going to lose their crop. These people were hopeless.

"That's ridiculous."

"I know that now, but then . . . You didn't hear the things that Todd said in his sermons, not most of them. You blame me for letting him take you up the hill, but you were protected from the worst of it up there. As Todd got deeper and deeper into his paranoia, I'd guess you'd call it, his sermons got longer and darker. And then people would leave, and he'd tell us he had spies out there in the world, and those people would be dead within a year. And then we'd hear that they *were* dead."

"He was lying to you."

"Yes. But again, I didn't know that then. Not for sure."

"You could've asked him to look them up on the internet."

"Honey, I didn't even know what the internet was. Your father had to go take special computer classes just to do what he did for Todd. And because of it, Todd monitored us much more than the others. There were cameras and microphones in our house. We were with him all the time. There was barely any time where the two of us were alone, and never a time where we felt safe expressing our thoughts. And this is me saying this now, with the benefit of hindsight. Then, it was all looks between us, I guess, at night, in bed, when at least Todd couldn't see us."

"Are you trying to make me feel sorry for you?"

"No. I'm only trying to explain."

"How you killed Todd?"

"Yes."

"Seems like you waited a bit too long."

She held her hands out in front of her, flat, as if telling some invisible someone to stop. Was she seeing things? Was she completely unhinged? She couldn't have killed Todd, could she?

"I kept him away from you," she said. "When Liam took you . . . that was me."

"You know Liam?"

"No, but I'd heard of him, like we all had. I was able to get a message to his family after they left with Aaron."

"You're shitting me."

She frowned. "What does that mean?"

"You were the one who told Liam to come get me?"

"Did you think I was going to let Todd . . ."

"That's exactly what I thought. What had you ever done to make me think anything different?"

She lowered her hands and rested them on her thighs. "I couldn't do that to you, Jessica. No. Your father told me one night that he'd received an email from Aaron's parents, offering help if we needed it. He'd deleted it before Todd could see it, but he memorized the address just in case. When the time came, he told them about your birthday coming up. They knew what it meant."

"And you arranged for me to go to the farmers' market that day?"

"Yes. I saw Liam approach you. I was worried you weren't going to keep your cool."

"Keep my . . . what? What?"

"It's an expression—"

"I know the expression. What about when Tanya took me shopping for the dress? Did you arrange that too?"

"Did you think she didn't notice that you'd left the store?"

My mother was calling me a moron, but she was right. I should've noticed, but I was so indoctrinated that I didn't. I thought I was getting away with something. I was proud of myself for being so brave. Instead, it was my mother, and my father, the whole time, letting me go. The whole narrative of my life since I was seventeen was unraveling right there in the cornfield.

"I did think that, yes."

"And you thought I didn't care, or didn't know, what Todd was planning?"

"Either. Both."

She shook her head slowly from side to side. "I failed you."

"You got me out."

"Yes, but not Kiki."

I felt a stab of pain. "Todd wasn't interested in her, though."

"Not while you were there."

The consequence of what she was saying hit me all at once. I dropped to my knees on the hard ground and threw up. My mother crouched down behind me, rubbing my back, holding my hair away from my face.

I retched again, and then again, tasting bile. There was nothing left inside me, but my stomach wouldn't give up.

Finally, it subsided. I spat and rocked back on my heels, away from the mess I'd made.

"Come into the house," my mother said.

"No. Finish it."

"Are you sure?"

I looked her in the eye. My own face was buried in hers. "Please."

"Todd was so angry when you left. He suspected us of helping you. He brought all the children down from the hill, and we had to stay in the Gathering Place for weeks. He wouldn't let us sleep. He'd take us away one by one, interrogating us, even the little kids. He left your aunt and uncle, and Kiki, and your father and me for last. Tanya and Tom didn't know anything. I'd told Tanya to let you use the phone because your father had gotten a message that his mother was dying. And that if she got caught, she was to say that you had escaped, briefly, but since you came back, she didn't want to get you in trouble. That's the story she told Todd. She came out of that meeting with a welt across her cheek.

"I was shaking so hard in my meeting with him, I almost passed out. Todd knew I was keeping something from him, but I stuck to my story, that your dad was worried about his mother, so I'd arranged to have you call them. You hadn't been able to get through because they must've changed their number. I told him over and over that I had no idea how to communicate with anyone outside of the LOT other than by making a phone call, which was true. And he knew from the phone logs, which he checked carefully each month, that no calls had been made. And then . . . and then I told him I was disappointed that he couldn't complete the ritual with you. He got this horrible look on his face and said that it didn't matter. Your replacement had been there all along."

"Kiki," I said.

"Kiki."

"You should have killed him then."

"I wanted to, but I didn't see how I could. Everyone was so paranoid. He broke all the couples up and matched us with someone else so there wouldn't be any loyalties. I had to share a house with one of the other men for months. And he isolated Tanya and Tom, sent them up the hill, and then . . . and then it all seemed to return back to normal."

"Normal?"

"Three months after you left, Todd let us out of the lodge, and life went on."

I struggled to get to my feet. "Not for Kiki, though, right, Mother?"

She looked very sad, but it wasn't enough for me. "No, she wasn't the same after that."

"We all killed her, each and every one of us."

"Yes."

"So that's why you killed Todd? Because of what he did to Kiki?"

"In part."

"Why, then?"

"Kiki didn't tell you?"

It was a mean thing to say, though I don't think she meant it that way. She was as surprised as I was at the secrets Kiki had kept from me.

"She didn't tell me any of this."

"I would've thought . . . but maybe she blocked it out. That's what Tanya always thought, because she never took any interest after . . . That's why we raised her instead of Tanya, so it would be easier for—"

"What the fuck are you talking about?" I grabbed her by the arm and shook her. She seemed surprised by my touch. Was she reliving the experience of killing him? What the hell was going on?

"It was because of Serene. Todd started paying too much attention to her, even though she was only four. And it might have been fatherly, but I couldn't take that chance, not after Aaron and . . ."

"But what's Serene got to do with Kiki?"

She looked at me, and I could see the truth in her eyes before she spoke it. "Because she's Kiki's daughter. Hers and Todd's."

"How did she do it?" Liam asks when I've paused for more than a minute. He's kept his word and let me tell it without asking any questions.

"There were all kinds of mushrooms growing in the woods, some good, some bad. She got herself put on kitchen duty and made Todd a special omelet for breakfast one morning."

"How come the police didn't figure it out?"

"They never called the police. They put out the word that Todd was dead and had a funeral. Covington was the one who told me."

"The local coroner didn't do anything?"

I shrugged. "Why would he? No one had paid any attention to the LOT for years. It was like a tacit agreement or something. Todd was probably paying them off in some way since none of us ever went to school or had our shots or whatever."

Liam shifted next to me. "He played closer to the rules than you'd think, actually. Paid taxes, applied for and received a homeschooling permit. He knew how to keep the cops away. And everyone else."

"If there'd only been one welfare check."

"Yeah, I thought of that," he says, "but my aunt and uncle begged me not to."

"Why?"

"They didn't want all the kids separated from their parents, which they surely would've been."

"But their parents were the ones who put them in danger."

"No guarantee that the foster system would have been any better."

"Who were they to decide that? Or you?"

He rubs at his face. "I made a choice to respect their wishes. They didn't want to put Aaron through an investigation, have him testify, any of it. So instead, I did what I could. I got out as many as I could."

His voice is shaking with emotion, but I feel angry now. For having to relive that horrible day with my mother, even though I brought it up. And with Liam, for not saving enough of us.

"Did you know?" I ask. "Did you know my mother was the one who reached out to you?"

"No."

I'm not sure I believe him, but who am I to call him out?

"How come you never told me about Kiki?" Liam asks.

"I was ashamed."

"Why?"

"First because I left her behind. And then because it was my fault she died."

"I hardly think . . ."

I turn on my side, my back to him. "Please don't, Liam, okay?"

"Okay."

I watch the shadows move across the wall, waiting for Liam's next question.

"Where is she now?" he asks eventually.

"Who?"

"Your mother."

"Why? You think I should turn her in?"

"No."

"I won't."

"I understand."

He slips his arm around me, and I press into him because even though he can't keep the nightmares away, he is the one who's come the closest to doing so.

"You can't turn her in either," I say.

"You don't trust me."

"It's not that. She's my mother. I have to protect her, and even though she was the worst mother in the world, she saved me. She trusted me to keep her secret, and now I've broken that by telling you. I'd rather you just forget that I said anything."

Liam stays quiet for a minute, but he doesn't roll away from me. Not yet.

"Is this what you were dreaming about earlier?" he asks.

"I'm not sure. I never remember my dreams."

"You shouldn't blame yourself."

"Shhh."

"Is Serene with your mother?"

"Yes."

"Do you think that's a good idea?"

"She seemed happy there. She thinks they're her parents. My aunt and uncle thought it was better for Kiki if Serene was raised by my parents, to help her forget the connection. I guess it worked in a way. Besides, I'm not equipped to raise a kid, assuming I could even get custody. Clearly."

Liam hugs me tighter then, and whispers in my ear, "I think you'd be a great mother."

And that's supposed to be so romantic, isn't it? Maybe that's why he said it, or maybe he actually thinks that. But I can't be anyone's mother. I might be able to turn my life around, like JJ imagines, but that would be a step too far.

But like so many things, I can't say this to Liam.

Instead, I say, "Thank you," and let him rock me gently to sleep.

Chapter 40

Unraveling

That night when I told Liam about what my mother did, and some of what happened to Kiki, that could've been the beginning of something between us, something more real because we'd brushed so many secrets aside. Instead, it ended up being the beginning of a wall. It's made up of bricks of things that I've known for years but have only started bothering me now that my watertight compartments have broken down. Things like why Liam didn't call Child Services, and how many things could've been changed and saved if he had.

Kiki would be whole and alive. Serene would never have come to be. Todd would be in jail and exposed, maybe dying, surrounded by other harmers of children, bottom-feeders all. And I could be living a normal life, could have found happiness with an ordinary guy who did ordinary things. I could have a career, never have killed Jessie, never have known Jessie at all.

I know a lot of this isn't fair. Todd didn't make Jessie. She was out there, already rotten, waiting for the opportunity to arise. Our paths could have crossed anyway, and maybe I would've made the same choices. Or maybe I would have chosen to let go, let *her* go, if I were happy. If the LOT were a distant memory that had lost its power to harm or shape me.

The bricks are not all of my making. Liam builds them too. I'm holding back details from him, things that happened with Jessie, things that happened to Kiki. I suspect he's unsure of whether I've actually given up the search for Jessie. It seems out of character for me to have done so after my dogged pursuit. But I don't have the energy to keep up the pretense that I'm still looking for her, even if it creates suspicion.

He is suspicious of me in general now. He'll start to ask questions, like whether I've checked in with the sergeant in Jackson lately, and I'll bite back that I'm not under investigation, and he should drop it, but I'm not sure he ever will. Not till Jessie's found.

Another brick I help him build involves the choice I made about my mother. To let her be. To let her raise Serene. To let her and the other leftovers live in their utopia on a quiet farm in Connecticut.

And then there's all the rest of the secrets, the biggest bricks of all.

I don't tell him that I've recovered the money. Not that this is the biggest thing I'm keeping from him, but still. I made my way through the labyrinth of Jessie's passwords and used the various passports I found to identify her two substantial offshore bank accounts and liquidate them. I'm not a thief, though, so when I unlocked the final key, I used some more tricks I learned from Liam and his cohorts along the way and found a way to send JJ her portion securely, and set up a trust for Serene. I kept my promise to Five and set up a real photography prize in her name in Jackson supplied by an anonymous donation, then salted away the rest of it offshore for myself, for a rainy day.

I don't tell Liam that I spend my mornings in the bathroom reading the Jackson paper online, looking for signs that Jessie's popped up. As a result, that town is so alive in my mind that I feel like I know many of the locals, those who show up in the paper on a regular basis, anyway. Sometimes I forget, and I start telling Liam a story I read that day, and he gets this puzzled expression on his face. I tell him it's my way of keeping track of the investigation, setting up a Google Alert for stories that mention the town, but like so many things I say to him now, I'm not sure he believes me.

There are so many secrets, it's hard to keep track.

In the end I think this is what breaks us. Opening up to him enough for him to see, or sense, the vast ocean of things I've kept to myself was a mistake. People always say that it's bad to keep secrets, that they corrode trust. But I don't think that's true. It's *knowing* there are secrets that you'll never have access to that rubs away at us. I can't tell him everything about me, but what I have said is too much.

It doesn't happen all at once, us falling apart. That would be easier. There isn't any dramatic fight; we could get past that, forgive each other, and make up with sex. Instead, one night, needing more sleep than I can get with Liam watching over me, I don't go to his place. I don't answer his texts. I just fall into the best sleep I've had in months in my own bed.

In the morning, I watch JJ's new show on my iPad as I listen to my roommates rumble around, going through their morning routines. Then I start looking for apartments on Craigslist.

I need some space to write, I tell Liam. I found my original thesis in a box at the back of my closet. After I sent it to my old editor at FeedNews, they had to print a retraction. While it was more time in the public eye, at least this time it was positive press and got me an assignment. I mostly have to write on spec, and my articles are fact-checked to infinity, but I sell them, and it's a foothold to getting back my career.

JJ's right that people like a second-chance story. She's making a comeback, too. Her first episode is about a foster house, not an orphanage exactly, but a family who takes twenty children at a time. Cooking's a major deal in this house, so she spent a week with them, teaching the kids how to make a week's worth of basics, then opened it up to donations. They flood in and the show goes viral. JJ's back, winning smile firmly in place, eternal optimism achievable. She tells me to write about it, and it's one of the first pieces I sell.

Liam visits my new apartment, but he doesn't like it. He doesn't ask me to move in with him, though, either. We work best in transience, I've decided. Or maybe that's just me. I don't know how to keep my secrets with someone I also depend on to make sure there's toilet paper in the house and milk in the fridge.

Maybe we could have found a way. I like to think that. As the nightmares recede and I have things to do to occupy myself, I'm not thinking all day long about what JJ and I did.

As the months pass without a body being discovered.

Then I get a text.

"Something's been bugging me since that day at the dive bar last summer," Covington says one day in early June, almost a year to the day since I met Jessica Two. He wanted to drop by to see the new place, he'd said.

"What day at the dive bar?" I ask, trying to keep my voice even, as if I've forgotten all about that conversation.

"When I told you my theory about Todd last year," Covington says. He looks tall in my tiny apartment, as if he might not fit on most of the furniture.

I go to the fridge in the alcove kitchen and grab the beer I know he wants. "That someone killed him?"

"Yeah."

I walk into the living room and hand him the beer, keeping my hands steady. "Have you been talking to Liam?"

"What? Why?"

"Nothing. Have a seat," I say. He sits, and I do the same on the couch across from him. They only got delivered last week, these couches, my first purchase with the money I got back from Jessie.

Covington takes a swig of his beer, then holds it awkwardly between his hands.

"What's going on, Cov?"

"It's been bugging me, like I said."

"What?"

He makes eye contact briefly, then looks away. "Your reaction."

I try to think back. We were drunk when he brought that up. I'm sure I denied knowing anything about it. Called it out for the silly thought it was.

"What do you mean?"

"You didn't seem surprised."

"I . . . What?"

"It didn't seem like news to you." Covington takes what I can only consider as a nervous sip of his beer, then puts it down on the table.

"What are you suggesting? That I somehow snuck back into the LOT and killed Todd?"

"No."

"Then what?"

He doesn't say anything.

"What, Covington? Jesus."

He glances at me again, then away. "How did Kiki die?"

I do not like the direction this is going in. "I told you, she killed herself."

"You didn't tell me that, actually."

"I didn't?"

"No. You told me she died, and that the funeral had been family only, and you said something about an accident."

"It was an accidental overdose. That's what I said."

"That's not what you said. And that's not true."

I look to the door. He's between me and it, though if I move fast enough, I'd probably get out before he reacts. But there's no point in trying to escape him. Better to sit here and learn what he knows, then make a plan.

"What business is it of yours how she died?" I ask. "Just because you shared a kiss—"

"It was more than that. I cared for her. And she cared for me."

I shrug. "She left you and went to Ohio."

He winces. "She needed to clear her head before we could start a real relationship."

"Fucking Todd."

"Yeah, him. But also, you."

"Me?"

"You wanted her to be something she wasn't."

"You don't know what you're talking about."

"I'm only telling you what Kiki told me."

I swallow my pain. I need to stay focused and not get distracted.

"She killed herself, okay?" I say. "I was ashamed to tell people. It felt like my fault."

"Why?"

"For a lot of reasons I don't have to discuss with you." I consider my words. "But how do you know what happened to Kiki? You been investigating me, Covington? Putting your Liam training to good use?"

"I wanted some answers."

"What did you come here to say?"

He stands and starts to pace back and forth in the small space.

"Todd's death was bugging me," he says. "It got me thinking about Kiki. How I'd never known what happened to her because I'd shoved all those feelings away after I found out she was dead because that was easier. Then that stuff with that girl, that other Jessica who defrauded you, something there was bugging me, too, and I couldn't quite place it. So, I started digging around, and, well, I ended up going to see your parents."

"My parents?"

"In Connecticut."

My stomach's in knots. "You have a nice reunion?"

Covington grimaces. "Ugh, no. It was awful seeing them all together. But Kiki's mom was nice to me. She showed me some pictures she had of Kiki, and that's when I noticed it."

"What?"

"Her name on the front of the photograph album. Her *real* name."

"Jessica Katherine Williams," I say.

He nods. "And her birthday."

"The same day as me."

"The same. I'd forgotten about that. Kiki mentioned it once, but I never thought about the two of you having the same name because I'd always known her as Kiki. Even in the LOT."

"We called her that since she was two. Before you were born."

"Her mother said. But not why they gave you the same name."

"It was a kind of joke between them, I think. The two families. That's what my mother told me. Because it was funny that two cousins were born on the same day in the same place, so why not take it a step further. Jessica was Todd's mother's name."

"That's weird."

"They were weird, in case you hadn't noticed."

"Anyway, the more I thought about it," Covington says, "the more it seemed like too many coincidences. Too many Jessicas." He picks up his beer and drains it. "And then your mother told me what she did."

"What?"

What the actual fuck? What is wrong with her?

"She told me what she did to Todd," Covington says. "And why."

"She told you about Serene?"

He nods. "I think it was because she could tell that I cared about Kiki. But I'm not sure. She seems a bit off."

"She is, obviously. Your parents too. Because they're living there also, right?" I say. "That's how you knew how to find my parents?"

"They can't seem to quit one another."

"Apparently. You never suspected about Serene?"

He shakes his head. "After you left, there was this strange three months or so where we were all forced to live in the Gathering Place together, but then all the kids were sent back up the hill, including me and the few others who'd been allowed to stay with their parents. I didn't see my parents for months, only Todd and the guardians. When we were allowed to come back down the next summer, Kiki was living in the house she built with Sarah. Only we were supposed to call them Tori and Thalia. And your parents had Serene. They told us that she was your mom's kid."

"She was too old to have a kid."

"I know that now, but I was only fourteen. I didn't understand that kind of stuff." He looks at me. "Did you know?"

"No. Kiki never told me."

"I wondered. Anyway, once I learned all of that, I decided to go to Kiki's college in Ohio."

"What? Why?"

"Because I wanted to know what had really happened to her."

"And you didn't trust me to tell you."

"Frankly? No. That's how I found out about her suicide. There was an article in the school newspaper about her." He reaches into his pocket. "I also found this."

He hands it to me. It's a newspaper clipping. I unfold it. It's a picture of Kiki and her roommate from college. They've got their arms around one another and are laughing into the camera. They're wearing Hawaiian leis for some luau party. Did she tell me about that? I can't remember. My eyes trail away from a happy-looking Kiki to her roommate, Jessie. Only she went by the name Karen then.

"That's her, isn't it?" Covington says. "Jessica Two? I recognized her from the wanted poster I found online."

They'd used a picture of Jessie from the school where she worked. She didn't look that different at thirty from how she had looked at twenty-four.

"It's her." My hands flutter at my sides. I'm not mad, or scared. Not yet, anyway. "Why are you here, Covington? To tell me all of this?"

"No." He pulls out his phone. "I read this online this morning."

I take it from him. It's a wire story that hadn't made it into the *Jackson Hole News & Guide* yet. A badly decomposed body was found in Jackson Lake. Female. Late twenties to early thirties. They haven't been able to identify it, but they think it might be associated with a woman who's wanted by the authorities for theft and identity fraud who was last seen in Jackson.

Jessie.

"Is this her too?" Covington asks.

"How am I supposed to know?"

"Come on, Jess."

I stare at him.

"Look, I don't know all the details," Covington says, "but I think I've figured out enough. And I'm not saying I blame you, okay? I might've done the same in your place."

"Why are you here, then?"

"I came to warn you. Liam's been asking questions too. About Kiki. Once this gets out . . . He's not stupid, Jess."

"I know."

He puts his hands on his knees. "That's what I came here to say."

"So what now?"

He stands. "I'm going to go."

"Just like that?"

"Just like that."

He moves toward the door. I stand to follow him. I feel detached from my body, strangely disconnected.

"You okay for money?" Covington asks with his hand on the knob.

"Yeah."

"Good. Just . . . don't leave without telling him goodbye, okay?"

"Who, Liam?"

"He wouldn't take that well."

"He'll be all right."

Covington shakes his head. "He's in love with you."

"He's never told me that. Not really." Only that one text last summer. Same, he'd written. Same.

"Would've thought it was obvious. Anyway, tell him something, okay? Something he can live with."

He opens the door, stops, then leaves without saying anything more.

I sink back into the couch, and the world tilts away from me.

So close, I think. I came so close to getting away with it.

Ohio, May 5, 2016

Dear Jess,

By the time you get this, I won't be here anymore. That sounds more dramatic than I wanted, but I'm not quite sure how to do this. The actual part, I've figured out. I've been seeing a doctor and she's given me pills, only I haven't been taking them. I've saved them and saved them, and I'll take them all at once. Then, hopefully, I'll fall asleep.

They'll find me in the room I shared with *her*. I don't know what made her do it. I would've given her the money if she'd asked. I never cared about it, anyway—that's why I told her about it in the first place. About Todd, all of it. This isn't because she took the money. I loved her, you see? I thought she felt the same. I trusted her. I shared myself with her. She was the first person in my life that I chose. That felt different and so much less complicated than what we'd been through. I thought it was real, but it wasn't. She betrayed me, and it's that I can't live with. Another person I love letting me down like that.

And oh, now I'm letting *you* down. I let people down, I do. Ask your mother. She'll explain. I can't write down why. I've locked it away so deep I can't let it out. But go see her after you get this. Ask her and she'll tell you, and then, maybe, you'll understand.

I love you so much, Jess. I know you think you failed me, but you didn't.

And now I'll be free from all of it for real this time.

Forgive me.

Love, Kiki

June 10, 2021

Dear Liam,

Have I told you enough, my love, for you to understand?

I started writing this as a way to pass the time, and to process what happened. I've had so much time to fill this last year while I watched us disintegrate and I waited to be discovered. Only, if I'm being honest, I didn't think I would be. I truly thought I'd get away with it. All the planning would pay off. So, I was also writing this as, maybe, my true comeback piece. A book. A novel. Who knows? I'd change enough details, if need be. Some chapters I'd take out entirely and replace with the stories I've told you.

But things are not working out like I planned, and I don't want to leave you with questions, so . . . Here's what I did. The unvarnished truth.

That piece I wrote about the Land of Todd, the one that started my career—I wrote that about Kiki. Maybe you've worked that out now that you know about her. I didn't ask her permission, and she wasn't happy about it. It was a shitty thing to do, but I knew she'd forgive me, and I knew it would help me make my mark, so I did it anyway. That should have been a clue to myself. A warning that I wasn't as far away from Todd as I thought.

If I heard it, I ignored it.

Jessie was Kiki's roommate at the school she went to in Ohio. Her name was Karen Rivers then, a name I'd find out later was fake. I don't know what she did before she became Karen. If she'd done anything truly bad already. Perhaps she was escaping a terrible childhood, trying to start over. It's possible those stories she told me about foster care were true. Or maybe her life was idyllic and she was born that way. Nature versus nurture. What would I have been if Todd had never gotten ahold of me? So many questions.

It doesn't matter why, though; it only matters what.

The consequences. The ripple effects.

Bad luck for Kiki to end up roommates with her. Worse luck still when Kiki told her about the money from the settlement. Jessie befriended her, seduced her, gained her trust, and took all Kiki's money. And then she disappeared.

Kiki was devastated. Not about the money, she wrote me, but about the betrayal of her trust. I get that, but I've never understood why she felt like killing herself was the only option. Why she couldn't reach out to me for help. That's probably my fault. If I'd done the right thing from the beginning and gotten her proper help, she would've made a different choice.

You can drive yourself crazy with what-ifs, I've learned.

I don't know what Jessie thought would happen. I presume she didn't know Kiki would take it badly and that her betrayal would be one straw too many for Kiki to bear.

Didn't know or didn't care. Another thing that's impossible to know and doesn't matter in the end.

But I do know that she had no idea Kiki would send me a letter before she did it, telling me what had happened, why she was ending her life. Because of who. Which meant I knew something Jessie didn't. I knew about *her*. That she was responsible for Kiki's suicide.

I told the police what she'd done; that's how I found out about her fake identity. But she was missing. Living under some other name, maybe in another state. They said it wasn't going to be easy to find her.

I thought I could do better. I started off trying to track her down. I used the skills you taught me, and the revelation I had one night, something I'd overlooked. Kiki's driver's license was missing. When I collected her things from her dorm, it wasn't there. I couldn't find her Social Security card, either, or the birth certificate I'd helped her get. I was sure Karen was using it, because who would look for a dead girl?

Turned out I was right. Karen was living as Jessica Williams outside Chicago. I held on to that information for a while, watching her from afar. I'm not sure why I didn't turn her in immediately. Maybe I was thinking of revenge, even then. And then she moved to Wilmington and floated that story about winning the lottery, and I couldn't help but wonder. Why would she draw attention to herself like that?

I looked into it and found the police report that she'd filed after "Jessica" stole her money. And there it was—her whole new scam laid out. She'd realized how much easier it was to take someone's money when you had their ID. There's no photograph on a birth certificate or a Social Security card. If you find someone with the same name, you're all set. But she had to be careful. If she was going to use Kiki's identity, she had to have an alibi. Be hiding in plain sight. If she played the victim card, she might escape detection if anyone ever went looking.

I'm not sure what tipped her off that there were other Jessica Williamses. Maybe it was something as simple as a Google Alert. I get a dozen hits a week for someone with my name. I just prayed that Kiki hadn't told her about me. How our parents had given us the same name when we'd been born on the same day.

I used a guy I'd met researching a piece to help me track down the other Jessicas. There are eight of us in North America. I watched all of them as closely as I could. I was worried about JJ when I saw her get famous, and sure enough, once that piece was written about her, Jessie struck. It was like watching a car wreck in slow motion. The piece. JJ tweeting that she was going to that cooking exhibition. Her going silent. Then those terrible tweets from her account. I saw it all and it felt like there was nothing I could do to stop it. But it solidified what I wanted to do. If I could get someone to help me.

I struggled with that for a while until it struck me.

Who better to ask than JJ?

It took a while to gain JJ's trust, but I'd learned a thing or two living in the Land of Todd. I worked on her slowly, and in the end I'm not sure she'd even say that what we did was my idea. It was something we agreed on together.

This was the plan. In the end, it was simple. Step 1: make myself a perfect target and get Jessica to take my money. Step 2: act like I had "tracked" down another victim, i.e., Jessie. Step 3: meet Jessie and get her to believe my story and agree to help me. Step 4: have JJ "appear" on Facebook from the same online trap I laid for Jessie. Step 5: get us all together. Step 6: use one of the other Jessicas as bait to get Jessie somewhere we could expose her and finish her.

That last part JJ and I left unspoken. But we both understood.

What else? I was the one who made sure my plagiarism was uncovered. I was the leaker. I knew it would cause a fuss, and I was delighted when it worked.

JJ and I were careful. We communicated through a secure messaging app and wiped our messages constantly. If anyone went looking, the only thing they'd find were the Facebook messages from last summer, when she reached out to me when I was with Jessie.

And I used you, my love, to redo all the things I'd done in the first place. Find Jessie. Find the other Jessicas.

Jessie went along with all of it, even though I realize now because of what she said on Jackson Lake about researching all of us that she must've known who I was from the beginning. How she must've been laughing inside, thinking she was taking me too. She really couldn't help herself, which is what I had been counting on.

Not everything went according to plan, but we were nimble. We adjusted. We shuffled the cards enough times to keep her following the wrong one.

We won. We took her money, and also her life.

Like she'd taken Kiki's. Like she'd taken JJ's. Like she thought she was taking mine.

I should've left you out of it, but I needed an alibi too. To leave a trail that would look like someone trying to put together a puzzle rather than carry out a plan.

The one thing I didn't plan was that night at your apartment, or the days that followed.

I almost gave it up then. I almost called it off.

But what if I could have it all? You *and* revenge. You and justice for Kiki.

Too tempting.

I'm sorry. I did a bad thing, but there's a certain justice to it, isn't there? And we're going to have to pay. Despite all our plans, JJ and I will both have to disappear.

Please, don't try to find me.

Please, let me go.

There are others who need you, and I've been too much trouble from the get-go.

Love, Jess

ACKNOWLEDGMENTS

This is my tenth published novel. Such a crazy sentence to write. When I sat down all those years ago (fourteen by the time you read this) to write I did not know what, I never could have imagined that I'd be here. Ten books. More than a million copies sold worldwide. Bestsellers in several countries. They tell you to dream big, but I never would've gotten this right.

I've gotten a lot of help along the way. My agent, Abigail Koons, and the team at Park & Fine. My editors, Jodi Warshaw at Lake Union and Laurie Grassi at Simon & Schuster Canada. The editors who acquired me in the first place in Canada, in the US, and in many countries around the world. The publishing and marketing teams at Lake Union and Simon & Schuster Canada. My sister, Cam, for reading as I write and fixing my mistakes. My mom for being the eagle-eye finder of typos on the final-pass pages. My writer peeps: Randy Susan Meyers and Matt Norman for reading an early draft of this and helping me craft it; Shawn Klomparens; my writing partners and daily partners in crime, Elyssa Friedman and Kim Roosevelt, whose new (but forever) friendships have enriched my life; Therese Walsh for being a sounding board.

I also couldn't do this without my friends and family, and especially Tasha, Sara, Candice, my husband, David, and the reason this book exists in the first place: Christie Brown. Thank you for having such a common name that we got pulled over at every border crossing for two years! Because of you, this book exists.

Finally, thank you, dear reader, and especially if you've followed me from *Spin* to now. I write for you.

BOOK-CLUB QUESTIONS

1. When the novel opens, we learn that Jessica Williams has recently been fired for plagiarism but managed to finagle a good settlement on her way out the door by essentially blackmailing her employer. What were your initial thoughts about her character? Did you feel bad when she returned from Mexico and found out that all her settlement money was gone, or did you think that she somehow deserved it?

2. As we get to know Jessica, we realize certain things—for instance, how she was raised in a cult without a typical family structure. Did this make you change your perception of her character? Does it excuse some of the things she did later on?

3. Jessica has tried to move on from her upbringing and lead a "normal" life, but it seems as though her only real friendships are with The Twists, people who have also experienced a similar upbringing. She often repeats the "Toddisms" that were hammered into her as a child.

How difficult do you think it would be for someone to be "deprogrammed" after a childhood like that? What would be their challenges integrating into society afterward?

4. Jessica is determined to find the person who scammed her and get her money back. Do you think that determination and resilience is somehow a product of growing up in the LOT? Do you see any similarities between her and Todd?

5. Liam seems wary of Jessica's plans but is nonetheless keen to go along with her, and he acts like a pseudo father figure to her. Do you think he has been harboring feelings for her for some time, or is he merely taking advantage of a new opportunity? Did you believe Jessie when she said that he was with other women he's helped out? Jessica seems jealous whenever Liam interacts with another woman—do you think that's why she didn't introduce him to Kiki?

6. When looking for Jessica Two's other victims, Jessica finds "Jessie" (who we later learn is the scammer). Jessie is effectively "hiding in plain sight" and succeeding in her criminal activities. Why do you think she agrees to go along with Jessica and put that all at risk?

7. When Jessica and Jessie are in Philadelphia looking for JJ, they participate in a few scams themselves, beating the three-card monte man at his own game and running a Bar Bill con on an easy mark. Did this raise any red flags for you or make you suspect that there was more to know about Jessie and/or Jessica?

8. What are your thoughts on Jessica and Kiki's relationship? When Jessica left the LOT, she tried to get Kiki to go with her, but did she try hard enough? When Kiki does finally leave five years later, she's far more vulnerable than Jessica was. Is Jessica at fault for not getting "real" help for Kiki and for her suicide? Can you understand Jessica's desire for revenge?

9. Jessica's mother, Therese/Charlotte, was complacent during the hardships Jessica endured growing up, but reveals that she was instrumental in Jessica's escape from the LOT when she realized what Todd's intentions were. Do you believe her? Do you think she's fit to raise Kiki's daughter, Serene? Many of the former cult members are still living together—do you think they're carrying on Todd's vision or they simply don't know what to do with themselves?

10. It took Jessica many years of planning to find Jessica Two and enact her grand plan. Do you think there is something pathological in that? Even with all that planning, things still didn't work out perfectly. Do you think Jessica intended to kill Jessica Two from the start?

11. When Jessica Two's body is found, Jessica realizes that she needs to disappear and writes a goodbye letter to Liam. Were you disappointed that the body turned up? Do you think Jessica should face the consequences of her actions? Do you think she will get away with everything?

ABOUT THE AUTHOR

Photo © 2016 Jason Trott

Catherine McKenzie is the #1 Amazon Charts bestselling author of ten novels, including *I'll Never Tell*, *The Good Liar*, *Fractured*, and *Hidden*, which have been translated into numerous languages. Her books are routinely chosen as best of the month by Goodreads, and *Smoke* was an Amazon Top 100 Book of 2015. An avid skier and runner and a graduate of McGill University, the internationally bestselling author practices law in Montreal, where she was born and raised. Visit Catherine online at www.catherinemckenzie.com.

differentials tended to be small, while diet (40 percent sweet potatoes, 31 percent vegetables and 28 percent grain), as Sidney Gamble discovered in his famous 1920s study of Ting hsien in Hebei, differed little except in quantity between most rural income groups.[6]

Although these farms are often described as the first shoots of rural capitalism, Huang has shown that northern managerial farms "resembled capitalist enterprises only in their use of wage labor: they clearly failed to generate any real advances in labor productivity, whether through economies of scale, increased capital use, or technological improvement." Likewise, the elite kinship networks so central to the highly commercialized economies of the lower Yangzi or the Pearl River deltas were peripheral in the more egalitarian north.

Huang argues that the harsher northern environment and relatively greater frequency of natural disasters were crucial factors in differentiating its social structures and land-tenure patterns from the south.[7] In a climate zone where, as we have seen, annual rainfall variability exceeded 30 percent and irrigation was the exception rather than the rule, average rates of return on agriculture were generally too marginal to attract substantial merchant capital. But the environmental instability of agriculture was counterbalanced by the deeply anchored monolithic character of the smallholder social order supported by a towering imperial state.[8]

If to most foreigners the cultural and ecological landscapes of the north epitomized China's inability to modernize, to others they represented the very essence of China's epochal achievement as a civilization. Francis Nichols, the American journalist who, as we saw earlier, traveled to Zian in 1901 to report on famine relief and the Boxer aftermath for the Christian Herald, discovered Jeffersonian as well as Confucian virtues in the Shaanxi yeomanry. Although the peasants were poor, "there is a complete absence of that condition that we call 'poverty.' … By Shensi roadsides one finds some professional beggars, most of whom are opium-victims, but here are very few 'unemployed,' except as the result of a universal calamity like a famine or a flood. Shensi farms seldom contain more than 3 or 4 acres, but they often remain in the possession of one family for generations. No one ever seems to desire more land or hold it solely for the purpose of selling it again." Moreover, Nichols discovered that Qing despotism, supposedly embodied in the mandarin suppression of all free speech, was belied by a rambunctious civil culture of irreverent political gossip and scalding public criticism.[9]

In "hidden Shensi," where he temporarily swelled the foreign population, Nichols was overwhelmed by the cultural and agronomic continuity of contemporary peasant life with ancient Han civilization. As a courageous critic of imperialist calumnies against the Chinese, he is easily forgiven for romanticizing peasant traditionalism as well as for failing to recognize the changed relations of production that were partly responsible for hideous starvation during the 1899–1901 drought. Everywhere in Shaanxi, the declining economic and ecological viability of smallholder agriculture over the course of the nineteenth century was expressed by increased peasant dependence upon cash crops like opium and cotton. Nichols's admirable farmers were almost universally entrapped in a hopeless system of petty commodity production on subminimal plots that annually wagered household survival on fickle market prices and rainfall patterns. At the same time, vital rural handicrafts were under siege from manufactured imports. Although the only indications of overseas trade (as opposed to traditional inter-Asian trade) that Nichols could find in the markets of Zian were imported cotton thread and some cotton fabrics (marked "Fall River, Massachusetts"), these were potent enough symbols of the destabilizing impact of the world market upon inland China.[10]

The Commercialization of Subsistence

The so-called "single whip" reforms under Zhang Juzheng in the late sixteenth century, which transmuted corvées and revenues-in-kind into cash taxes, had inexorably monetarized subsistence production. As immigration and high fertility rates supported by Qing antifamine policies began to rebuild populations in the provinces devastated by late Ming warfare (especially Henan, Shaanxi and Shanxi, where as much as one-third of the cultivated land had been depopulated) to their historical maximums, the customs of partible inheritance generated growing pressure on farmland.[11] In the absence of the European alternatives of rapidly growing cities and overseas colonies to absorb supernumerary agricultural labor, Qing China struggled to sustain its standard of living within traditional parameters of land use and agricultural technique.

Initially, there was stunning success. In her recent study of Shaanxi's densely populated Wei River Valley—the site of terrible mortality in 1877–78 and again in 1899–1901—Laura Murray confirms the role of new world crops (especially sweet potatoes and maize) and marginal land reclamation in accommodating population growth at constant levels of per capita output through the mid eighteenth century. By the 1780s, however, the Wei Valley peasantry was caught in what Murray (borrowing from Mark Elvin) characterizes as a "high-level equilibrium trap" in which increasing labor inputs realized diminishing returns in crop yield. With average cultivated land per capita reduced to three-quarters of an acre, even the most intense efforts by Wei farmers could barely produce the caloric minimum of grain to maintain their continued labor. In this context, cash crops' higher value per unit of land made them irresistibly attractive to the poorest strata of the peasantry.[12]

Commercialization on these terms was usually more "a gamble for survival" than an exercise in optimal resource utilization, and cash crops were immediately sold to purchase food and pay taxes, not used to accumulate capital or land. As Murray emphasizes, "land use tended to shift from grain crops to cash crops when population density reached the point that average holdings were too small to supply adequate subsistence grains ... Many families [were only] able to survive on plots too small for subsistence farming because of the higher value of cash crops. Most counties with a high level of commercialization also had grain deficits, and their residents depended on complex trade networks."[13]

The Wei Valley case was probably typical of the logic of subsistence cash-cropping throughout north China. "From their differing perspectives, Chao Kang, Philip Huang, and Ramon Myers have all shown that faced with diminishing farm size, the vast majority of peasants were able to sustain their livelihoods only by the ability to intensify, to turn to subsidiary occupations, and to switch to cash crops."[14] Huang, in particular, cautions against the common assumption of development theorists that such peasants, simply because of their dependence on commodity networks, were suddenly transformed into the competitive, incipient capitalist subjects of neoclassical economics. "This kind of market involvement should not be mistaken for entrepreneurial marketing, nor should such peasant behavior be mistaken for profit-maximizing rationality. Theirs was the rationality of survival, not of profit maximization." Moreover, Huang offers a useful distinction between the "survival-driven commercialization" so common in north China and the "extraction-driven commercialization" in the more class-stratified Yangzi Delta, where peasants were forced into the market primarily to earn rent payments to landlords and interest payments to moneylenders.[15]

North China peasants, within the limits of a relatively uniform ecology, embraced several alternative systems of cash crop subsistence. Throughout the Yellow River plain, for example, villages commonly sold wheat to the cities or distilleries (like those around Linqing on the Grand Canal) and used the cash to buy coarse grains—millet, sorghum and buckwheat—for their own diet. Likewise in Shandong, along the route of the Jiaozhou–Jinan railroad, tobacco monoculture supplanted grain production on much of the best farmland. Peanuts were commercially important by the eve of the Boxer uprising in southern Hebei as well as in the semi-arid foothills just north of the Great Wall.[16]

Opium cultivation, meanwhile, was a primitive form of import substitution, embraced, despite its theoretical illegality, by magistrates and merchants throughout northwest and southwest China. In Shanxi the governor had sponsored opium cultivation as early as 1852 in a desperate attempt to bolster revenues and peasant incomes. Poppies quickly supplanted so much grain acreage that missionaries, like the American Presbyterian Dr. Elkins, blamed the extreme famine mortality of 1877–78 on the opium boom.[17] In the Wei Valley, opium got a later start, becoming a major commercial crop only after 1870, when fiscally strapped county governments began to encourage its export to other parts of northern China. Once established, however, its growth was dramatic. By 1890, opium had become the livelihood of a majority of the peasantry in the eastern counties of the valley.[18]

For marginal peasants everywhere in China, however, the most important cash crop was cotton. It had two principal virtues. In the first place, there was huge, relatively stable internal demand. Second, peasants could

Figure 11.1 Home Cotton Spinning
Spinning cotton yarn was often the margin of survival on undersized farm plots.

add value by processing cotton as spun yarn and woven fabric. Moreover, from the merchant standpoint, rural surplus labor was more rationally exploited at home than in the workshop. "Once the marginal product of labor fell below the subsistence wage," Madeleine Zelin explains, "it became more economical for merchants to contract or purchase goods from household producers than to produce them themselves using hired labor. Surplus labor was thus retained at home, where the peasant and his family, wishing to garner whatever they could from their residual productivity, were willing to work for less than subsistence wages. The system was possible because the equipment needed to produce yarn, cloth, and other handicraft items was relatively cheap, and problems of marketing were solved by the dense network of rural markets in place by the early Qing."[19]

Originally, the north China plain had been simply a periphery to the lower Yangzi textile revolution, exchanging raw cotton for cotton cloth. The northern winters, however, gave peasant households a long slack time in which they could concentrate on spinning and weaving for household use and sale. In Arthur Smith's famous account of Village Life in China (1899), the Shandong-based missionary marveled at the grim dedication of north China's peasants-cum-handloom weavers: "In some regions every family owns a loom (one of the clumsy machines exiled from the West a century ago) and it is not uncommon for the members of a family to take turns, the husband weaving until midnight, when the wife takes up the task till daylight (often in cellars two-thirds underground, damp, unventilated, and unwholesome)."[20]

As in pre-industrial Europe, a vast system of cotton handicrafts emerged, centered on the Yellow River Delta, which, in turn, stimulated the further conversion of cereal acreage to cotton in counties as far away as the loess plateaux. Simultaneously, new world crops like maize and sweet potatoes, which demanded less labor for higher yields, allowed producers to devote more land and labor to all phases of cotton production. Thus by the middle of the eighteenth century, north China was second only to the lower Yangzi in cotton cultivation, which "replacing grain, occupied an estimated 20–30% of all agricultural land."[21] It was not rare to find counties near river or canal transport, as in southern and central Hebei, where 80 to 90 percent of the population derived its principal subsistence from trading cotton cloth (sold as far away as Korea) for millet. Indeed for poorer peasants forced to lease land, "there was often no choice at all: once rental terms on land that could grow cotton came to be set according to the market potential of that crop, no tenant could really afford to grow cereals."[22]

In good years, therefore, cash cropping allowed basically "sub-subsistence" farms to survive in great numbers. Although cotton required twice as much labor per mu as sorghum or millet, this was not a problem in an "involuted" economy where labor was abundant and land was scarce. But cotton cultivation in north China "cut both ways," as Huang has emphasized in his study of the Hebei–northwest Shandong region. "The smallholder found that, though his returns became higher, so too did his expenses. The risks from natural or man-made disaster were thus correspondingly greater." Whereas millet and sorghum depend upon the late summer monsoon, cotton requires ample rainfall or irrigation in the spring: "a relatively dry season at best, with only 10–15 percent of the total annual precipitation." To the extent that households derived increasing subsistence from the sale of cotton or cotton handicrafts, their survival was mortgaged more precariously than before against ENSO fluctuations.

"Drought in the spring could bring total disaster to a household completely dependent on cotton."[23]

The boom–bust cycle of cotton production also reinforced social stratification, enlarging the ranks of poor peasants or laborers dependent upon seasonal or permanent wage labor. Since partible inheritance dissolved most village-level concentrations of wealth after a generation or two, the growth of a rich peasant class in north China in the Victorian era was less dramatic than the accumulation of mendicancy and instability below. Unlike the Yangzi Delta, agrarian immiseration in the North was not counterbalanced by the consolidation of big mercantile or agrarian capital. In drought-ravaged northern Shaanxi, where survivors of the Long March would regroup in 1935, "it could be said that socioeconomic differences within the region were really a matter of varying depths of poverty."[24] Reliance on the market only exacerbated the radical nakedness of these pauper layers in face of the threats of drought and flood. Huang cites the apprehensions of a mid-nineteenth-century magistrate in a Shandong county where most of the sown land was dedicated to cotton. "The rich do not store grain, and the poor rely entirely on hiring out and the board that comes with wage labour. Once confronted with natural disaster and bad harvests, they are at a complete loss."[25]

Micro-commercialization in addition added new exposures to such man-made disasters (often interacting with the natural) as commodity cycles, price inflation and monetary speculation. The diversion of so much cultivable acreage from grain production made tens of millions of formerly autonomous peasants directly dependent upon the grain trade and the price ratio between cash crops and subsistence cereals. Folk textiles, meanwhile, faced the competition after 1880 of factory-produced imports from India and Japan. Handspun yarn declined from 98 percent of China's consumption in 1876 to little more than 40 percent in 1900, and cotton merchants were transformed from peddlers of domestic production into salesmen of foreign yarn. India's export to Asia, principally China, meanwhile increased from 21.3 million pounds in 1878 to nearly 300 million pounds in 1905.[26] The most spectacular surge in yarn imports—40 percent in value in a single year—occurred, ominously enough, between 1898 and 1899.[27]

"A peasant spinner," Huang emphasizes, "simply could not overcome the overwhelming advantage of a technology by which, according to one estimate, he could be outproduced by as much as 8,000 percent by a worker using a power spindle. The result was a product so cheap it sometimes sold close to the cost of raw cotton."[28] It was not surprising that rural Chinese were baffled by the origin of such cheap thread. Thus a Shaanxi spinner whom Francis Nichols interviewed in 1901 "accounted for [the cheapness of American cotton thread] by the theory that the United States was an island not far from China. When I told him that the country from which the thread came was 18,000 li from the plain of Sian, he shook his head dubiously. 'The thread would cost more,' he said, 'if it had to be brought such a long distance.'"[29] Although handloom weaving, which benefited from better factory-made yarn, would struggle on against machine competition for another generation, the collapse of cotton spinning in the 1890s had profound repercussions for the poorest strata of north China peasants.

Esherick in his study of the social origins of the Boxer movement, as we have seen, argues that western Shandong became the seedbed of revolt in the late 1890s precisely because of its combined vulnerability to natural disaster and foreign textile imports. The changed course of the Yellow River after 1855 and the consequent silting up of the Grand Canal, combined with an increased frequency of flood and drought, had made the depressed regions along the Shandong–Hebei and Shandong–Jiangsu–Henan borders ever more dependent on cotton handicrafts for sheer survival. "Too isolated and too lacking in alternative resources to enjoy any of the stimulative effects that the treaty port economies sometimes generated in their more immediate hinterlands," western Shandong was economically devastated in the 1890s by the loss of its traditional markets to factory-made Indian cotton yarn and cloth.[30] The imports were the dragons' teeth, sown by the world market, that eventually grew into peasant insurrection.

Depletion of the Granaries

The commercialization of subsistence in north China was only weakly supported by long-distance grain trading. The raw cotton and cotton handicrafts, wheat, tobacco and opium grown by poor peasants were principally exchanged within "cellular" local markets usually coinciding with county boundaries or, more rarely, with the north China regional system.[31] There was an insufficient two-way flow of goods between the periodically grain-deficit north and the surplus-producing Yangzi Valley to protect against harvest shortfalls on a large scale. As late as 1900, the inter-regional trade of farm products was only 7 percent of total empire-wide production.[32] Regular long-distance grain trading was confined to east–west corridors within southern China—for example, from Sichuan and Hunan down the Yangzi River, or from Guangxi to Guangdong—where economic specialization was most developed. By contrast, the flow of grain from south to north, frequently against the gravity of market prices, required the heavy lifting of the imperial tribute system. Ironically, as northern peasants increasingly staked their survival on cash crops, they became, if anything, more dependent on the state's capacity to ensure the inter-regional redistribution of grain outside of market mechanisms. And this depended, in the first place, on the empire's fiscal health.[33]

"The eighteenth century," Susan Naquin and Evelyn Rawski emphasize, "was a period of surplus revenues for the Qing state: bulging treasuries and a fat Privy Purse, the product not only of peace and prosperity but also of the successful tightening of control over tax remittances from the provinces under Yongzheng [emperor]."[34] On the eve of the French Revolution, the Qing treasury still had a surplus of 70 million taels, but this was rapidly expended in costly military campaigns or squandered by corrupt courtiers. By the time that the Jiaqing emperor took the throne in 1796, the Golden Age had ended and fiscal crisis was becoming chronic. The turning point was a millenarian peasant uprising in the disaster-prone border region of western Shandong ("repeatedly afflicted by either drought or flooding of the Huai and Yellow Rivers").[35] The ensuing decade-long war (1796–1804) against the White Lotus rebels—"the first major human calamity (renhuo) in about 120 years"—sapped both the treasury and tribute grain reserves.[36] "The food supply priorities of the state shifted to provisioning large numbers of troops": a diversion that would become almost total during the later Taiping, Nian and Muslim civil wars.[37]

Immensely costly flood catastrophes, which had no equivalent in the eighteenth century, also conspired to push the late Qing state deep into insolvency. There were no less than seventeen consecutive years of flooding between 1839 and the final Yellow River cataclysm of 1855.[38] "The cost to the state in social disruption, lost agricultural income, and relief and repair funds was immense. Combined with the expense of the Opium War and the state's already weakened fiscal conditions, these floods left the state treasury barren."[39] Even greater calamities, of course, followed in the 1850s when the rain-swollen Yellow River hijacked the course of the Daqing River (one of its ancestral channels) to switch deltas from the Yellow Sea to the Gulf of Bohai just as the Taiping revolution was cutting off Beijing's all-important revenues and grain tributes from the Yangzi Valley.

The Qing fiscal system, as we saw earlier, was additionally undermined by price inflation rooted in China's opium-generated trade deficits as well as the exchange perturbations that followed the Great Powers' adoption of the gold standard in the 1870s. Despite desperate efforts to insulate taxes from monetary erosion by maintaining a favorable copper/silver ratio, Wang Yeh-chien has estimated that the real value of land revenues declined by almost two-thirds from the Golden Age of the 1750s to the Boxer uprising. From the mid nineteenth century the Qing had mixed success in using commercial taxes, special surcharges and customs revenue to arrest the erosion of their traditional agrarian tax-base. Their increasing reliance on tax farmers to collect old and new revenues only increased the illegal "leakage." At the end of day, however, the fiscal crisis came to weigh most heavily upon provincial and county governments, which depended even more than Beijing on land revenue yet were increasingly expected to shoulder additional responsibilities for self-defense, flood control, irrigation and famine relief.[40]

Fiscal crisis directly translated into reduced administrative capacity and indirectly into diminished peasant food security, at least in areas poorly served by the inter-regional rice trade. The ever-normal and charity granary systems which stored as much as 48 million shih of reserve rice, wheat and millet in the high Qing were rapidly depleted.[41] "Even in the early eighteenth century, when the population of China was not much more than half of its 1840 (or 1930) level, this amount probably represented little more than 3 or 4 per cent of the nation's grain output."[42] Will cites an edict of 1799 complaining that only one-quarter of the ever-normal granaries had stored their full quotas.[43] Reduced to these levels, the imperial granaries were no longer able to act as an economic flywheel "normalizing" grain prices. By the 1820s, according to R. Bin Wong, the empire-wide grain reserves had fallen below 30 million shih; by the 1850s, they were under 20 million.[44] Twenty years later, at the onset of famine in 1876, there was probably less than 10 million shih left in the entire system.[45]

At a local level, this was often equivalent to complete collapse. Even in the Golden Age, the ever normal mechanism of restocking granaries with autumn purchases had broken down in much of the northwest. Granaries in Shaanxi and Gansu were forced to distribute grain more frequently than they could afford by their own account, and the ensuring deficit had to be financed by Beijing.[46] From the calamitous watershed of the White Lotus Rebellion, the regional disequilibrium between annual harvest and minimum consumption was exacerbated by a vicious circle of declining agricultural productivity, ethno-religious warfare and government insolvency.[47] Gentry-managed community and charity granaries, which took up some of the burden of food security elsewhere (Hunan and Sichuan, for example), were ineffective in braking the decline of state granaries in the impoverished loess areas. As a result, granary inventories in some counties of Shaanxi had fallen to less than 10 percent of their quotas by the early 1870s.[48] On the eve of the great drought, in other words, northwest China was ripe for catastrophe.

The empire-wide rundown in ever-normal granary inventories was also accompanied by an increasing diversion of tribute grain flows from the inland north China plain. Although, as Dwight Perkins points out, the "amount of grain going north to Peking was trivial in comparison to total national output (0.2–0.3 per cent)," it represented about 15 percent of the revenues of the central government, and, as we saw in the case of the 1743 drought, constituted a strategic famine reserve close at hand in north China. Most of the tribute was supplied by four provinces (Jiangsu, Jiangxi, Anhui and northern Zhejiang), and there was intense lobbying by the Jiangnan elites to substitute the maritime route for the Grand Canal. "Beginning in the 1870s, the coastal steamer rapidly replaced grain-tribute junks on the Grand Canal. By the 1890s, the only substantial amounts of grain carried by canal junk were the shipments of millet from Shantung." Beijing's port of Tianjin (Tientsin) boomed as a result, while the older Canal entrepôts with their large workforces of bargemen and laborers (key constituencies of the Boxer uprising) declined into permanent depression.[49] Although the imperial granaries at Tongzhou, near Beijing, were still theoretically available for relief campaigns, Will shows that by the end of the Jiaqing reign in 1820 tribute grain had ceased to play a major role in combating famine.[50]

As the state infrastructure deteriorated, the Empire increasingly relied on a combination of cash handouts and local philanthropy to relieve famines. In 1831, the Daoguang emperor, noting "the wretched condition" of the imperial granaries, "remarked that 'for this reason, when a province is hit by calamity, [the local authorities] rarely ask that [the victims] be aided with ever-normal grain; in general, they content themselves with applying for silver from the provincial treasury and converting it into copper cash to be distributed [to the population].'"[51] Although the Tongzhi reformers temporarily returned to a vigorous hands-on approach to famine relief when the region around the capital was successively baked by drought and drowned by flood in 1867–68, it was a last hurrah for Confucian statecraft in the heroic mode of Fang Guancheng. Henceforth Beijing's principal response to weather disasters was the tardy donation of cash. As we have seen in the accounts of the 1877 and 1899 famines, the resort to monetary relief had fatal flaws.[52]

The market, for example, was frequently unable to accommodate emergency demand. Either the explosion in grain prices quickly exceeded the minimal survival value of cash relief, or, as in the extreme case of Shanxi, there was simply not enough grain locally available at any price. Attempts to purchase and transport large amounts of grain at one time into the loess highlands only produced catastrophic traffic pile-ups like that at Guguan Pass in 1877. Unlike the Yangzi Valley, where water transport of rice remained cheap and efficient, grain commerce in the drier northern provinces, especially during droughts, suffered from the paucity of navigable waterways. In John Lossing Buck's epic study, Land Utilization in China, only two out of fifty-one northern villages had access to water transport in contrast to twenty-three out of eighty in the south.[53] From the perspective of a society dependent on commercial grain for survival during famine, overland transport was staggeringly expensive and inefficient. Summarizing the Royal Asiatic Society's extensive 1893–94 investigations of inland communications in China, T. Kingsmill marveled that a civilization so brilliant in its development of water transport could entirely abdicate road construction. "Probably no country in the world," he wrote, "has paid so little attention to roads," especially in the north where "neglect culminates."[54]

Table 11.1

Transport in the North China Plain: Comparative Efficiency

	Tonnage	Cost Index
River junks	40–100 tons	1.0
Carts	1 ton	3.3
Pack mules	.125 ton	8.2
Coolies	.09 ton	8.6

Source: Data from George Cressey, *China's Geographic Foundations*, New York 1934, p. 179.

Mary Wright long ago suggested that deliberate neglect of inland arteries of transport was rational policy from Beijing's point of view. State-power in imperial China was frequently equated with immobilization of the peasantry and their isolation from disruptive ideological or economic influences. The Qing, in this interpretation, were no more eager to encourage the peasantry to move around the country than they were to invite foreign powers to use railroads to bring troops and cheap factory goods into the interior. Even the reformers of the 1860s "were interested in improved communications only in so far as they might affect maritime defense and the food supply of the capital."[55] This neglect, however, would over time grow into a principal popular grievance. The Communists in Shaanbei and other northern base areas in the late 1930s won great popularity for making road-building a top priority of their rural reconstruction program.[56]

Corruption and Devolution

The monetarization of relief also made it even easier for venal officials to pilfer funds. The rampant practice in the nineteenth century of selling local offices to generate relief funds dramatically expanded the number of lower-level fiscal predators. The ever-normal granaries and the grain-tribute administration were especially lush targets for corrupt officials in the Rasputin-like mold of Heshen, the notorious late-eighteenth-century minister of revenue with whom the Qianlong emperor probably had a homosexual liaison. As Will points out, everyone in late Qing China, from the emperor to secret societies, believed that honesty and efficiency in local government had declined dramatically from the 1790s:

> As early as 1801, the year the Jiaqing emperor closely supervised the special measures carried out in Zhili in the wake of severe flooding, he was struck by the troubling thought that the skyrocketing cost of relief in other provinces was perhaps better explained by the profits made by the "clerks and runners" than by the number of ruined peasants pure and simple; and later in the reign, various memorials spoke of the extortions exacted by investigators and subbureaucrats, unauthorized deductions from provincial funds, registers of disaster victims drawn up without verification of any kind, distribution centers established with attention to actual needs, gruel containing sand, fraudulent exchange rates in converting silver to copper, and other abuses.[57]

By the coronation of the unhappy Xiangong emperor a half-century later, these abuses, seemingly magnified by the Qings' inability to defend Chinese sovereignty, had become core revolutionary grievances. As prolonged drought turned into famine through much of Guangxi and Guangdong in 1848–49, "corrupt local magistrates connived with local grain merchants to manipulate distributions from the local granaries so as to drive the already exorbitant rice price higher."[58] When, ultimately, rice became "as high as the price of pearls," starving peasants attempted to open granaries and were slaughtered by the magistrates' troops. As a direct result, countless thousands flocked to the angry millenarian banner of "God's Chinese Son," Hong Xiuquan. Later, in the summer of 1852, when the Taiping kings paused in Daozhou (southern Hunan) to issue their famous proclamations against the Qing, they accused their rulers of "withholding public relief from victims of flood, famine and other natural calamities in order to decrease the Chinese population."[59] The benevolent eighteenth-century welfare state of the Yongzheng emperor was not even a distant memory. "Whenever floods and droughts occur, [the Manchus] do not show the slightest compassion; they sit and watch the starving people wander by until the bleached bones grow like wild weeds."[60]

The Tongzhi Restoration did little to restore popular confidence in local government's ability to provide protection against disaster. Despite the reformers' rhetorical exaltation of the social compact between the Qing and the peasantry, one of their most significant initiatives (in the name of rewarding the loyal elites who had fought the Taiping) was a vast sale of Confucian merit that increased the caste of degree-holders from 1.1 million to 1.45 million.[61] The venal appetite of this enlarged gentry explains why peasants were groaning under new fiscal oppressions while Beijing was simultaneously complaining that it was broke. Granary administration, in particular, was treated as a spoils system by local collusions of corrupt officials and grain merchants. By 1893, when the first Western study of Chinese finances was completed, more than half of the north's tribute grain was estimated as lost to pilferage.

> The officials in charge of the granaries juggle with the rice, and every few years a great scandal occurs; old and decayed rice is paid out in the place of new rice, weights and measures are falsified, the Manchu soldiery are found to be selling their nominal rights for what they will fetch, and to be actually buying eatable rice in the market, and so on. Peking, in short, is like a filthy colony of rats, each official living in a hole of his own, and preying, when he can and where he can, upon the public storehouse.[62]

Although honest local officials still struggled heroically to restock the granaries, their efforts were everywhere undercut by corrupt subordinates. Murray cites the example of a magistrate in Shaanxi's Han-ch'eng county—which in the early 1890s had not yet recovered from the 1877–78 disaster—who conscientiously bought up grain surpluses during good years to fill twenty local granaries. When drought destroyed the harvest in 1900, he turned confidently to his reserves only to find that the granary administrators had secretly sold off two-thirds of the inventory.[63] As a result, the county was almost depopulated by famine. (When the empress-mother arrived in Zian at the end of the famine, she ordered a thorough review of the famine-relief accounts "that ended in cutting off the heads of three of the most prominent mandarins of the province.")[64]

In face of such obdurate corruption and overwhelmed by fiscal exigencies, the imperial government disengaged itself even further from direct administration of food security. As Mary Rankin, Mark Elvin and others have emphasized, the formidable state capacities of the eighteenth century were gradually devolved to the non-office-holding gentry during the long nineteenth-century siege by imperialism and domestic rebellion. Nouveaux riches merchants and landowners increasingly coordinated tax collection, local law-and-order, flood control and famine relief. When the resources of the locally managed zhenju (relief bureaus) and their privately stocked charity granaries were inadequate to the task, the late Qing state turned to the wealthy Jiangnan elites, who donated rice and cash, provided assistance with transportation, and opened their city gates to famine refugees from the north. But this makeshift system, which failed so catastrophically in 1877 and 1899, was never a real alternative to the vertically integrated state infrastructure of the previous century with its abilities to maintain local ever-normal granaries as well as to carry out the inter-regional transfers that "alone made large-scale and long-lasting famine relief possible."[65]

The reconstruction of the granary system and restoration of peasant food security, accordingly, became central demands of all anti-Qing revolutionaries. Long before Mao's "Yenan Way," the Taipings in their utopian manifesto, *The Land System of the Heavenly Dynasty*, had envisioned a more directly "communist" system for redistributing the entire agricultural surplus through new state granaries.

> All land under heaven will be cultivated in common by all who live under heaven … [The produce from] all land under heaven will circulate to equalize abundance and scarcity. The produce of one locality where the harvest is good will be transported to give relief to another place where famine occurs … At harvest time the *liang-ssu-ma* [headmen of twenty-five households] will supervise the *wu-chang* [headmen of five households] and

> will, after deducting [quantities of grain] sufficient for food for each of the persons belonging to the twenty-five households until the next harvest, [collect] the surplus and send it to the state granaries.[66]

Paying the Bill for the Golden Age

North China's history has been shaped by its paradoxical position within the larger spatial economy of the Empire: economically peripheral, it remained the administrative core. The geographical separation of economic and political power in China—equivalent to the distance between London and Berlin—has been unique for a land-based state. Since the early Sung Dynasty, the greater part of the economic surplus had been produced in the lower Yangzi Valley, but the largest center of surplus consumption usually has been in the north (Chang'an, Dadu, Kaifeng and Beijing) on the edge of the steppe, close to the nomadic sources of Jurchen, Mongol and Manchu military hegemony.

The extraordinary transportation infrastructure—comprising the Grand Canal, its feeder waterways and storage depots—used to move surplus wealth from south to north also made it possible for the Qings to ecologically stabilize northern agriculture with vital imports of rice, fuel, timber and stone. In the mid eighteenth century, as we have seen, the imperial bureaucracy could mobilize famine relief more effectively than any European polity. Yet a century later, Beijing seemed almost powerless to intervene in one of the most deadly chain reactions of civil war, foreign intervention, climate disaster, disease and famine in history. This collapse in state capacity to control the natural as well as social environments has long vexed historians of modern China. "Why did ecological degradation," asks Kenneth Pomeranz in a recent forum, "which up until the mid-eighteenth century was arguably under better control than in Europe or Japan assume crisis proportions thereafter?"[67]

Recent scholarship suggests the necessary distinction between two discrete, if ultimately convergent, environmental crises, developing at separate tempos and levels in the social formation. In the first case, peasant land clearances in the mountainous watersheds of the Yellow, Wei and Huai Rivers accelerated the erosion cycle with inevitably devastating consequences for the plains below. In the second case, the mid-Victorian fiscal crisis of the Qing state, which coincided with skyrocketing costs of flood control arising from increased sedimentation, led to the gradual devolution of hydraulic management to a pauperized peasantry and unwilling gentry. North Chinese agriculture was thus exposed to the most severe climate stress in 200 years (the extreme ENSO cycles of the 1870s and 1890s) precisely when the state was in full retreat from its traditional ecological mandates.

The Qing Golden Age in the eighteenth century, Robert Marks reminds us, was based on a "massive remaking" of Chinese environmental space. Population growth under a system of partible inheritance between 1750 and 1850, at least partly induced by the rising "protoindustrial" demand for family labor in rural handicraft production, put increasing stress on agro-ecological carrying capacity. Unlike Europe, this population explosion was not absorbed through the parallel growth of urban centers or emigration to overseas colonies. Indeed, according to Maddison, "by 1820 the Chinese degree of urbanisation was not much greater than it had been a thousand years earlier," and actually declined from the early Qing (6.8 percent of population) to the late Qing (5.9 percent).[68] As in India, the long economic recession in the first half of the nineteenth century—due in China's case to the negative balance of trade and silver outflows caused by opium imports—caused widespread urban unemployment and pushed many workers into the countryside.[69]

Instead, the eighteenth-century population boom (estimates, as we have seen, range wildly from a 33 percent to a 200 percent increase) was largely accommodated by ecologically unsustainable settlement in formerly uncultivated mountains, foothills and wet lowlands. Peasant pioneers and improving landowners brought nearly 25,000 square kilometers of new land under the plough during the eighteenth century—most of it hilly or periodically inundated. The immediate advantages were great.[70] Legendary profits were made clear-cutting the forests that still protected the watersheds of China's great rivers. Worrisome congestion in the fertile valleys and plains was temporarily relieved by mass emigration into foothill and mountain peripheries where New World crops like maize and sweet potatoes allowed cultivators to wrest a living from sandy, unfertilized soils previously regarded as untillable. At the same time, land-hungry peasants and urban speculators built dikes to reclaim hundreds of thousands of acres of rich marsh and bottom land for commercial agriculture.

By the last quarter of the eighteenth century, however, the marginal returns from forestry and land conversion were near the vanishing point. Manchuria aside, Rhoads Murphey estimates that Chinese forests "were already largely gone by 1820, almost wholly by 1860."[71] Too many peasants clung to eroding hillsides or struggled to drain malarial wetlands. Overflow basins that managed flood waters, as well as reservoirs that stored water for irrigation in dry spells, had been ill-advisedly turned into fields, with predictably disastrous results.[72] Thus the great clearances that had subsidized the Golden Age became root causes of intractable ecological crisis during the century that followed. This previously little-understood environmental history of Qing population growth has been admirably explored in recent case-studies of the Pearl River watershed (Marks) and the Dongting Lake region in the middle Yangzi Valley (Perdue). In both regions, the early windfalls of virgin soil cultivation were inevitably followed by environmental degradation and increased vulnerability to natural hazards. Nature collected the bill for eighteenth-century prosperity in deferred payments of drought, flood and famine.[73]

The Denudation of North China

The greatest downstream tragedies, however, took place in the system of the Yellow River and its major tributaries. Shaanxi's Wei River Valley, studied by several authors, is a sobering example. At the end of the Ming Dynasty, the foothills of the Chinling Mountains, which formed the valley's southern border, were still heavily wooded. During the early and mid-Qing, however, huge "timber factories" mobilizing armies of 3,000 to 5,000 woodcutters and laborers systematically denuded the forests. Subsequently, thousands of poor peasants from congested counties as far away as Szechwan and Hupei were officially encouraged by tax exemptions and other subsidies to emigrate to the region. (Edward Vermeer stresses the perverse role of Qing tax policies that often rewarded the exploitation of marginal lands while penalizing farmers for improvements on existing, high-quality plots.)[74] New World crops allowed cultivation on soils that were "too sandy, too acidic, too infertile and drought-prone to have sup-

Figure 11.2 Hillside Farms in Shaanxi
As farming deforested hillsides the erosion rate increased exponentially.

ported settled populations in any numbers in the past."[75] Maize and potatoes, especially, could be cultivated on sloping, unterraced hillsides with thin soil layers otherwise unsuitable for rice or wheat. However, the price of this cheap subsistence was increased erosion that eventually became catastrophic.

Within a few generations, geomorphological forces had crossed a dynamic threshold and gullies grew with alarming speed, deepening sometimes by several hundred feet within the span of a single human lifetime. "By the mid-nineteenth century," writes Murray, "the mountains became barren and the rivers were blocked up."[76] The first modern European visitors, like Baron von Richthofen in 1870, gave vivid accounts of the silting up of the famous Qing irrigation systems, particularly the magnificent complex that had made the Wei plain a hearth of civilization. Similarly, many of the areas in the loess country that Marco Polo had praised for verdancy and the abundance of mulberry trees had become treeless near-deserts by Victorian times.[77] Although foreigners often confused modern and ancient decay (serious hydraulic deterioration in the Wei Valley dated back to Tang times), the nineteenth century administered the environmental coup de grace.

For peasants, meanwhile, the easy living of early pioneer days became an increasingly grim battle for survival on eroding islands of semi-arable soil. "On the lower slopes, by the later nineteenth century, there had been up to a century of maize cultivation with only limited fertilizer; yields began to fall drastically. Potato crops began to suffer seriously from disease … Yields were unstable; the price of food began to rise, doubling in the nineteenth century, owing to the increasing population and static or declining supplies."[78] Eventually many mountain farmers were unable to produce their own family subsistence, so they turned to fruit trees as a cash crop. "This specialization," Murray explains, "was regarded by the authors of the local history as particularly precarious, because the profit of the entire year depended on a single harvest. Many of the fruit growers were extremely poor, lacking even adequate food and clothing."[79]

The mid-century civil wars completed the denudation of China's surviving forested watersheds:

> Accounts of the time … repeatedly mention wanton destruction of forests by the Taipings, and equally massive assaults by the Imperial forces in their effort to deny shelter to the rebels. The major weapon seems to have been fire. There are descriptions of former forests which by the 1860s consisted only of blackened stumps over hundreds of square miles. All of this activity was concentrated in the remaining area within, or around the edges of, the major center of population in China proper which still had some vestigial forest cover. The mountainous far west was unaffected, but forests there were of little use to the rest of China, where the vast majority of the people lived. Those forests were in turn heavily exploited in the course of the great Muslim rebellions and their suppression, concentrated in Yunnan and in Shensi-Kansu, between 1855 and 1878.[80]

Depopulation and ecological devastation was perhaps most extreme in Shaanxi, where genocidal ethnic warfare killed or displaced an estimated 90 percent of the Muslim population and left much of the province outside the Wei Valley a wilderness for the Chinese Communists to resettle a full half-century later. As Pauline Keating points out, the financially

Figure 11.3 A Silted-up Channel in the Wei Valley

strapped Qing "invested only in the pacification of Shaanxi, not its reconstruction."

> In the absence of both an official resettlement strategy and a sustained program of infrastructural repair and development, local economic systems disintegrated. Whole villages were deserted, the distances between settlements became longer, transport routes fell into disrepair (a process made swifter by the rapid erosion of earthen constructions in loess country), and market centers and trading networks disappeared. Water wells, irrigation and drainage systems, cropland embankments, granaries, and pathways were not maintained.[81]

The same dismal sequence, if less apocalyptically, was repeated everywhere throughout the foothills and loess plateaux of northwest China. "It seemed as if humans had set out to reduce their original environment to only two types of land: carefully maintained, productive, private farmland, and ruthlessly exploited, unproductive, common wasteland."[82] Nor was deforestation, as an account from turn-of-the-century Shandong makes clear, the last stage in the economic exploitation of the foothills and mountains. "All the boys of the village big enough to walk and carry a basket are sent out over the hillsides to collect grass, twigs, and any kind of herbage that can be used as fodder or fuel. Each boy carries an iron grubbing hook, and thus equipped he clambers up the slopes, working away at this task with cheerful energy. Through the industry of this army of human locusts the mountains are denuded of herbage and even roots often grubbed up."[83] The stubble that remained on the slopes was burnt to provide fertilizing ash run-off for fields downhill.[84]

As the last local sources of firewood were exhausted, a fuel and lumber famine began to undermine agriculture throughout north China. Despite vast, although poorly mined, coal deposits in Shandong and Shanxi, the rural poor could seldom afford coal, and the breakdown of the Grand Canal system, to be discussed in a moment, inflated its price as well as that of imported wood from central China. Cheap Manchurian timber was available in the coastal cities, but was generally not imported into the interior.[85] "Demand for construction material," wrote an American authority on Chinese forestry in the 1920s, "has been reduced to supply, until in northern Shensi about the only articles of wood within a house are chopsticks, and only the door and the paper window lattice of the house are of wood."[86] Likewise in southwest Shandong, Pomeranz estimates that the fuel supply per peasant household at the time of the Boxer upheaval was barely a quarter of what was traditionally held to be the subsistence minimum. Scarce cattle dung, therefore, had to be burnt for heat and less fertilizer was applied to the soil.[87] Alternatively, more intensive efforts had to be made gathering residual vegetation from the hillsides, thus ensuring their complete denudation.[88]

As in India, deforestation enhanced the frequency of hydrological drought by lowering water tables, increasing runoff, and ruining irrigation systems and reservoirs with sedimentation.[89] Fatalistic peasants, all too conscious that they were involuntary actors in a vicious circle of poverty and environmental destruction, quoted Mencius to each other: "mountains empty—rivers gorged." The acceleration of the erosion cycle became nearly exponential. The American forestry expert W. C. Lowdermilk estimated in 1930 that slope denudation in Shanxi and Shandong in the previous century or so had "increased superficial runoff fifty-fold." But the "rate of erosion is increased from one hundred to several thousand-fold."[90] As a result, visitors frequently encountered deforestation's ubiquitous monuments: great stone bridges completely mired in sediment:

> Their arches were partially or entirely blocked by silt, although they had been designed originally to accommodate a deeper, more regular flow of water. One might in fact have derived a round measure of the chronology of deforestation and siltation in many areas by fixing the date of the bridges (many of them as old as Ming, some more recent) as an indication of the time when the streams were less silt-laden and comparing this with the depth and apparent recency of deposition since.[91]

Traveling in 1923 through northern Shaanxi, the future redoubt of Mao's Long Marchers, Lowdermilk was stunned by the extent to which overcultivation had eroded the landscape into badlands. As soil exhaustion in the eighteenth century led to the substitution of pasturage for agriculture, shepherds began to systematically burn off shrub cover to open land for grass. "The result was that 50% of the groundspace in the region was occupied by erosion gullies, some several hundred feet deep."[92]

Erosion on this scale led to radical changes in the composition of the sediment load carried downstream. For millennia, the Yellow River and its tributaries had conveyed rich loess silt to replenish and fertilize the north China plain. By the nineteenth century, however, accelerated erosion had removed the deep loess cover in many parts of the watershed and the highlands were beginning to erode bedrock and sand instead. As early as 1810, Shaanxi officials were already worried about the vast quantities of sand and gravel that were annually washed from the deforested hillsides, clogging up irrigation ditches and canals in the valleys below. ("People suffer greatly because of this!")[93] By the end of the century, flood-deposited sand was smothering some of the best cropland in north China.

Finally, the denudation of the mountains and hills directly affected the water supply available during droughts in the plains below. "In addition to erosion and flooding," Murphey explains, "deforestation had the predictable effect of lowering the water table, especially critical in north China with its heavy dependence on shallow traditional wells, which increasingly ran dry. Without adequate cover, especially on slopes, to retain and absorb rainfall, ground water reserves were not recharged as they should be by slow release and seepage."[94] In a fuel-famished economy that lacked cheap energy sources (even bullocks) for running hydraulic pumps, the lowering of the water tables below the reach of manually operated windlasses or level poles was a constant and sometimes deadly frustration. Drought-stricken peasants knew that there was plenty of water underneath their fields but had no means to pump it to the surface. It was not until after Liberation that suitably deep wells with electric pumps revolutionized farming in the north China plain.

The Crisis of River Conservancy

Sedimentation in the Yellow River Delta is a problem in hydraulic control that dwarfs the challenge of all other civilized rivers except perhaps the modern Mississippi. Twentieth-century measurements show that each cubic meter of river water carries an astonishing hundred pounds of silt in suspension. "Approximately one and one-half billion tons of loess are eroded annually in the Yellow River basin. Half of that amount settles out of suspension as the river slows down across the floodplain, and half of it is carried to the sea."[95] (Alternately, before construction of the post-Liberation upstream dam system, the Yellow had a 40 percent silt content at flood stage.)[96] Deposited on the nearly flat north China plain, the sediment will either force the river into chaotic and rapidly changing meanders like a great writhing snake or, if the channel is constricted by human engineering, will lead to the rapid buildup of the riverbed high above the plain.[97] Although the mandarin engineers of the Yellow River Conservancy developed extraordinary expertise in using the diked power of the river to scour deeper and faster channels, sedimentation eventually overcame their most ingenious efforts at streamlining the flow.

There were, in fact, two warring schools about how to tame the Yellow River. One school of river managers wanted to confine the river between high, narrowly spaced levees to maximize its channel-deepening power and emancipate more floodplain for tillage, while the other advocated lower levees set five to ten kilometers apart. "These two strategies," Charles Greer writes, "represent more than different technical approaches to controlling the river. Their roots lie in different philosophical outlooks. Needham associates the construction of close, strong dikes with a Confucianist tendency to curb nature, analogous to the reliance by this school of thought on strict ethical codes for shaping human behavior. He associates widely separated, low levees with the Taoist approach of letting nature

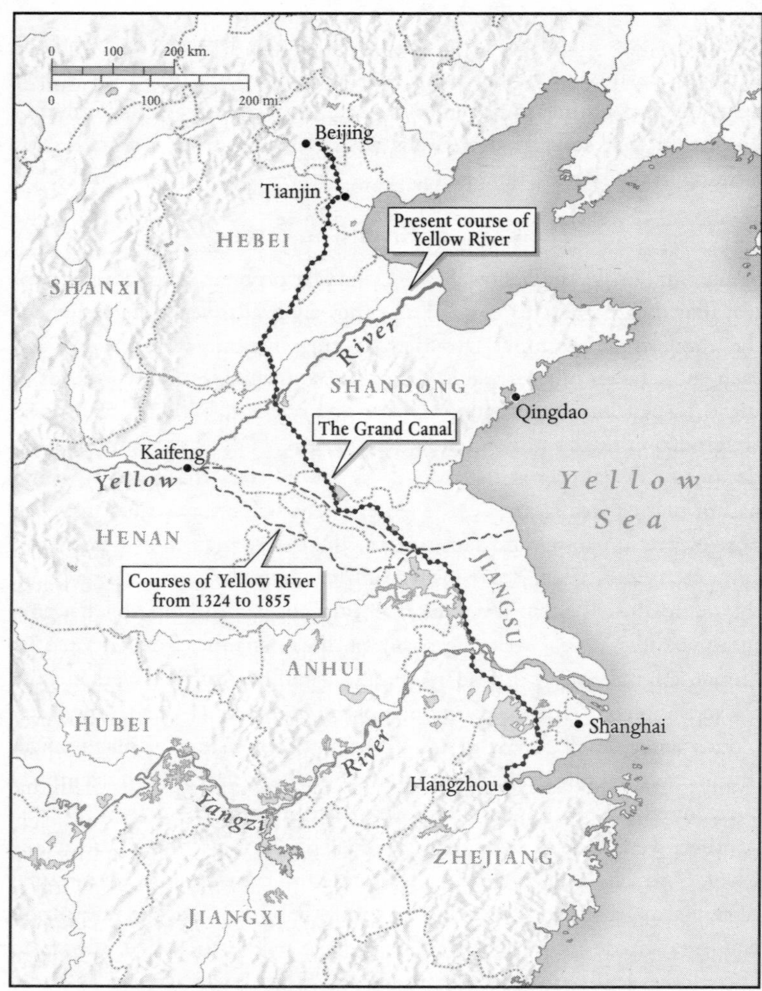

Figure 11.4 The Grand Canal and the Yellow River

follow its own course."[98] Even the Taoists, however, were ultimately forced to respond to the rising bed with higher levees and revetments, as well as more cutoffs, overflow basins, drainage canals and polders.

This inexorable construction program in turn required a growing army of hired labor (the Qing had abolished the Mings' hated corvée), specialist river troops and their overseers. Thus the hydraulic evolution of the river produced a corresponding expansion in the scale, complexity and financial burden of its Conservancy. Soaring costs were aggravated by "excessive bureaucratization" and rampant corruption (especially in the procurement of the sorghum stalks used in revetments) that ultimately sped the system toward collapse.[99] The rising river bed also generated bitter social conflict everywhere along the Yellow's course. "Newer, higher dikes," Vermeer writes, "diverted the flood problem to less well protected flood-prone areas. The city walls might offer protection for county capitals, but the countryside was left to its own devices." Likewise the widespread conversion, usually illegal, of polders and reservoirs to fields increased the river's pressure against its levees and exacerbated the chance of a catastrophic breach.[100]

Inevitably, despite the most arduous efforts of the Conservancy's hydraulic experts, the defenses would fail after an unusually heavy summer monsoon, most likely in a major La Niña year. Angry brown waters would engulf hundreds, even thousands of villages, as in 1898 on the eve of the Boxer Rebellion. More than 1,500 such floods have been recorded since the time of the Han: they are north China's "ordinary" disasters and a major cause of its chronic peasant unrest. Every few centuries, however, cumulative sedimentation, modulated by human action (including both flood control and war), would so reshape the topography of the plain that the river would break free into a completely different channel. Thus, eight times in written history the Yellow River has radically switched its path to the sea, moving hundreds of miles from the Yellow Sea to the Gulf of Bohai and back again.[101] These epochal changes of channel, by regionally redistributing the costs of flood control, have had complex political repercussions: indeed, have determined the fate of dynasties.

In 1800, the Yellow River flood-control system, redesigned by the great engineer Pan Jixun between 1577 and 1589, was more than 200 years old. As Randall Dodgen points out, the river "had gone longer without a change of course, but it had never been held in one course for so long by dint of human labor and engineering."[102] It was the singular misfortune of the Qings that this inescapable hydraulic cycle, which in its final stages

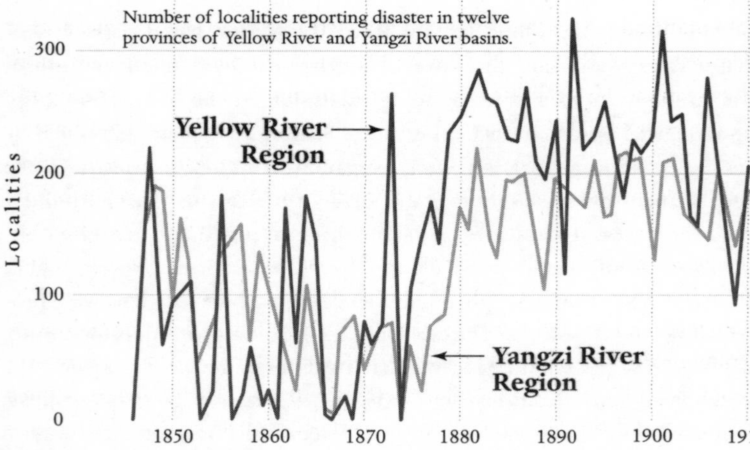

Figure 11.5 Yellow and Yangzi Regions Disaster Reporting
Source: B. Stavis, "Ending Famines in China," in Garcia and Escudero, p. 117.

entailed almost geometrical increases in the costs of dike construction, reached its crisis point in coincidence with economic recession and the most destructive civil war in history. Already by the early nineteenth century, more than 10 percent of the Imperial budget was devoted to increasingly desperate efforts to control the path of the Yellow River, "an expense totally without parallel in the eighteenth century."[103] Thereafter, as we saw in chapter 9, the Qing treasury was rapidly emptied by the forced outflow of silver to purchase opium from British India, the depletion of the Yunnan copper mines, the costs of the Opium Wars, and, finally, the Taiping catastrophe, which cut off tribute from the middle Yangzi provinces for almost a decade.

As early as 1837, Conservancy officials had warned Beijing that, despite huge expenditures on reinforcement, many of the dikes in Henan were too weak to withstand high water. In the event, the three successive floods of 1841–43, coincident with the First Opium War, dealt crippling blows to the Qing's simultaneous effort to contain both imperialism and the river. As Dodgen points out, "the cost to the state in social disruption, lost agricultural income, and relief and repair funds was immense. Combined with the expense of the Opium War and the state's already weakened fiscal condition, these floods left the state treasury barren."[104] For another decade, during the last years of the Daoguang emperor, troops and engineers gamely struggled to restore control over a river seemingly becoming wilder each year. "It was not until a second series of floods took place in 1851, 1852 and 1853 that the Qing's commitment to Yellow River conservancy began to waver. Concerned with the growing scope of the Taiping Rebellion, the state slowed the pace of repairs and redirected funds to the struggle against the rebels."[105]

While Beijing was thus diverted, the Yellow in 1855 broke free of its old channel, hijacked the course of the Daqing River, and poured downgrade through Honan and Shandong, drowning hundreds of thousands of peasants and millions of acres of fertile farmland. Flood refugees, ruined farmers and displaced transportation workers, in turn, swelled the ranks of the Nian rebels and local "Turban bandits" who controlled a vast swathe of territory from the Huai River to the new course of the Yellow. (Most of the Nian, Jonathan Spence points out, were "poor peasants or ex-peasants struggling to survive in a bleak environment of worked-out soil, harsh winters, and unstable river systems subject to appalling floods.")[106] The alliance of the Taiping and Nian in the aftermath of the channel-switching catastrophe might have doomed the Qing had not a simultaneous civil war amongst the Taiping leaders in Nanking fatally splintered the Kingdom of Heavenly Peace.

Fighting desperately for its survival on multiple fronts, meanwhile, the Empire was powerless to control nature in the Yellow River plain. Only after the defeat of the Taipings in 1865 could Beijing focus again on the complex, almost overwhelming, problem of the unleashed Yellow River. Arguing that neglect of the hydraulic infrastructure had been a principal cause of the Taiping and Nian revolts, the Qing hero Zeng Guofan made "repair of old waterworks and the construction of new and improved systems … a cardinal point in Restoration planning." His expensive schemes for forcing the Yellow back into its old channel and for developing new irrigation in eastern Hebei, however, collided with other equally ambitious plans for military modernization and the reconquest of Central Asia. The Manchu generals, not surprisingly, were a more powerful lobby than millions of ruined peasants in Shandong and Hebei. Even established water agencies, like the General Office for the Control of the Huai, "unable to compete with the armies for funds," were forced to close up shop, and thus "water control continued to be dealt with in piecemeal fashion."[107]

The resulting decline in hydraulic control after 1870, in the Yangzi as well as the Yellow River basins, has been graphically depicted by B. Stavis as a sudden spike in locally reported disasters (see Figure 11.5).

Abdicating Hydraulic Control

The Tongzhi Restoration's failure to resolve the flood control crisis ignited an epic battle between regional elites. The wealthy Jiangan gentry, for their part, were delighted by the northern migration of the Yellow River, which relieved them of their traditional burden in taxes, labor duties, flood relief and periodic flood damage. On the other side, local gentry in western Shandong faced ruin: by the early 1880s the channel had grown high above the plain and flooding had become chaotic and almost impossible to contain. Then "in 1886–87, it briefly appeared that the river gods had come to Shandong's aid as the Yellow broke its banks in Henan and returned to a southern course. Shandong peasants were said to have resisted government requisitions of millet stalks to repair the break, while Shandong officials lobbied Beijing to let the river resume its old course. But the province's political weight was no match for that of Jiangnan and its powerful governor-general … After a year's respite, the breach was repaired and the river returned to continue its devastation of northwest Shandong."[108]

This political decision to keep flood waters channeled through the north China plain, Esherick points out, reflected the emergent control of the rich coastal cities over inter-regional resource flows. It was also a decisive step in the long campaign by the Jiangnan commercial elites to shift the transport of Beijing's annual grain tribute from the Grand Canal to coastal shipping.[109] Indeed one of the major consequences of the Yellow River's change of channel was to cut off the clear waters of the Wen River that fed the Grand Canal and kept critical sections navigable during El Niño droughts. Periodic attempts to use the Yellow River to replenish the Canal were no solution since its waters deposited too much silt. As a result, traffic along the Canal began its steep decline, with only the smallest boats able to proceed along the stretches vulnerable to drought.[110] As we have seen, the resulting bottleneck was fatal to relief efforts during the 1876–78 drought-famine. In the 1890s the water-starved northern sections of the Canal were abandoned, and in 1901 the grain tribute was formally consigned to coastal shipping and the new railroad between Tianjin and Beijing. The decline of the Canal redounded to the great profit of the two British-owned steamship lines—the Ewo (Jardine Matheson & Co.) and Taikoo (Butterfield & Swire)—who from the 1870s dominated the maritime transport of rice, cotton and other staples.[111] (Japan, by contrast, banned foreign flags from its coastal trade.)

This abdication of hydraulic control in inland north China was perhaps the most portentous consequence of the growing imperialist pressure on the Qing. "The foreign onslaught," writes Pomeranz, "destroyed basic principles of Ming-Qing statecraft, particularly a commitment to social reproduction that had often required rich areas to subsidize the infrastructure of poorer ones. Instead foreign pressures helped impart a quasi-mercantilist logic to the actions of a state that was struggling to survive. Resources had to be used where they did the most to protect China's autonomy from direct intervention or the consequences of foreign debt or both." In effect, Beijing resorted to "regional triage" by abandoning the costly upkeep of the Yellow River dikes and the Grand Canal in order to concentrate on creating new armies, coastal arsenals and flood-control works around the mouth of the Yellow River "where major floods seemed likely to provide excuses for further foreign encroachment." Whereas in the eighteenth century Qing policies had served to reduce regional inequalities, using tribute grain as a tool to regulate the flow of resources within the Empire, the decision to place all bets on the coastal-oriented economy exploded regional differentials. The Yangzi landlords, coastal merchants and British shipping interests profited directly from this neomercantilist orientation, while the inland North now became peripheralized in every sense.[112]

Except in the Tianjin-Beijing region, which was now provisioned by sea, the ruin of the Grand Canal system grievously undermined food security in the north, especially in the event of drought-famines, which tended to be longer in duration and larger in area than flood-famines. It also wrecked the economies of the famous canal towns and grain depots. From the jobless ranks of former boatmen and Canal laborers the Boxers recruited some of their most militant leaders and fighters; as did the Communist Party in the 1930s and 1940s from their descendants.[113]

Moreover without the Canal to transport timber and stone, it became increasingly difficult to keep the Yellow River within its embankments. "Lacking stone, brick, or often even wood, dike builders used various inferior materials. The most common was gaoliang (a type of sorghum) stalks … At best, they might last three years; one to two years was common, and improperly cut stalks, lacking the plant's roots, would decay in months."[114] In 1891 Beijing disbanded most of the specialized battalions of "river troops" (ying) who maintained the dikes and devolved responsibility for flood control, like famine relief, to the impoverished counties of the plain. Within a generation, fully one-fifth of the region's net income and an equivalent proportion of its labor-time were consumed in Sisyphean efforts to defend agriculture against almost annual flood destruction.[115]

This unraveling of centralized hydraulic control had repercussions at every level of environmental management. In contrast to India, where the traditional hydraulic infrastructure in dry regions consisted of free-standing improvements (wells, ditches and tanks) that seldom depended upon a massive central project, public works in north China functioned only as an integrated and coordinated hierarchy. Flood control, canal management and local irrigation were largely inseparable. Shuili ("water benefits") or village-level irrigation farming, as well as local drainage, depended upon the hegong ("riverworks"): regional networks of dikes, levees and master canals. A hegong system like the Yellow River Conservancy may have been designed for flood control rather than irrigation (diversion of water from the raised river channel was outlawed because of the danger of breaching the dikes), but its reliable operation was the prerequisite for stable agriculture of any kind. "Until the main drainage arteries are made effective," wrote the American agricultural expert Loessing Buck in 1938, "local drainage systems will be of limited value."[116] Poor water management, in turn, exacerbated the problem of land scarcity. Marshes formed where the Yellow River dikes bisected local streams, and vast sections of valuable cropland were lost to waterlogging, salinization and sand sedimentation.

Finally, as in India, "small irrigation" lost much of its state sponsorship during the recessions and fiscal retrenchments of the nineteenth century. On a macro-scale, Maddison calculates an absolute decline in irrigated cropland from 21.7 million hectares (or 29.4 percent of arable) in 1820 to 20 million hectares (18.5 percent) in 1952.[117] On a regional scale, studies of Shaanxi's Wei Valley contrast the attention given to irrigation under the early Qing to its political neglect in the nineteenth century. Thus in the aftermath of the drought of 1690–92, a famous mandarin, Wang Hsin-Ching, published a treatise on famine administration in the Wei Valley urging the government to help peasants tap plentiful groundwater reservoirs. Given the region's unreliable transport links with the surplus-producing provinces, Wang advocated well-digging and self-sufficiency as the "only 'solid and reliable' plan for preventing future drought-famines."[118] Later agricultural reformers in the loess region echoed Wang's recommendations about peasant-managed irrigation while specifically warning against large-scale, centrally managed projects that encouraged official corruption, pitted upstream against downstream villages, and were ultimately unsustainable. There is considerable evidence, moreover, that Shaanxi's eighteenth-century governors authorized significant investment in wells, irrigation and drainage under the direct supervision of energetic hsien magistrates.[119] The result in many cases was a 200 percent to 300 percent increase in the output of grain and cotton.[120]

In the tumult of the nineteenth century, irrigation subsidies were more or less abandoned. The predictable consequences were a sharp decline in agricultural productivity and a concomitant increase in vulnerability to drought and flood. Murray points to Ching-yang, traditionally the richest county in the entire Wei Valley, where "agriculture was crippled" by the late nineteenth century as a result of the deterioration of the irrigation system. "A similarly depressing scene was revealed in the 1882 history of Hua-chou, located in the southeastern sector of the valley, where neglect of water control was also blamed for the decline of local agriculture. Not only had the irrigation ditches often become useless, but the natural waterways had silted up, and flooding along the riverbanks had destroyed much of the county's best farmland."[121] Neglect of irrigation (only 6.8 percent of cultivated acreage in north China in 1932) continued through the Republican period. The famous Mass Education Movement study (1926–33) of Ting Hsien in Hebei concluded that 30,000 additional small wells were needed in this single county to fully realize its agricultural potential.[122]

The failure of successive warlord, Guomindang and Japanese occupation governments to improve local irrigation, like their similar inability to tame the Yellow River, became powerful factors in rallying the northern peasantry behind the program of the Communist Party. After Liberation (and despite the costs of the Korean intervention), water conservancy was duly accorded the highest priority in successive agricultural plans, and, according to E. Vermeer, "during 1946–1954 the State funds expended on anti-flood work on the Yellow River constituted 22-fold the total invested during the period 1914–1932." Dam construction and dike repair in the 1950s was followed in the early 1970s by a pump-well revolution in the north China plain which (measured from 1949) increased pump horsepower 400-fold and quadrupled the irrigated acreage along the Yellow River.[123] Irrigation, in tandem with the expansion of the chemical fertilizer industry, was the most important productive force unleashed by China's agrarian reforms just as it was the principal engine powering India's contemporaneous "Green Revolution."

Yet real environmental stability in north China has proven elusive. Modern hydraulic control has been achieved in the style of the Colorado Basin or Soviet Central Asia: at the cost of enormous wastage without systematic efforts at recycling. Indeed, by the 1990s, the profligate water-use made possible by reservoirs and electric pumps had both dried up the lower Yellow River (which now fails to reach the Bohai Sea most of the year) and lowered the water table 60 meters in the Beijing region. The northern water shortage, according to experts, is "without a doubt the country's most serious ecological problem," a direct threat to further breakneck economic expansion. The recent intensification of the ENSO cycle only magnifies the danger of growth-choking drought. Accordingly, Beijing has opted for the ultimate "Confucian fix": a vast scheme to divert northward millions of acre-feet from the headwaters of the Yangzi, and possibly from the upper reaches of the Mekong and Irrawaddy. Even more than the controversial Three Gorges Dam on the Yangzi, such diversions are fraught with unpredictable environmental and geopolitical hazards.[124]

12

Brazil: Race and Capital in the Nordeste

Definition of "drought": "a strategic element in the process of accumulation by large rural production units in the Northeast."

— G. Dias

Nineteenth-century Brazil, also a subcontinent much visited by El Niño, shared two other things in common with contemporary India. First, while nominally independent, its economy, especially in the Nordeste, was so dominated by English investors and creditors that it has become the classic example of an "informal colony" in modern literature on economic dependency.[1] Second, economic development on a national scale ground to a halt during the second half of the nineteenth century with no appreciable increase in per capita income or productivity. While per capita GDP soared by 600 percent between 1800 and 1913 in the United States and even 150 percent in Mexico, there was zero growth in Brazil. A fabulous coffee boom in the São Paulo region was counterbalanced by the equally spectacular economic retrogression of the Nordeste.[2] As in the case of the Deccan, a formerly core region was transformed into a periphery of hunger. Even the *zona da mata*, the Nordeste's lush littoral, suffered a drastic decline in nutrition as real wages plunged 60 percent from 1870 to 1890.[3] Whereas in India, however, increasing vulnerability to famine went hand in hand with notable infrastructural modernization in the late nineteenth century, the modern history of the *sertão* is striking for the absence of any significant state developmental role until the 1960s and the threat of revolution.

Informal Colonialism and State Capacity

British commercial and financial hegemony in Brazil had ancient roots in Portugal's vassalage to London during the seventeenth and eighteenth centuries. When the Bragança monarchy was relocated under "tremendous British pressure" to Brazil in 1808, the immediate payoff was a commercial treaty that gave British imports preference over those from Portugal. Then in 1827 Emperor Dom Pedro, in return for British recognition of his slave empire, codified dependency in one of the most inequitable trade agreements in history: a nonreciprocal treaty that limited taxes on British imports to 15 percent ad valorum while allowing the British to impose 300 percent tariffs on Brazilian coffee. The Commercial Treaty, according to Cain and Hopkins, transformed Brazil into a "virtual British protectorate."[4] Although the United States made substantial commercial inroads during the 1850s, the Civil War cotton boom re-established British preeminence. On the eve of the *Grande Seca*, Britain supplied 51 percent of Brazil's imports and consumed 37 percent of its exports.[5]

But the deepest level of British hegemony was financial. Chronic trade deficits were repeatedly financed by punitive British loans whose interest payments generated permanent budget deficits which, in turn, were financed by yet more foreign bonds.[6] "The London Rothschilds were the empire's exclusive bond-raising agents, the leading exporters and importers were all British, and all the early railroads were British owned or financed. The largest British bank, the London and Brazilian, had considerably greater financial resources than the semi-official Bank of Brazil."[7] The domestic banking system was stunted and undeveloped. As late as 1888, thirteen of the twenty Brazilian provinces had no local banks at all, and the total capital of the entire national banking system was only US$48 million. The state bank largely confined itself to the conservative management of the money supply in the interest of its British creditors.[8]

Domestic capital formation as a consequence was severely bridled. "The foreign banks were notorious ... [for] their reluctance to make long-term loans to agriculture or domestic concerns."[9] Commerce, in turn, was skewed toward foreign middlemen and British imports, above all in the Nordeste. In 1890s Bahia, for example, only one of eleven licensed exporters was Bahian; and twenty-four of sixty-four import houses specialized in imported British textiles.[10] Foreign capital, moreover, vigilantly policed the growth of any saplings of competitive, indigenous industrialism like that imagined in the utopian *literatura do Norte* of Franklin Tavora. ("If capital and credit were mobilized, if agriculture, industrial and artistic markets were put in place, we would see at every turn a Manchester or a New York ...")[11] When local entrepreneurs occasionally tried to increase value-added income by setting up cotton-related manufactures, British exporters punctually retaliated. Warren Dean cites the telling example of a sewing thread mill in Alagoas that was purchased by an English firm for the sole purpose of dismantling it and dumping the machinery into the São Francisco River.[12]

Despite its elites' vast aspirations to a modernizing tropical empire, the developmental autonomy of the Brazilian state was thus circumscribed by foreign debt, a primitive banking system and the volatility of its export income. Leff argues that in land-rich Brazil, as contrasted to India and Japan, there was "little pressure of population on land," thus "Ricardian rent, the basis for land taxation, was small." The Empire, as well as the conservative Republic that succeeded it in 1889, relied on export taxes for revenue, but "until the end of the nineteenth century, the volume and growth of Brazil's foreign trade were too small to permit a high level of government expenditure."[13] In the 1890s, as coffee prices stalled then fell, debt service soared to half the federal budget.[14] As drought and famine again desolated the Nordeste, the Republic was hard-pressed even to pay for the bullets to kill Conselheiro's followers.

The adoption of the international gold standard during the 1870s "automated," as it were, Brazil's unequal exchange relationships. Although Rio might balk at British attempts to steer its foreign policy, London retained through the early 1900s quasi-veto power over major capital flows within the Brazilian economy. When some Brazilians protested the draconian terms of the Funding Loan of 1898, which confiscated the entirety of customs revenue for debt repayment, they were forceably reminded that dreadnaughts were the City's debt collectors of last resort. "Lord Rothschild, anticipating that the resolve of the recipients might weaken, took care to point out, in a manner which was unauthorised but managed to sound authoritative, that the alternative, repudiation, would involve not only 'the complete loss of the country's credit' but might also 'greatly affect Brazil's sovereignty, provoking complaints that could arrive at the extreme of foreign intervention.'"[15]

Informal colonialism, however, did not affect Brazil's regions equally. If the northeastern sugar *fazendas* were the very paradigm of dependence upon British capital, the southern coffee industry was relatively more independent. "The paulistic market," Ruthanne Deutsch points out, "was never the private sphere of influence of a single country or a single financial combine."[16] First linked to the coast by railroad in 1872, the fertile São Paulo region was supplying half of the world's coffee by the 1890s. An informal pact between the Republican parties of São Paulo and Minas Gerais after the overthrow of the Empire in 1889 "guaranteed these two states control of the economic policy of the central government," supplanting the old landowning elites of Rio who had been the chief beneficiaries of the Empire. The new dispensation was sweetened, however, by an elaborate system of bribes and concessions that buttressed the local power of the *coroneis* in the smaller states.[17]

Despite its nationalist rhetoric, the "Revolution of 1889–91," as Dean emphasizes, did nothing to address export dependency or the financial dominance of the City of London. Indeed, with the consolidation of Paulista power, Brazil became a monoculture. "It is remarkable that Brazil, a country of immense territory and varied resources, participated in world trade essentially as a planter of a single crop: coffee."[18] The developmental ambitions of the new Republic, moreover, were almost entirely concentrated on railroad construction in the dynamic coffee-growing core. "National integration" meant little more than the Paulistas in Congress occasionally scratching the backs of other oligarchs. Unlike Victorian India with its impressive railroads and inter-regional grain trade, Brazil until the early twentieth century remained an "archipelago" of distinctive economies separated by dauntingly high internal costs of transportation. Indeed, "class interests were so disparate as to raise serious questions concerning the validity of using the nation as a unit of analysis."[19]

Table 12.1

Unequal Regional Development
(Per Capita Product)

	1872	1900	Change
Ceará	£2.2	£0.8	–275%
Rio Grande do Norte	£0.4	£0.2	–100%
Bahía	£4.0	£3.9	–3%
São Paulo	£3.1	£15.7	+506%

Source: Mirçea Buescu, "Regional Inequalities in Brazil During the Second Half of the Nineteenth Century," in Barioch and Levy-Leboyer, p. 352.

The rise of the coffee states inevitably accelerated the decline of the northern sugar littoral. Contemporary Brazilians are used to thinking of their country as "Belindia: Belgium in the south, India in the north," but as Deutsch shows, "around 1870, the quality of life and the level of economic development in the Nordeste rivaled, if it did not surpass, that of the Southeast."[20] This quickly changed, however, as real per capita income in the once economically dominant north fell by 30 percent (to 1913) in tandem with the collapse of its chief exports. Sugar and cotton, which in 1822 comprised 49 percent of Brazil's export income, contributed barely 3 percent in 1913 against the 60 percent represented by coffee.[21] Meanwhile, local markets were supplanted by warehouses at railroad hubs and town life atrophied. The rapid urbanization of the southeast after 1880 contrasted with relative deurbanization in the north.[22]

The dismal decade of the 1890s, which combined drought with the international deflation of commodity prices and a national financial panic, was particularly devastating in the Nordeste. By 1897, for example, the transport price of sugar exceeded the selling price offered by brokers, and numerous plantations and *usinas* (sugar refineries) went belly up.[23] ("Only southern Bahia's cacao region avoided the overall economic decline of the 1890s, chiefly because prices for cacao on the world market rose during this period and planters were able to profit from cheaper labor costs because of an influx of migrants driven from the *sertão* by drought.")[24]

Eugenics and Economic Involution

As Leff has pointed out, it is not immediately obvious why the late-nineteenth-century Nordeste should have undergone such extraordinary economic devolution. Certainly other primary producers made up for falling export prices with higher productivity and increased output. "In view of the rapid growth of world demand for cotton and sugar during the nineteenth century, Brazil's failure to expand its exports of these products much more vigorously seems astonishing." His own explanation hinges on the exchange-rate consequences of Brazilian coffee's dominant position in the world market. Under the gold standard system, strong coffee earnings led to the automatic appreciation of the milreis, which in turn raised northern sugar and cotton prices to uncompetitive levels. The Nordeste's biggest problem, in this view, was its monetary integration with the rest of Brazil. "The coffee-dominated exchange rate," writes Leff, "squeezed factor returns and priced ever-larger quantities of the northeast's sugar and cotton out of the world market."[25]

The decline of export competitiveness brutally pruned the foliage of the Nordeste's class structure. If successive southern-dominated governments assuaged the great northern oligarchs with regular political kickbacks (often in the guise of "drought aid"), more modest *fazendeiros* were left to the mercy of market forces. From about 1875, control over production began to pass into the hands of the owners (often foreign or foreign-born) of modernized usinas. "The capability of the usinas to handle a greater load of cane called for further monopolistic consolidation of land resources; in the wake of this process, small and middle landowners became uprooted."[26] The fate of ex-slaves, of course, was unimaginably more difficult in an economic system that no longer required the same huge levies of labor-power. As the Nordeste's economy slumped into a coma, supernumerary labor was either pushed into the *sertão*'s "black, barren fields of hunger" (Tavora) or induced to gamble with disease and exploitation in the rubber forests of Amazonas.

What did *not* happen in the last quarter of the nineteenth century was what neoclassical theory would have predicted as an automatic reflex: the emigration of northern labor to southeastern growth poles. Instead, beginning in the late Empire, national and local governments began to heavily subsidize mass immigration from Italy, Germany and Portugal. Even the elites of the Nordeste fervidly embraced "Europeanization." An extraordinary example was Bahia during the terrible "Two Eights" drought-famine of 1888–89. While state authorities were roadblocking *retirantes'* route to the cities and forcibly interning them by the thousands in camps, they continued efforts to lure European immigrants with expensive subsidies (few were tempted).[27]

Southeastern coffee planters, for their part, wanted only "white" overseas laborers after Emancipation, and soon made this federal policy in the new Republic. (The racial preference was later amended to include Japanese as well as southern Europeans.) "Why were the coffee planters in the southeast more willing to finance immigration from Europe than from the northeast?" Leff believes that "part of the answer may have been the prevalent racial attitudes on the part of the coffee planters, which led them to prefer European to mulatto workers," while Deutsch points to "cultural biases on the part of Southeastern planters against native Brazilian workers."[28]

Both understate racism as public policy. Gerald Greenfield has shown how Liberal discourse about drought and development in the late 1870s revolved around urban perceptions of the "dark, primitive world of the hinterland" and "retirante inferiority and aversion to labor."[29] "To the extent that Brazil during the latter portion of the nineteenth century embraced the tenets of positivism, enlightenment notions of progress, and the concomitant scientific racism of thinkers like Buckle and Spencer, the backlanders became not merely curiosities from a bygone age, but detriments to the nation's progress. Evolving institutions of national culture, largely based in Rio and revealing marked influence from Western Europe and the United States, stressed the nation's great potential while lamenting the inadequacies, intellectual as well as moral, of much of the nation's population."[30] The Brazilian Republic, moreover, was probably the first government anywhere explicitly committed to large-scale "positive Eugenics." Leading fin de siècle savants like the Bahian scientist Nina Rodrigues corroborated fears that "race mixing was responsible for all social deviance such as banditry, religious heresy, and the like."[31] Whereas mass European immigration into the United States in the 1890s was conceived as simply providing human fuel for the economy, Brazil's elites also wanted to use immigration to radically transform the nation's racial physiognomy. They were obsessed with "de-Africanizing" and "whitening" Brazil.

The War of Canudos, as we have seen, became a macabre racial allegory driven by elite fears of the northern poor whom they denigrated as *caboclos*: a racial caste strongly marked by admixture of Indian ancestry with Portuguese and African. The demonized figure of Antonio Conselheiro was frequently invoked to justify the urgency of Europeanization. ("Always insecure over the rest of Brazil's whispers that Bahia's leading families had intermixed so much with the *gente de cor* during the heyday of slavery, the Bahians seized the conflict as a way to demonstrate their commitment to continued progress on the European model.")[32] In this way, European immigration became the deliberate substitute for either developing the *sertão* and/or letting the northern poor move southwards.

As a result, scientific racism helped create the mother of all dual labor markets. "The highly elastic supply of labor from overseas meant that output could expand at a rapid pace in Brazil's advanced sector without raising the wages of workers in the rest of the economy."[33] By 1889 the British consul in Pernambuco reported to London "that labor there was cheaper than anywhere in the world except in Asia."[34] As Celso Furtado famously argued, the Nordeste, following the pattern of previous export booms and busts in Brazilian history, regressed on a diet of super-cheap labor. As in Victorian India or late Qing China, the glut of labor-power created massive disincentives to productivity-raising capital investment (the usinas being a partial exception). "This economic 'involution,' as Furtado called it, was the opposite of development because each historical export boom until coffee (brazilwood, sugar, gold, and contemporaneous with coffee, rubber) led to retrogression, not to sustained growth."[35]

Ecological Decline

Since the emergence of the great *fazendas de gado* in the late seventeenth century, the ecology and economy of the *sertão* repeatedly have been reshaped by El Niño droughts. The "Leather Age" of the eighteenth century, when *fazendeiros* made legendary fortunes selling their longhorned cattle and *carne do Ceará* (dried beef) to coastal sugar plantations and the gold mines of Minas Gerais, was brought to an end by the terrible drought of 1791–93, which decimated the semi-wild herds. Some of the big *fazendeiros* clung to their feudal domains, while others moved to the coast and became absentee landlords, but even more let their cattle ranges be broken up into impoverished shards.[36] The ecology of the *sertão* was ill-suited to the pressures of many small, marginal ranches. "As a matter of fact," Kenneth Webb has argued, "the sertão is not really very good for cattle," but was adapted to this use when the herds were forced out of the *zona da mata* by the sugar boom. The productivity of the *sertão* with its scant forage was notoriously low. "The carrying capacity of the land was determined not by how many head of cattle were supported by one hectare of *caatinga*, but rather how many hectares of land were required by one beef critter."[37] A typical ranch of 1,000 hectares, for example, might sustain only 50 scrawny cattle; and even the biggest *fazendas* (10,000 hectares or more) rarely pastured herds larger than 1,000.[38]

In the early nineteenth century, large numbers of subsistence farmers and laborers as well as fugitive slaves, mostly from the adjacent *agreste* of Pernambuco or Bahia, began to move into the sertão for the first time. "Agriculture required little or no investment," writes Chandler in her study of the Cearán *sertão* of Inhamuns, "and although it was even more susceptible to the disastrous effects of droughts than cattle, recovery was much easier."[39] The vast northeast interior became a frontier safety valve for the social contradictions of the coastal slave economy. "The *sertão* absorbed the surplus population of the *zona da mata* during the stagnant periods of the sugar industry, and benefited from the labors and energies of those who, for economic, psychological, or whatever reason, could not integrate themselves into the famous *casa grande e senzala* sugar culture."[40] Between 1822 and 1850, the Empire officially supported this immigration by recognizing homestead claims on land formerly belonging to the *sertão*'s fast-disappearing indigenous peoples.

As the greatest twentieth-century authority on Nordeste agriculture, Jose Guimaraes Duque, has emphasized, most of the new settlers brought labor-intensive, mid-latitude farming techniques ill-suited to the dry tropical climate and infertile soils of the *sertão*.[41] This 650,000-square-kilometer region—Euclydes da Cunha pointedly named his famous book *Os Sertões* rather than *O Sertão*—encompasses a stunning variety of landscapes and local climates. But only the fertile bottomlands along the rivers corresponded to the immigrants' experience and these were monopolized by the cattle *fazendas*, their orchards and loyal tenants. So the newcomers moved into the humid *serras* (uplands). These hilly soils gave good harvests for a year or two, but quickly lost their fertility. After tragic trial and error, they eventually adapted a semi-nomadic swidden style of agriculture: two years of cultivation followed by eight years of fallow and cattle-grazing.[42] But population pressure eventually forced thousands into the dry *sertão* or *caatinga*—characterized by shallow rocky soils and spiny cacti—where ownership was unestablished or where they squatted at the pleasure of the big *fazendeiros* whose gunmen might remove them at will.[43]

After the termination of legal squatting in 1850, most new immigrants to the *sertão* simply became *parceiros* (sharecroppers) on *fazenda* land. Although the backlands were still popularly identified with the picturesque figure of the free-ranging *vaqueiro,* the great majority of the population by mid-century were threadbare subsistence farmers, *parceiros* or migratory *agregados* (day-laborers). "In the mid-nineteenth century," estimates Levine, "certainly less than 5% and probably less than 1% of the rural population owned land."[44] These poor *sertanejos,* unlike the slaves of the *zona de mata*, were nominally free men, but access to land and water was as tenuous as the life of a laborer confronted by the *capangas* of an angry landowner. The most powerful *fazendeiro* in each rural municipio typically held the rank of "coronel" in the old imperial Guardia Nacional, and the system of boss-controlled voting and elite violence, which originated in the coastal sugar plantations then spread to the *fazendas*, became known as *coronelismo*. It was the "essential partner to economic exploitation, allowing landlords to squeeze the maximum possible surplus from their work-force, eliciting submissiveness and crushing any resistance or attempts to challenge their monopoly over the land."[45] As Hamilton Monteiro has emphasized, high levels of routine violence—whether between squatters and *fazendeiros* or between competing elite *parentelas*—organized and directed the relations of production in the Victorian *sertão.*[46]

The slow deterioration of the landscape under the pressure of overgrazing—visible since the late eighteenth century—was accelerated by the slash-and-burn agriculture of the rural poor who cultivated maize, beans and manioc. "In the caatinga especially, impermeable, crystalline rock formations are common, which slope towards the rivers, facilitating rapid run-off, soil erosion, silting up of rivers and evaporation."[47] Poverty became synonymous with the lack of water and clear title to the land. A small number of big *fazendas*, the enduring centers of oligarchical power, monopolized the perennial water sources and were usually well protected from drought, but the rest of the population in the *semi-arido* was pitifully dependent upon the erratic rainfall. Every year the *sertanejo* made a desperate wager with a devil we know as El Niño:

> The lives of all the dwellers of the backlands were inescapably linked to the fluctuations of the seasons, but none so closely, hence so vulnerable, as the small subsistence farmer. In November and December he would burn off the dry stalks remaining from the previous season, preparing to plant his beans, corn, and manioc in the ashes of the previous crop; if the land had yielded poorly the past year, he might move to a new location. When the first rains arrived, usually in January, he would plant his seeds and hope for their continuance.
>
> In seasons of relatively light rainfall, those able to plant in the *baixos* [pockets of rich soil in streambeds] were better off than those on the higher ground, but they ran the risk of losing their crops to flash floods which might sweep down the creekbeds without warning with heavy local showers upstream. If heavy showers came before the seedlings had taken firm hold, they would be washed out; frequently, plants sprouted only to wither as the rains stopped. In such cases, the farmer would plant again, and if necessary, a third or fourth time. Exhibiting astonishing tenacity and patience, he would plant time and time again, reserving only a minimal stock of seed for food until the harvest.
>
> At intervals, the rain would fail completely, or hold off so long as to make a successful harvest impossible. Only then would the stubborn back-

> lands farmers leave their homes and move toward the better-watered hills, the coast, or, as a last resort, to the towns and cities like "... so many errant ants hunting food wherever they could find it, crossing and recrossing the roads and on them meeting others in similar condition." In the towns they would seek work, or failing that, surrender their pride and beg, but only until such time as they could safely return to their plots of ground.[48]

The drought-famine of 1825, which killed 30,000 in Ceará alone, exposed the full ecological precariousness of the *sertão*'s hybrid cattle and subsistence farming economy in the absence of systems of water storage and irrigation.[49] It caused "such widespread mortality and human dislocation," according to Cunniff, "as to alter radically the settlement and economic patterns of the region." In effect, it revealed that the biological endowments of the *sertão* were being dangerously mined out. "Cattle were grazed beyond the areas of natural pasture, into the previously shunned arid land and onto the wooded hills, where they came into conflict with the similarly expanding agriculture of the slopes." What cattle on the overstocked ranges did not eat up was quickly stripped away as firewood or fodder by squatters. The infinite network of cattle trails worn into the sterile, friable soil accelerated erosion. In the classic pattern, as the sparsely wooded hillsides were denuded, runoff increased while water tables and springflows declined. It was evident both to the *sertanejos* themselves as well as the occasional foreign visitor that they were desertifying parts of the backlands and probably altering the climate as well. Some dreamed of a vast irrigation network of wells, dams and reservoirs; others envisioned reforestation "as the route back to the mythical once-verdant *sertão*."[50]

But there was no source of investment to stabilize or reverse the *sertão*'s ecological decline. The backward cattle industry, little changed since the seventeenth century, supported the autocratic power of the local *coroneis* but failed to generate an accumulable surplus for irrigation works had such inclinations towards improvement existed amongst the *sertão*'s oligarchs. Even on the great *fazendas*, hydraulic engineering consisted simply of shallow wells (*cacimbas*) in creek beds that were dug by hand every May as the surface waters dried up. The few small reservoirs actually built during the nineteenth century were so unusual as to become objects of local awe.[51]

As discussed earlier, the capacity of any layer of government to sponsor irrigation works was constrained by what might be called "triple peripheralization": the underdevelopment of the Brazilian financial system vis-à-vis British capital; the Nordeste's declining economic and political position vis-à-vis São Paulo; and the *sertão*'s marginality within state politics vis-à-vis the plantation elites of the coast. Politicians endlessly proposed irrigation schemes, but none were built. Ironically, the State's impotence to develop the *sertão* was inverted by the littoral elite into the racist caricature of the indolent, backward *sertanejo*.

The Cotton Boom

The socio-ecological crisis in the backlands was temporarily hidden from view (as in India and Egypt) by the cotton boom that accompanied the US Civil War. The abdication of the irrigation debate, as Cunniff points out, had ultimately fatal consequences. "Ironically, the most prosperous period in the history of the sertão was to compound the errors and continue the trends of the previous years; the relative affluence of the 1860s was in large part responsible for the horrors of the 1870s."[52] A drought-resistant variety of arboreal cotton was introduced in the *sertão* and exports to English textile mills from the port of Recife increased from 165,265 kilos in 1845 to nearly 8 million kilos in 1871.[53] Prices almost doubled from 885 reis in 1861 to 1,600 reis in 1863, and "the cotton boom at its zenith reached into nearly every corner of the sertão."[54] The mirage of prosperity was reinforced by the remarkable absence of drought between 1845 and 1869.

But high cotton prices were only a magnet that attracted yet more "landless, directionless subsistence farmers" to the backlands. The labor required during the short vegetative cycle of cotton did not amortize the annual subsistence cost of slaves, so it was usually cultivated by free labor.[55] "Although it is evident that some larger landholders turned to cotton, it was essentially the crop of the poor, who had no previous agricultural investment to hinder their plunge into its culture." As workers deserted the plantations of Pernambuco for the cotton frontier of Ceará's Carirí valley, the sugar barons complained bitterly about the growing labor shortage.[56] By 1876 the poorest stratum of the *sertão* social order, the landless *agregados*, comprised fully 40 percent of the population of Ceará (epicenter of the 1877 drought).[57]

Although it should have been evident after Appomattox that high-quality US cotton would soon flood the world market, the Cotton Supply Association of Manchester, whose overriding interest (as we saw in Berar) was a permanently overstocked buyer's market in raw cotton, fiercely lobbied Brazilians to bring even more acreage under cultivation. Before long, however, the return of short-staple Southern cotton drove down the price of the varieties that Manchester had promoted so zealously in Egypt, India and Brazil.

Desperate *sertanejos* tried to compensate by producing yet more cotton. But as cotton patches blossomed in the most remote corners of the *sertão*, the producers were caught in a vise between falling world market prices and high, rigid costs of overland transport to the nearest river ports. Unlike India, the Nordeste lacked a railroad infrastructure, and unlike China, which also suffered from transportation bottlenecks, it lacked a huge domestic market to encourage value-added cotton handicrafts. The only hope for saving the *sertão*'s cotton industry was a crash program of railroad and road construction in the interior. As Cunniff explains, the imperial government toyed in the late 1860s with a plan to build a railroad from Ceará's capital of Fortaleza to the major cotton center of Uruburetama, but the project was abandoned in 1868 after the completion of a only few kilometers of track. As with irrigation, there was neither state capacity nor obvious foreign interest to take up the challenge of developing the *sertão*.[58]

By 1869, when a new drought devastated subsistence crops in many parts of the backlands, the same British cotton buyers who had orchestrated the boom a decade before were rejecting the Nordeste's "inferior," "poorly processed" cotton shipments. The *sertanejos*—once again pariahs—had nowhere to turn. "From subsistence farmers and herdsmen, a large proportion of backlanders had been converted into the marginal commercial farmers and agricultural laborers existing in an extremely precarious economic state, more vulnerable than ever to sudden crisis by virtue of the fact that their traditional ties to the large landholders had been greatly weakened or broken."[59] As in north China, the commercialization of agri-

Table 12.2

Rise and Fall of the *Sertão* Cotton Boom

	Pernambuco		Ceará	
	Kilos Exported	Price	Kilos Exported	Price
1860	1.3 million	–	0.8 million	–
1862	2.8 million	–	0.7 million	–
1864	8.4 million	1.00	1.0 million	1.00
1866	18.2 million	.62	2.1 million	.74
1869	15.2 million	.71	–	.49
1871	16.8 million	–	7.3 million	.35
1873	15.2 million	.47	5.1 million	.35
1875	11.1 million	.35	5.8 million	–
1877	2.6 million	–	.06 million	.24

Price: 1864=1.00
Source: Adapted from data in Cunniff, Table II-1, p. 81, and Johnson, *Sharecroppers of the Sertão*, Table 1, p. 20.

culture in the *sertão* had less to do with seedlings of rural capitalism than with increased social and ecological marginality.

To make matters worse, the overextension of cotton cultivation during the 1860s had been matched by the expansion of the cattle population: from 1.2 million in Ceará in 1860 to 2 million in 1876. Like the pauper cotton-growers, the *fazendeiros* had recklessly increased the size of their herds, despite legislation attempting to stabilize land/cattle ratios, to compensate for falling beef and leather prices. Soil degradation and erosion were accelerated. Moreover the combined pressure of cotton and cattle on the soil left less room for traditional subsistence crops, and Cunniff finds indications that the Nordeste "was entering a period of famine even before the great drought devastated the area." The epidemiological evidence includes the appearance of beriberi in Ceará and Paraiba in 1872—attributed to the *sertanejos*' increasing dependence on cheap, poorly milled rice imported from India—as well as outbreaks of smallpox, cholera and yellow fever.[60]

The international shockwaves from the collapse of the US railroad boom, which inaugurated the depression of 1873–79, reached the *sertão* in 1874. "The most drastic deflation in the memory of man," it depressed even further the prices of the agricultural exports that were now the faltering livelihood of *agregados* as well as *fazendeiros*. The small trickle of domestic credit, inadequate even in boom times, dried up completely. "By the end of the year the majority of banks [in the Nordeste] suspended loans. In 1875 the Banco Maua begged for a moratorium, while the Banco National stopped payments and the director of the Banco Alemão committed suicide. There was no way to control the ensuing panic."[61]

The provincial governments, meanwhile, were wrestling with public debts they could no longer finance. At the edge of default, several provinces, led by Pernambuco, imposed onerous taxes on foodstuffs sold at regional fairs. This despised legislation fatefully coincided with simultaneous efforts by the imperial government to introduce the metric system and reinforce conscription (a measure that was widely feared as an attempt to "enslave" freedmen). The resulting explosion was known as the Quebraquilos ("smashing the kilos") revolt. Throughout the *agreste* and *sertão* regions of Paraiba, Pernambuco, Rio Grande do Norte and Alagoas, armed crowds systematically destroyed decimal weights and measures and burned tax records.[62] The revolt was finally crushed by imperial troops, forcing many rebellious *sertanejos* to flee into the hills where they became *cangaceiros* preying on the *fazendas* and towns.[63] Thus, on the eve of the Grande Seca, local government in the Nordeste was bankrupt, malnutrition and beriberi were widespread, rioting had broken out in some of the towns, the poor were pillaging *fazendas*, and banditry was the only growth sector in the economy.

The Irrigation Charade

Large northern landowners, needless to say, welcomed the emergence of this overstocked labor-supply without realizing that they were, in effect, embracing their own underdevelopment. Indeed, as we have seen, they protested violently against anything, like Conselheiro's saintly and autarchic city of Canudos, that appeared to threaten their abundance of labor. Elsewhere such a surfeit of immiseration might have produced a social revolution, but the northeastern littoral had the vastness of the *sertão* as a social safety-valve. Indeed, from the 1870s onward, the Nordeste was effectively capitalized on the fluxes of labor between the backlands and the coast. Potentially explosive accumulations of poor and unemployed laborers in the littoral were diverted into the subsistence economy of the *sertão*, then periodically regurgitated towards the coast by drought. The *sertão*, in effect, provided welfare for the poor, while drought guaranteed that desperate laborers would always be available to depress wages on the coast. Even in the Ceará *sertão*, virtually depopulated by the great *secas* of the 1870s and 1890s, local oligarchs as we have seen were able to find profit as labor contractors for Pará and Amazonas.

Thus while the *coroneis* had the most avid interest in "drought relief" (which they largely intercepted), they were little disposed toward any real development or ecological stabilization of the *sertão*. The all-out national mobilization to destroy Canudos was in stark contrast to official apathy over the fate of *sertanejos* in the four successive El Niño droughts between 1888 and 1902. The great domestic debate of the 1890s, symptomatically, was not over arresting the decline of the Nordeste, but between Paulistas who urged more state spending in the southeast and the opposition, which wanted to bolster Brazil's international credit after the milreis lost half of its value to runaway inflation between 1892 and 1897. The Rothschilds rescued the government in 1898 with a £10 million loan in return for a surcharge on import duties and a deflationary budget that left no spare change for public works.[64]

The economic and political hegemonies, respectively, of the British and the Paulistas, plus the northeastern oligarchs' deepening investment in their own underdevelopment, thus explains much of the structural context of the century-long burlesque of "irrigating the *sertão*." In the wake of successive El Niños, national commissions and visiting foreign irrigation experts drew up sweeping, never-implemented plans for stabilizing agriculture and human settlement in the backlands. The few hydraulic projects that were actually built, beginning with the Acude Quixada reservoir in Ceará in 1899, "stored water which benefited large landowners and protected their cattle by providing pasture and watering facilities but ... left most of the low-income agricultural population untouched."[65] Only 500 hectares of the *sertão* had actually been irrigated by 1941, and twenty-seven years later, when a military dictatorship worried about possible Guevarist *focos* in the Nordeste hired Israeli consultants to conduct the first comprehensive irrigation survey, conditions of life for millions of drought-stricken and immiserated *sertanejos* were little different from the days when Conselheiro and Cícero first preached Apocalypse on the backroads of Ceará.[66]

Glossary

agregado	Tenant or tolerated squatter (literally, one who lives by favor on another's land); same as *morador.*
agreste	Intermediate zone between the drought-stricken *sertão* and humid coastal zona de mata.
bajra	Pearl millet: extremely drought resistant and more nutritious than higher-status grains.
bania	Moneylender (and usually trader).
beata(o)	Lay ascetic.
caatinga	Thorny scrub forest.
caboclo	Mixed-race person.
cangaceiro	Outlaw.
cash	Bronze coin (1/1000th of a tael).
coronel	Rural political boss (plural: *coroneis*).
cultuurstelsel	"Culture system": obligatory regime of agricultural export production in the Netherlands East Indies.
dacoit	Robbery/expropriation.
Deccan	Peninusular interior of India south of the Narmada River; also the volcanic Deccan Plateau.
durbar	State meeting of officials.
Encilhamento	Speculative bubble in the early Brazilian Republic.
ENSO	El Niño-Southern Oscillation.

fazenda Cattle ranch (in the Nordeste).
fazendeiro Rancher (*hacendado*).
fellah Peasant (plural *fellahin*).
flagelado "Scourged one" (drought victim).
gente de cor People of color.
gram Pulse grown during *rabi.*
hsien Chinese county.
ITCZ Intertropical Convergence Zone (of trade winds).
jagunco Pejorative term for herdsmen of the *sertão*/follower of Conselheiro.
jawar *Sorghum vulgare.*
khatedar Equivalent of *ryot* in Berar.
kaoliang All-purpose sorghum: milled for grain while stalks used in construction.
kharif Growing season of crops harvested in the autumn.
lakh 100,000.
makhzan Government/royal power (Morocco).
malguzar Landowner, often with tenants (India's Central Provinces).
mandioca Cassava (the root is poisonous unless carefully prepared).
maund Unit of weight (82 lbs.).
milreis Nineteenth-century Brazilian currency.
MSLP Mean Sea Level Pressure .
mu One-sixth of an acre (China).
NAO North Atlantic Oscillation.
Nian rebellion Vast peasant uprising north of the Huai River (1851–68) led by Zhang Luoxing and defeated by U. S. Grant's host, Li Hongzhan.
Nordeste Eight states of the Brazilian northeast whose vast interior is the *sertão*.
parceiro Sharecropper.
rabi Growing season of crops harvested in the spring.
retirante Refugee (Brazil).
ryot Peasant (Deccan).

ryotwari	System by which each peasant is assessed separately for revenue.
sabha	Association.
seca	Drought.
sertão	Backland region of Brazil's Nordeste.
sertanejo	Resident of the *sertão*.
shi	Measure of grain: about 176 pounds in weight.
SOI	Southern Oscillation Index.
sowcar	Moneylender (also *sahukar*).
SPCZ	South Pacific Convergence Zone.
SST	Sea surface temperature.
takavi	State-backed agricultural loan (also *taqavi* and *tagai*).
tael	Chinese ounce of silver; nineteenth-century monetary unit.
taluk	Indian revenue division.
talukdar	Large landowner.
teleconnection	Correlation between widely separated climate events.
thermocline	The sharp temperature gradient separating warm surface layer of ocean from deeper cold water.
Warm Pool	Trade Wind–driven pooling of very warm surface water in the western Pacific (Indonesia and Queensland); it drives earth's largest tropical convection system; both migrate towards the International Date Line during El Niño events.
vaqueiro	Cowboy (in Brazil's Nordeste).
zamindar	Property-holder under permanent settlement (Bengal).
zemstvo	Provincial and county council.
zona de mata	Well-watered zone of sugar cultivation on the coast of the Nordeste.

Notes

Preface

The epigraph is from John Hidore, *Global Environmental Change: Its Nature and Impact,* Upper Saddle River, N.J. 1996, p. 96.

1. William McFeely, *Grant: A Biography,* New York 1981, pp. 453, 457–60 and 471.
2. Ibid., pp. 458–71.
3. John Russell Young, *Around the World with General Grant,* subscription edn. (American News Company in 20 parts), New York 1878–79, pp. 242 and 246.
4. Ibid., pp. 266–7 and 274.
5. Ibid., pp. 278 and 284–5.
6. Ibid., p. 622.
7. Ibid., p. 624.
8. "On this occasion 'our distinguished guest,' the double Ex-President of the 'Great Western Republic,' who got as drunk as a fiddle, showed he could also be as profligate as a lord. He fumbled Mrs. A., kissed the shrieking Miss B.—pinched the plump Mrs. C. black and blue—and ran at Miss D. intent to ravish her. Finally, after throwing all the … female guests into hysterics by generally behaving like a must elephant, the noble beast was captured by main force and carried (quatre pattes dans l'air) by six sailors … which relieved India of his distinguished presence. The marine officer … reports that, when deposited in the public saloon cabin, where Mrs. G. was awaiting him … this remarkable man satiated there and then his baffled lust on the unresisting body of his legitimate spouse, and copiously vomited during the operation. If you have seen Mrs. Grant you will not think this incredible" (Lytton quoted in McFeely, p. 473).
9. Adam Badeau, *Grant in Peace,* Hartford 1887, pp. 310–11.
10. Quoted in McFeely, p. 474.
11. Young, p. 414.
12. Hang-Wei He, *Drought in Northern China in the Early Guang Xu (1876–1879),* Hong Kong 1980, pp. 36–7 (in Chinese).
13. Quoted in McFeely, p. 557 fn43.
14. J.T. Headley, *The Travels of General Grant,* Philadelphia 1881, p. 444.
15. William Digby, *"Prosperous" British India: A Revelation from Official Records,* London 1901, p. 118.
16. Ibid., p. 122.
17. Alfred Russel Wallace, *The Wonderful Century: Its Successes and Its Failures*, London 1898, p. 341.
18. David Landes, *The Wealth and Poverty of Nations*, New York 1998, p. 437.
19. W. Arthur Lewis, *Growth and Fluctuations, 1870–1913*, London 1978, pp. 29, 187 and 215 especially.

20. Karl Polanyi, *The Great Transformation*, Boston 1944, p. 160.
21. Ibid., pp. 159–60.
22. Slavoj Žižek, *The Spectre Is Still Roaming Around! An Introduction to the 150th Anniversary Edition of the Communist Manifesto*, Zagreb 1998, p. 17.
23. Rosa Luxemburg, *The Accumulation of Capital,* trans. Agnes Schwarzchild, London 1951 [1913], pp. 370–71.
24. Bertolt Brecht, *Poems 1913–1956,* London 1976, p. 204.
25. See chapter 7.
26. Jill Dias, "Famine and Disease in the History of Angola, c. 1830–1930," *Journal of African History* 22 (1981).
27. P. Wright, *An Index of the Southern Oscillation*, University of East Anglia, Climate Research Unit Publication, Norwich 1975; and William Quinn et al., "Historical Trends and Statistics of the Southern Oscillation, El Niño, and Indonesian Droughts," *Fish. Bull.* 76 (1978).
28. George Kiladis and Henry Diaz, "An Analysis of the 1877–78 ENSO Episode and Comparison with 1982–83," *Monthly Weather Review* 114 (June 1986). Although they "resist the temptation to compare the 'intensity'" of the two events, they point out that the 1876–78 event lasted longer and was associated with sea-level pressure anomalies across a larger area of the tropics (p. 1046).
29. Peter Whetton and Ian Rutherfurd, "Historical ENSO Teleconnections in the Eastern Hemisphere," *Climatic Change* 28 (1994), p. 243.
30. Michael Watts, *Silent Violence: Food, Famine and Peasantry in Northern Nigeria*, Berkeley 1983.
31. David Arnold, *Famine: Social Crisis and Historical Change*, London 1988.
32. Alfred Sauvy, "Trois mondes, une planete," *L'Observateur* 118 (14 Aug. 1952), p. 5.
33. See the discussion in chapter 9; also the much-awaited study by Kenneth Pomeranz, *The Great Divergence: China, Europe, and the Making of the Modern World Economy*, Princeton, N.J. 2000, which appeared while this book was in proof.

A Note on Definitions

1. See Kevin Trenbeth, "General Characteristics of El Niño-Southern Oscillation," in M. Glantz, R. Katz, and N. Nichols (eds.), *Teleconnections Linking Worldwide Climate Anomalies,* Cambridge 1991, pp. 13–42.
2. Rolando Garcia, *Drought and Man: The 1972 Case History, vol. 1, Nature Pleads Not Guilty,* Oxford 1981, p. 157.
3. *Report on the Famine in the Bombay Presidency, 1899-1902, vol. 1,* Bombay 1903, p. 3; and J. A. Crawford, *Report on the Famine in the Hyderabad Assigned Districts in the Years 1899 and 1900,* Nagpur 1901, p. 2. On China, see Pierre-Etienne Will, *Bureaucracy and Famine in Eighteenth-Century China,* Stanford, Calif. 1990.
4. Amartya Sen, P*overty and Famines: An Essay on Entitlement and Deprivation,* Oxford 1984, p. 1. Also Meghnad Desai, "The Economics of Famine," in G. Harrison (ed.), *Famine,* Oxford 1988.
5. Arnold, pp. 44–5 and 85.
6. Amarita Rangasami, "'Failure of Exchange Entitlements' Theory of Famine: A Response," in *Economic and Political Weekly* 20:41 (12 Oct. 1985), p. 178.
7. Michael Watts, "Drought, Environment and Food Supply," in Michael Glantz (ed.), *Drought and Hunger in Africa: Denying Famine a Future,* Cambridge 1987, p. 205.
8. Michael Watts,"Heart of Darkness" in Stephen Reyna (ed.), *The Political Economy of African Famine,* New York 1991, p. 44.
9. Alexander De Waal, *Famine That Kills: Darfur, Sudan, 1984-1985,* Oxford 1989, pp. 6 and 10.
10. *Report of the Commissioners Appointed to Enquire into the Famine in Bengal and Orissa 1866,* vol. 1, Calcutta 1867, p. 24.
11. Klein, "Plague, Polity and Popular Unrest," p. 731.
12. Maharatna, pp. 7–8.
13. David Washbrook, "The Commercialization of Agriculture in Colonial India: Production, Subsistence and Reproduction in the 'Dry South,' c. 1870–1930," *Modern Asian Studies* 28:1 (1994), p. 151.
14. Klein, p. 735.
15. Inga Glendinnen, *Reading the Holocaust,* Cambridge 1999, p. 14.

1. Victoria's Ghosts

1. William Digby, *The Famine Campaign in Southern India: 1876–1878,* 2 vols., London 1878, p. 505; references are to vol. 1 unless otherwise noted.
2. "Philindus," "Famines and Floods in India," *Macmillan's Magazine*, Jan. 1878, pp. 244–5.
3. Digby, pp. 7 and 13.
4. British Parliamentary Papers, *Report of the Indian Famine Commission*, part 1, *Famine Relief*, cd. 2591, London 1880, p. 191. On the revolutionary role of Burmese rice surpluses in the imperial economy, see Cheng Siok-hwa, *The Rice Industry of Burma, 1852–1940,* Kuala Lumpur 1968.
5. Cornelius Walford, *The Famines of the World*, London 1879, p. 126.
6. Meerut district officer quoted in Elizabeth Whitcombe, *Agrarian Conditions in Northern India*, vol. 1 of *The United Provinces Under British Rule, 1860–1900,* Berkeley 1972, p. 195.
7. Letter from Madras Government to Government of India, 30 Nov. 1876, quoted in B. Bhatia, *Famines in India, 1850–1945*, Bombay 1963, p. 94.
8. *The Nineteenth Century*, Sept. 1877, p. 177.
9. Christophe Guilmoto, "Towards a New Demographic Equilibrium: The Inception of Demographic Transition in South India," *The Indian Economic and Social History Review* (hence, *IESHR*) 29:3 (1992), p. 258.
10. Digby, pp. 38 and 361.
11. Andrew Roberts, *Salisbury: Victorian Titan*, London 1999, p. 215.
12. *The Times*, 9 Jan. 1877; Aurelia Harlan, *Owen Meredith*, New York 1946, pp. 218–20; and Bernard Cohn, "Representing Authority in Victorian India," in Eric Hobsbawm and Terence Ranger, eds., *The Invention of Tradition*, Cambridge 1983, pp. 179–208.
13. Digby, vol. 1, p. 46.
14. R. Neelankanteswara Rao, *Famines and Relief Administration: A Case Study of Coastal Andhra, 1858–1901,* New Delhi 1997, p. 120.
15. Roberts, p. 218.
16. For Lytton as a war hawk within Disraeli's government, see R. Ensor, *England: 1870–1914*, Oxford 1936, p. 62; and Lt.-Col. R. Osborne, "India Under Lord Lytton," *Contemporary Review*, Dec. 1879, p. 555 (Liberal view). On the effects of the Gold Standard on Indian finances, see Lance Brennan, "The Development of the Indian Famine Codes," in Wolf Tietze, ed., *Famine as a Geographical Phenomenon*, Dordrecht 1984, pp. 94 and 97.
17. "Swinburne called Lytton's poem 'Lucille' an 'infamous imposture' in that the plot, characters, situations, and even minute descriptions were borrowed from George Sand's novel *Lavinia*. The accusation of plagiarism was also made by Lytton's father" (John Lowe Duthie, "Lord Lytton and the Second Afghan War: A Psychohistorical Study," *Victorian Studies* [Summer 1984], p. 471).
18. Janet Oppenheim, *"Shattered Nerves": Doctors, Patients and Depression in Victorian England,* Oxford 1991, pp. 173–4.
19. Roberts, p. 220.
20. Adam Smith, *An Inquiry into the Nature and Causes of the Wealth of Nations* (1776), fifth edn., London 1930, pp. 27–8.
21. S. Ambirajan, *Classical Political Economy and British Policy in India,* Cambridge 1978, p. 63.
22. Osborne, p. 553; Hari Srivastava, *The History of Indian Famines*, Agra 1968, p. 131; Digby, pp. 50–51; and David Steele, *Lord Salisbury: A Political Biography*, London 1999, p. 98. Compare also to Bentham: "*Laissez faire*, in short, should be the general practice: every departure, unless required by some great good, is a certain evil." In a notable dissent from ultra-orthodoxy, however, John Stuart Mill criticized the policy of absolute nonintervention when large numbers of lives were at stake: "Direct measures at the cost of the state, to procure food from a distance are expedient when, from peculiar reason, the thing is not likely to be done by private speculation" (quoted in Rao, pp. 250).
23. Steele, p. 98 (it is unclear whether this is a direct quotation or paraphrase from a letter from Lytton to Sir John Strachey, Oct. 1877).
24. Angus Maddison, *Moghul Class Structure and Economic Growth: India and Pakistan Since the Moghuls,* New York 1971, p. 40.
25. Derived from Bhatia, Table 5, p. 38.
26. Quoted in John Caldwell, "Malthus and the Less Developed World: The Pivotal Role of India," *Population and Development Review* 24:4 (Dec. 1998), p. 683.

27. From *Parliamentary Papers*, 1881, 68, "Famine Commission —Financial Statement," quoted in Sheldon Watts, *Epidemics and History: Disease, Power and Imperialism*, New Haven, Conn. 1997, p. 203.
28. Caldwell, p. 683.
29. Quoted in Roberts, pp. 85–6.
30. Quoted in Steele, pp. 95 and 102.
31. "General Tremenheere on Missions," *Calcutta Review* 128 (1877), p. 278.
32. Salisbury in Steele, p. 98.
33. Government of India, *Report of the Indian Famine Commission, 1878*, Part I, Famine Relief, London 1880, p. 59.
34. Digby, pp. 173-4
35. K. Suresh Singh, *The Indian Famine 1967*, New Delhi 1975, p. 242.
36. Digby, p. 105.
37. Ibid., pp. 103–4.
38. "Famine and Debt in India," *The Nineteenth Century*, Sept. 1877, p. 184; and Jairus Banaji, "Capitalist Domination and the Small Peasantry: The Deccan Districts in the Late Nineteenth Century," in Gyan Prakash, ed., *The World of the Rural Labourer in Colonial India*, Delhi 1992, p. 124.
39. Correspondent for the *Calcutta Statesman* quoted in Digby, pp. 276–81.
40. Digby, pp. 46–7 and 265; and Bhatia, pp. 94–5. For the quarrel between Lytton and Wodehouse, see *The Times*, 5 Feb. 1877.
41. Bhatia, pp. 85–7.
42. *The Economist* 32 (July 1874), p. 802.
43. See Ambirajan, p. 92.
44. Quoted in ibid., p. 96.
45. *The Times*, 5 Feb. 1877.
46. Copy of Victoria's telegram to the Imperial Assemblage, 1 Jan. 1877, in Huntington Library (San Marino), Grenville Papers (Stowe Collection), 3rd Duke of Buckingham and Chandos, STG India, box 2 (file 7).
47. Secretary of State for India quoted in A. Loveday, *The History and Economics of Indian Famines*, London 1914, p. 57.
48. De Waal, p. 32.
49. "Although no one person can be blamed for the deficiencies of the relief policies, Trevelyan perhaps more than any other individual represented a system of response which increasingly was a mixture of minimal relief, punitive qualifying criteria, and social reform" (Christine Kinealy, *This Great Calamity: The Irish Famine, 1845–52*, Dublin 1994, pp. 349–50).
50. Cf. Rao, p. 118, and Currie, p. 47.
51. Digby, p. 52.
52. Ibid., pp. 85 and 135.
53. Anonymous, "The Indian Famine: How Dealt with in Western India," *Westminster Review*, Jan. 1878, p. 145.
54. Quoted in "Indian Famines," *Edinburgh Review*, July 1877, p. 80. Of all common cereals, rice is the most incomplete in amino acids. See discussion of rural diet and protein deficiencies in Paul Greenough, *Prosperity and Misery in Modern Bengal*, Oxford 1982, p. 70 passim.
55. S. Partridge, medical inspector of emigrants, in *Indian Economist*, 15 Oct. 1870, p. 45 (cited in Dadabhai Naoroji, *Poverty and Un-British Rule in India*, London 1901, p. 25).
56. Quoted in "The Indian Famine: How Dealt with in Western India," p. 145. Cornish hoisted Temple by his own petard by publishing in parallel columns Temple's contrasting views on nutrition requirements in the 1874 and 1876 famines —see his account in *The Times*, 18 May 1877.
57 Digby, pp. 55, 74–5, 85, 113, and 135; and Bhatia, p. 96. For Temple's point of view, see *The Story of My Life*, vol. 1, London 1896, esp. 289–94.
58. Digby, vol. 2, pp. 247 and 252.
59. Kohei Wakimura, "Famines, Epidemics and Mortality in Northern India, 1870–1921," in Tim Dyson (ed.), *India's Historical Demography: Studies in Famine, Disease and Society*, London 1989, pp. 285–6 (on grain prices).
60. *The Times*, 9 July 1877.

61. Digby, vol. 2, pp. 203–4.
62. Digby, p. 26.
63. Rev. A. Rowe, *Every-Day Life in India*, New York 1881, pp. 347–8.
64. Quoted in Kerby Miller, *Emigrants and Exiles: Ireland and the Irish Exodus to North America*, New York 1985, p. 283.
65. Rowe, pp. 204 and 372–3.
66. Quoted in "The Indian Famine: How Dealt with in Western India," p. 153.
67. Digby, p. 340.
68. S. Mehrotra, "The Poona Sarvajanik Sabha: The Early Phase (1870–1880)," *IESHR* 3 (Sept.1969), pp. 305 and 310.
69. Quoted in Digby, pp. 341–2. Lytton's granite face towards India's starving children in these months—like Temple's repudiation of his own "excessive charity" in 1874 —perhaps needs to be seen in a tormented psychological context: perhaps his father's (Bulwer Lytton's) cruel attacks on his "unmanly repining" after the death of his little son in 1871 (Harlan, p. 205).
70. Rowe, p. 345.
71. Digby, p. 283.
72. Harlan, p. 214.
73. "The Sabha humbly submits that no small portion of the success [in restoring rations and reducing deaths] is due to the attitude of complaint and watchfulness taken up by the native and European press …" Letter to Temple, 16 May 1877, quoted in Digby, p. 355.
74. Lytton in a letter to Sir Louis Mallet (11 Jan. 1877), quoted in Ambirajan, p. 93.
75. Quoted in Brennan, p. 97.
76. Digby, pp. 148–50 and 361–2.
77. Ira Klein, "Imperialism, Ecology and Disease: Cholera in India, 1850–1950," *IESHR* 31:4 (1994), pp. 495 and 507; David Arnold, "Cholera Mortality in British India, 1817–1947" in Dyson, p. 270; and Rita Colwell, "Global Climate and Infectious Disease: The Cholera Paradigm," *Science* 274 (20 Dec. 1996), p. 2030.
78. Cecil Woodham-Smith, *Florence Nightingale: 1820–1910*, New York 1983, p. 338.
79. Digby, pp. 361–5; and Richard Tucker, "Forest Management and Imperial Politics: Thana District, Bombay, 1823–1887," *IESHR* 16:3 (1979), p. 288 (quote).
80. Washbrook, "The Commercialization of Agriculture in Colonial India," *Modern Asian Studies* 28:1 (1994), p. 131; and W. Francis, *Bellary District*, Madras 1904, p. 135.
81. Digby, vol. 2, p. 148.
82. Kate Currie, "British Colonial Policy and Famines: Some Effects and Implications of 'Free Trade' in the Bombay, Bengal and Madras Presidencies, 1860–1900," *South Asia* 14:2 (1991), p. 43.
83. Loveday, p. 60.
84. Cf. Ira Klein, "When the Rains Failed: Famine, Relief, and Mortality in British India," *IESHR* 21:2 (1984), p. 195; and Charles Elliot, *Report on the History of the Mysore Famine of 1876–1878*, pp. xx–xxix.
85. Klein, p. 195.
86. Elliot, p. 42.
87. Klein, pp. 196–7.
88. Victoria's speech in *The Economist*, 18 Aug. 1877.
89. A clipping from August 1877 in Grenville Papers, STG India, outsized box (file 5).
90. Ibid.
91. Mary Lutyens, *The Lyttons in India*, London 1979, pp. 111–12. The Madras Government, on the other hand, described its relief workers as "an industrious, hardworking set, fully alive to the grave situation they were in, and grateful for the work provided for them" (*Report on the Buckingham Canal [Koitadatam] Division During the Madras Famine*, Box 2[a], Grenville Papers, STG India).
92. Digby, pp. 206–23.
93. Rev. J. Chandler quoted in Digby, vol. 2, p. 148.
94. David Arnold, "Famine in Peasant Consciousness and Peasant Action: Madras, 1876–78," *Subaltern Studies* 3 (1984), pp. 86–7 and 93; and "Dacoity and Rural Crime in Madras, 1860–1940," *The Journal of Peasant Studies*, p. 163.
95. Sharma, p. 359.
96. Neville Nicholls, "Complex Climate-Human-Ecosystem Interactions in the 1877 El Niño,"

Abstracts, Second International Climate and History Conference, Norwich 1998, pp. 65–6; and J. Mayer, "Coping with Famine," *Foreign Affairs* 53:1 (Oct. 1974), p. 101.

97. *The Times*, 9 July 1877.
98. Digby, p. 241.
99. Ibid., pp. 243–4.
100. Reprinted as James Wilson, *The Government of India in Relation to Famines and Commerce,* London 1878, pp. 9 and 13.
101. D. Rajasekhar, "Famines and Peasant Mobility: Changing Agrarian Structure in Kurnool District of Andhra, 1870–1900," *IESHR* 28:2 (1991), pp. 143 (quote), 144 and 150.
102. This is the hardly unbiased recollection of a relief official, Lepel Griffin, told to *Harper's Weekly* many years later during the famine of 1896 ("Indian Famine," 7 Nov. 1896, pp. 489–90).
103. Bhatia, pp. 98–101.
104. Quoted in Osborne, p. 563 (his emphasis).
105. Ibid., pp. 563–7.
106. Wakimura, p. 286.
107. Osborne, p. 564.
108. Ibid., pp. 553 and 565.
109. Digby singles out Knight's *Statesman* for praise for sending a correspondent to spend six months reporting from the famine districts of Bombay, Madras and Mysore (Digby, p. 22). The *Statesman's* scathing editorials and similarly critical letters from missionaries were published in pamphlet form as *Sir George Couper and the Famine in North Western Provinces* (Calcutta 1878). This excerpt is from Bhatia, p. 100.
110. Cf. Kaushalya Devi Dublish, *Revolutionaries and Their Activities in Northern India*, Delhi 1982, pp. 3–4; and Mehrotra, pp. 310–11.
111. John McLane, *Indian Nationalism and the Early Congress*, Princeton, N.J. 1977, p. 45. On widespread British anxiety that the 1876–77 famine might lead to "revolution," see Ems Namboordiripad, *A History of the Indian Freedom Struggle*, Trivandrum 1986, p. 136.
112. Premansukumar Bandyopadhyay, *Indian Famine and Agrarian Problems*, Calcutta pp. 97–103.
113. Nightingale, quoted in *The Nineteenth Century*, 8 Sept. 1878.
114. F. B. Smith, *Florence Nightingale*, London 1982, p. 146.
115. "When I wrote these notes in 1873, or read them in 1876, I little dreamt that they would so soon obtain such terrible confirmation as the present deplorable famines have given them" (D. Naoroji, *Poverty and Un-British Rule in India*, London 1901, pp. 60 and 141); and R. Masani, *Dadabhai Naoroji: The Grand Old Man of India*, London 1939, p. 192.
116. Quoted in Osborne, p. 568.
117. Bandyopadhyay, p. 104.
118. Ibid., pp. 106 (Gladstone) and 113 (funds spent).
119. Brennan, p. 98.
120. Ibid., p. 108.
121. Ibid., pp. 103–7.
122. Carol Henderson, "Life in the Land of Death: Famine and Drought in Arid Western Rajasthan," Ph.D. diss., Columbia University 1989, p. 66.
123. H. M. Hyndman, *The Bankruptcy of India,* London 1886, p. 26.
124. Naoroji, pp. 212 and 216.
125. Brennan, p. 107.
126. Bandyopadhyay, p. 109; and 1880 Report quoted in *Report of the Indian Famine Commission, 1901*, Calcutta 1901, p. 2.
127. McLane, p. 49.
128. Masani, p. 295.

2. 'The Poor Eat Their Homes'

The statement by the governor of Shanxi appeared in the *Imperial Gazette* (15 March), translated in *The Times* (London), 21 June 1877.

1. Cf. *L'Exploration* [Paris] 6 (1877), p. 43; and K. De Silva, *A History of Sri Lanka*, Berkeley 1981, p. 308.

2. George Kiladis and Henry Diaz, "An Analysis of the 1877–78 ENSO Episode and Comparison with 1982–83," *Monthly Weather Review* 114 (1986), pp. 1035 (quote), 1037–9 and 1046.
3. Eric Foner, *Reconstruction: America's Unfinished Revolution, 1863–1877*, New York 1988, pp. 512–13. "1873 is a great economic divide. It was the peak of the trading boom of the mid-nineteenth century" (Derek Beales, *From Castlereagh to Gladstone, 1815–1885*, New York 1969, p. 232).
4. Eric Hobsbawm, *The Age of Capital 1848–1875*, London 1975, p. 46.
5. The extensive plantation economy of Oceania, usually associated with copra and sugar, actually started with the cotton boom of the 1860s. See the preface in Brij Lal, Doug Munro and Edward Beechert, *Plantation Workers: Resistance and Accommodation*, Honolulu 1993, pp. 3–4.
6. P. Cain and A. Hopkins, *British Imperialism: Innovation and Expansion, 1688–1914*, London 1993, p. 371.
7. *The Times* (21 June 1877) blamed the famine on the refusal of the Qing to allow European investors to build a mainline railroad into interior northern China.
8. On the 1867–68 famine in Hebei (Xhili), see Mary Wright, *The Last Stand of Chinese Conservatism: The T'ung-Chih Restoration, 1862–1874*, Stanford, Calif. 1957, p. 135.
9. R. H. Tawney, *Land and Labour in China*, London 1932, p. 77.
10. UK, Foreign Office, *Parliamentary Papers*, China No. 2 (1878), pp. 1–2.
11. Rev. Timothy Richard, quoted in Paul Bohr, *Famine in China and the Missionary*, Cambridge, Mass. 1972, p. 14.
12. Will, *Bureaucracy and Famine*, p. 36.
13. Frederick Williams, *The Life and Letters of Samuel Wells Williams*, New York 1889, p. 432.
14. Bohr, p. 15.
15. *Parl. Papers*, No. 2, p. 3.
16. Richard, pp. 98 and 117.
17. Cited in the *Pall Mall Gazette*, 1 May 1877.
18. Bohr, p. 15; and Timothy Richard, *Forty-Five Years in China* (third edn.), New York 1916, p. 119.
19. Quoted in *Parl. Papers*, No. 2, p. 11.
20. Bohr, pp. 60–63 and 218.
21. *Times* (London), 1 May 1877.
22. Bohr, pp. 35–41 and 227.
23. *Parl. Papers*, No. 2, p. 6.
24. Srinivas Wagel, *Finance in China*, Shanghai 1914, p. 23.
25. *Parl. Papers*, No. 2, p. 6.
26. Arthur Smith, *Village Life in China*, Boston 1970 [1899], p. 116. See also Kamal Sheel, *Peasant Society and Marxist Intellectuals in China*, Princeton, N.J. 1989, p. 12.
27. Joseph Esherick, *The Origins of the Boxer Uprising*, Berkeley 1987, p. 101.
28. David Faure, "Local Political Disturbances in Kiangsu Province, China: 1870–1911," Ph.D. diss., Princeton, N.J. 1975, pp. 162–3.
29. Will, p. 49.
30. Faure, pp. 162–5, 275 and 468.
31. John Hidore, *Global Environmental Change*, Upper Saddle River, N.J. 1996, p. 96.
32. *Parl. Papers*, No. 2, p. 6. Two members of the China Inland Mission had attempted to found a mission in Henan in 1875 but were quickly driven out. With enormous difficulty a foothold was finally achieved in Chowkiakow in 1884, but missionaries had little success and most were forced to flee during the uprising in 1900 (Marshall Broomhall [ed.], *The Chinese Empire: A General and Missionary Survey*, London 1907, pp. 159–61).
33. Resumes in *L'Exploration* [Paris] 6 (1878), pp. 172 and 416.
34. Elizabeth Perry, "Social Banditry Revisited: The Case of Bai Lang, a Chinese Brigand," *Modern China* 9:3 (July 1983), p. 362.
35. Milton Stauffer, *The Christian Occupation of China*, Shanghai 1922, p. 211.
36. In Ping-ti Ho, *Studies on the Population of China, 1366–1953*, Cambridge, Mass. 1959, p. 232.
37. S. Wells Williams, *The Middle Kingdom*, vol. 2, New York 1883, p. 736.
38. On Shanxi's dependence on Wei Valley surpluses, see Helen Dunstan, *Conflicting Counsels to Confuse the Age: A Documentary History of Political Economy in Qing China, 1644–1840*, Ann Arbor 1996, pp 250–51.
39. *Parl. Papers*, No. 2, pp. 5–7.

40. *Gazette* (15 March), translated in *The Times*, 21 June 1877.
41. *New York Times*, 24 February 1878.
42. Harold Hinton, *The Grain Tribute System of China (1845–1911)*, Cambridge, Mass. 1956, pp. 42–3.
43. *Parl. Papers*, No. 6 (1878), p. 2.
44. Bohr, p. 43.
45. *The Times* (London), 21 June 1877.
46. A. Broomhall, *Hudson Taylor and China's Open Century: Book Seven (It Is Not Death to Die!)*, London 1989, pp. 170 and 467 ff 13. See also Adrian Bennett, *Missionary Journalist in China: Young J. Allen and His Magazines, 1860–1883*, Athens, Ga. 1983, p. 174.
47. Bohr, pp. 16–21.
48. Hang-Wei He, *Drought in North China in the Early Guangxu (1876–1879)* [in Chinese], Hong Kong 1980, p. 15.
49. William Soothill, *Timothy Richard of China*, London 1924, p. 102.
50. Richard, p. 130.
51. Syndicated to the *New York Times*, 6 July 1878.
52. *Parl. Papers*, No. 6, p. 1.
53. A. Broomhall, *China's Open Century: Book Seven*, pp. 111 and 163.
54. James Legge (trans.), *The Famine in China. Pictures Illustrating the Terrible Famine in Honan That Might Draw Tears from Iron. Extracts from a Translation of the Chinese Texts*, London 1878 (Trinity College Library [Dublin] pamphlet collection).
55. Lillian Li, "Introduction: Food, Famine, and the Chinese State," *Journal of Asian Studies*, 41:4 (Aug. 1982), p. 700.
56. *Records of the General Conference of the Protestant Missionaries of China* (Shanghai, 10–24 May 1877), Shanghai 1878, p. 446.
57. A. Broomhall, *China's Open Century, Book Seven,* p. 115; and Arthur Smith, *The Uplift of China* (revised edn.), New York 1912, p. 175.
58. Arnold, *Famine*, p. 137.
59. Rudolf Wagner, "The *Shenbao* in Crisis: The International Environment and the Conflict Between Guo Songtao and the *Shenbao*," *Late Imperial China* 20:1 (June 1999), p. 117.
60. Quoted in B. MacGillivray, *A Century of Protestant Missions in China*, Shanghai 1907, pp. 78–9.
61. Williams, p. 433.
62. Ibid., p. 184.
63. A. Broomhall, *China's Open Century: Book Six,* pp. 169 and 246.
64. Ibid., pp. 176–7
65. *Parl. Papers*, No. 2, p. 7.
66. A. Broomhall, *China's Open Century: Book Six,* p. 169.
67. Ibid., pp. 175 and 181.
68. Euclydes da Cunha, *Rebellion in the Backlands* (*Os Sertões*), trans. Samuel Putnam, Chicago 1944, p. 41.
69. Professor and Mrs. Louis Agassiz, *A Journey to Brazil*, Boston 1869, p. 459.
70. Herbert Smith, *Brazil: The Amazon and the Coast,* New York 1879, p. 400.
71. Da Cunha, p. 24.
72. Ibid., p. 410.
73. Roger Cunniff, "The Great Drought: Northeast Brazil, 1877–1880," Ph.D. diss., University of Texas, Austin 1970, p. 128.
74 Pierre Denis, *Brazil*, London 1911, p. 330.
75. Ibid., p. 129.
76. Smith, pp. 411–13.
77. Rodolfo Theofilo, *Historia da seca do Ceará, 1877–1880*, Rio de Janeiro 1922, p. 120.
78. Smith, ibid.
79. Cunniff, pp. 248–50.
80. Account of 11 November 1877 cited in Billy Jaynes Chandler, *The Feitosas and the Sertão dos Inhamuns*, Gainesville, Fla. 1972, p. 162.
81. Cunniff, pp. 152–3.
82. Chandler, pp. 160–61.
83. Rodolfo Theofilo, quoted by Anthony Hall in *Drought and Irrigation in North-East Brazil*, Cambridge 1978, p. 5.

84. Gerald Greenfield, "Migrant Behavior and Elite Attitudes: Brazil's Great Drought, 1877–1879," *The Americas* 43:1 (July 1986) p. 73; and Cunniff, ibid.
85. Smith, pp. 415–6.
86. Cunniff, p. 163.
87. Father Cícero Romão Baptista describing conditions in Ceará's Carirí Valley (ibid., p. 202).
88. Smith, p. 417.
89. Cunniff, pp. 166 and 192.
90. Ibid., pp. 206–11 and 242.
91. Smith, p. 419.
92. Cunniff, pp. 212–13; Smith, pp. 419–35; Kempton Webb, *The Changing Face of Northeast Brazil*, New York 1974, pp. 30–32; and Hall, p. 5.
93. Nicanor Nascimento quoted in Josué de Castro, *Death in the Northeast*, New York 1969, pp. 51–2.
94. Chandler, pp. 164–5.
95. Cunniff, p. 299
96. Ibid., pp. 292–3.

3. Gunboats and Messiahs

The quote from Mirza Asadullah Khan Ghalib appears in Sugata Bose and Ayesha Jalal, *Modern South Asia*, Delhi 1999, p. 43.

1. Hilary Conroy, *The Japanese Seizure of Korea: 1868–1910*, Philadelphia 1974, pp. 90–91. See also Han Woo-Keun, *The History of Korea*, Seoul 1970, p. 403.
2. Reynaldo Ileto, "Religion and Anti-colonial Movements," in Nicholas Tarling (ed.), *The Cambridge History of Southeast Asia*, vol. 2, Cambridge 1992, pp. 220–21.
3. Kiladis and Diaz, p. 1038.
4. Han Knapen, "Epidemics, Droughts, and Other Uncertainties on Southeast Borneo During the Eighteenth and Nineteenth Centuries," in Peter Boomgaard, Freek Colombijn, and David Henley, *Paper Landscapes: Explorations in the Environmental History of Indonesia*, Leiden 1997, p. 140.
5. Henry Forbes, "Through Bantam and the Preanger Regencies in the Eighties," reprinted in Pieter Honig and Frans Verdoorn (eds.), *Science and Scientists in the Netherlands Indies*, New York 1945, pp. 112–13.
6. Knapen, p. 144.
7. W. Hugenholz, "Famine and Food Supply in Java, 1830–1914," in C. Bayle and D. Kolff (eds.), *Two Colonial Empires*, Dordrecht 1986, pp. 169–71.
8. M. Ricklefs, *A History of Modern Indonesia Since c. 1300*, 2nd edn., Stanford, Calif. 1993, pp. 121–23; C. Faseur, "Purse or Principle: Dutch Colonial Policy in the 1860s and the Decline of the Cultivation System," *Modern Asian Studies* 25:1 (1991), p. 34.
9. J. Furnivall, *Netherlands India: A Study of Political Economy*, Cambridge 1944, pp. 138 and 162. For a synthesis of current research on the *cultuurstelsel*, see R. Elson, *Village Java under the Cultivation System, 1830–1870*, Sydney 1994.
10. Hugenholz, ibid.
11. Alfred McCoy, "Sugar Barons: Formation of a Native Planter Class in the Colonial Philippines," *The Journal of Peasant Studies*, 19:3/4 (April/July 1992), pp. 109–14.
12. Violeta Lopez-Gonzaga, "Landlessness, Insurgency and Food Crisis in Negros Island," in *Famine and Society*, p. 111.
13. Angel Martinez Duesta, *History of Negros*, Manila 1980, pp. 253, 259–61, 378–9, 400, and 412–13.
14. Michael Billig, "The Rationality of Growing Sugar in Negros," *Philippine Studies* 40 (1992), pp. 156–7.
15. Filomeno Aguilar, *Clash of Spirits: The History of Power and Sugar Planter Hegemony on a Visayan Island*, Honolulu 1998, p. 166.
16. Ibid.
17. Ibid., pp. 166–70.
18. Myriam Dornoy, *Politics in New Caledonia*, Sydney 1984, pp. 19, 24–5 and 26.
19. Linda Latham, "Revolt Re-examined: The 1878 Insurrection in New Caledonia," *Journal of Pacific History* 10:3 (1975), p. 62.

20. Martyn Lyons, *The Totem and the Tricolour,* Kensington, NSW 1986, p. 61.
21. Ibid.
22. Latham, p. 49.
23. Lyons, pp. 58–65.
24. Louise Michel, *The Red Virgin: Memoirs of Louise Michel,* Birmingham 1981, p. 114.
25. Sharon Nicholson, "Environmental Change Within the Historical Period," in J. Adams, A. Goudie and A. Orme, *The Physical Geography of* Africa, Oxford 1996, pp. 75 and 79; and Jill Dias, "Famine and Disease in the History of Angola, c. 1830–1930," *Journal of African History* 22 (1981), pp. 366–7.
26. Dias, p. 368.
27. Ibid., p. 366.
28. Ibid.
29. Ibid., pp. 368–9.
30. Donald Morris, *The Washing of Spears*, London 1966, p. 267.
31. See Charles Ballard, "Drought and Economic Distress: South Africa in the 1800s," *Journal of Interdisciplinary History*, 17:2 (Autumn 1986), pp. 359–78.
32. *Nature*, 28 March 1878, p. 436.
33. Morris, p. 254.
34. Shula Marks, "Southern Africa, 1867–1886," in Roland Oliver and G. Sanderson (eds.), *The Cambridge History of Africa*, vol. 6, Cambridge 1985, pp. 381 and 387.
35. Morris, p. 267.
36. Cain and Hopkins, p. 372.
37. On the centrality of the labor-supply question to British strategy, see Marks, p. 380; and Jeff Guy, *The Destruction of the Zulu Kingdom*, London 1979, p. 45.
38. T. Davenport, *South Africa: A Modern History*, 4th edn., Toronto 1991, p. 128.
39. Morris, p. 286.
40. Guy, p. 49.
41. Michael Lieven, "'Butchering the Brutes All Over the Place': Total War and Massacre in Zululand, 1879," *History* 84:276 (Oct. 1999), pp. 621 and 630.
42. Karl Butzer, "History of Nile Flows," in P. Howell and J. Allan (eds.), *The Nile: Sharing a Scarce Resource*, Cambridge 1994, p. 105.
43. *The Times* (London), 2 Jan. 1878.
44. Luxemburg, p. 437. Luxemburg devoted most of a chapter to debt imperialism and the ensuing famine in Egypt (pp. 429–39).
45. Lady Gordon quoted in Roger Owen, *The Middle East in the World Economy, 1800–1914*, 2nd edn., London 1993, p. 142.
46. Wilfred Blunt, *Secret History of the British Occupation of Egypt*, New York 1922, pp. 8–9.
47. Roger Owen, *Cotton and the Egyptian Economy: 1820–1914*, Oxford 1969, p. 147.
48. Juan Cole, *Colonialism and Revolution in the Middle East: Social and Cultural Origins of Egypt's 'Urabi Movement*, Princeton, N.J. 1993, pp. 87–8.
49. Cited in Theodore Rothstein, *Egypt's Ruin*, London 1910, pp. 69–70.
50. Cole, ibid.
51. Quoted in the Earl of Cromer, *Modern Egypt*, vol. 1, London 1908, p. 35.
52. Cole, pp. 87–8. See also Allan Richards, "Primitive Accumulation in Egypt, 1798–1882," *Review* 1:2 (Fall 1977), pp. 46–48.
53. "The Winter of 1876–7 in Algiers," *Symons' Monthly Meteorological Magazine*, October 1877, pp. 132–3.
54. Charles-Robert Ageron, *Les Algeriens musulmans et la France (1871–1919),* vol. 1, Paris 1968, pp. 380–81.
55. Ibid., pp. 378–9.
56. Ageron, *Histoire de l'Algerie contemporaine*, vol. 2, Paris 1979, p. 202.
57. Julia Clancy-Smith, *Rebel and Saint: Muslim Notables, Populist Protest, Colonial Encounters*, Berkeley 1994, p. 224.
58. Ageron, *Histoire*, pp. 201–2, 211 and 220.
59. Jean-Louis Miege, *Le Maroc et l'Europe (1830–1894),* vol. 3, Paris 1962, pp. 383–4, 403, 419 and 441. On the monetarization of agrarian taxation, see Edmund Burke III, *Prelude to Protectorate in Morocco, Precolonial Protest and Resistance, 1860–1912*, Chicago 1976, p. 22.

60. Miege, pp. 382–3, 390 and 398.
61. Quoted in Cornelius Walford, *The Famines of the World*, London 1879, p. 19.
62. Miege, pp. 385–8 and 393.
63. Ibid., pp. 395–7, 450–53 and 458.
64. *Nature*, 28 March 1878, p. 436.
65. Walford, p. 49.
66. Letter to *Nature*, 4 April 1878; Doug Munro and Stewart Firth, "Samoan Plantations: The Gilbertese Laborers' Experience, 1867–1896," in Lal, et al. (eds.), *Plantation Workers: Resistance and Accommodation*, Honolulu 1993, p. 111; and Kiladis and Diaz, p. 1040.
67. Enrique Florescano and Susan Swan, *Breve historia de la sequia en Mexico*, Xalapa (Ver.) 1995, p. 57.
68. Walford, p. 70.
69. Kiladis and Diaz, p. 1042. It was the second wettest winter in San Francisco, the first elsewhere in Northern California.
70. Walford (1879), p. 299.
71. H. Diaz, "A Possible Link of the 1877–78 Major El Niño Episode and a Yellow Fever Outbreak in the Southern United States," *Abstracts*, Second International Climate and History Conference, University of East Anglia, Norwich 1998.
72. W. Quinn and V. Neal, "The Historical Record of El Niño Events," in R. Bradley and P. Jones (eds.), *Climate Since AD 1500*, London 1992, p. 638.
73. *Nature* (1878), p. 447.
74. Marx to N.F. Danielson (19 February 1881) in *Karl Marx and Friedrich Engels on Colonialism*, Moscow n.d., p. 337.
75. Romesh Chunder Dutt, *Open Letters to Lord Curzon*, Calcutta 1904, pp. 3–4.
76. Kohei Wakimura, "Famines, Epidemics and Mortality in Northern India, 1870–1921," in Tim Dyson (ed.), *India's Historical Demography*, London 1989, pp. 288–90.
77. Klein, "When the Rains Failed," pp . 199 and 210.
78. William Digby, "Famine Prevention Studies," in Lady Hope, *General Sir Arthur Cotton: His Life and Work*, London 1900, pp. 362–3.
79. Rajasekhar, "Famines and Peasant Mobility," p. 132.
80. Washbrook, p. 141.
81. Rajasekhar, p. 134.
82. Ibid., pp. 142 and 150 (quote).
83. Rao and Rajasekhar, p. A-82.
84. Figures from Hugh Tinker, *A New System of Slavery: The Export of Indian Labour Overseas, 1830–1920*, Oxford 1974, pp. 49 and 305.
85. Srivastava, p. 226.
86. Zhang Jiacheng, Zhang Xiangong and Xu Siejiang, "Droughts and Floods in China During the Recent 500 Years," in Jiacheng (ed.), *The Reconstruction of Climate in China for Historical Times*, Beijing 1988, p. 46 (driest year); Hang-Wei He, pp. 36–7 (quote); Will, *Bureaucracy and Famine*, p. 30 ("the worst drought in North China's premodern history was undoubtedly that of 1876–79"); A. Broomhall, *China's Open Century, Book Six*, p. 466 fn44 (official estimate); and Cahill, p. 7. Susan Cotts Wakins and Jane Menken estimate that 12 percent of the population died in five northern provinces ("Famines in Historical Perspective," *Population and Development Review* 11:4 (Dec. 1985), p. 651.)
87. *Report of the China Famine Relief Fund*, Shanghai 1879, p. 7; and Lillian Li, "Introduction: Food, Famine, and the Chinese State," *Journal of Asian Studies*, 41:4 (Aug. 1982), p. 687. This is the same range of mortality earlier quoted by Tawney in his famous study (p. 76).
88. This is based on articles in *China's Millions* used by A. Broomhall, *China's Open Century, Book Six*, p. 181.
89. Ibid., p. 181; Soothill, p. 101. Richard, it should be noted, believed that the death toll throughout nine affected provinces was somewhere between 15 and 20 million (Soothill, p. 103).
90. Arnold, p. 21.
81. Burke, p. 23.
92. Miege, p. 443.
93. Luis Felipe de Alencastro (ed.), *Historia da vida privada no Brasil: Imperio*, São Paulo, 1997, p. 312.
94. Seymour Drescher, "Brazilian Abolition in Comparative Perspective," in Rebecca Scott, et al. (eds.), *Abolition of Slavery in Brazil*, Durham, N.C. 1988, p. 32.

95. Quoted in de Castro, p. 53.
96. Cunniff, p. 283.
97. Arup Maharatna, *The Demography of Famines: An Indian Historical Pespective*, Delhi 1996.

4. The Government of Hell

R. Anatase quoted in Harold Marcus, *The Life and Times of Menelik II*, Oxford 1975, pp. 136–7.

1. Cf. Avner Offer, *The First World War: An Agrarian Interpretation,* Oxford 1989, pp 85, 89; Dan Morgan, *Merchants of Grain*, New York 1979, esp. pp. 32–6; and Carl Solberg, *The Prairies and the Pampas: Agrarian Policy in Canada and Argentina, 1880–1930*, Stanford, Calif. 1987, esp. p. 36.
2. Eric Stokes, *The Peasant and the Raj*, Cambridge 1978, p. 275.
3. Quoted in Neil Charlesworth, "Rich Peasants and Poor Peasants in Late Nineteenth-Century Maharashtra," in Dewey and Hopkins (eds.), p. 108.
4. Christopher Baker, *An Indian Rural Economy, 1880–1955: The Tamilnad Countryside*, Bombay 1984, p. 135.
5. Gilbert Fite, *The Farmers' Frontier, 1865–1900*, New York 1966, p. 96.
6. The Nordeste was an exception: the improvement in weather could not make up for the decline in the earnings of sugar and cotton. Recession on the coast, moreover, turned into depression in the hinterlands. "In the *sertão*, even formerly independent cowherds reverted to marginal activities, selling goat hides and working for pitiful wages on the ranches of large landowners. Bankrupt agriculturalists sold or abandoned their land and moved to cities" (Levine, p. 37).
7. See Donald Meinig's brilliant studies of bonanza wheat belts and rainfall modification theories, "The Evolution of Understanding and Environment: Climate and Wheat Culture in the Columbia Plateau," *Yearbook of the Association of Pacific Coast Geographers* 16 (1954); and *On the Margins of the Good Earth: The South Australian Wheat Frontier, 1869–1884*, Chicago 1962. (It should be noted that South Australia's climatic boom–bust cycle was in antiphase to most other regions, with humid years in the late 1870s and severe drought in the early 1880s. Unlike eastern Australia, its weather has little correlation with ENSO.)
8. Jonathan Raban, *Bad Land: An American Romance*, New York 1996, p. 208. He refers to the drought of 1917–20 that broke the wartime wheat boom in eastern Montana.
9. Meinig, *On the Margins*, p. 207.
10. See "Filtered Normalised Monthly Anomalies of MSLP and SST Since 1871," in Rob Allan, Janette Lindesay and David Parker, *El Niño Southern Oscillation and Climate Variability*, Collingwood, Vic. 1996, pp. 188–201.
11. Peak grain prices in the pre-Depression United States (which reflect global, not just local, harvest conditions)—e.g., 1891–92, 1897–98, 1908–09, 1914–19 and 1924–25—correlated to observed El Niño events (price trend from Wilfred Malenbaum, *The World Wheat Economy, 1885–1939,* Cambridge, Mass. 1953, p. 29).
12. Fite, pp. 108–9 and 126–7. Drought in 1892–93 again produced great distress throughout the Great Plains. The famous hunger-fighter Louis Klopsch, the publisher of New York's *The Christian Herald*, reported incredulously from Nebraska that "there was really a famine in one of the richest agricultural regions of the United States" and that thousands faced death from cold or starvation unless they received immediate relief (quoted in Charles Pepper, *Life-Work of Louis Klopsch: Romance of a Modern Knight of Mercy*, New York 1910, pp. 245–6).
13. Florescano and Swan, pp. 57 and 113–14.
14. Bhatia, pp. 168–9.
15. Digby, *Prosperous British India*, London 1901, p. 129.
16. Bhatia, pp. 172–8.
17. Carol Henderson, "Life in the Land of Death: Famine and Drought in Arid Western Rajasthan," Ph.D. diss., Columbia University 1989, p. 42.
18. Navtej Singh, *Starvation and Colonialism: A Study of Famines in the Nineteenth Century British Punjab, 1858–1901*, New Delhi 1996, pp. 89–91.
19. Ibid.
20. Digby considered this an accurate estimate of total famine mortality ("*Prosperous*" *British India*, p. 129).
21. "Hume to Every Member of the Congress Party" (16 Feb. 1892, quoted in Edward Moulton, "Allan

O. Hume and the Indian National Congress: A Reassessment," in Jim Masselos (ed.), *Struggling and Ruling: The Indian National Congress 1885–1985*, New Delhi 1987, p. 11.

22. For an 1888 account of depopulation in Shaanxi, see George Jamieson, "Tenure of Land in China and the Condition of the Rural Population," *Journal of the China Branch of the Royal Asiatic Society* (for 1888), Shanghai 1889, p. 91.
23. Allan, Lindesay and Parker, pp. 188–91.
24. Cf., T. L. Bullock (consul at Chefoo), "The Geography of China," *The Journal of the Manchester Geographical Society,* 14:4–6 (April–June 1896), p. 129; John Freeman, "Flood Problems in China," *Proceedings, American Society of Civil Engineers,* May 1922, pp. 1113 and 1137–8; Alvyn Austin, *Saving China: Canadian Missionaries in the Middle Kingdom,* Toronto 1986, pp. 36–8; A. Broomhall, *China's Open Century: Book Seven,* pp. 97–8; *Spectator* syndicated in *New York Times*, 5 March 1888; and C. Vorosmarty, et al., "Drainage Basins, River Systems, and Anthropogenic Change: The Chinese Example," in James Galloway and Jerry Melillo, *Asian Change in the Context of Global Climate Change*, Cambridge 1998, p. 212.
25. Han Woo-Keou, *History of Korea*, p. 404.
26. George Lensen, *Balance of Intrigue: International Rivalry in Korea and Manchuria, 1884–1899*, vol. 1, Tallahassee 1982, p. 118.
27. Han Woo-Keou, pp. 404–13.
28. Richard Robbins, Jr., *Famine in Russia: 1891–1892*, New York 1975, pp. 6–10.
29. Ibid., pp. 12–13 and 170–71.
30. Leroy Vail and Landeg White, *Capitalism and Colonialism in Mozambique: A Study of Quelimane District*, Minneapolis 1980, pp. 100–101.
31. Denis, p. 351.
32. Graciliano Ramos, *Barren Lives*, Austin, Tex. 1971, p. 121.
33. Arthur Dias, *The Brazil of Today*, Nivelles 1903, pp. 249–50.
34. Ralph Della Cava, *Miracle at Joãseiro*, New York 1970, p. 31.
35. James McCann, *People of the Plow: An Agricultural History of Ethiopia, 1800–1900*, Madison, Wis. 1995, p. 89.
36. Richard Pankhurst, *The History of Famine and Epidemics in Ethiopia Prior to the Twentieth Century*, Addis Ababa 1986, pp. 62–3.
37. William Jordan, *The Great Famine: Northern Europe in the Early Fourteenth Century*, Princeton, N.J. 1996, p. 36.
38. McCann, p. 89.
39. Pankhurst, pp. 59 and 91–2.
40. Holger Weiss, "'Dying Cattle': Some Remarks on the Impact of Cattle Epizootics in the Central Sudan During the Nineteenth Century," *African Economic History* 26 (1998), p. 182.
41. Richard Pankhurst, *Economic History of Ethiopia, 1800–1935*, Addis Ababa 1968, pp. 216–20.
42. James McCann, *From Poverty to Famine in Northeast Ethiopia: A Rural History, 1900–1935,* Philadelphia 1987, pp. 73–4.
43. Chris Prouty, *Empress Taytu and Menelik II*, London 1986, p. 101.
44. Pankhurst, *The History of Famine*, pp. 71–2 and 100.
45. Marcus, *Menelik II*, pp. 135, 139 and 143 fn2.
46. Haggai Erlich, *Ethiopia and Eritrea During the Scramble for Africa: A Political Biography of Ras Alula, 1875–1897*, East Lansing 1982, p. 141.
47. Pankhurst, *History of Famine*, pp. 74–85 and 96; and *Economic History*, pp. 216–20. McCann (*People of the Plow*) questions accounts of cannibalism, "since no such practices have been reported from recent famines of equal or greater severity" (p. 90).
48. Pankhurst, *The History of Famine*, pp. 87–8.
49. Ibid., p. 91.
50. Harold Marcus, *A History of Ethiopia*, Berkeley 1994, p. 94.
51. A. Donaldson Smith, "Expedition through Somaliland to Lake Rudolf," *Geographical Journal* 8 (1896), p. 127.
52. Pankhurst, *The History of Famine*, pp. 86–9, 105.
53. Marcus, p. 143.
54. Father Joseph Ohrwalder (edited by F. Wingate), *Ten Years' Captivity in the Mahdi's Camp*, London 1897, p. 283.
55. P. Holt, *The Mahdist State in the Sudan: 1881–1898*, Oxford 1958, pp. 157–60.

56. Ibid., pp. 160 and 165–7.
57. Ibid., pp. 171–3. See also Augustus Wylde, *Modern Abyssinia*, London 1901, p. 106.
58. Alexander De Waal, *Famine that Kills: Darfur, Sudan, 1984–1985*, Oxford 1989, pp. 63–4.
59. Ohrwalder, p. 306.
60. Holt, pp. 174–5.
61. C. Rosignoli, "Omdurman during the Mahdiya," *Sudan Notes and Records* 48, Khartoum 1967, p. 43.
62. Rudolf Slatin Pasha, *Fire and Sword in the Sudan*, London 1897, p. 274.
63. Ibid., p. 273.
64. Ibid., pp. 274–5.
65. Rosignoli, *Sudan Notes*, p. 42.
66. Catherine Coquery-Vidrovitch, "Ecologie et historie en Afrique noire," *Histoire, economie et société* 16:3 (1997), p. 501;
67. Richard Pankhurst, *The Ethiopians*, Oxford 1998, pp. 183–9.
68. Marcus, pp. 92–3.
69. On the 1896 drought-famine in Ethiopia, see Coquery-Vidrovitch, p. 503. For a recent overview of Ethiopian climate history, see Maria Machado, Alfredo Perez-Gonzalez and Gerardo Benito, "Paleoenvironmental Changes During the Last 4000 years in the Tigray, Northern Ethiopia," *Quaternary Research* 49 (1998), pp. 312–21.
70. Sir John Elliot, "Address to the Sub-section Cosmical Physics," reprinted in *Symon's Meteorological Magazine* 465 (Oct. 1904), p. 147.
71. Malenbaum, pp. 178–9.
72. For a discussion of drought and dearth in Upper Egypt and the Sudan, see A. Milne, "The Dry Summer on the Upper Nile," *Scottish Geographical Magazine* 16 (1900), pp. 89–91. Tolstoy's observations on the agrarian crisis that began with the 1896–97 crop failures ("La Famine en Russie en 1898") was published in *La Revue socialiste* (Paris), 1898, pp. 129–42. In Milan, the army massacred 80 bread rioters on 8 May 1898 (see Offer, p. 220).
73. David Landes, *The Unbound Prometheus: Technological Change and Industrial Development in Western Europe from 1750 to the Present*, Cambridge 1969, p. 231.
74. Elizabeth Isichei, *A History of African Societies to 1870*, Cambridge 1997, p. 293.
75. David Arnold, "Touching the Body: Perspectives on the Indian Plague, 1896–1900," *Subaltern Studies* 5 (1987), p. 74.
76. Esherick, p. 300; and David Little, *Understanding Peasant China*, New Haven, Conn. 1989, pp. 152–3 (quote).
77. Arthur Smith, *China in Convulsion*, vol. 1, Edinburgh 1901, p. 219; and A. Broomhall, *China's Open Century, Book Seven*, p. 306.
78. Della Cava, p. 55.
79. Charles Ambler, *Kenyan Communities in the Age of Imperialism*, New Haven, Conn. 1988, p. 3.
80. John Lonsdale, "The European Scramble and Conquest in African History," in Oliver and Sanderson, p. 692.

5. Skeletons at the Feast

The quote appears in H. M. Hyndman, *The Bankruptcy of India*, London 1886, p. vi.

1. "Presidential Address at Lucknow Congress," (Dec. 1899) in Romesh Chunder Dutt, *Romesh Chunder Dutt*, New Delhi 1968, p. 202.
2. Loveday, p. 65.
3. Michelle McAlpin, "Price Movements and Fluctuations in Economic Activity (1860–1947), in Dharma Kumar (ed.), *Cambridge Economic History of India*, Cambridge 1983, pp. 886–8. See also Sir John Strachey, *India*, London 1894, pp. 184–5.
4. Augustin Filon, "L'Inde d'aujourd'hui d'apres les ecrivains indiens: I. La Situation economique et la vie publique," *Revue des deux mondes*, Nov.–Dec. 1899, p. 381.
5. Rashmi Pande, *The Viceroyalty of Lord Elgin II*, Patna 1986, p. 131.
6. Premansukumar Bandyopadhyay, *Indian Famine and Agrarian Problems*, Calcutta, p. 231.
7. The steep decline of British agriculture is vividly illustrated by the contrast between the harvest of 80

million bushels in 1884 and the meager 37 million bushels harvested in 1895 (Marcello de Cecco, *The International Gold Standard: Money and Empire*, New York 1984, p. 25).

8. Thus in an October 1896 letter the collector of Godavari complained that despite a bountiful local harvest, grain prices "depend almost entirely on the condition in other parts of India" (quoted in A. Satyananarayana, "Expansion of Commodity Production and Agrarian Market," in Ludden [1994], p. 207). Satyananarayana provides a useful overview of the complex debate on the degree of integration and automatic price movement in local, national and international markets by the late nineteenth century.
9. G. Chesney, "Famine and Controversy," *The Nineteenth Century*, March 1902, pp. 479 (preexisting drought in Central Provinces and Rajputana) and 481 (price of millet).
10. *The Times*, 18 Jan. 1897.
11. Quoted in B. Bhatia, "The 'Entitlement Approach' to Famine Analysis," in G. Harrison (ed.), *Famine*, Oxford 1988, pp. 39–40.
12. Moulton, p. 17.
13. Bandyopadhyay, p. 140.
14. *Spectator*, 30 Jan. 1897.
15. "From Ahmednagar," 16 Oct., in *New York Times*, 22 Nov. 1896.
16. Margaret Denning, *Mosaics from India*, Chicago 1902, pp. 168–9.
17. "Sir Edwin Arnold on the Famine in India," reprinted from the *North American Review* (March 1897) in the *Review of Reviews*, April 1897, p. 459.
18. "Pestilence and Famine in India," *Spectator*, 16 Jan. 1897, p. 81.
19. S. N. Kulkarni, *Famines, Droughts and Scarcities in India (Relief Measures and Policies)*, Allahabad 1990, p. 16; and Hari Srivastava, *The History of Indian Famines*, Agra 1968, pp. 205 and 226; Bandyopadhyay, pp. 14–16.
20. Bandyopadhyay, ibid.
21. Ibid., p. 231.
22. Ibid., p. 39.
23. As Currie points out, most of the apparatus of the New Poor Law of 1834 was imported into India, except "under normal conditions, there was no commitment to the maintenance of the 'deserving' poor" (p. 49) .
24. Singh, p. 110.
25. George Lambert, *India, The Horror-Stricken Empire*, Elkhart, Ind. 1898, p. 144.
26. Loveday, pp. 88–9.
27. Lambert, pp. 99–100.
28. Pepper, p. 59.
29. Ibid., pp. 318–19.
30. G. Thomas, *History of Photography in India, 1840–1980*, Pondicherry 1981, p. 28. For a British howl of protest against "misleading" famine photographs, see J. Rees, "Fighting the Famine in India," *The Nineteenth Century*, March 1897, pp. 358–61.
31. Sir Andrew Fraser, *Among Rajas and Ryots*, London 1911, pp. 111–25.
32. John McLane, *Indian Nationalism and the Early Congress*, Princeton, N.J. 1977, p. 71.
33. On Tilak and the Irish, see H. Brasted, "Irish Models and the Indian National Congress, 1870–1922," in Masselos, pp. 31–2.
34. E. Pratt, "India and Her Friends," *Westminster Review*, June 1897, p. 647.
35. McLane, p. 29.
36. H. Birdwood, "The Recent Epidemics of Plague in Bombay," *Journal of the Manchester Geographical Society*, 1898, pp. 141–3. See also Alok Sheel, "Bubonic plague in south Bihar: Gaya and Shahabad districts, 1900–1924," *IESHR*, 35:4 (1998), pp. 426–7.
37. Rajnarayan Chandavarkar, "Plague Panic and Epidemic Politics in India, 1896–1914," in Terence Ranger and Paul Slack (eds.), *Epidemics and Ideas*, Cambridge 1992, p. 213.
38. F. B. Smith, *Florence Nightingale*, London 1982, p. 125.
39. Ira Klein, "Urban Development and Death: Bombay City, 1870–1914," *Modern Asian Studies* 20:4 (1986), p. 748.
40. Radhika Famasubban and Nigel Crook, "Spatial Patterns of Health and Morality," in Sujata Patel and Alice Thorner (eds.), *Bombay: Metaphor for Modern India*, pp. 148–51.
41. Klein, p. 734.

42. See the *Spectator*, 16 January 1897, p. 81.
43. On unrest over grain prices, see Kulkarni, p. 16; on rioting, David Arnold, *Colonizing the Body: State Medicine and Epidemic Disease in Nineteenth-Century India*, Berkeley 1993, pp. 214 and 230.
44. Ira Klein, "Plague, Policy and Popular Unrest in British India," *Modern Asian Studies*, 22:4 (1988), p. 737.
45. Arnold, p 204.
46. Chandavarkar, p. 207.
47. Nayana Goradia, *Lord Curzon: The Last of the British Moghuls*, Delhi 1993, p. 123.
48. "Four of every five patients who entered Bombay hospitals perished there," Klein, "Plague, Policy and Popular Unrest," p. 742.
49. Arnold,"Touching the Body," p. 71.
50. McLane, p. 30.
51. Cf. D. Tahmankar, *Lokamanya Tilak*, London 1956, p. 68 passim; N. Kelkar, *Life and Times of Lokamanya Tilak*, Delhi, p. 338 passim; Richard Cashman, *The Myth of the Lokamanya*, Berkeley, pp. 123–50; and Romesh Chunder Dutt, *The Economic History of India in the Victorian Age*, 2nd edn., London 1906, p. 456 (quote).
52. I. Catanach, "Plague and the Indian Village, 1896–1914," in Peter Robb (ed.), *Rural India: Land, Power and Society Under British Rule*, London 1983, pp. 218 and 227.
53. Chandavarkar, p. 210.
54. Catanach, ibid.
55. *India in 1897*, quoted in Filon, p. 381. In his study of the history of famine in a poor district of Bihar, K. Suresh Singh observes that although "the [1896–97] famine was the most lethal in Palamau's recorded history … officially it was reported that 'no deaths were caused by starvation'" (*The Indian Famine 1967*, New Delhi 1975, p. 32).
56. "The Famine in India," *Missionary Review of the World*, April 1897, p. 286.
57. He judged 1897, not 1857 or 1877, to be India's "most calamitous year of the century"; see Ramabai Ranade (ed.), *Miscellaneous Writings of the Late Hon'ble Mr. Justice M.G. Ranade*, Delhi 1992 (reprint), p. 180.
58. Singh, *Starvation and Colonialism*, pp. 98–9.
59. Dutt, pp. 219–22 (Indian National Congress); *Famine and Agrarian Problems*, pp. 193 (Bilaspur) and 227 (Hamilton in House of Commons).
60. This claim (supposedly based on testimony by Sir Charles Lyall in 1898) was made by "E.C." in "The Indian Famine," *Westminster Review* 155:2 (1901), p. 135.
61. D.E.U. Baker, *Colonialism in an Indian Hinterland: The Central Provinces, 1820–1920*, Delhi 1993, pp. 174, 194 and 202.
62. F. Merewether, *A Tour Through the Famine Districts of India*, London 1898, pp. 129–30. Merewether's account of the Jubbulpur poorhouse was scoffed at by J. Rees in *The Nineteenth Century* (March 1897), who claimed that conditions were not radically different than in Limehouse or Mile End. "If the misery and destitution of London itself were collected within a ring fence, it is doubtful if a visitor from the east would think it other than a sad spectacle" (p. 359).
63. See Pepper, p. 78.
64. *The Memoirs of Julian Hawthorne*, ed. Edith Hawthorne, New York 1938, p. 295.
65. Julian Hawthorne, "India Starving," *Cosmopolitan* 23:4 (August 1897), pp. 379–82
66. Ibid. Dr. Louis Klopsch of the *Christian Herald* penned equally shocking accounts from the Ahmedabad poorhouse where prostrate victims were left out in the open, to be eaten by flies in the 110-degree heat. "On inquiring why these people were exposed to the relentless rays of the sun without shelter or shade, I was told that they had been brought in from the neighboring villages on carts and were to remain under observation for twenty-four hours in order to determine whether symptoms of contagious disease developed. They had come in during the afternoon, they had lain there for three or four hours, they were to remain there all night and to stay there all the next forenoon. Possibly the evening of the next day they would be admitted to the inhospitable shelter of the Ahmedabad poor-house. Myriads of flies were feasting on each individual bundle, and the eyelids, mouths, nostrils and ears were all besieged with battalions of flies gorging themselves on the helpless victims of the India famine." Klopsch found the "indescribable misery" of the small children almost "unbearable" to relate (quoted in Pepper, pp. 79–80).
67. W. Aykroyd, *The Conquest of Famine*, London 1974, pp. 64–7.

68. Rudyard Kipling, "William the Conqueror," in *The Day's Work*, London 1898, p. 203.
69. Ibid., pp. 380–81.
70. Caption on photographs, inside front cover, *Cosmopolitan* 23:3 (July 1897).
71. Bandyopadhyay, p. 51.
72. For example, *Harper's Weekly* in 1900 claimed: "The famine of 1877 killed some ten million beings; that of 1897, about sixteen millions; whilst the present one will probably break the record with twenty million" (p. 350). See also Digby, *"Prosperous" British India*, p. 129.
73. C. Ramage, *The Great Indian Drought of 1899*, Boulder 1977, pp. 1–3. Ramage is a world authority on the Indian monsoon.
74. See D. Mooley and B. Parthasarathy, "Fluctuations in All-India Summer Monsoon Rainfall During 1871–1978," *Climate Change* 6 (1984), pp. 287–301.
75. Ramage, p. 6.
76. Bombay Government, *Report on the Famine in the Bombay Presidency, 1899–1902*, vol. 1, Bombay 1903, p. 114.
77. Ramage, p. 4.
78. Pierre Loti, *India*, English translation by George Inman, London 1995, pp. 145–6.
79. Bombay, *Report*, vol. 1, p. 3.
80. Vaughan Nash, *The Great Famine and Its Causes*, London 1900, p. 12.
81. Scott, pp. 142–3.
82. Frederick Lamb, *The Gospel and the Mala: The Story of the Hyderabad Wesleyan Mission*, Mysore 1913, p. 49.
83. Scott, pp. 31–2.
84. Singh, pp. 113–18.
85. Bombay, *Report*, vol. 1, pp. 3 and 83 (artisans and mill workers).
86. Charlesworth, "Rich Peasants and Poor Peasants," pp. 110–11.
87. McLane, pp. 26–7.
88. C. J. O'Donnell, *The Failure of Lord Curzon*, London 1903, pp. 37–41.
89. Quoted in C. Ramage, p. 5.
90. O'Donnell, p. xviii.
91. Nash, p. 171.
92. Bandyopadhyay, pp. 63–7 and 226.
93. Bernard Semmel, *The Liberal Ideal and the Demons of Empire*, Baltimore 1993, p. 109. "Never since the Crimean War, never perhaps since the death of Castlereagh in 1822," wrote Dutt, "has Imperialism been so rampant in England; never have the higher instincts of humanity and justice, of respect towards rival nations, and fairness towards subject nations, been at a lower ebb" (quoted in Romesh Chunder Dutt, *Romesh Chunder Dutt*, New Delhi 1968, p. 63).
94. S. Thorburn, *Problems of Indian Poverty*, Fabian Tract No. 110, London, March 1902, p. 226 (he is writing about 1899–1901).
95. See figures in *The Times* (London), 17 Feb. 1900.
96. Scott, p. 153.
97. Ibid.
98. Eddy, p. 25.
99. On Naoroji's and Dutt's disenchantment with British Liberalism and the former's turn towards the Socialists, see Masani, pp. 201, 400–402 and 432; Dutt, pp. 62–3 and 79; and J. K. Gupta, *Life and Work of Romesh Chunder Dutta, CIE*, Calcutta 1911 (reprinted Delhi 1986), pp. 240–44, 318–19 and especially 458. On demoralization and lack of direction within the Indian National Congress during the famines, see McLane, pp. 130–31. On British Christian socialists and imperialism, see Peter d'A. Jones, *The Christian Socialist Revival 1877–1914*, Princeton, N.J., esp. pp. 198–205; and on Fabian imperialism, see Francis Lee, *Fabianism and Colonialism: The Life and Political Thought of Lord Sydney Olivier*, London 1988.
100. Raymond Challinor, *The Origins of British Bolshevism*, London 1977, p. 15 (Falkirk SDF). At the 1904 Amsterdam Congress of the Socialist International, which branded "Great Britain with the mark of shame for its treatment of India," a thousand delegates (including Hyndman, Jaurès, Luxemburg and Lenin) stood in silence in commemoration of the Indian famine dead, then gave Naoroji a rapturous applause when he declared that the liberation of India from hunger and the drain of wealth "rests in the hands of the working classes. Working men constitute the immense

majority of the people of India, and they appeal to the workmen of the whole world, and ask for their help and sympathy" (Masani, pp. 431–2).

101. Nash, pp. 179–80.
102. Ibid., pp. 19–33.
103. Ibid., pp. 19, 173 and 181.
104. Bombay, *Report*, vol. 1, p. 91
105. Klein, p. 752.
106. Ibid., p. 54.
107. On Kholapur, see Merewether, pp. 27–8.
108. Goradia, pp. 71–4 and 146.
109. Scott, pp. 113–14.
110. Loti, pp. 171–2.
111. Ibid., p. 172.
112. Kuldeep Mathur and Niraja Jayal, *Drought, Policy and Politics*, New Delhi 1993, p. 63.
113. Scott, p. 107.
114. "The outturn of crops which was in the previous year 27,710,258 Indian maunds fell in 1899–1900 to 1,174,923 Indian maunds" (R. Choksey, *Economic Life in the Bombay Gujarat [1800–1939]*, Bombay 1968, p. 171).
115. Ibid; and Scott, pp. 107–8. Choksey estimates that about half of the cattle (or 800,000 head) in Gujarat perished (p. 176).
116. Sherwood Eddy, *India Awakening*, New York 1911, p. 24.
117. Scott, ibid.
118. Quoted in Pepper, pp. 82–3.
119. Vasant Kaiwar, "The Colonial State, Capital and the Peasantry in Bombay Presidency," *Modern Asian Studies*, 28:4 (1994), p. 813.
120. Bombay, *Report*, p. 100.
121. Choksey, p. 44.
122. Eddy, ibid.
123. Klein, "When the Rains Failed," p. 205.
124. J. Coe, "Congress and the Tribals in Surat District in the 1920s," in Masselos, pp. 60–62.
125. "A lady writing from Ahmedabad," quoted in ibid., p. 36.
126. Choksey, p. 44.
127. Bombay, *Report*, p. 95.
128. Nash, pp. 9–10.
129. David Hardiman, "The Crisis of Lesser Patidars: Peasant Agitations in Kheda District, Gujarat, 1917–34," in D. Low (ed.), *Congress and the Raj*, London 1977, pp. 55–6.
130. Baker, p. 231.
131. Ibid., p. 198.
132. Bombay, *Report*, pp. 5–6.
133. Tim Dyson, "On the Demography of South Asian Famines—Part 1," *Population Studies* 45 (1991), pp. 16 and 22.
134. Dutt, *Romesh Chunder Dutt*, p. 252.
135. Arup Maharatna, *The Demography of Famines: An Indian Historical Perspective*, Delhi 1996, p. 15 (Table 1.1); Stein, "The Making of Agrarian Policy in India," p. 18; and Lewis , p. 173.
136. Speech to the Legislative Council, Simla, 19 Oct. 1900 (in Curzon, *Lord Curzon in India: Being a Selection of His Speeches ...* , London 1906, p. 394.
137. Bombay, *Report*, p. 103.
138. Tim Dyson, "Indian Historical Demography: Developments and Prospects," in Dyson (ed.), *India's Historical Demography: Studies in Famine, Disease and Society*, London 1989, p. 5; and J. A. Crawford, *Report on the Famine in the Hyderabad Assigned Districts in the Years 1899 and 1900*, vol. 1, Nagpur 1901, p. 8.
139. *The Lancet*, 16 May 1901.
140. Digby, "*Prosperou" British India*, pp. 137–9.
141. Klein, "When the Rains Failed," p. 186 (on Davis); and Pierre Le Roy, *Le Faim dans le monde*, Paris 1994, p. 16.
142. Maharatna, pp. 15 and 63–7.

143. Chandavarkar, p. 203.
144. Srivastava, p. 269.
145. Ibid., p. 219; and B. Tomlinson, *The Economy of Modern India, 1860–1970* (*The New Cambridge History of India,* 3:3), Cambridge 1993, p. 83.
146. Bandyopadhyay, pp. 192 and 200.
147. Sumit Sarkar, *Modern India: 1885–1947*, Madras 1983, p. 36.
148. Wakimura, p. 301; and Choksey, p. 44.
149. *Report of the Indian Famine Commission, 1901*, Calcutta 1901, p. 7; Klein, "When the Rains Failed," p. 204 fn33.

6. Millenarian Revolutions

The epigraph appears in Euclydes da Cunha, *Rebellion in the Backlands* (*Os Sertões*), trans. Samuel Putnam, Chicago 1944, p. 133.

1. Pepper, *Life-Work of Louis Klopsch*, p. 172.
2. Francis Nichols, *Through Hidden Shensi*, New York 1902, pp. 2–9; Marshall Broomhall, *The Chinese Empire: A General and Missionary Survey*, London (China Inland Mission) 1907, p. 206 (mortality figures).
3. Broomhall, pp. 228–35 and 242. Arthur Tiedemann draws attention to comparable suffering in northern Anhui. "A Jesuit priest at Mengcheng observed, for example, that so many people were dying in the city that the naked dead and dying had to be dumped outside the city walls to be devoured by hungry dogs" ("Boxers, Christians and the Culture of Violence in North China," *Journal of Peasant Studies* 25:4 [July 1899], p. 156).
4. According to Wilkinson (Table 3, p. 144) 75 of 90 Shenxi districts reported crop disaster in 1898. The drought continued through 1900 (67 districts) and was punctually followed by war and brigandage affecting agriculture in 68 districts.
5. On the centrality of *fengshui* doctrines to the popular Chinese interpretation of the crisis, see Smith, vol. 1, p. 57.
6. Esherick, p. 299.
7. Tiedemann (p. 159) cites the *North-China Herald* on "a general crop failure in the wheat-exporting area of northwestern Shandong" previous to the inundation.
8. Ibid., pp. 175–7.
9. Quoted in Pepper, p. 164.
10. Paul Cohen, *History in Three Keys: The Boxers as Event, Experience, and Myth*, New York 1997, p. 69.
11. *New York Times*, 25 March 1899.
12. Lu Yao, "The Origins of the Boxers," *Chinese Studies in History*, 20:3–4 (1987), p. 54.
13. Esherick, pp. 179–80.
14. Pepper, pp. 164–5. A year later, however, the navy did provide Klopsch with a transport, the *Quito*, to carry 5,000 tons of Kansas relief grain to India.
15. Harlan Beach, "The History of Christian Missions in China," in G. Blakeslee (ed.), *China and the Far East*, New York 1910, p. 274.
16. Endymion Wilkinson, "Studies in Chinese Price History," Ph.D. diss., Princeton University 1970, p. 52.
17. Smith, vol. 2, p. 573.
18. S. Teng, *The Nien Army and Their Guerrilla Warfare, 1851–1868*, Paris 1961, p. 127.
19. Smith, vol. 1, pp. 155–6.
20. Elizabeth Perry, "Social Banditry Revisited: The Case of Bai Lang, a Chinese Brigand," *Modern China* 9:3 (July 1983), pp. 361, 366 and 369.
21. Esherick, pp. 174, 223 and 281–2.
22. Smith, p. 219.
23. Ibid., p. 244.
24. Lu, p.52.
25. Cohen, pp. 35, 77–82 (first quote) and p. 95 (second quote); Tiedemann, p. 156.
26. Lu, p. 55.
27. Qi Aizhang, "Stages in the Development of the Boxer Movement and Their Characteristics,"

Chinese Studies in History 20:3–4 (1987), p. 115. In the same issue, Liao Yizhong ("Special Features of the Boxer Movement") denies the existence of any "anti-feudal" dimension, although his citations are from Shandong, not Hebei (pp. 186–7).

28. Broomhall, vol. 7, p. 374.
29. Georges Lefebvre, *The Great Fear of 1789: Rural Panic in Revolutionary France*, New York 1973.
30. Eva Price, *China Journal, 1889–1900: An American Missionary Family During the Boxer Rebellion*, New York 1989, pp. 199 and 203–4. See also Sarah Alice (Troyer) Young, letter from Shanxi (2 Dec. 1899) in coll. 542, box 1, folder 7, Billy Graham Center.
31. Price, pp. 204 and 222.
32. Cohen, p. 172. For similar populist, anti-foreign reactions to the drought in the Beijing region, see E. Ruoff (ed.), *Death Throes of a Dynasty: Letters and Diaries of Charles and Bessie Ewing, Missionaries to China*, Kent, Ohio 1990, p. 68 (letters of Sept. and Oct. 1899).
33. Price, pp. 191–4, 199 and 209.
34. Archibald Glover, *A Thousand Miles of Miracle in China*, London 1904, pp. 6, 85, 195 and 244 (song).
35. Price, p. 224.
36. Austin, p. 75.
37. Esherick, pp. xv–xvi, 282 and 291–2.
38. Smith, vol. 2, p. 716. The Japanese, in contrast to the barbarities of their armies in China in the 1930s, were the honorable exception, and were praised by all independent observers for their humane and respectful treatment of Chinese civilians.
39. E.J. Dillon, "The Chinese Wolf and the European Lamb," excerpted in the *New York Times*, 27 Jan. 1901.
40. Ibid.
41. Joseph Page, *The Revolution That Never Was: Northeast Brazil, 1955–1964*, New York 1972, pp. 26–7.
42. Vera Kelsey, *Seven Keys to Brazil*, New York 1941, p. 172.
43. Robert Levine, *Vale of Tears: Revisiting the Canudos Massacre in Northeastern Brazil, 1893–1897*, Berkeley 1992, pp. 34–8.
44. Levine, pp.193–203 and 229.
45. Ibid., pp. 139, 151 and 159–61.
46. Ibid., pp. 132–3 and 229–31.
47. Ibid., pp 142–6.
48. On the drought in 1898 and 1900, see Charles Wagley, *An Introduction to Brazil*, London 1971, p. 41. According to historical statistics from the International Research Institute for Climate Prediction (University of California, San Diego), the 1897–98 drought in the Nordeste had a rainfall anomaly of –8.15 cm/month. In the following century, the next most severe drought (1915) measured –3.3 cm/month. Moreover, all years from 1897 through 1906 were in the driest historical tercile and had rainfall anomalies of at least –1.4 cm/month. (database at iri.ucsd.edu/hot_nino/impacts/ ns_amer/ index).
49. Levine, pp. 164–5.
50. Ibid., p. 177.
51. Ibid., p. 178.
52. Da Cunha, p. 475.
53. Levine, p. 190.
54. Della Cava, ibid.
55. Levine, p. 148.
56. Della Cava, p. 89.
57. C. Kim and Han-Kyo Kim, *Korea and the Politics of Imperialism, 1876–1910*, Berkeley 1967, pp. 116–17.
58. Pierre van der Eng, "The Real Domestic Product of Indonesia, 1880–1989," *Explorations in Economic History* 1992, pp. 355 and 358.
59. Furnivall, p. 232.
60. See R. Elson, "The Famine in Demak and Grobogan in 1849–50; Its Causes and Circumstances," *Review of Indonesian and Malaysian Affairs* 19:1 (1985).
61. Hugenholz, pp. 178–9

62. R. Elson, "From 'States' to State: The Changing Regime of Peasant Export Production in Mid-Nineteenth Century Java," in J. Lindblad (ed.), *Historical Foundations of a National Economy in Indonesia, 1890s–1990s*, Amsterdam 1996, p. 128.
63. Ricklefs, pp. 124–5.
64. Hugenholz, ibid.
65. H. Dick, "The Emergence of a National Economy, 1808–1990s," in Linblad, p. 36.
66. Ricklefs, pp. 151–3.
67. Martinez Duesta, p. 260.
68. Ken De Bevoise, *Agents of Apocalypse: Epidemic Disease in the Colonial Philippines*, Princeton, N.J. 1995, pp. 60–62 and 447.
69. Ibid., pp. 41–2 and 158–60.
70. Ibid., pp 63–6, 177 and 181–2.
71. Ibid., p. 65.
72. Brian Linn, *Guardians of Empire: The US Army and the Pacific, 1902–1940*, Chapel Hill, N.C. 1997, p. 14.
73. De Bevoise, pp. 13 and 65; see also Matthew Smallman-Raynor and Andrew Cliff, "The Philippines Insurrection and the 1902–04 Cholera Epidemic: Part I—Epidemiological Diffusion Processes in War," *Journal of Historical Geography* 24:1 (1998), pp. 69–89.
74. Billig, p. 159.
75. Violeta Lopez-Gonzaga and Michelle Decena, "Negros in Transition: 1899–1905," *Philippine Studies* 38 (1990), p. 112.
76. McCoy, pp. 120–22.
77. Robin Palmer, "The Agricultural History of Rhodesia," in Palmer and Parsons, p. 223.
78. S. Nicholson, "The Historical Climatology of Africa," in Wigley , pp. 262–3.
79. John Reader, *Africa: A Biography of the Continent*, New York 1998, p. 587.
80. Coquery-Vidrovitch, pp. 495 and 502; A. Milne, "The Dry Summer on the Upper Nile," *Scottish Geographical Magazine* 16 (1899), pp. 89–90; and Quinn, "A Study of Southern Oscillation–Related Climatic Activity," p. 144.
81. On the drought-famine in Swaziland in 1896–97, see Neil Parsons and Robin Palmer, "Introduction: Historical Background," in Palmer and Parsons (eds.), *The Roots of Rural Poverty in Central and Southern Africa*, Berkeley 1977, p. 17.
82. Terence Ranger, *Revolt in Southern Rhodesia, 1896–7*, London 1967, p. 148.
83. John Iliffe, *Famine in Zimbabwe*, pp. 21–30.
84. Charles Ambler, *The Great Famine in Central Kenya 1897–1900*, Nairobi 1977, pp. 122–8 and 143. (On the plague and the railroad, see Peter Curson and Kevin McCracken, *Plague in Sidney: The Anatomy of an Epidemic*, Kensington, p. 31.)
85. H. J. Mackinder, *The First Ascent of Mount Kenya*, ed. K. Michael Barbour, London 1991, pp. 82–5. This account was never published in the author's lifetime, its editor explains, to prevent disclosure of an atrocity: eight of the expedition's Swahili porters were executed at Mackinder's order (pp. 22–3).
86. Ambler, ibid.
87. D. Low, "British East Africa: The Establishment of British Rule, 1895–1912," in Vincent Harlow et al. (eds.), *History of East Africa*, vol. 2, Oxford 1965, pp. 4–5.
88. Marcia Wright, "East Africa, 1870–1905," in Oliver and Sanderson, p. 576.
89. Isichei, p. 454; and Ambler, p. 146.
90. Low, pp. 16–17.
91. Mackinder, p. 99.
92. Frederick Cooper, *From Slaves to Squatters: Plantation Labor and Agriculture in Zanzibar and Coastal Kenya, 1890–1925*, New Haven, Conn. 1980, pp. 59–60 and 220–22.
93. Low, pp. 110–11.
94. Ibid., p. 111; and Wright, p. 576–7.
95. James Giblin, *The Politics of Environmental Control in Northeastern Tanzania, 1840–1940*, Philadelphia 1992, pp. 90–91, 114–15, and 124–7
96. Leroy Vail and Landeg White, *Capitalism and Colonialism in Mozambique: A Study of Quelimane District*, Minneapolis 1980, pp.
97. Allen and Barbara Isaacman, *The Tradition of Resistance in Mozambique: The Zambesi Valley 1850–1921*, Berkeley 1976, p. 115.

98. Ibid., pp. 134–42.
99. Palmer, ibid.
100. Ambler, p. 149.
101. Tomlinson, p. 195.
102. Jairus Banaji, "Capitalist Domination and the Small Peasantry: The Deccan Districts in the Late 19th Century," in Gyan Prakash (ed.), *The World of the Rural Labourer in Colonial India*, Delhi 1994, p. 123.
103. Sumit Guha, *The Agrarian Economy of the Bombay Deccan*, p. 192.
104. Banaji, pp. 123–4; Arnold, "Famine in Peasant Consciousness," p. 42.
105. Charlesworth, *Peasants and Imperial Rule: Agriculture and Agrarian Society in the Bombay Presidency, 1850–1935*, Cambridge 1985, pp. 109–10.
106. Sir John Strachey, *India: Its Administration and Progress*, London 1911, p. 249.
107. Guha, pp. 149–58.
108. Vasant Kaiwar, "The Colonial State, Capital and the Peasantry in Bombay Presidency," *Modern Asian Studies* 28:4 (1994), p. 822.
109. Philip Huang, *The Peasant Economy and Social Change in North China*, Stanford, Calif. 1985, pp. 85–105.
110. Philip Huang, *The Peasant Family and Rural Development in the Yangzi Delta, 1350–1988*, Stanford, Calif. 1990, p. 71.
111. Huang, *Peasant Economy*, p. 17.
112. Fritjof Tichelman, *The Social Evolution of Indonesia*, The Hague 1980, p. 33.
113. D. R. Gadgil, *The Industrial Evolution of India in Recent Times, 1860–1939*, Delhi 1971, p. 180; and Daniel Little, *Understanding Peasant China*, New Haven, Conn. 1989, p. 92.
114. Jan Breman and E. Valentine Daniel, "Conclusion: the Making of a Coolie," in Daniel, Bernstein and Brass (eds.), *Plantations, Proletarians and Peasants in Colonial Asia*, London 1992, p. 290.
115. Pauline Keating, *Two Revolutions: Village Reconstruction and the Cooperative Movement in Northern Shaanxi, 1934–1945*, Stanford, Calif. 1997, pp. 27–8.
116. Ibid., p. 33.
117. Ibid., pp. 10–13, 23 and 30. Between 1920 and 1936 18,350,000 people were officially estimated to have died of famine in China, mostly in the north (E. Vermeer, *Water Conservancy and Irrigation in China*, The Hague 1977, p. 32).

7. The Mystery of the Monsoons

The quote is from Frater, *Chasing the Monsoon*, New York 1991, p. 190.

1. "Climate" and "weather" differ not only in time-scale (mean versus individual value), but also in causal level. As Kevin Trenberth has pointed out, "Climate variation results from the interactions between the atmosphere and the other spheres (hydrosphere, cryosphere, biosphere, etc.) in the Earth system. Weather variations occur from instabilities within the atmosphere itself and are much more short-lived" (see ENSO Colloquium, July 1997, at www.dir.ucar.edu/esig/enso).
2. Why not, then, an Atlantic "El Niño" as well? The trade winds also pool warm water off Brazil and leave a cold tongue off Africa, but the Atlantic Ocean apparently does not provide a wide enough basin for ENSO-scale fluctuations to initiate or become a self-sustaining system. See F. Jin, "Tropical Ocean-Atmosphere Interaction, the Pacific Cold Tongue, and the ENSO," *Science* 274 (4 Oct. 1996), pp. 77–8.
3. Richard Grove, "The East India Company, the Raj and the El Niño: The Critical Role Played by Colonial Scientists in Establishing the Mechanisms of Global Climate Teleconnections, 1770–1930," in Richard Grove, Vinita Damodaran, and Satpal Sangwan, *Nature and the Orient: The Environmental History of South and Southeast Asia*, Delhi 1998, pp. 301–23.
4. Frederik Nebeker, *Calculating the Weather: Meteorology in the 20th Century*, San Diego 1995, p. 12. By 1880 there were 121 meteorological stations in India including Burma and Ceylon (*Nature*, 23 August 1883, p. 406).
5. Blanford virtually founded modern monsoon meteorology, and his 1877 book, *The Indian Meteorologist's Vade-Mecum*, "became the most widely used textbook on tropical meteorology for the rest of the century" (see Gisela Kutzbach, "Concepts of Monsoon Physics in Historical Perspective," in Jay Fein and Pamela Stephens [eds.], *Monsoons*, New York 1987, p. 181).

6. "On the Barometric See-Saw Between Russia and India in the Sun-Spot Cycle," *Nature,* 18 March 1880, p. 477. See also his *Report on the Meteorology of India in 1878,* Calcutta 1880.
7. On China, see "On the Barometric See-Saw," p. 480.
8. The first use of the term *teleconnection* was apparently A. Angstroem, "Teleconnections of Climate Changes in Present Time," *Geogr. Ann.* 17 (1935), pp. 242–58.
9. Richard Grove, *Green Imperialism: Colonial Expansion, Tropical Island Edens and the Origins of Environmentalism, 1600–1860,* Cambridge 1995, p. 446.
10. J. Norman Lockyer and W. Hunter, "Sun-Spots and Famines," *The Nineteenth Century,* Nov. 1877, p. 601.
11. *Nature,* 17 Aug. 1899, p. 374.
12. Douglas Hoyt and Kenneth Schatten, *The Role of the Sun in Climate Change,* Oxford 1997, pp. 36 and 144–5.
13. For a dessicationist perspective—influenced by Marsh's *The Earth as Modified by Human Action*—on the famine of 1876, see "Philindus," "Famines and Floods in India," *Macmillan's Magazine,* Feb. 1878 (quote from p. 256).
14. Lockyer and Hunter, p. 599.
15. See the discussion by Lloyd's expert Henry Jeula in Cornelius Walford's *The Famines of the World: Past and Present,* London 1879, pp. 94–6.
16. Meldrum also virtually accused Hunter of plagiarizing his 1875 research on Madras rainfall; see "Sun-Spots and Rainfall," *Nature,* 4 April 1878, pp. 448–50. Hunter's earlier reservations about a sunspot signature in higher latitude rainfall can be found in "Rainfall in the Temperate Zone in Connection with the Sun-Spot Cycle," *Nature,* 22 Nov. 1877, pp. 59–61.
17. See, for example, the richly sardonic critique of Hunter's speculations by Richard Proctor: "Sun-Spot, Storm, and Famine," *Gentleman's Magazine,* Dec. 1877, pp. 705–6.
18. E. Archibald, "W. W. Hunter: The Cycle of Drought and Famine in Southern India," *Calcutta Review* 131 (1878), p. 129; and for an account of Strachey's paper "On the Alleged Correspondence of the Rainfall at Madras with the Sun-spot Period, and on the True Criterion of Periodicity in a Series of Variable Quantities," read before the Royal Society in May 1877, see letter of B. Stewart to W. S. Jevons, 5 June 1877, in *Papers and Correspondence of William Stanley Jevons,* vol. 4, ed. R. Collison Black, London 1977, p. 203.
19. See C. Meldrum, "Sun-Spots and Rainfall," 4 April 1878, pp. 448–50; E. Archibald, "Indian Rainfall," 25 April 1878, p. 505; and S. Hill, "Indian Rainfall," 20 June 1878, p. 193.
20. Blanford, "On the Barometric See-Saw," pp. 477–8.
21. Kutzbach, p. 199.
22. Archibald, pp. 148–9.
23. Cunniff, p. 195. Cunniff points out, however, that Tomas Pompeu, an ardent "rainmaker" and author of *Memoria sobre a clima e seccas do Ceará* (1878), had been "the first Brazilian to correlate sunspots and droughts" (ibid.).
24. "The Rainfall of Brazil and the Sun-Spots," *Nature,* 8 Aug. 1878, p. 384; and Joaquim Alves, *Historia das secas (Seculos XVII a XIX),* Fortaleza 1953, p. 123.
25. Cunniff, pp. 183–9.
26. Hoyt and Schatten, p. 163.
27. "The Periodicity of Commercial Crises and Its Physical Explanation," *Journal of the Statistical and Social Inquiry Society of Ireland* 7 (1878); "Commercial Crises and Sun-Spots I," *Nature,* 14 Nov. 1878; and "Commercial Crises and Sun-Spots II," *Nature,* 24 April 1879.
28. Walford, pp. 292–3.
29. W. Jevons, "Economic Policy," in R. Smyth (ed.), *Essays in Economic Method,* London 1962, p. 26.
30. Philip Mirowski, "Macroeconomic Instability and the 'Natural' Processes in Early Neoclassical Economics," *Journal of Economic History* 44:2 (June 1984), p. 346.
31. Ibid., p. 349. In an earlier letter to his brother, Jevons admitted that "my theory of crises has the appearance of being a little too ingenious … but I have great confidence in its substantial truth" (14 Nov. 1878 in *Papers and Correspondence,* vol. 4, p. 293).
32. Letter to *The Times,* published 17 Jan. 1879, ibid., vol. 5, pp. 10–11.
33. Letter to *The Times,* published 19 April 1879, ibid., vol. 5, pp. 44–8.
34. On Jevons's interest in Brazilian *secas,* see his letter to his brother, 18 June 1879, vol. 5, p. 65. While she never saw sunspots, Rosa Luxemburg in *The Accumulation of Capital* (1913) accepted part of

Jevons's argument, agreeing that "periodical famines in India ... recurring at intervals of ten or eleven years, were ... among the causes of periodical crises in England," p. 286).

35. Quoted in Proctor, p. 701.
36. Ibid., p. 165.
37. Indeed, the indefatigable Archibald, after a quarter-century's statistical labor, claimed that droughts in southern India followed minima, while those in the north coincided with maxima: a decidedly confusing (or, as he put it, "spasmodic") conclusion (*Nature,* 2 Aug. 1900, p. 335).
38. Quoted in Kutzbach, p. 200.
39. Colin Ramage, *Monsoon Meteorology,* New York 1971, p. 239.
40. A. Meadows, *Science and Controversy: A Biography of Sir Norman Lockyer,* Cambridge, Mass. 1972, pp. 284–6.
41. Cf. report on Hildebrandsson's recent papers in *Nature,* 17 Aug. 1899; and Allan, Lindesay and Parker, p. 12.
42. Kutzbach, p. 202. See, for example, Gilbert Walker, *Outlines of the Theory of Electromagnetism,* Cambridge 1910.
43. Ibid., p. 203 (the analogy to geopolitics is mine).
44. Halford Mackinder, "The Geographical Pivot of History," *Geographical Journal* 23 (1904), p. 422.
45. Mark Cane, "El Niño," *Ann. Rev. Earth Planet. Sci.* 14 (1986), p. 44. On the other hand, contemporary geodesists—like John Hayford in America—had achieved spectacular results (the figure of the earth) through massive computations where the "sheer bulk of information" was most important. (See the discussion of turn-of-the-century geodesy in Naomi Oreskes, *The Rejection of Continental Drift: Theory and Method in American Earth Science,* New York 1999, pp. 234–5.)
46. Donald Mock, "The Southern Oscillation: Historical Origins," NOAA (www.ced. noaa.gov/-dm/pubs/mock81).
47. Allan, Lindesay and Parker, p. 13. Walker's concept of the SO was partly anticipated by C. Brooks and H. Braby's 1921 article "The Clash of the Trades in the Pacific" (*Q. J. R. Meteorol. Soc.* 47, pp. 1–13).
48. Peter Webster and Song Yang, "Monsoon and ENSO: Selectively Interactive Systems," *Q. J. R. Meteorol. Soc.* 118 (1992), p. 878.
49. Ibid.
50. Ibid., p. 17.
51. Allan, Lindesay, and Parker, p. 14.
52. See the brief history of the Bergen School in Nebeker, pp. 49–57 and 84–6.
53. H. Berlage, "Fluctuations of the General Atmospheric Circulation of More Than One Year: Their Nature and Prognostic Value," *K. Ned. Meteorol. Inst. Meded. Verh.* 69 (1957); and Allan, Lindesay and Parker, p. 5 (quote). An even earlier precursor of Bjerknes's focus on ocean–atmosphere interaction was J. B. Leighly's "Marquesan Meteorology" (*Univ. Calif. Publ. Geogr.* 6:4 [1933], pp. 147–72), although as J. Wallace et al. note, "The lack of citations of this remarkable paper indicates that it had little or no impact on the field at the time" (J. Wallace et al., "On the Structure and Evolution of ENSO-Related Climate Variability in the Tropical Pacific: Lessons from TOGA," *Journal of Geophysical Research* 103:C7 [29 June 1998], p. 14,242).
54. E. Rasmusson and T. Carpenter, "Variations in Tropical Sea Surface Temperature and Surface Wind Fields Associated with the Southern Oscillation/El Niño," *Mon. Wea. Rev.* 110 (1982), pp. 354–84.
55. J. Bjerknes, "Atmospheric Teleconnections from the Equatorial Pacific," *Mon. Wea. Rev.* 97 (1969), p. 170.
56. Thomas Levenson argues that John Leighy, studying the weather of the Marquesas Islands in 1933, had glimpsed this complex wind/sea surface temperature interaction in microcosm, but his work was not resurrected until 1978, a decade after Bjerknes's breakthrough (*Ice Time: Climate, Science and Life on Earth,* New York 1989, pp. 70, 72).
57. George Philander, "Learning from El Niño," *Weather* 53:9 (Sept. 1998), p. 273.
58. Bjerknes, ibid.
59. K. Wyrtki, "El Niño: The Dynamic Response of the Equatorial Pacific Ocean to Atmospheric Forcing," *Journal of Physical Oceanography* 5, pp. 572–84; and "The Response of Sea Surface Topography to the 1976 El Niño," *Journal of Physical Oceanography* 9, pp. 1223–31. Also see the characterization of Wyrtki's contribution in Allan, Lindesay and Parker, pp. 19 and 24–5.
60. There is also a deep ocean transfer of heat through thermohaline convection—the famous "conveyor

belt"—driven by subduction of water masses in the Nordic Sea and Antarctica, but it works very slowly on wavelengths of decades or more. It constitutes the long-term memory of the coupled atmosphere–ocean system.

61. On the "capacitator" analogy, cf. Joel Gunn, "Introduction," special issue of *Human Ecology* (22:1 [1994]) on global climate change, p. 11; and Peter Webster and Timothy Palmer, "The Past and the Future of El Niño," *Nature* 390 (11 Dec. 1997), p. 562.
62. There is considerable debate about which is the more important control over the ENSO cycle: heat storage in the Warm Pool or the internal wave dynamics of the Pacific. The latter is given priority in the famous "dampened oscillator" or "delayed action oscillator" model of ENSO developed by P. Schopf and M. Suarez in 1988 ("Vacillations in a Coupled Ocean–Atmosphere Model," *J. Atmos. Sci.* 45 , pp. 549–66). Their revision of Wyrtki was a response to the puzzling absence of a "canonical" buildup of sea level and sea surface temperature in the western Pacific before the massive 1982–83 El Niño.
63. Michael McPhaden, "Genesis and Evolution of the 1997–98 El Niño," *Science* 283 (12 Feb. 1999), p. 953.
64. See G. Kiladis, G. Meehl and K. Weickmann, "The Large-Scale Circulation Associated with Westerly Wind Bursts and Deep Convection over the Western Equatorial Pacific," *J. Geophys. Res.* 99 (1994), pp. 18527–44.
65. S. G. Philander, "El Niño and La Niña," *J. Atmos. Sci.* 42 (1985), pp. 451–9.
66. Richard Barber in Michael Glantz, *Currents of Change: El Niño's Impact on Climate and Society,* Cambridge 1996, p. 167.
67. Richard Kerr, "Big El Niños Ride the Back of Slower Climate Change," *Science* 283 (19 Feb. 1999), p. 1108.
68. For the most sweeping case for El Niño–like forcing of world climate on nested time-scales from the seasonal to the orbital, see Mark Cane and Amy Clement, "A Role for the Tropical Pacific Coupled Ocean–Atmosphere System on Milankovitch and Millennial Timescales: Parts I & II," in Peter Clark, Robert Webb and Lloyd Keigwin (eds.), *Mechanisms of Global Climate Change at Millennial Time Scales,* Washington, D.C. 1999.
69. Eugene Rasmusson, Xueliang Wang and Chester Ropelewski, "Secular Variability of the ENSO Cycle," Natural Research Council, *Natural Climate Variability on Decade-to-Century Time Scales,* Washington, D.C. 1995, pp. 458 and 469.
70. Henry Diaz and Roger Pulwarty, "An Analysis of the Time Scales of Variability in Centuries-Long ENSO-Sensitive Records in the Last 1000 Years," abstract, NOAA El Niño website; and Xiao-Wei Quan, "Interannual Variability Associated with ENSO: Seasonal Dependence and Interdecadal Change," Ph.D. diss., University of Colorado, Boulder 1998, p. 105.
71. Webster et al., "Monsoon Predictability and Prediction," *Journal of Geophysical Research* 103: C7 (29 June 1998), p. 14,457. See also C. Folland et al., "Large Scale Modes of Ocean Surface Temperature Since the Late Nineteenth Century," in Navarra (ed.).
72. For a sense of what a devilish business periodizing low-frequency ENSO variations has turned out to be, see Rasmusson, Wang and Ropelewski, "Secular Variability of the ENSO Cycle," pp. 458–69.
73. See the discussion in Chapter 3, Xiao-Wei Quan, pp. 89–137.
74. Richard Kerr, "In North American Climate: A More Local Control," *Science* 283 (19 Feb. 1999), p. 1109.
75. See N. Mantua, "A Pacific Interdecadal Climate Oscillation with Impacts on Salmon Production," *Bulletin of the American Meteorological Society* 78:6 (June 1997), pp. 1069–79.
76. Ben Kirtman and Paul Schopf, "Decadal Variability in ENSO Predictability and Prediction," *Journal of Climate* 11 (Nov. 1998), p. 2805.
77. Cf. Kerr, ibid. (quote); and Xiao-Wei Quan, p. 106.
78. Xiao-Wei Quan, pp. 109–10.
79. Although their cause is not yet known, compelling evidence that Dansgaard/Oeschger cycles have regulated climate instabilities in the Holocene as well as throughout the Quaternary is presented in Gerard Bond et al., "A Pervasive Millennial-Scale Cycle in North Atlantic Holocene and Glacial Climates," *Science,* 278 (14 Nov. 1997), pp. 1257–66.
80. Cf. Richard Kerr, "El Niño Grew Strong as Cultures Were Born"; and Donald Rodbell et al., "A 15,000-Year Record of El Niño–Driven Alluviation in Southwestern Ecuador," *Science* 283 (22 Jan. 1999).

81. Betty Meggers, "Archeological Evidence for the Impact of Mega-Niño Events on Amazonia During the Past Two Millennia," *Climatic Change* 28 (1994), p. 328–9.
82. Cf., Kirtman and Schopf, p. 2805 (quote); and K. Trenberth and T. Hoar, "El Niño and Climate Change," *Geophys. Res. Lett.* 24 (1997), pp. 3057–60.
83. *Summary Report,* NOAA/CIRES La Niña Summit, July 1998, p. 14.

8. Climates of Hunger

The quote is from Achebe, *A Man of the People*, New York 1966, pp. 161–2.

1. It is important to note that the famous protracted droughts of the 1930s in the US Great Plains, Australia and southern Africa occurred during one of the weakest periods of ENSO activity in the last 150 years.
2. Kiladis and Diaz, p. 1071.
3. Allan, Lindesay and Parker, p. 77.
4. Ibid., pp. 25–6.
5. Ibid.
6. Peter Webster, "The Variable and Interactive Monsoon," in Fein and Stephens, p. 305.
7. David Rodenhuis, "The Weather That Led to the Flood," in Stanley Changnon (ed.), *The Great Flood of 1993*, Boulder, Colo. 1996, pp. 44–5.
8. P. Webster et al., "Monsoons: Processes, predictability, and the prospects for prediction," *Journal of Geophysical Research* 103:C7 (19 June 1998), p. 14,459.
9. Alexander Gershunov, Tim Barnett and Daniel Cayan, "North Pacific Interdecadal Oscillation Seen as Factor in ENSO-Related North American Climate Anomalies," *EOS* 80:3 (19 Jan. 1998), pp. 25 and 29–30.
10. *Summary Report*, La Niña Summit, p. 10.
11. Kevin Trenberth, "The Different Flavors of La Niña," La Niña Summit, 1998, p. 2.
12. Greg O'Hare, "The Indian Monsoon, Part Two: The Rains," *Geography* 82:4 (1997), p. 335.
13. Seasonal distribution is everything. For example, the cyclone of 18–20 May 1877 dumped 20 inches of rain—half a year's precipitation—over Madras in three days during the height of the Great Drought. As Digby points out,"it did more harm than good" and the drought continued for six months more (Digby, *The Famine Campaign*, vol. 1, pp. 148–9).
14. K. Rao, *India's Water Wealth*, Delhi 1975, pp. 10 and 16.
15. J. Ju and J. Slingo, "The Asian Summer Monsoon and ENSO," *Q. J. R. Meteorol. Soc.* 121 (1995), pp. 1133–68. "Displacement of the IACZ into the Pacific results in the establishment of a separate convection zone over southeast Asia during Monsoon season. This draws air from a much reduced area compared to a normal Monsoon, because of the adjustment of the tropospheric circulation to competition from the central Pacific convergence. Weak Monsoon rainfall, and drought in extreme cases, is the result."
16. Webster et al., p. 14,476 (text differs from Table 2).
17. O'Hare, p. 349. See also Peter Webster and Song Yang, "Monsoon and ENSO: Selectively Interactive Systems," *Q. J. R. Meteorol. Soc.* 118 (1992), pp. 877–926; and Madhav Khandekar, "El Niño/Southern Oscillation, Indian Monsoon and World Grain Yields—A Synthesis," in M. El Sabh et al. (eds.), *Land-Based and Marine Hazards*, Kluwer 1996, pp. 79–95. Equatorial stratospheric wind oscillation may be a third independent variable interacting with ENSO and Eurasian snow cover. (See Khandekar, "Comments on 'Space–Time Structure of Monsoon Interannual Variability,' in *Journal of Climate* 11 (Nov. 1998), pp. 3057–9.)
18. Buwen Dong and Paul Valdes, "Modelling the Asian Summer Monsoon Rainfall and Eurasian Winter/Spring Snow Mass," *Q. J. R. Meteorol. Soc.* 124 (1998), pp. 2567–9.
19. R. Kripalani and A. Kulkarni, "Climatic Impact of El Niño/La Niña on the Indian Monsoon: A New Perspective," *Weather* 52:2 (1997), p. 45.
20. K. Krishna Kumar, Balaji Rajagopalan and Mark Cane, "On the Weakening Relationship Between the Indian Monsoon and ENSO," *Science* 284 (25 June 1999), pp. 2156–9. See also H. Annamalai and Julia Slingo, "The Asian Summer Monsoon, 1997," *Weather* 53:9 (Sept. 1998), pp. 285–6.
21. Ramasamy Suppiah, "Relationships Between the Southern Oscillation and the Rainfall of Sri Lanka," *International Journal of Climatology* 9 (1989).

22. Y. Kueh, *Agricultural Instability in China, 1931–1991,* Oxford 1998, p. 29.
23. Needham, p. 246.
24. Keith Buchanan, *The Transformation of the Chinese Earth*, London 1970, p. 80; Walter Mallory, *China: Land of Famine*, New York 1926, p. 43.
25. George Cressey, *China's Geographic Foundations: A Survey of the Land and Its People,* New York 1934, pp. 84–5.
26. The occurrence of several severe El Niños in the mid seventeenth century raises the possibility that the extraordinary agricultural crisis of the late Ming dynasty—seven years of drought followed by nine years of flooding—was ENSO-related: 1640 was the driest year in the last five hundred (cf. Zhang Jiacheng [ed.], *The Reconstruction of Climate in China for Historical Times*, Beijing 1988, p. 45; Manfred Domros and Peng Gongbing, *The Climate of China*, Berlin 1988, p. 198; and Jiacheng Zhang and Zhiguang Lin, *Climate of China*, Shanghai 1992, p. 330).
27. Ye Zongwei and Wang Cun, "Climatic Jumps in the Flood/Drought Historical Chronology of Central China," *Climate Dynamics* 6 (1992), p. 158.
28. Ding Yihui, *Monsoons over China*, Dordrecht 1996, p. 290–92.
29. A pioneering consideration of SO's possible role in drought and flood was Tu Chang-Wang, "China Weather and the World Oscillation," in Academia Sinica, *Collected Scientific Papers: Meteorology 1919–1949*, Beijing 1954.
30. Shao-Wu in Glantz, *Currents of Change,* p. 173; as well as Kueh, pp. 159–61.
31. Wei-Chyung Wang and Kerang Li, "Precipitation Fluctuation over a Semiarid Region in Northern China and the Relationship with El Niño/Southern Oscillation," *Journal of Climate* (July 1990), p. 769.
32. Wang Shao-wu, "La Niña and Its Impact on China's Climate," La Niña Summit, 1998, p. 1.
33. Wang and Li, p. 777.
34. Ding Yihui, pp. 273, 285.
35. See the La Niña impact map for 1898 in Allan, Lindesay and Parker, p. 139.
36. For weather conditions in 1876, cf. Broomhall, p. 166; and *Parl. Papers*, China No. 2 (1878), p. 1.
37. Chenglan Bao and Yanzhen Xiang, "Relationship Between El Niño Event and Atmospheric Circulation, Typhoon Activity and Flooding," in W. Kyle and C. Chang (eds.), *Proceedings*, Second International Conference on East Asia and Western Pacific Meteorology and Climate (Hong Kong, Sept. 1992), Singapore 1993, p. 239.
38. Yihui, pp. 286–7.
39. PRC, National Environmental Protection Bureau, *The Yellow River Runs Dry and Its Sustainable Development* (in Chinese), Beijing 1997: cited in Z. Yang et al., " Yellow River's Water and Sediment Discharge Decreasing Steadily," *EOS* 79:48 (1 Dec. 1998), p. 592.
40. Zhenhao Bao et al., "Drought/Flood Variations in Eastern China During the Colder (1610–1719) and Warmer (1880–1989) Periods and Their Relations with the Southern Oscillation," *Geographical Reports of Tokyo Metropolitan University* 33 (1998), p. 10.
41. Hengyi Weng et al., "Multi–Scale Summer Rainfall Variability Over China," *Journal of the Meteorological Society of Japan* 77:4 (1999), pp. 845–57.
42. Cf. Jasper Becker, *Hungry Ghosts: Mao's Secret Famine*, New York 1996; and Philip Short, *Mao: A Life*, London 1999, pp. 504–10 (on the severity of the drought). There is no necessary discrepancy between the characterization of the 1958 drought as the most severe *throughout* China and the study (cited in fn 35) that finds other droughts in *north* China to have been more extreme.
43. Y. Kueh, *Agricultural Instability in China, 1931–1991,* Oxford 1998. See also Penny Kane, *Famine in China, 1959–61: Demographic and Social Implications,* London 1988.
44. Jean Dreze and Amarya Sen, "Introduction," in Dreze, Sen and Hussain, *The Political Economy of Hunger: Selected Essays*, Oxford 1995, pp. 18–19.
45. J. Murphy and P. Whetton, "A Re-analysis of a Tree Ring Chronology from Java," *Proceedings of the Koninklijke Nederlandse Akademic van Weterschappen* B92:3 (1989), pp. 241–57.
46. Christine Padoch and Nancy Peluso (ed.), *Borneo in Transition: People, Forests, Conservation, and Development,* Oxford 1996, p. 3. See also H. Brookfield, L. Potter and Y. Byron, *In Place of the Forest: Environmental and Socio–Economic Transformation in Borneo and the Eastern Malay Peninsula,* Tokyo 1995.
47. See rainfall anomaly tables for Indonesia and the Philippines since 1896, International Research Institute for Climate Prediction, UCSD (iri.ucsd.edu/hot_Niño/impacts).

48. US Naval Intelligence Division, *Netherlands East Indies,* Vol. 1, Geographical Handbook Series, Washington D.C. 1944, p. 338. On a drought belt in eastern Java and southernmost New Guinea, see Glenn Trewartha, *The Earth's Problem Climates*, Madison, Wis. pp. 202–3.
49. Knapen, pp. 126–7.
50. Jean-Paul Malingreau, "The 1982–83 Drought in Indonesia: Assessment and Monitoring," in Michael Glantz, Ricard Katz, and Maria Krenz (eds.), *Climate Crisis: The Societal Impacts Associated with the 1982–83 Worldwide Climate Anomalies*, New York 1987, pp. 11–18; and Eric Hackert and Stefan Hastenrath, "Mechanisms of Java Rainfall Anomalies," *Monthly Weather Review* 114 (April 1986), p. 746.
51. R. Kane, "El Niño Timings and Rainfall Extremes in India, Southeast Asia and China," *International Journal of Climatology* 19 (1999), pp. 653–72.
52. See the webpage iripred.ido.columbia.edu/research/ENSO/tables/phil 1.html.
53. Famine chronology from Martinez Duesta, p. 260 (my correlation to ENSO).
54. Lopez-Gonzaga, pp. 113–15.
55. Data from Relief Web (www.reliefweb.int), 3 Aug. 1998.
56. See the chart in Glantz, Katz and Krenz, pp. 90–91.
57. Quoted in Allan, Lindesay and Parker, p. 9.
58. Ann Young, *Environmental Change in Australia Since 1788,* Melbourne 1996.
59. Ian Anderson, "Parched Papua Prays for Rain," *New Scientist*, 20 Sept. 1997, p. 18.
60. Jean Nicet and Thierry Delcroix, "ENSO-related Precipitation Changes in New Caledonia, Southwestern Tropical Pacific: 1969–98," *Monthly Weather Review* 8:2 (August 2000), pp. 3001–6.
61. Andrew Sturman and Nigel Tapper, *The Weather and Climate of Australia and New Zealand*, Melbourne 1996, pp. 367–70.
62. Pao-Shin Chu, "Hawaiian Drought and the Southern Oscillation," *Inter. J. Climatol.* 9 (1989), p. 628.
63. Thomas Schroeder, "Climate Controls," in Marie Sanderson (ed.), *Climate and Weather in Hawaii*, Honolulu 1993, p. 17.
64. "Summary of Drought Around the World, August–September 1998," National Drought Mitigation Center.
65. Antonio Moura and Jagadish Shukla, "On the Dynamics of Droughts in Northeast Brazil: Observations, Theory and Numerical Experiments with a General Circulation Model," *Journal of the Atmospheric Sciences* 34 (December 1981), pp. 2653 (quote) and 2654.
66. Webb, p. 44.
67. Vernon Kousky, "Frontal Influences on Northeast Brazil," *Monthly Weather Review* 107 (1979), pp. 1140–53.
68. Hall, pp. 16–17.
69. Gilbert Walker, "Ceará (Brazil) Famines and the General Air Movement," *Beitr. z. Phys. der freien Atmosphare* 14 (1928), pp. 88–93.
70. Cf. José Gasques and Antonio Magalhaes, "Climate Anomalies and Their Impacts in Brazil During the 1982–83 ENSO Event," in Glantz, Katz and Krenz, pp. 31–2; and Pao–Shin Chu, "Brazil's Climate Anomalies and ENSO," in Michael Glantz, Richard Katz, and Neville Nicholls (eds.), *Teleconnections Linking Worldwide Climate Anomalies*, Cambridge 1991, pp. 56–61.
71. Cf. Rodolfo Teofilo, *A Seca de 1915*, Forteleza 1980, 129–31; and Kiladis and Diaz, pp. 1038–40.
72. Pao–Shin Chu, pp. 64–5.
73. See Kiladis and Diaz, ibid.; and data at iri.ucsd.edu/hot_Niño/impacts/ns_amer/index.html.
74. C. Caviedes, "The Effects of Enso Events in Some Key Regions of the South American Continent," in Stanley Gregory (ed.), *Recent Climate Change,* London 1988, pp. 252–3 and 264.
75. Carlos Malpica, *Cronica del Hambre en el Peru,* Lima 1966, pp. 161–3.
76. Caviedes, ibid.
77. Gregory Asner, Alan Townsend and Bobby Braswell, "Satellite Observation of El Niño Effects on Amazon Forest Phenology and Productivity," *Geophysical Research Letters* 27:7 (1 April 2000), p. 981.
78. Betty Meggers, "Archeological Evidence for the Impact of Mega-Niño Events on Amazonia During the Past Two Millennia," *Climatic Change* 28 (1994), p. 330.
79. Allan, Lindesay and Parker, p. 65.
80. Miguel Gonzalez, "Probable Response of the Paraná River Delta (Argentina) to Future Warmth and Rising Sea Level," *J. Coast. Res. Spec. Issue* 17 (1995), pp. 219–20.

81. José Rutllant and Humberto Fuenzalida, "Synoptic Aspects of the Central Chile Rainfall Variability Associated with the Southern Oscillation," *International Journal of Climatology* 11 (1991), pp. 63 and 65.
82. For the 1896 drought, see Antonio del Bajio, *Crisis alimentarias y subsistencias populares en Mexico*, vol. 1, Mexico, D.F. 1987, p. 162.
83. A. Filonov and I. Tereshchenko, "El Niño 1997–98 Monitoring in Mixed Layer at the Pacific Ocean near Mexico's West Coast," *Geophysical Research Letters* 27:5 (1 March 2000), p. 705.
84. During the drought corn prices soared 130 percent while minimum agricultural wages fell 28 percent (Moises Gonzalez Navarro, *Cinco crisis mexicanas*, Mexico, D.F. 1999, p. 19). See also Florescano and Swan, *Breve historia*, pp. 124–6 and 161; del Bajio, pp. 166–71; and Friedrich Katz, *The Life and Times of Pancho Villa*, Stanford, Calif. 1998, pp. 48–50.
85. Gonzalez, p. 31.
86. See Midwestern Climate Center (Champaign, Ill.), "El Niño and the Midwest" (http://mcc.sws. uiuc. edu/elNiño.html).
87. Jennifer Phillips, et al., "The Role of ENSO in Determining Climate and Maize Yield Variability in the US Cornbelt," *International Journal of Climatology* 19 (1999), pp. 877–88.
88. Stanley Changnon, "Impacts of El Niño's Weather," in Changnon (ed.), *El Niño 1997–1998: The Climate Event of the Century*, Oxford 2000, pp. 151, 165.
89. Julia Cole and Edward Cook, "The Changing Relationship Between Enso Variability and Moisture Balance in the Continental United States," *Geophysical Research Letters* 25:24 (15 Dec. 1998), pp. 4529–32.
90. Research in progress reported by Arthur Douglas, Creighton University (www.ncdc. noaa.gov/ogp/ papers/douglas.html).
91. Cf. Charlotte Benson, "Drought and the Zimbabwe Economy: 1980–93," p. 246; and Bill Kinsey, "Dancing with El Niño," pp. 276–7, both in Helen O'Neill and John Toye (eds.), *A World Without Famine?*, New York 1998.
92. J. Lindesay and C. Vogel, "Historical Evidence for Southern Oscillation–Southern African Rainfall Relationships," *International Journal of Climatology* 10 (1990), p. 679; and Mark Cane, Gidon Eshel and R. Buckland, "Forecasting Zimbabwean Maize Yield Using Eastern Equatorial Pacific Sea Surface Temperature," *Nature* 370 (21 July 1994), pp. 204–5.
93. Vincent Moron and M. Neil Ward, "ENSO Teleconnections with Climate Variability in the European and African Sectors," *Weather* 53:9 (Sept. 1998), p. 288.
94. S. Mason and M. Jury, "Climatic Variability and Change over Southern Africa: A Reflection on Underlying Processes," *Progress in Physical Geography* 21:1 (1997), pp. 23–50.
95. Lindesay and Vogel, ibid.; and Cane, Eshel and Buckland, p. 204.
96. Tsegay Wolde-Georgis, "The Impact of Cold Events on Ethiopia," La Niña Summit, 1998, pp. 1–2. See also Y. Seleshi and G. Demaree, "Rainfall Variability in the Ethiopian and Eritrean Highlands and Its Links with the Southern Oscillation Index," *Journal of Biogeography* 22 (1985); and Tesfaye Hale, "Causes and Characteristics of Drought in Ethiopia," *Ethiopian Journal of Agricultural Sciences* 10:1–2 (1988).
97. Based on Coquery-Vidrovitch, p. 503; and Glantz, Katz and Krenz, "Appendix: Climate Impact Maps," pp. 81–105.
98. Cf. P. Hutchinson, "The Southern Oscillation and Prediction of 'Der' Season Rainfall in Somalia, *Journal of Climate* 5 (May 1992), p. 525; and Gerard Beltrando, "Interannual Variability of Rainfall in the Eastern Horn of Africa and Indicators of Atmospheric Circulation," *International Journal of Climatology* 13 (1993), pp. 533 and 543.
99. M. Hulme, "Global Climate Change and the Nile Basin," in P. Howell and J. Allan (eds.), *The Nile: Sharing a Scarce Resource*, Cambridge 1994, p. 148.
100. G. Trewartha, *The Earth's Problem Climates*, Madison, Wis. 1981, p. 134.
101. A. Gouldie, "Climate: Past and Present," in W. Adams, A. Goudie and A. Orme (eds.), *The Physical Geography of Africa*, Oxford 1996, p. 38.
102. Matayo Indeje, Frederick Semazzi and Laban Ogallo, "ENSO Signals in East African Rainfall Seasons," *International Journal of Climatology* 20 (2000), p. 20.
103. Cf. G. Farmer, "Rainfall Data Bases and Seasonal Forecasting in Eastern Africa" in Gregory, pp. 197–9; and Peter Usher, "Kenya and ENSO: An Observation and La Niña Prediction," La Niña Summit, 1998.

104. Indeje, Semazzi and Ogallo, pp. 30 and 44–5.
105. Jennifer Phillips and Beverly McIntyre, "ENSO and Interannual Rainfall Variability in Uganda: Implications for Agricultural Management," *International Journal of Climatology* 20 (2000), p. 171–82.
106. Allan, Lindesay and Parker, p. 22.
107. Bette Otto-Bliesner, "El Niño/La Niña and Sahel Precipitation During the Middle Holocene," *Geophysical Research Letters* 26:1 (1 Jan. 1999), pp. 87–8.
108. Abdel Kader Ali, "El Niño Events and Rainfall Variations in the Sahel Region of Africa," *Bulletin of the Egyptian Geographical Society* 70 (1997), pp. 77 (see Fig. 3) and 81–3.
109. M. Neil Ward et al., "Climate Variability in Northern Africa: Understanding Droughts in the Sahel and the Mahgreb," in Navarra (ed.), p. 138.
110. According to the Center for Ocean-Atmosphere Prediction Studies, ENSO (1944–96) was in a warm phase 21 percent of the time; cold phase, 28 percent; and neutral phase, 51 percent; see the COAPS website. A 1950–1997 timeframe, however, gives warm phase, 31 percent; cold phase, 23 percent; and neutral, 46 percent (NCAR News–La Niña website).
111. Cf. "History's Favorite Hitman," *Hong Kong Standard,* 22 May 1998; and "El Niño," *The Irish Times,* 28 May 1998.
112. D. Harrison and N. Larkin, "El Niño-Southern Oscillation Sea Surface Temperature and Wind Anomalies, 1946–1993," *Reviews of Geophysics* 36:3 (Aug. 1998), p. 391. For an opposing view, however, see B. Dong et al., "Predictable Winter Climate in the North Atlantic Sector During the 1997–1999 ENSO Cycle," *Geophysical Research Letters* 27:7 (1 April 2000), pp. 985–8.
113. Moron and Ward, p. 289.
114. Kiladis and Diaz, pp. 1041–2.
115. M. Halpert and C. Ropelewski, "Surface Temperature Patterns Associated with the Southern Oscillation," *Journal of Climate* 5 (1992). See also X. Rodo, E. Baert and F. Comin, "Variations in Seasonal Rainfall in Southern Europe During the Present Century: Relationships with NAO and ENSO," *Climate Dynamics* 13 (1997).
116. Alfredo Rocha, "Low-Frequency Variability of Seasonal Rainfall over the Iberian Peninsula and ENSO," *International Journal of Climatology* 19 (1999), p. 889.
117. A. Meshcherskaya and V. Blazhevich, "The Drought and Excessive Moisture Indices in a Historical Perspective in the Principal Grain-Producing Regions of the Former Soviet Union," *Journal of Climate* 10 (Oct.1997), pp. 2670–82.
118. Trevor Davies, "Guest Editorial—Hubert Lamb," *Weather* 53:7 (July 1998) p. 199. These data sets recently have been used to generate a landmark atlas (Allan, Lindesay and Parker, 1996) of the global oceanic and atmospheric patterns accompanying ENSO warm and cold phases since 1871.
119. Cf. William Quinn, "A Study of Southern Oscillation–Related Climatic Activity for AD 622–1900, Incorporating Nile River Flood Data," in Henry Diaz and Vera Markgraf (eds.), *El Niño: Historical and Paleoclimatic Aspects of the Southern Oscillation,* Cambridge 1992; and Quinn, Victor Neal and Santiago Antunez de Mayolo, "El Niño Occurrences over the Past Four and a Half Centuries," *Journal of Geophysical Research* 92:C13 (15 Dec. 1987), p. 14,454.
120. Whetton and Rutherfurd, p. 225.
121. See discussion of data sources in Allan, Lindesay and Parker, pp. 59–60.
122. Charles Ballard, "Drought and Economic Distress: South Africa in the 1800s," *Journal of Interdisciplinary History* 17:2 (Autumn 1986), pp. 359–78.
123. Charlesworth, *Peasants and Imperial Rule,* p. 76.
124. My rough annual ratios would, of course, be better expressed as seasonal ratios.
125. On modification of ENSO cycle by changes in Pacific Ocean circulation, see Robert Dunbar et al., "PEP-1 Contributions to Increased Understanding of Past Variability in Enso and Its Teleconnections," poster session *Abstracts,* IGBP PAGES Open Sciences Meeting, "Past Global Changes and Their Significance for the Future," London, 20–23 April 1998; and for a discussion of a shortened, intensifed ENSO, see Tahl Kestin et al., 'Time-Frequency Variability of ENSO and Stochastic Simulations," *Journal of Climate* 11 (Sept. 1998), pp. 2260–61.
126. "Simultaneous correlation between ENSO and the monsoon is very robust over the past 140 years. The sole exception, the drop during the recent decades, obviously is of great interest, and perhaps a cause for concern": K. Kumar et al., "Epochal Changes in Indian Monsoon–ENSO Precursors," *Geophysical Research Letters* 26:1 (1 Jan. 1999), p. 78. "Before 1900, the ENSO influence on US moisture balance was more extensive than in later periods": Julia Cole and Edward Cook, "The

Changing Relationship Between ENSO Variability and Moisture Balance in the Continental United States," *Geophysical Research Letters* 25:24 (15 Dec. 1998), p. 4530.

127. Quinn et al, "El Niño Occurrences," p. 14,459.
128. D. Rind, "Complexity and Climate," *Science* 284 (2 April 1999), p. 106.
129. Brent Yarnal and George Kiladis, "Tropical Teleconnections Associated with El Niño/Southern Oscillation (ENSO) events," *Progress in Physical Geography* 9 (1985), pp. 541 and 544.
130. Quinn and Neal, p. 627.
131. David Engield and Luis Cid, "Low-Frequency Changes in El Niño-Southern Oscillation," *Journal of Climate* 4 (Dec. 1991), p. 1139.
132. Eugene Rasmusson, Xueliang Wang and Chester Ropelewski, "Secular Variability of the ENSO Cycle," in National Research Council, *Natural Climate Variability on Decade-to-Century Time Scales*, Washington, D.C. 1995, pp. 458–70.
133. D. Harrison and N. Larkin, "El Niño-Southern Oscillation Sea Surface Temperature and Wind Anomalies, 1946–1993," *Reviews of Geophysics* 36:3 (Aug. 1998), pp. 386–91.
134. T. Baumgartner et al., "The Recording of Interannual Climatic Change by High–Resolution Natural Systems: Tree-Rings, Coral Bands, Glacial Ice Layers, and Marine Varves," *Geophysical Monograph* 55 (1989), pp. 1–14.

9. The Origins of the Third World

The epigraph is from Isaacs, *Scratches on Our Minds: American Images of China and India*, New York 1958, p. 273.

1. For a typically cavalier view, see Roland Lardinois, "Famine, Epidemics and Mortality in South India: A Reappraisal of the Demographic Crisis of 1876–1878," *Economic and Political Weekly* 20:111 (16 March 1985), p. 454.
2. Emmanuel Le Roy Ladurie, *Tmes of Feast, Times of Famine: A History of Climate Since the Year 1000*, Garden City, N.Y. 1971, p. 119.
3. Raymond Williams, *Problems in Materialism and Culture*, London 1980, p. 67.
4. When it served their interests, of course, the British could switch epistemologies. In the case of late-nineteenth-century China, for example, the British and their allies primarily blamed Qing corruption, not drought, for the millions of famine deaths.
5. Kueh, pp. 4–5.
6. Jared Diamond, *Guns, Germs, and Steel: The Fates of Human Societies*, New York 1997, pp. 424–5.
7. Re 1743–44: "another exceptional period in the eastern hemisphere, which corresponds with QN El Niño of 1744, although conditions were more markedly dry in the east in 1743" (Whetton and Rutherfurd, pp. 243–6).
8. "The first Qing emperor envisioned ever–normal granaries in county seats, charity granaries in major towns, and community granaries in the countryside. Ever–normal granaries were to be managed by members of the magistrate's staff, who were directed to sell, lend, or give away grain in the spring and to make purchases, collect loans, and solicit contributions in the autumn" (Pierre-Etienne Will and R. Bin Wong [with James Lee, Jean Oi and Peter Perdue], *Nourish the People: The State Civilian Granary System in China, 1650–1850*, Ann Arbor, Mich. 1981, p. 19).
9. Will, *Bureaucracy and Famine*, Chapters 7 and 8.
10. Ibid., pp. 86 and 189.
11. John Post, *Food Shortage, Climatic Variability, and Epidemic Disease in Preindustrial Europe: The Mortality Peak in the Early 1740s*, Ithaca, N.Y. 1985, p. 30.
12. Will, p. 270.
13. Jean Oi and Pierre-Etienne Will, "North China: Shandong During the Qianlong Period," in Will and Wong, pp. 369–70. ENSO correlations based on Quinn chronology.
14. "Introduction," in Will and Wong, p. 21. China's roads, on the other hand, remained miserable, and were a major obstacle to market integration as well as famine relief.
15. Wilkinson, pp. 122–9.
16. R. Bin Wong, "Decline and Its Opposition, 1781–1850," in Will and Wong, p. 76.
17. Helen Dunstan, *Conflicting Counsels to Confuse the Age: A Documentary Study of Political Economy in Qing China, 1644–1840*, Ann Arbor, Mich. 1996, p. 251.

18. Wilkinson, pp. 122–9. See also Will, "The Control Structure," in Will and Wong, pp. 220–21.
19. Jane Leonard, "'Controlling from Afar': Open Communications and the Tao-Kuang Emperor's Control of Grand Canal–Grain Transport Management, 1824–26," *Modern Asian Studies* 22:4 (1988), p. 666.
20. Joseph Needham, *Science and Civilization in China*, vol. 4, Cambridge 1971, p. 326.
21. Will, p. 257.
22. Jacques Gernet, *A History of Chinese Civilization*, 2nd edn., Cambridge 1996, p. 468.
23. Dwight Perkins, *Agricultural Development in China, 1368–1968*, Chicago 1969, p. 176.
24. Endymion Wilkinson, "Studies in Chinese Price History," Ph.D. diss., Princeton University 1970, p. 31.
25. Will, p. 32.
26. J. A. G. Roberts, *A Concise History of China*, Cambridge, Mass. 1990, p. 173.
27. On the special tribute granaries at Luoyang and Shanzhou organized during the Kangxi reign, see Will and Wong, pp. 32 and 301.
28. Food security in the mid eighteenth century may have consumed 10 percent of annual Qing revenue. As Wong emphasizes, "For a state to spend such sums for this purpose on a regular basis for well over a century is likely unique in the early modern world" ("Qing Granaries and Late Imperial History," in Will and Wong, p. 477).
29. Sanjay Sharma, "The 1837–38 Famine in U.P.: Some Dimensions of Popular Action," *IESHR* 30:3 (1993), p. 359.
30. Bhatia, p. 9.
31. Darren Zook, "Developing India: The History of an Idea in the Southern Countryside, 1860–1990," Ph.D. diss., University of California, Berkeley 1998, p. 158. The Raj was built upon mythology and hallucination. As Zook points out, the British universally attributed the ruins scattered through the Indian countryside to the decadence of native civilizations, when, in fact, many were direct memorials to the violence of British conquest (p. 157).
32. Sugata Bose and Ayesha Jalal, *Modern South Asia*, Delhi 1999, p. 43.
33. Ashok Desai, "Population and Standards of Living in Akbar's Time," *IESHR* 9:1 (1972), p. 61.
34. Chetan Singh, "Forests, Pastoralists and Agrarian Society in Mughal India," in David Arnold and Raachandra Guha (eds.), *Nature, Culture, Imperialism: Essays on the Environmental History of South Asia*, Delhi 1996, p. 22.
35. Habibul Kondker, "Famine Policies in Pre-British India and the Question of Moral Economy," *South Asia* 9:1 (June 1986), pp. 25–40; and Kuldeep Mahtur and Niraja Jayal, *Drought, Policy and Politics*, New Delhi 1993, p. 27. Unfortunately, contemporary discussion of famine history before 1763 has been contaminated by Hindu-versus-Muslim bickering. See, for example, the apparent anti-Muslim bias in Mushtag Kaw, "Famines in Kashmir, 1586–1819: The Policy of the Mughal and Afghan Rulers," *IESHR* 33:1 (1996), pp. 59–70.
36. C. Blair, *Indian Famines*, London 1874, pp. 8–10.
37. David Hardiman, "Well Irrigation in Gujarat: Systems of Use, Hierarchies of Control," *Economic and Political Weekly*, 20 June 1998, p. 1537.
38. Commission quoted in W. R. Aykroyd, *The Conquest of Famine*, London 1974, p. 51. See also John Richards, *The Mughal Empire* (*The New Cambridge History of India, 1*:5), Cambridge 1993, p. 163.
39. Bagchi, pp. 11–12 and 27.
40. J. Malcolm, *A Memoir of Central India*, vol. 1, London 1931, p. 7, quoted in D. E. U. Baker, *Colonialism in an Indian Hinterland: The Central Provinces, 1820–1920*, Delhi 1993, p. 28.
41. Baker, p. 52.
42. J. Richards and Michelle McAlpin, "Cotton Cultivating and Land Clearing in the Bombay Deccan and Karnatak: 1818–1920," in Richard Tucker and J. Richards (eds.), *Global Deforestation and the Nineteenth-Century World Economy*, Durham 1983, pp. 71 and 74.
43. Ibid.
44. Nash, p. 92.
45. Greenough, *Prosperity and Misery*, p. 59.
46. C. Walford, "The Famines of the World: Past and Present," *Journal of the Statistical Society* 41:13 (1878), pp. 434–42. I cite Walford elsewhere from the expanded 1879 book version of this article.
47. Michael Watts, *Silent Violence: Food, Famine and Peasantry in Northern Nigeria*, Berkeley 1983, pp. 462–3. This "negotiation," of course, is two-sided and must include climate shock as an independent variable.

48. Watts, pp. 267 and 464.
49. Hans Medick, "The Proto-Industrial Family Economy and the Structures and Functions of Population Development under the Proto-Industrial System," in P. Kriedte et al. (eds.), *Industrialization Before Industrialization*, Cambridge 1981, p. 45.
50. Ibid., pp. 44–5.
51. Lewis, *Growth and Fluctuations*, p. 189.
52. Cited in Clive Dewey, "The End of the Imperialism of Free Trade," p. 35.
53. Kenneth Pomeranz, *The Making of a Hinterland: State, Society, and Economy in Inland North China, 1853–1937*, Berkeley 1993.
54. Paul Bairoch, "The Main Trends in National Economic Disparities Since the Industrial Revolution," in Paul Bairoch and Maurice Levy-Leboyer (eds.), *Disparities in Economic Development Since the Industrial Revolution*, London 1981, p. 7.
55. Paul Bairoch, "International Industrialization Levels from 1750–1980," in *Journal of European Economic History* 11 (1982), p. 107.
56. Fritjof Tichelman, *The Social Evolution of Indonesia*, The Hague 1980, p. 30.
57. Prasannan Parthasarathi, "Rethinking Wages and Competitiveness in Eighteenth-Century Britain and South India," *Past and Present* 158 (Feb. 1998), pp. 82–7 and 105–6.
58. Dutt, cited in Eddy, p. 21.
59. Philip Huang, *The Peasant Family and Rural Development in the Yangzi Delta, 1350–1988*, Stanford, Calif. 1990.
60. Wong, p. 38.
61. F. W. Mote, *Imperial China, 900–1800*, Cambridge, Mass. 1999, p. 941.
62. Kenneth Pomeranz, "A High Standard of Living and Its Implications," contribution to "E. H. R. Forum: Re-thinking 18th Century China," Internet, 19 Nov. 1997.
63. Pomeranz, "Two Worlds of Trade, Two Worlds of Empire: European State-Making and Industrialization in a Chinese Mirror," in David Smith et al., *States and Sovereignty in the Global Economy*, London 1999, p. 78 (my emphasis).
64. See S. Patel, "The Economic Distance Between Nations: Its Origin, Measurement and Outlook, *Economic Journal*, March 1964. (There is some discrepancy between his figures for the aggregate non-European world and the later estimates of Bairoch and Maddison.)
65. Albert Feuerwerker, *The Chinese Economy, 1870–1949*, Ann Arbor, Mich. 1995, pp. 32–3.
66. Paul Bairoch, "Geographical Structure and Trade Balance of European Foreign Trade, from 1800–1970," *Journal of European Economic History* 3:3 (Winter 1978), p. 565. Ch'en cites 1866 as the beginning of the serious penetration of imported textiles into China (p. 64).
67. Jack Goldstone, "Review of David Landes, *The Wealth and Poverty of Nations*," *Journal of World History* 2:1 (Spring 2000), p. 109.
68. Carl Trocki, *Opium, Empire and the Global Political Economy*, London 1999, p. 98.
69. Brian Bond, *Victorian Military Campaigns*, London 1967, pp. 309–11.
70. See O'Rourke and Williamson, pp. 53–4.
71. Historians traditionally contrast the Meiji and Tonzhang restorations, but as Goldstone suggests, the more significant comparison is between the Taipings and Japan. "What if China's old imperial regime, like Japan's, had collapsed in the mid nineteenth century, and not fifty years later, what then? What if the equivalent of Chiang Kai-shek's new model army had begun formation in the 1860s and not the 1920s? Would Japan still have been able to colonize Korea and Taiwan? What would have been the Asian superpower?" (Goldstone, ibid.).
72. "India wealth supplied the funds that bought the national debt back from the Dutch and others, first temporarily in the interval of peace between 1763 and 1774, and finally after 1783, leaving Britain nearly free from overseas indebtedness when it came to face the great French wars from 1793" (Ralph Davis, *The Industrial Revolution and British Overseas Trade*, Leicester 1979, pp. 55–6).
73. P. Cain and A. Hopkins, *British Imperialism: Innovation and Expansion, 1688–1914*, London 1993, p. 334.
74. For a recent review, see Young Goo-Park, "Depression and Capital Formation: The UK and Germany, 1873–96," *Journal of European Economic History* 26:3 (Winter 1997), especially pp. 511 and 516.
75. Giovanni Arrighi, *The Long Twentieth Century: Money, Power and the Origins of Our Times*, London 1994, p. 263.

76. A. Latham, *The International Economy and the Undeveloped World, 1865–1914*, London 1978, p. 70. Latham, it should be noted, is notoriously apologistic for British colonialism in India, arguing that the subcontinent's "relatively low growth overall is due largely to climatic factors, not to any deleterious effect of British colonial policy" (See A. Latham, "Asian Stagnation: Real or Relative?", in Derek Aldcroft and Ross Catterall (eds.), *Rich Nations–Poor Nations: The Long-Run Perspective*, Cheltenham 1996, p. 109).
77. Robin Moore, "Imperial India, 1858–1914," in Andrew Porter (ed.), *The Oxford History of the British Empire: The Nineteenth Century*, Oxford 1999, p. 441.
78. Marcello de Cecco, *The International Gold Standard: Money and Empire*, New York 1984, p. 30.
79. Ravi Palat, et al., "Incorporation of South Asia," p. 185. According to these authors, the apparent exceptions to Indian deindustrialization in fact proved the rule: cotton spinning was integral to the production of an export surplus from the China trade while jute manufacture was an "island of British capital ... initiated, organized, and controlled by British civil servants and merchants" (p. 186).
80. Ibid., pp. 37–8.
81. J. Stamp, *British Incomes and Property*, London 1916, p. 36.
82. Cain and Hopkins, pp. 338–9.
83. Eric Hobsbawm, *Industry and Empire: An Economic History of Britain Since 1750*, London 1968, p. 123.
84. The same question, of course, could be asked of Indonesia, which in the late nineteenth century generated almost 9 percent of the Dutch national domestic product. See Angus Maddison, "Dutch Income in and from Indonesia, 1700–1938," *Modern Asian Studies* 23:4 (1989), p. 647.
85. Eric Stokes, "The First Century of British Colonial Rule in India: Social Revolution or Social Stagnation?" *Past and Present* 58 (Feb. 1873), p. 151.
86. Dietmar Rothermund, *An Economic History of India*, New York 1988, p. 36; Dutt, *Open Letters*, p. 48.
87. Lu Aiguo, *China and the Global Economy Since 1840,* Helsinki 2000, pp. 34, 37 and 39 (Table 2.4).
88. J.W. Wong, *Deadly Dreams: Opium and the Arrow War (1856–1860) in China*, Cambridge 1998, pp. 390 and 396. The British tea imports from China, which opium also financed, were the source of the lucrative tea duty that by mid-century almost compensated for the cost of the Royal Navy (pp. 350–55).
89. Lu Aiguo, p. 36.
90. Latham, *The International Economy*, p. 90. India (including Burma) also earned important income from rice exports to the Dutch East Indies.
91. Ibid., pp. 409–10. See also M. Greenberg, *British Trade and the Opening of China*, Cambridge 1951, p. 15.
92. Latham, pp. 453–4.
93. Ibid., pp. 81–90. After Japan's victory in 1895, however, its textile exports began to crowd India and Britain out of the Chinese market (p. 90).
94. Cain and Hopkins, p. 425.
95. Jerome Ch'en, *State Economic Polices of the Ch'ing Government, 1840–1895*, New York 1980, p. 116.
96. Latham, ibid.
97. John Hobson, "The Military-Extraction Gap and the Wary Titan: The Fiscal Sociology of British Defense Policy, 1870–1913," *Journal of European Economic History* 22:3 (Winter 1993), p. 480.
98. Historians have yet to address Chi-ming Hou's complaint in 1963 that "no serious studies have ever been made of the effects of such wars on the Chinese economy" ("Some Reflections on the Economic History of Modern China, 1840–1949," *Journal of Economic History* 23:4 [Dec. 1963], p. 603).
99. Bohr, p. 24.
100. Michelle McAlpin, "Price Movements and Fluctuations in Economic Activity," in Dumar (ed.), *Cambridge Economic History of India*, p. 890.
101. John McGuire, "The World Economy, the Colonial State, and the Establishment of the Indian National Congress," in I. Shepperson and Colin Simons (eds.), *The Indian National Congress and the Political Economy of India, 1885–1985*, Avebury 1988, p. 51.
102. Nash, p. 88.
103. McAlpin, "Price Movements," ibid.

104. Bandyopadhyay, *Indian Famine*, p. 130.
105. De Cecco, pp. 62 and 74. "[Indians] considered fiscal pressure to be unduly high, in view of the fact that the Indian government's budget was every year in surplus and the country had a trade surplus year after year; in addition to which the government had a substantial credit balance" (p. 74).
106. Krishnendu Ray, "Crises, Crashes and Speculation," *Economic and Political Weekly* (30 July 1994), pp. 92–3. By 1913 the Government of India's account in London was £136 million (ibid.).
107. Dieter Rothermund, "The Monetary Policy of British Imperialism," *IESHR* 7 (1970), pp. 98–9.
108. Wilkinson, pp. 34, 41–3, 52.
109. Wright, *The Last Stand of Chinese Conservatism*, p. 166.
110. Ch'en, p. 120.
111. Aiguo, p. 48.
112. Wilkinson, pp. 34, 41–3, 52.
113. Lewis, p. 216.
114. Charlesworth, pp. 13 and 22.
115. Tomlinson, "Economics: The Periphery," p. 68 (Table 3.7).
116. Quoted in Bipan Chandra, "Colonial India: British versus Indian Views of Development," *Review* 14:1 (Winter 1991), p. 102.
117. Bagchi, p. 27.
118. William Lavely and R. Bin Wong, "Revising the Malthusian Narrative: The Comparative Study of Population Dynamics in Late Imperial China," *Journal of Asian Studies* 57:3 (Aug. 1998), pp. 714–48.
119. Esther Boserup, *The Conditions of Agricultural Growth: The Economics of Agrarian Change Under Population Pressure,* Chicago 1967.
120. Angus Maddison, *Chinese Economic Peformance in the Long Run,* Paris 1998, p. 39. See also Zhang Kaimin, "The Evolution of Modern Chinese Society from the Perspective of Population Changes, 1840–1949," in Frederic Wakeman and Wang Xi (eds.), *China's Quest for Modernization: A Historical Perspective*, Berkeley 1997.
121. Pomeranz, p. 121.
122. Gernet, p. 560.
123. Martin Heijdra, "The Socio-Economic Development of Ming Rural China (1368–1644)," Ph.D. diss., Princeton University 1994, pp. 50–56; and Mote, pp. 903–6.
124. Mote, p. 906.
125. Pomeranz, "Two Worlds of Trade," pp. 81–3.
126. Patrick O'Brien, "Intercontinental Trade and Third World Development," *Journal of World History* (Spring 1997), p. 91.
127. Hardiman, "Well Irrigation in Gujarat," p. 1533. He is characterizing the conclusions of Anil Agarwal and Sunita Narain (*Dying Wisdom: Rise, Fall and Potential of India's Traditional Water Harvesting Systems*, Delhi 1997).
128. Feuerwerker, p. 21.
129. Maddison, *Chinese Economic Performance,* p. 30.
130. As the geographer Joshua Muldavin has emphasized, economic and ecological poverty are not equivalent: Households with identical levels of economic poverty can have extremely different levels of vulnerability to climatic instability or disaster ("Village Strategies for Maintaining Socio–Ecological Security in the post-Mao Era," unpublished paper, UCLA Department of Geography, 1998).

10. India: The Modernization of Poverty

The quotation in the epigraph is from Romesh Chunder Dutt, *Open Letters to Lord Curzon*, Calcutta 1904, p. 27.

1. Maddison, *Chinese Economic Performance,* p. 67. Revisionist attempts to claim an increase in per capita income in Victorian India despite an undeniable collapse in life expectancy are dealt with, rather devastatingly, by Irfan Habib in "Studying a Colonial Economy — Without Perceiving Colonialism," *Modern Asian Studies* 19:3 (1985), pp. 368–74.
2. H.M. Hyndman, *The Awakening of Asia*, London 1919, p. 22.
3. B. Tomlinson, *The Economy of Modern India, 1860–1970*, Cambridge 1993, p. 31.
4. Sumit Guha, "Introduction," in Guha (ed.), *Growth, Stagnation or Decline? Agricultural Productivity in British India*, Delhi 1992, pp. 45–6.
5. Kingsley Davis, *Population of India and Pakistan*, Princeton, N.J. 1951, p. 8. Measured from the "good decade" of the 1880s to 1911–21, Irfan Habib (Table 2, p. 373) finds that male life expectatancy declined by 22 percent.
6. Laxman Satya, "Cotton and Famine in Berar, 1850–1900," Ph.D. diss., Tufts University 1994, pp. 50 and 155. See also Peter Harnetty, *Imperialism and Free Trade: Lancashire and India in the Mid-Nineteenth Century*, Vancouver 1972.
7. Dewey, "The End of the Imperialism of Free Trade," p. 51.
8. Stanley Wolpert, *A New History of India*, Oxford 1989, p. 248.
9. Satya, pp. 21–7, 36–7, 50–51, 72, 155, 162, 188–90 and 333; and "Introduction" to book version (*Cotton and Famine in Berar, 1850–1900*, Delhi 1997), p. 25.
10. Satya, p. 182 (export); and Vasant Kaiwar, "Nature, Property and Polity in Colonial Bombay," *Journal of Peasant Studies* 27:2 (Jan. 2000), p. 7 (acreage).
11. Satya, p. 182.
12. Charlesworth, p. 81.
13. Satya, pp. 68 and 298.
14. Ibid., p. 200.
15. Ibid., pp. 148, 281–2 and 296.
16. Tim Dyson, "The Historical Demography of Berar, 1881–1980," in Dyson (ed.), *India's Historical Demography: Studies in Famine, Disease and Society*, London 1989, pp. 181–2.
17. David Washbrook, "The Commercialization of Agriculture in Colonial India: Production, Subsistence and Reproduction in the 'Dry South,' c. 1870–1930," *Modern Asian Studies* 28:1 (1994), p. 131.
18. Ibid., pp. 137 and 161. In another article, Washbrook claims that the average cultivator had only half the dry land acreage needed for subsistence ("Economic Development and Social Stratification in Rural Madras: The 'Dry Region' 1878–1929" in Dewey and Hopkins [eds.], pp. 70–72).
19. David Washbrook, *The Emergence of Provincial Politics: The Madras Presidency, 1870–1920*, Cambridge 1976, p. 69.
20. Washbrook, "Commercialization of Agriculture," p. 145.
21. Ibid., p. 146.
22. Richards and McAlpin, p. 83
23. Washbrook, "Commercialization of Agriculture," p. 153.
24. As elsewhere in India, British land settlements in the 1860s had transformed the conditional tenure of Mogul or (in this case) Maratha tax farmers into a simulacrum of an English squirearchy. The ranks of the *malguzars,* however, were severely pruned in the terrible repression that followed 1857. Rebel leaders were shot from cannon, hanged or, in one case, even crucified by vengeful British officers. See D. E. U. Baker, pp. 101–6.
25. On the credit system and merchant hypothecation of harvests, see T. Raghavan, "Malguzars and Peasants: The Narmada Valley, 1860–1920," in David Ludden (ed.), *Agricultural Production and Indian History*, Delhi 1994, pp. 309 and 339–40.
26. Baker, p. 124
27. Peter Harnetty, "Crop Trends in the Central Provinces of India, 1861–1921," *Modern Asian Studies* 11:3 (1977), p. 347.
28. Baker, p. 106.

29. Ibid., p. 147.
30. Ibid., p. 151.
31. Ibid., pp. 129 and 150.
32. Raghavan, p. 311.
33. Ibid., pp. 137–41.
34. Ibid., pp. 182–3; Solberg, *The Prairies and the Pampas*, p. 36 (Table 3.3).
35. Singh, *Starvation and Colonialism*, p. 220.
36. Neeladri Bhattacharya, "Lenders and Debtors: Punjab Countryside, 1880–1940" in Bose (ed.), *Credit, Markets and the Agrarian Economy*, p. 200.
37. Singh, *Starvation and Colonialism*, p. 220.
38. Ibid., p. 221.
39. Hardiman, "Introduction," pp. 13–14.
40. Colin Fisher, "Planters and Peasants: The Ecological Context of Agrarian Unrest on the Indigo Plantations of North Bihar, 1820–1920," in Clive Dewey and A. Hopkins (eds.), *The Imperial Impact: Studies in the Economic History of Africa and India*, London 1978, pp. 125–31.
41. Carl Trocki, *Opium, Empire and the Global Political Economy*, London 1999, p. 67.
42. Binay Chaudhuri, "Growth of Commercial Agriculture," *IESHR* 7:2 (1970), pp. 231, 246–9.
43. Ibid., p. 251. On sugar, see Shahid Amin, *Sugar and Sugarcane in Gorakhpur: An Inquiry into Peasant Production for Capitalist Enterprise in Colonial India*, Delhi 1983.
44. Raghavan, p. 336.
45. Shahid Amin, "Small Peasant Commodity Production and Rural Indebtedness: The Culture of Sugarcane in Eastern U.P., c. 1880–1920" in Sugata Bose (ed.), *Credit, Markets and the Agrarian Economy of Colonial India*, Delhi 1994, p. 124.
46. Sarkar, pp. 30–31.
47. Bipan Chandra quoted in D. Rothermund, *Phases of Indian Nationalism*, Bombay 1970, p. 264 fn19.
48. Burton Stein, *A History of India*, London 1998, p. 263.
49. Lance Davis and Robert Huttenback, *Mammon and the Pursuit of Empire: The Economics of British Imperialism*, Cambridge 1988, pp. 101 (quote) and 135.
50. Vasant Kaiwar, "The Colonial State, Capital and the Peasantry in Bombay Presidency," *Modern Asian Studies* 28:4 (1994), p. 800.
51. David Washbrook, "Economic Development and Social Stratification," p. 69.
52. Bagchi, pp. 6 and 38.
53. Kaiwar, p. 793.
54. Guha, pp. 27 and 70.
55. Scott, p. 21.
56. Osborne, p. 554.
57. Charlesworth, pp. 193–5.
58. Quoted in ibid., p. 40.
59. C. Baker, "The Markets," in Sugata Bose (ed.), *Credit, Markets and the Agrarian Economy of Colonial India*, Delhi 1994, p. 192.
60. David Washbrook, "Progress and Problems: South Asian Economic and Social History, c. 1720–1860," *Modern Asian Studies* 22:1 (1988), p. 90.
61. Christopher Baker, *An Indian Rural Economy, 1880–1955: The Tamilnad Countryside*, Bombay 1984, p. 156.
62. B. Chaudhuri, "Agrarian Relations in Bengal: 1859–1885," in N. Sinha (ed.), *The History of Bengal (1757–1905)*, Calcutta 1967, pp. 318–20.
63. Kaiwar, p. 800.
64. Martha Chen, *Coping with Seasonality and Drought*, Delhi 1991, p. 119.
65. David Ludden, *Peasant History in South India*, Princeton, N.J. 1985, p. 122.
66. Chetan Singh, p. 44.
67. Satya, p. 299.
68. Atuluri Murali, "Whose Trees? Forest Practices and Local Communities in Andhra, 1600–1922," p. 100.
69. Madhav Gadgil and Ramachandra Guha, "State Forestry and Social Conflict in British India," in Hardiman (ed.), *Peasant Resistance*, p. 275.

70. Hardiman, "Introduction," pp. 47–8.
71. Satya, p. 120.
72. Baker, pp. 157 and 161.
73. V. Saravanan, "Commercialisation of Forests, Environmental Negligence and Alienation of Tribal Rights in Madras Presidency, 1792–1882," *IESHR* 35:2 (1998), p. 139; and Ramachandra Guha, "An Early Environmental Debate: The Making of the 1878 Forest Act," *IESHR* 27:1 (1990), p. 67.
74. Nash, pp. 21, 125 and 164–5.
75. Ludden, "Introduction," pp. 23–4.
76. Jos Gommans, "The Silent Frontier of South Asia, c. AD 1000–1800," *Journal of World History*, 9:1 (1998), p. 17.
77. Ludden, "Introduction," pp. 23–4.
78. Neeladri Bhattacharya, "Pastoralists in a Colonial World," p. 70.
79. Charlesworth, pp. 77 and 295.
80. Sumit Guha, pp. 58–61, 65–6.
81. Bandyopadhyay, p. 163.
82. Kaiwar, p. 57.
83. Bhattacharya, p. 65.
84. Ibid., pp. 56–7.
85. Kaiwar, "Nature, Property and Polity," p. 14.
86. Sumit Guha, pp. 83 and 121–3. See also H. Mann, *A Study of Rainfall in the Bombay Deccan, 1865–1938*, Bombay 1955.
87. Satya, pp. 72, 116 and 122.
88. Hardiman, "Well Irrigation in Gujarat," p. 1534.
89. Satya, ibid.
90. *The Finances and Public Works of India* (pp. 7–8), quoted in Elizabeth Whitcombe, *Agrarian Conditions in Northern India*, vol. 1, *The United Provinces Under British Rule, 1860–1900,* Berkeley, Calif. 1972, p. 2.
91. Under Company rule, of course, infrastructural investment had been infamously nugatory. Thus John Bright once demonstated in Parliament that the Corporation of Manchester spent more on public works in 1856 than the East India Company had expended on all of India during the preceding fourteen years (cited in Lady Hope, p. 258).
92. Elizabeth Whitcombe, "Irrigation," in Dharma Kumar (ed.), *The Cambridge Economic History of India, Volume Two: 1757–c. 1970*, Cambridge 1983, p. 703.
93. General Sir Arthur Cotton, *The Madras Famine*, London 1877, p. 5. See also Florence Nightingale, letter to the *Illustrated News*, 29 June 1877.
94. "Discussion with Woodrow Wyatt," *The Collected Works of Mahatma Gandhi,* vol. 83 (no. 473, 13 April 1946), Ahmedabad 1981, pp. 404–5.
95. S. Sharma, "Irrigation," in V. Singh, *Economic History of India: 1857–1956*, Bombay 1966, pp. 165; and Whitcombe, "Irrigation," pp. 678, 703–7.
96. *Famine and Agrarian Problems*, p. 232.
97. Ian Stone, *Canal Irrigation in British India*, Cambridge 1984.
98. Whitcombe, *Agrarian Conditions*, p. 11.
99. Quoted in Stone, p. 88.
100. Ibid., p. 154; and Whitcombe, *Agrarian Conditions*, p. 81.
101. Tomlinson, p. 76.
102. Whitcombe, *Agrarian Conditions*, pp. xi and 75.
103. Quoted in Whitcombe, "The Environmental Costs of Irrigation in British India: Waterlogging, Salinity, Malaria," p. 247.
104. *Papers on the Revenue Returns of the Canals of the North-Western Provinces* (1865), quoted in Stone, p. 75.
105. Ibid., p. 260.
106. Whitcombe, "Irrigation," pp. 716–17 and 720 (quote).
107. C. J. O'Donnell, *The Failure of Lord Curzon*, London 1903, p. 99.
108. Ludden, "Introduction," pp. 104 and 146.
109. Kaiwar, "Nature, Property and Polity," pp. 23 and 25.
110. The *Nasik Gazetteer,* 1883, quoted in Kaiwar, ibid.

111. Hyndman, *The Bankruptcy of India*, p. 128.
112. See Ranabir Chakravarti, "The Creation and Expansion of Settlements and Management of Hydraulic Resources in Ancient India," in Grove, Damodaran and Sangwan, pp. 87–105.
113. Hardiman, "Small–Dam Systems of the Sahyadris," p. 204.
114. Jonathan Mabry and David Cleveland, "The Relevance of Indigenous Irrigation," in Mabry (ed.), *Canals and Communities: Small-Scale Irrigation Systems*, Tucson, Ariz. 1996, pp. 227–8 (quote) and 236 (efficiency).
115. M. Quraishi, *Drought Strategy*, Delhi 1989, p. 42. On the other hand, private exploitation of underground water resources since the 1960s has led to a profligate drawing down of the water table and a wholly avoidable water crisis.
116. "But for their listless acceptance of the worst miseries in the hand of fate, India would ages ago have been fertilized by a system of irrigation, and saved almost from the possiblity of Famine. The Natives are one of the most improvident as well as helpless races on earth" (*The Times*, 23 Jan. 1877).
117. Col. J. Anderson of the Madras Engineers quoted in "Philindus," "Famines and Floods in India," *Macmillan's Magazine*, Jan. 1878, p. 237.
118. Grove, pp. 134–5.
119. Lady Hope, p. 194. See also G. Rao, "Canal Irrigation and Agrarian Change in Colonial Andhra: A Study of Godavri District, c. 1850–1890," *IESHR* 25:1 (1988).
120. Quoted in Zook, pp. 163–4.
121. Bagchi, pp. 28–9.
122. William Wedderburn, *Agricultural Banks for India*, p. 27.
123. Fawcettt in *The Times* quoted in George Chesney, "Indian Famines," *The Nineteenth Century*, Nov. 1877, p. 618.
124. Berar, p. 197.
125. H.M. Hyndman, *The Indian Famine*, London 1877, p. 12; and John Dacosta, *Facts and Fallacies Regarding Irrigation as a Prevention of Famine in India*, London 1878, pp. 2–4. Similar arguments are advanced in "A Journalist," *The Great Lesson of the Indian Famine*, London 1877 (pamphlet collection, Trinity College Library, Dublin).
126. Bandyopadhyay, p. 115.
127. Baker, p. 472.
128. Ludden, *Peasant History*, p. 146 (see Table 5).
129. *The Hindu* (Madras), 10 May 1900.
130. Navtej Singh, *Starvation and Colonialism: A Study of Famines in the Nineteenth Century British Punjab, 1858–1901*, New Delhi 1996, p. 8.
131. Satya, p. 85.
132. R. Carstairs, *The Little World of an Indian District Officer*, London 1912, pp. 364–5.
133. Kaiwar, "Nature, Property and Polity," p. 23.
134. Nash, p. 2.
135. Ravinder Kumar, *Western India in the Nineteenth Century*, London 1968, p. 325.
136. Ludden, "Introduction," pp. 104 and 146.
137. David Mosse, "Colonial and Contemporary Ideologies of 'Community Management': The Case of Tank Irrigation Development in South India," *Modern Asian Studies* 33:2 (1999), p. 315.
138. Hardiman, "Well Irrigation in Gujarat," p. 1541.

11. China: Mandates Revoked

The epigraph is from Wolfgang Bauer, *China and the Search for Happiness*, New York 1976, p. 257.

1. Karl Wittfogel, *Oriental Despotism: A Comparative Study of Total Power*, New Haven, Conn. 1957, p. 290.
2. Susan Naquin and Evelyn Rawski, *Chinese Society in the Eighteenth Century*, New Haven, Conn. 1987, pp. 22, 146 and 219; and Will, *Bureaucracy and Famine*, pp. 64–5.
3. Huang, *Peasant Family*, p. 42 (also pp. 74–6).
4. Kamal Sheel, *Peasant Society and Marxist Intellectuals in China*, Princeton, N.J. 1989, p. 94.
5. Little, *Understanding Peasant China*, p. 92.
6. Sidney Gamble, *Ting Hsien: A North China Rural Community*, New York 1954, pp. 52, 64 and 110.

7. Huang, *Peasant Family*, p. 5.
8. Huang, *Peasant Economy*, pp. 102–6 and 152.
9. Nichols, pp. 128–9.
10. Ibid., pp. 248–50.
11. Huang, *Peasant Economy*, p. 115.
12. Laura Murray, "New World Food Crops in China: Farms, Food and Families in the Wei River Valley, 1650–1910," Ph.D. diss., University of Pennsylvania, 1985, pp. 43–4.
13. Ibid., pp. 45, 68, 82 and 138.
14. Madeleine Zelin, "Modernization and the Structure of the Chinese Economy in the Nineteenth and Twentieth Centuries," in Frederic Wakeman and Wang Xi (eds.), *China's Quest for Modernization: A Historical Perspective*, Berkeley 1997, p. 93.
15. Huang, *Peasant Family*, pp. 102–6.
16. Huang, *Peasant Economy*, p. 124; and Will, pp. 178 and 180–81.
17. Dr. J. Edkins, *Opium: Historical Note on the Poppy in China*, Shanghai 1898, p. 66.
18. Murray, pp. 74–5 and 79.
19. Zelin, p. 108.
20. Arthur Smith, *Village Life in China* (1899), Boston 1970 (reprint), pp. 210–11.
21. Naquin and Rawski, p. 143.
22. Huang, *Peasant Economy*, pp. 7 and 118–19.
23. Ibid., p. 60.
24. Pauline Keating, *Two Revolutions: Village Reconstruction and the Cooperative Movement in Northern Shaanxi, 1934–1945*, Stanford, Calif. 1997, p. 15.
25. Huang, *Peasant Economy*, pp. 107–8 and 114.
26. Kamal Sheel, *Peasant Society and Marxist Intellectuals in China*, Princeton, N.J. 1989, pp. 54–7; and K. Chaudhuri, "Foreign Trade and Balance of Payments," in Dharma Kumar (ed.), *The Cambridge Economic History of India, Volume 2,* Cambridge 1983, p. 853.
27. Calculated from Table 7 in Albert Feuerwerker, *The Chinese Economy, ca. 1870–1911*, Michigan Papers in Chinese Studies, Ann Arbor, Mich. 1969.
28. Huang, *Peasant Economy*, p. 132.
29. Nichols, p. 248.
30. Esherick, pp. 72–3.
31. Wilkinson, pp. 198–9.
32. Perkins, *Agricultural Development in China, 1368–1968*, Chicago 1969, pp. 119 and 136.
33. On long-distance commercial flows, see R. Bin Wong, "Food Riots in the Qing Dynasty," *Journal of Asian Studies* 41:4 (Aug. 1982), pp. 768–9.
34. Naquin and Rawski, p. 219.
35. Esherick, p. 40.
36. Will, p. 291.
37. "Decline and Its Opposition," in Will and Wong, p. 91.
38. Manfred Domros and Peng Gongbing, *The Climate of China*, Berlin 1988, p. 198.
39. Randall Dodgen, "Hydraulic Evolution and Dynastic Decline: The Yellow River Conservancy, 1796–1855," *Late Imperial China* 12:2 (Dec. 1991), pp. 51 and 55–6.
40. Wang Yeh-chien, *Land Taxation in Imperial China, 1750–1911*, Cambridge, Mass. 1973, pp. 113, 121 and 125–6.
41. Kung-Chuan Hsiao, *Rural China: Imperial Control in the Nineteenth Century*, Seattle 1960, p. 146.
42. Perkins, p. 164. (As explained in Chapter 9, however, the population in 1700 may have been much higher than Perkins assumes.)
43. Will, p. 276.
44. Wong, p. 783.
45. Perkins, p. 164.
46. R. Bin Wong, "The Grand Structure, 1736–1780," in Will and Wong, pp. 60–61.
47. On the crisis in Shaanxi's granaries, see "Decline and Its Opposition," ibid., p. 78.
48. Hsiao, p. 154.
49. Perkins , pp. 150–51.
50. Will, p. 289.
51. Will, pp. 276–7.

52. There were exceptions, of course, as in Gansu in 1810 where "the large sum of one million taels was allotted for a comprehensive and apparently successful effort to reach the stricken population" (Will, p. 296).
53. *Land Utilization in China: Statistics*, Nanking 1937, p. 344, Table 2.
54. T. Kingsmill, "Inland Communications in China," *Journal of the China Branch of the Royal Asiatic Society* (for the year 1895–96), Shanghai 1899, pp. 3 and 147.
55. Wright, p. 175 (also pp. 176–80).
56. Keating, p. 25.
57. Ibid., p. 314. "Corruption had always been a way of life in China, but in the nineteenth century it reached unprecedented proportions, not to be exceeded until the first half of the twentieth century" (Victor Lippit, "The Development of Underdevelopment in China," in Philip Huang (ed.), *The Development of Underdevelopment in China: A Symposium*, White Plains, N.Y. 1980, p. 67).
58. Jonathan Spence, *God's Chinese Son: The Taiping Heavenly Kingdom of Hong Xiuquan*, New York 1996, p. 158.
59. Jen Yu-wen, *The Taiping Revolutionary Movement*, New Haven, Conn. 1973, pp. 54 and 94. "Toleration of corrupt and rapacious officials" and the "selling of offices through bribes" were another two of the "ten major crimes" of the Qing (p. 94).
60. Spence, p. 161.
61. Roberts, pp. 181–2.
62. E. Parker, "The Financial Capacity of China," *Journal of the China Branch of the Royal Asiatic Society* (1893–1894), Shanghai 1898, pp. 97–8.
63. Murray, p. 270.
64. Nichols, p. 235.
65. Murray, pp. 315 and 318.
66. Ibid., p. 183.
67. Kenneth Pomeranz, EH.NET Forum: "Rethinking 18th-Century China," Internet, 16 Dec. 1997.
68. Maddison, pp. 34–5.
69. Hans Van De Ven, "Recent Studies of Modern Chinese History," *Modern Asian Studies*, 30:2 (1996), p. 241.
70. Robert Marks, *Tigers, Rice, Silk, and Silt: Environment and Economy in Late Imperial South China*, Cambridge 1998, pp. 277 and 307.
71. Rhoads Murphey, "Deforestation in Modern China," in Richard Tucker and J. F. Richards (eds.), *Global Deforestation and the Nineteenth-Century World Economy*, Durham 1983, p. 111. He cautions, however, that "it is not known, or discoverable by any means, what China's forest cover was at any point in the nineteenth century, or the extent of net depletion in the course of that century" (p. 114).
72. Anne Osborne, "The Local Politics of Land Reclamation in the Lower Yangtzi Highlands," *Late Imperial China* 15:1 (June 1994), p. 2.
73. Marks, ibid.; and Peter Perdue, *Exhausting the Earth,* Cambridge, Mass. 1987.
74. Eduard Vermeer, "Population and Ecology along the Frontier in Qing China," in Elvin and Liu, pp. 249–51 and 261. Since Qing tax rates were essentially capped, the easiest way to increase land revenues was by encouraging the expansion of land area under cultivation.
75. Anne Osborne, "Barren Mountains, Raging Rivers: The Ecological Effects of Changing Landuse on the Lower Yangzi Periphery in Late Imperial China," Ph.D. diss., Columbia University 1989, p. 158.
76. Murray, p. 278.
77. Von Richtofen's letters to the *North China Herald* (1870–72) are discussed in W. Lowdermilk, "Forestry in Denuded China," *Annals of the American Academy* 15 (Nov. 1930), pp. 137–8.
78. Frank Leeming, *The Changing Geography of China*, Oxford 1993, p. 50.
79. Murray, p. 69.
80. Murphey, p. 119.
81. Keating, pp. 23–4.
82. Vermeer, p. 235.
83. Eliot Blackwelder, "A Country That Has Used Up Its Trees," *The Outlook* 82 (24 March 1906), pp. 693–700.
84. Murphey, p. 116.

85. Lowdermilk, p. 137.
86. Ibid., p. 139.
87. Pomeranz, p. 124.
88. On this process in Shandong and Liaotung, see Cressey, pp. 208–9.
89. Will, p. 129.
90. Lowdermilk, pp. 130 (proverb) and 140 (erosion rate).
91. Murphey, pp. 126–7.
92. W. Lowdermilk, "A Forester's Search for Forests in China," *American Forests and Forest Life* 31 (July 1925), p. 239.
93. Vermeer, pp. 273–4.
94. Murphey, p. 125.
95. Charles Greer, *Water Management in the Yellow River Basin of China*, Austin, Tex. 1979, p. 18.
96. Murphey, pp. 124–5.
97. Greer, p. 33.
98. Ibid. The struggle to control the Mississippi in the late nineteenth and early twentieth centuries produced its own version of warring hydraulic schools with the Army Corps as unconscious Confucians and civilian engineers like Charles Ellet and James Eads as spontaneous Taoists. See the fascinating account (pp. 19–93) in John Barry, *Rising Tide*, New York 1997.
99. Randall Dodgen, "Hydraulic Evolution," pp. 36 fn1 and 50–51. In a significant dissent from the mainstream of late Imperial historians, Dodgen argues that the "crisis of the Yellow River control system was the product of riparian realities, and was not primarily determined by Qing institutional vitality or decline" (p. 59).
100. Vermeer, p. 265.
101. Mark Elvin and Su Ninghu, "Action at a Distance: The Influence of the Yellow River on Hangzhou Bay Since A.D. 1000," in Mark Elvin and Liu Ts'ui-jung (eds.), *Sediments of Time: Environment and Society in Chinese History*, Cambridge 1998, pp. 344–407.
102. Randall Dodgen, "Controlling the Dragon: Confucian Engineers and the Yellow River in the Late Daoguang, 1835–1850," Ph.D. diss., Yale Univesity 1989, p. 40.
103. Will, p. 292; also Naquin and Rawski, p. 24.
104. Dodgen, "Hydraulic Evolution," p. 55.
105. Ibid., p. 56.
106. Jonathan Spence, *The Search for Modern China*, New York 1990, p. 185; and Teng, p. 40.
107. Wright, pp. 161–3.
108. Esherick, pp. 14–15.
109. Ibid.
110. Pomeranz, *The Making of a Hinterland*, p. 179.
111. Jurgen Osterhammel, "Britain and China," in Andrew Porter (ed.), *The Oxford History of the British Empire: The Nineteenth Century*, Oxford 1999, p. 160.
112. Ibid., pp. 3, 15–16, 131 and 157–60.
113. Esherick, p. 292.
114. Pomeranz, p. 183.
115. Ibid., p. 16.
116. Buck quoted in Kueh, p. 117.
117. Maddison, p. 30.
118. Murray, pp. 128 and 266.
119. Naquin and Rawski, p. 24.
120. Modern studies of the impact of irrigation in Shaanxi cited in E. Vermeer, *Water Conservancy and Irrigation in China*, The Hague 1977, p. 182.
121. Murray, pp. 276–7.
122. Vermeer, p. 172 fn26; and Sidney Gamble, *Ting Hsien*, p. 235.
123. Vermeer, pp. 7, 182, 187 and 288–9 (quote).
124. James Kynge, "Yellow River Brings Further Sorrow to Chinese People," *Financial Times*, 7 Jan. 2000.

12. Brazil: Race and Capital in the Nordeste

The definition in the epigraph is from G. Dia et al., "Drought as a Social Phenomenon in Northeastern Brazil," in Rolando Garcia and José Escudero, *Drought and Man, Volume 3: The Roots of Catastrophe*, Oxford 1986, p. 106.

1. Cf. Bradford Burns, *A History of Brazil,* Berkeley, Calif. 1970, p. 102; Andre Gunder Frank, *Capitalism and Underdevelopment in Latin America: Historical Studies of Chile and Brazil,* New York 1967, pp. 162–4; and Emilia Viotta da Costa, *The Brazilian Empire: Myths and Histories,* Chapel Hill, N.C. 1985, pp. 21–4.
2. Nathaniel Leff, "Economic Development in Brazil, 1822–1923," in Stephen Haber (ed.), *How Latin America Fell Behind,* Stanford, Calif. 1997, pp. 1, 35; and Warren Dean, "The Brazilian Economy, 1870–1930," in Leslie Bethall (ed.), *The Cambridge History of Latin America,* vol. 5 (1870–1930), Cambridge 1986, p. 685.
3. Jaime Reis, "Hunger in the Northeast: Some Historical Aspects," in Simon Mitchell (ed.), *The Logic of Poverty: The Case of the Brazilian Northeast,* London 1981, pp. 50–52.
4. Cain and Hopkins, p. 298.
5. Stephen Haber and Herbert Klein, "Hunger in the Northeast: Some Historical Aspects," in Haber (ed.), p. 251; and Alan Manchester, *British Preeminence in Brazil: Its Rise and Decline,* Chapel Hill, N.C., pp. 337–40.
6. Bertha Becker and Claudio Egler, *Brazil: A New Regional Power in the World-Economy*, Cambridge 1992, p. 32.
7. Dean, p. 708.
8. Stephen Haber, "Financial Markets and Industrial Developments," in Haber (ed.), p. 151.
9. Ruthanne Deutsch, "Bridging the Archipelago: Cities and Regional Economies in Brazil, 1870–1920," Ph.D. diss., Yale University 1994, p. 190.
10. Levine, *Vale of Tears,* p. 55.
11. Quoted in David Jordan, *New World Regionalism*, Toronto 1994, p. 35.
12. Dean, p. 708.
13. Leff, p. 53–4.
14. Cain and Hopkins, p. 303.
15. Ibid., pp. 303–4.
16. Deutsch, p. 167.
17. Dean, p. 723; and Winston Fritsch, *External Constraints on Economic Policy in Brazil, 1889–1930,* London 1988, p. 3.
18. Dean, p. 696.
19. Nathaniel Leff, *Underdevelopment and Development in Brazil,* vol. 1, London 1982, p. 7.
20. Deutsch, pp. 3–5. In Jeffrey Williamson's well-known 1960s study of regional inequality in twenty-four major countries, the polarization between Brazil's Northeast and its Center-South was the most extreme. (See the discussion in "Regional Inequality and the Process of National Development: A Description of the Patterns," in L. Needleman (ed.), *Regional Analysis: Selected Readings,* Baltimore 1968, pp. 110–15.)
21. Leff, "Economic Development," p. 35.
22. Deutsch, p. 86.
23. Leff, "Economic Development," p. 35.
24. Levine, p. 55.
25. Leff, "Economic Development," pp. 27, 35–6.
26. Eul-Soo Pang, *PCCLAS Proceedings* 8 (1981–82), p. 2.
27. Levine, p. 49.
28. Leff, "Economic Development," p. 39; and Deutsch, p. 163.
29. Gerald Greenfield, "The Great Drought and Imperial Discourse in Imperial Brazil," *Hispanic American Historical Review* 72:3 (1992), pp. 385 and 396.
30. Greenfield, "Migrant Behavior and Elite Attitudes," p. 83.
31. Eul-Soo Pang, *Bahia in the First Brazilian Republic*, Gainesville, Fla. 1979, p. 62.
32. Ibid., p. 56.
33. Leff, "Economic Development," p. 39.

34. J. Galloway, "The Last Years of Slavery on the Sugar Plantations of Northeast Brazil," *Hispanic American Historical Review* 51 (Nov. 1971), fn54.
35. Quoted in Joseph Love, *Crafting the Third World: Theorizing Underdevelopment in Rumania and Brazil,* Stanford, Calif. 1996, p. 163.
36. Sir Richard Burton, visiting the *sertão* in 1867, described one vast fazenda that used to run 66 kilometers along the São Francisco river divided into scores of impoverished and failing ranches (Hall, *Drought and Irrigation*, p. 33).
37. Webb, pp. 68, 81. In the twentieth century, palma, a spineless cactus, would be adopted as a forage crop ideally suited to the aridity of the *sertão* (pp. 84–5).
38. Chandler, *The Feitosas,* pp. 129–30.
39. Ibid., p. 137.
40. Webb, p. 115.
41. Webb summarizes Guimaraes Duque's landmark study, *Solo e agua no poligono das secas* (1949), pp. 85–8.
42. Allen Johnson, *Sharecroppers of the Sertão: Economics and Dependence on a Brazilian Plantation,* Stanford, Calif. 1971, pp. 17, 47–8.
43. Cunniff, pp. 14–15, 25 and 28–9.
44. Levine, p. 43.
45. Cunniff, p. 37.
46. Hamilton de Mattos Monteiro, *Crise agaria e luta de classes: o Nordeste brasileiro entre 1850 e 1889,* Brasilia 1980, pp. 157–63.
47. Hall, p. 17.
48. Cunniff, pp. 33–4.
49. Hall, p. 3.
50. Cunniff, pp. 55, 61; Webb, pp. 112–13.
51. Chandler, pp. 131–2.
52. Cunniff, pp. 65–6.
53. Hall, p. 4.
54. Cunniff, p. 80.
55. Webb, p. 116.
56. Ibid., p. 83.
57. Hall, p. 36.
58. Cunniff, 87–93.
59. Ibid., p. 96.
60. Cunniff, 104–6
61. Monteiro, p. 47.
62. Ibid., pp. 129–33 and 191–3.
63. Cunniff, p. 102.
64. Dean, p. 690.
65. Hall, p. 5.
66. "… one indication of how little times have changed lies in the reports of root poisoning suffered by the desperately hungry in 1970, reminiscent of the graphic accounts given by Theophilo a century earlier" (Hall, p. 12).

Index